The Two Roberts

Also by Damian Barr

You Will Be Safe Here
Maggie & Me

The Two
Roberts

DAMIAN BARR

CANONGATE

First published in Great Britain in 2025
by Canongate Books Ltd, 14 High Street, Edinburgh EH1 1TE

canongate.co.uk

3

Copyright © Damian Barr, 2025

The right of Damian Barr to be identified as the
author of this work has been asserted by him in accordance
with the Copyright, Designs and Patents Act 1988

No part of this book may be used or reproduced in any manner for the purpose
of training artificial intelligence technologies or systems. This work is reserved
from text and data mining (Article 4(3) Directive (EU) 2019/790)

British Library Cataloguing-in-Publication Data
A catalogue record for this book is available on
request from the British Library

ISBN 978 1 80530 154 7

Typeset in Bembo by
Palimpsest Book Production Ltd, Falkirk, Stirlingshire

Printed and bound by CPI Group (UK) Ltd, Croydon CR0 4YY

The manufacturer's authorised representative in the EU
for product safety is Authorised Rep Compliance Ltd,
71 Lower Baggot Street, Dublin D02 P593 Ireland
(arccompliance.com)

'Kiss me with rain on your eyelashes,
come on, let us sway together,
under the trees, and to hell with thunder.'
                      'Kiss Me . . .' by Edwin Morgan

For Mike,
thank you for making our life into art.

Prologue

The top of Kildoon Hill, Ayrshire

Late afternoon, 21 June 1934

The pair of them lie panting together, curled like commas, naked in the nest they've rolled in the high golden grass. They've never done it outside before but today is different — today is their last day.

From up here, their childhoods spread before them in fields of blue-reaching barley — rolling right up to the gates of the dark factories still just about making everything an empire could need. Salt dries the air. The distant sea is dancing sun-pennies, great ships greet one another coming and going from the Clyde. From up here, Bobby and Robert can see the whole world. But it can't see them.

Bobby feels the unlikely sun butter his body — he will stay like this for ever, Robert's arm draped round him. They will be forever twenty. He tries to look up at the sky without shifting — senses any movement could end this moment. He picks shapes out of the clouds — never in shortage over Ayrshire, even on this endless impossible afternoon.

'Rabbit!' says Bobby, still catching his breath. 'See? See its ears? Robert?'

Silence.

The high-blue wind, which wouldn't dream of ruffling a hair on either head, sets the cloud rabbit running. Bobby *pffts* his liquorice-black fringe off his eyes and squints up. 'He's on his back legs now. Look, he's at the dancin!'

Silence still.

A skylark peels straight up – close enough to nearly catch – spilling its song over the pair of them. A blessing, thinks Bobby. A witness, thinks Robert, reclaiming his arm and turning away. Bobby rolls over to Robert and his accusing back.

'Robert Colquhoun, are you listenin to me?'

Bobby takes this opportunity to observe Robert naked outdoors – he's not stopped looking since clocking him on their first day, never imagined another man would let him look, never mind look back. Already their first year at the art school is over, their lease is over and they cannot afford this unimagined summer. They are being split up. It is unbearable. It is unstoppable.

'Robert? Robert, have you died?'

Robert screws his eyes shut, hoping Bobby will get the idea for once. But the June sky won't be ignored and neither will Bobby. It is, unbelievably, too hot. Like a hound waking, Robert stretches his long pale legs, ploughing his heels into the rich black soil, then crumbling it between his toes to make his point. Robert has never felt more exposed. Every cell in his body is completely transparent. To say nothing of his soul. He half-opens his eyes and tries to see the pair of them, not as the law must, but as the sun might: two skites of pink-white-blue in a sea of midsummer gold. No more, no less. The stickiness drying round his balls tightens. He tries to cover himself.

Bobby laughs. 'You need an extra hand.'

Robert considers jumping up and running all the way to the sea, bombing in and never coming back up. 'Right,' he says, blinking, making a show of paying attention. 'Where's this rabbit then?'

'It's away now,' Bobby sing-song-sighs. 'A-way.' He pauses. 'Probably saw the farmer.'

Robert bolts up, grabbing around for his clothes. A trapdoor opens inside him.

'Awww,' Bobby laughs, sweeping his arms around their world of two. 'Am only kiddin on!'

'Not funny, Bobby! Not funny. We need to go.'

'We don't,' says Bobby, snapping the nearest golden stalk and tracing it down Robert's chest.

Robert shoos him away. 'We do. It's time.'

'It's not,' says Bobby. 'We don't.' He tries again with a different stalk.

'That tickles,' says Robert, not stopping him. 'Where's ma pants?' His cock is very clearly not interested in finding them. 'If anybody sees—'

'Nobody'll see,' Bobby promises, sitting astride Robert, clasping their hands in a kind of prayer. Bobby looks down into Robert's face, his eyes shining with more, more, more. Robert notes a nimbus around Bobby's head and then velvet as Bobby passes a hand over his eyes, closing them gently, before walking the other down to where they both need it to go, to where it might never go again.

PART ONE

Glasgow School of Art

1933–1938

Chapter 1

Maybole, Ayrshire

4 September 1933

Bobby MacBryde is on his way. He's going to the Glasgow School of Art — to the big palace of painting on top of Garnethill with the windows his mother says would take a month to clean. He's going to do Painting. He's getting away. Five years of tacking soles at Lees Boots and a lifetime it's taken to get here, to this morning, packing and repacking the khaki satchel his mother has made for him.

'You'll miss yer train,' she shouts from the scullery, where the light is always best in the morning. His wee sister Jessie is at school already. His wee brother John is out looking for work. Their father is, as always, at Lees.

'Ah won't,' says Bobby, ducking in to see her again, for the final, final time.

'Yer father's swapped a shift,' his mother continues, without looking up. 'So don't be late.' The dress she's unpicking is even more worn than her, but good cotton — washed, cut down and pressed it will do well round the back doors of the big houses in Ayr.

'Ah won't,' says Bobby, noting a bundle from McKay's the Butchers bleeding on the bunker, wrapped tight as a widow in the *Kilmarnock Herald and North Ayrshire Gazette*. 'You shouldnae have,' he says, noting the blurring headlines and wondering if this chicken was the freshest or cheapest.

'Acht, what's tick for?' his mother shrugs. 'We're good for it, eventually. And yer Auntie Maggie will be in the night as well.'

Bobby smiles thinking of his Auntie Maggie and her stories and her harmonica. He slings his new bag over his shoulder – it feels so light for all the hope it holds. As the strap settles, he remembers what it took to get here, to this moment.

His father took him out of school at fourteen – the same as everybody else. Despite the gentle protestations of Mrs Kennedy, his art teacher, Bobby was marched out the doors of Carrick Academy on the Friday and down the high street to Green's the Grocers where he was told to start first thing Monday. He got the Sunday off. Come Monday, he mounted the delivery bike, a cast-iron Clydesdale. His legs were found wanting. Wobbling off he lacked puff – his chest, as his mother was always warning him.

When he was ten, he'd spent two weeks at the Sanatorium in Ayr, tucked tightly into a skinny high bed, like an overdue bill in an envelope. He'd been on a ward with men even older than his father – the windows were never shut and sea-green curtains danced on the prescribed fresh air. At first, Bobby had been so bored he'd even missed Jessie and her wee dolly. When he did get home, he was given the only other bedroom and Jessie had to sleep on the scullery floor but never moaned, said she was cosy by the range.

So, Bobby should have known this job was beyond him, but he needed to do his bit in the house and save up for art school. Also, he'd always fancied a bike – it was one of the few things other boys had that he wanted too. You could go far on a bike, out of Maybole, all the way to Ayr, even to the golden sands of Troon. There was no chance of a bike in their house and he knew better than to ask. After a week of huffing from the shop at the corner of Weavers Vennel up to the folk that could afford deliveries, old Mr Green let him go. 'Aye but he's enough puff to chat up the wifies,' the grocer had winked to his father, who'd smiled thin as bootlaces.

Next day, Bobby had started at Lees, the finest factory in a town famed for cobbling. 'Stick in,' his father had warned him – he'd got him the job, despite lay-offs, because he was a tanner. Bobby could always sense when his father was home, the tang of something dead on the way to leather. So, Bobby stuck in. But he'd no intention of sticking about. He never sat still, chatting away to the girls either side as they all tapped in their tacks – hundreds of pairs of tacketties marching out of Lees every day, to every corner of the Empire. Bobby liked to think about all the places they'd go. One of his favourite books in Maybole Library was *The Times Atlas of the World* – it took two hands to turn the pages. Most of the world blushed pink.

With his mother's nimble fingers Bobby tap-tap-tapped the tacks even faster than he talked. But in his head he was always drawing – his beloved Mrs Kennedy had given him ten silver tubes of Winsor & Newton oils, each promising a world of colour. *Keep at it*, she'd told him, pressing the package into his hands, so nicely wrapped it had to be from a shop in Glasgow. Sometimes, from his workbench, he'd glimpse his father going on a break – tanners got their tea first because nobody wanted to sit with them. He would always wave and sometimes his father nodded back and when he did, Bobby would beam for all the world to see but the canteen doors were always already swinging.

For five whole years Bobby had sat there. Hour after hour. Boot after boot. Every hour the same. Every boot the same. Year by year the order books shrank. He learned to slow down so he didn't show the others up. At night, Bobby could still feel tacks between his teeth.

Sundays he got off for the Sabbath. Bobby's lot never bothered with chapel but he had his own places of worship – he snuck into the Picture House, preferring women's films because there were never any lads there. He would sit at the back so nobody saw him – once, he had to dodge his Auntie Maggie on the way out of a Greta Garbo; he's still not sure if she saw. After crying his eyes out at *Oliver Twist*, Bobby braved the library to ask for more Dickens. Maybole Public Library was the first building in town to get gas lights so Bobby could sit in there and read even when it was dark, which was most of the year. It was all free – you didn't even have to pay to get in. Soon, he'd read the place dry. But the library let you order books in. He'd been amazed by the arrival of art books, gilt and leather grimoires that smelled of the big houses where his mother bought and sold at the back door. He marvelled at whole-page prints of the Great Pictures and made plans to visit them all one day. Bobby saw no great mystery in the *Mona Lisa*. He knows from Lees what that smile means and it'll end with a ring on her finger, if she's lucky. He imagined himself clinging to *The Raft of the Medusa*, slipping off then being pulled back on by a wild-haired sailor crying *I won't let you go!* Bobby memorised rich Dutch still-lifes with glistening goblets and glassy-eyed birds and pearl-handled fruit knives that cost more than he could imagine. What do you do with an artichoke anyway?

Bobby had boosted his escape fund by drawing cartoons of his workmates – he 'borrowed' stubby pencils and brown paper from the pattern-making cupboard. He made big noses bigger, amplifying every wart into an Ailsa Craig. So long as he was equally unsparing, they'd all laugh. Folk crowded round him, pointing and laughing as familiar faces emerged. At first it felt strange to draw in front of people – to have an audience for something he'd always done in secret, in the art room at lunchtimes, or up on Kildoon Hill, just him and the sky. He doubted his colleagues would enjoy watching him try to get the perfect morning blue of the wild periwinkles. They admired his skill. This kind of looking was safe, he realised, because they were seeing themselves. Word spread, as it always did, and folk brought in that one photograph of their cousin that's away to Canada or Australia. Every now and then a tearful woman handed him a tissue-wrapped photo and he refused money for these, drew them in private. Bobby got good at telling the stories of every face but his own – disliked his pouty lips, which sat right on his mother and Jessie. Avoiding himself was easy because the only mirror in their house was a tile screwed to the wall over the scullery sink where his father shaved every morning, his face curled in steam. Anyway, there would always be somebody to catch him. A man shouldn't look at himself any longer than he needs to; Bobby knew the rules. So, he only ever saw himself in what people reflected back – if he could make them laugh or give them back a face they'd lost, he liked what he saw.

Every Sunday, whatever the weather, Bobby took the paper he'd scrounged and went up Kildoon Hill. He raced away from the houses until he ran out of road or puff. Auntie Maggie was always saying, 'You'll meet yourself coming back.' He huffed his way up the rubbly track, the same one marched by Roman soldiers who built the fort at the top. Bobby imagined their sandaled feet scuffed with faraway dust, swords hanging by their sides, dark eyes on a distant horizon. Why did they come here when they could be somewhere sunny? Where did they all go? He searched the faces at Lees wondering if any of them was ever Roman. Andrew, whose mother was a baker, had an olivey look. Sandra, sat next to him, was definitely an empress. Bobby was far from pale – his father claimed they're from the Black Irish, survivors of the Armada who washed up in Ireland and were welcomed with open – *laugh, nudge, wink*. If his ancestors did come from far away then maybe Bobby could find his way back.

Finally at the top, Bobby would sit himself down on the nearest driest rock and unpack his stuff, rushing to get it all down. Out at sea sits the burnt roll of Ailsa Craig, sometimes so close he thought he could swim to it. White splashes burst from the waves as gannets split the sky, exploding into the depths. Even if it wasn't that dry, and it rarely was, Bobby took his boots off, felt the cool grass between his toes. The hill was studded with wind-stunted wildflowers – he recited their names as he drew. For things he really loved, he broke into Mrs Kennedy's paints. Was he really good enough for the art school? When he stayed behind after the bell to avoid the walk home, she'd tell him all about the masterpiece of Mr Charles Rennie Mackintosh. She'd taken classes there herself. Bobby had written to them every year since he was taken out of school, but never heard back. Nothing. Not until he got the letter.

Auntie Maggie had marched him into Glasgow for his interview; his mother was up to her elbows at the steamie and his father was at Lees (or the Maybole Arms). It was only his third time on a train – he counted all his pleasures carefully. Then there was his first tram. Finally, they'd both stood outside staring up – they could hardly take it all in.

'In ye get,' she'd said, near kicking him up the stairs. 'I'll be here,' she'd said, with no clue how long he'd be.

Bobby had never done anything like this before so had arrived just as it was about to start. A young woman with mad curly hair rushed towards him asking 'MacBryde?' His arse didn't touch a chair – she propelled him down a long corridor towards tall double doors. 'Ready?' she asked, pushing the doors open and him through. At the far end of an officially echoey hall stretched a long table with three men sat behind. As Bobby crossed the parquet expanse, he felt them look him up and down. The baldy one picked up a sketch he recognised and rubbed the corner of the brown factory paper between thumb and forefinger, before wiping his hands on his heavy tweed trousers. Bobby sat down and did what he'd always done: talked and talked and talked – about all the pictures in all the books at the library, about the particular morning blue of the periwinkles on Kildoon Hill, about the colour of everything. Once or twice the young-looking one smiled and made a note. How long did he sit there talking for? A minute? An hour? A day?

When he came back out, Auntie Maggie was still stood exactly where she said she would be, her rare green eyes shining. She made him tell her everything. Twice. He let her hold his hand on the train until they got to Maybole. A letter nearly beat them home. Auntie Maggie couldn't read it herself but scried his face and hauled him out onto the front step and shouted to all of Weavers Vennel, the whole of Maybole, that Bobby MacBryde was going to the Glasgow School of Art and that Robert Burns had better watch his back because Ayrshire would soon have another name to sing.

All this goes through Bobby's head as he leans down to kiss his mother goodbye. She stops unpicking stitches for one whole second, her right thumb keeping her place, and half stands to kiss her eldest boy. He's away already, she thinks, knowing he was always going.

'Away you go. The train disnae care who you think you are. And don't be late – yer father will want to hear all about it.'

Bobby wonders if she believes that herself but is touched that she wants him to. 'Aye right,' he says, pulling the back door shut gently. He pauses in the dark bleachy close then steps out into his future, already so bright he needs to blink.

Chapter 2

The Ayrshire Express leans forward at Maybole Station, the end of the line running all the way to Glasgow, where Bobby has been three whole times – once to see the Christmas Tree at George Square, another time to the Baird Street Auxiliary Hospital for a chest X-ray and then for his big interview.

Bobby clatters over the red iron bridge, rusting with the town's fortunes. He's wearing the brand-new boots his Auntie Maggie gave him 'for all the way you've got to go'. As he'd tried them on she'd warned, 'Never forget where you come fae.' Maybe he'd tacked the soles on them? Today is all possibility. Right now, the stiff new leather is getting him nowhere fast.

The platform is nearly empty. Two porters stand by carts they've decanted on board. The tall thin one admires his pocket watch. The short fat one warms a whistle on his waistcoat. 'You've nearly missed her,' Lanky shouts over the warning engine. Bobby, feet killing him, penguin-walks to third class, a ridiculous cartoon.

'Art school we heard?' smirks the shorter one – Bobby recognises them both. His hand aches with the memory of what they did to him that day. He makes a fist. They stand back as he passes.

'Aye,' says Bobby, swinging a carriage door open. 'The Glasgow School of Art.'

'Oooh!' They nudge one another. 'The Glasgooow Schoool of Art!'

Bobby steps up in to the carriage with all the hauteur he can muster. His boots pinch. What would Garbo do? Safely above the pair, he turns and slams the door. The shorter one finally gets to blow his whistle.

'Get fucked, Laurel and Hardy!' Bobby shouts over a roar of steam from up front.

'You wish!' shouts the lanky one, bending over.

Bobby ignores them and turns to find a seat. He is greeted by a carriage of faces ranging from mortified to amused. He knows a fair few of them. Word will get home long before he does. At least Auntie Maggie will laugh. There's a window seat in the middle so he heads for it, stowing his satchel on the rack then plonking down, making sure to face forward.

The Ayrshire Express is in no rush. Stop by stop, the train fills, in reverse order of class. Eventually it's standing room only. Bobby is smooshed against the window by a wifie who clearly thinks she should be sat further up. Her hat looks like a hen house after a fox has got in. Pressed against greasy glass, Bobby glimpses flashes of fields between bouts of smoke. It reminds him of the news reel, all fast and important – the opposite of life in Maybole where time is measured in shifts or, lately, factories shutting.

He considers sketching the new faces crowded round him but his neighbour tuts theatrically every time he tries to restore his circulation. Finally risking her wrath, he leans out and over, contorting to retrieve his satchel. Bum back on seat, he unpacks a polar-fresh pad of paper and a box of charcoals, congratulations from Mrs Kennedy. His neighbour gawps as if he's pulled out a whole naked lady. An artist!

As they pull into Kilmarnock, Bobby admires the fancy ironwork arches and the sky darkens with soot from the mills that paid for it all. Doors slam up and down the train as they get ready to go again. Bobby's attention is drawn by a squad of soldiers who have just got on – more and more of them these days. They're loudly pleased with their new uniforms. 'Not our war,' his mother had said, when he'd told her about some Lees boys joining up – *Stick it to Hitler, better money and a chance to see the world.* 'You cannae see much fae a coffin,' his mother had said, furiously pressing a shirt, pausing at a cuff to say, 'They won't take you anyway. Not wi your chest.'

Machine-gun laughter strafes the carriage. Bobby sits up. He learned long ago to be alert to groups, especially ones with no girls – to gauge their mood, to be sure of a road out. The soldiers sway and jostle, landing jokes and kid-on punches. Stuck in the middle of them, with his back to the carriage, stands a tall man in a very obviously new black suit; Bobby's mother would pick it out a crowd. Bobby traces a perfect V of loose dark curls tapering towards a bright white collar but stopping respectably short. His shoulders are slender but not mean. He looks like an upside-down exclamation mark. The soldiers have him surrounded. He tries to break free without drawing attention. He has a portfolio wedged under one arm – one of them grabs at it. The train jolts and the man staggers backwards into the aisle – Bobby reaches out instinctively. The man steadies himself on the back of a seat, then turns. A face from a coin. A Roman coin. Or a film – Gary Cooper. Sleek black waves roll away from a high clear forehead. Cheekbones sear up to sea-coal eyes. Bobby fumbles for his charcoals without looking away. His neighbour watches him make his first mark then follows his gaze, trying to work out who he's sketching.

The man is much younger than his suit suggests. No glasses, no moustache, no pipe. They might even be the same sort of age. Bobby works quickly, stealing glances. He focuses on the head and shoulders. A bust. The hair isn't easy but Bobby presses on as the train pushes forwards – he feels the man's hair curl around his fingers then closes his eyes, pushing the thought away. He wills his cock to stay down, already blaming the inciting vibrations of the train. As he opens his eyes, his neighbour squints shamelessly at his work. Bobby sharpens the cheekbones he can already imagine kissing. He lifts his charcoal from the page. These thoughts are incriminating. Having them in public, on a packed train, then transmitting them to his hands and committing them to paper, might even be dangerous. But he can't stop. He's not growing out of them, as he'd hoped and even, once, prayed. He's heard the stories his mother brings back from the steamie: that beautiful young man found hanging off the railway bridge, that dirty old bastard caught in the toilets at Troon then sent to Australia. Bobby knows where his thoughts could lead. So, he keeps them secret – along with the memory of that lad who came through with the fair last summer. He tells himself these stories do at least mean he's not, as he feared, the only one. He only *feels* alone. All these laws must mean there are also lots of lawbreakers. Bobby thinks maybe he can trap his thoughts on paper, fix them in charcoal and make them safe – make them art. On and on he draws, picking up pace with the train. By the time they pull into Glasgow Central he's nearly forgotten where they're going.

As the train falters, his subject leans down to peer out and his neighbour howks herself up and stands waiting, one hand on her not inconsiderable hip, the other on his seat. He gets the hint and fetches her carpet bag. She adjusts her mad feathered cloche then peers down at his sketch one final time, uttering her verdict: 'The hair's wrang . . . the rest's no bad.'

'Thanks,' says Bobby, looking to his model. But he's gone. The carriage is nearly empty. Bobby packs away his charcoals, cursing as one snaps. He's last off. A vast glass roof zig-zags over the station and in the middle hangs the station clock, one face for each point on the compass. 'Mair faces than the toon clock,' is one of Auntie Maggie's favourite sayings. A sudden pang is replaced by the realisation he's nearly late for his first day.

Outside it's smirring with clammy September rain. He hops on the first tram, guessing, from all the portfolio carriers crushed on, it's going the right way. They birl up Hope Street then left up Sauchiehall Street and along, clanking and ringing all the way. The clatter reminds him of Lees and he wonders what Sandra is doing.

'Fares,' says the conductor swinging through and Bobby hands his over, like he does it every day. He is moving at speed through a city and not just any city.

'Mack!' shouts the conductor but he hardly needs to because the building fills every window. 'The Mack!'

The tram slows and Bobby leaps off with everybody else, landing so hard his boots nearly spark the wet cobbles. The rain has cleared the air for a minute. The art school is all glass, huge panes bounce the north light like sails catching a wind. It's not symmetrical but somehow feels it. Bobby supposes Mackintosh knew what he was doing. *I'm here. I get to look up at this every day for five years, if I'm good enough. Which I will be, I've got to be. How many days is that? What then?* He sways in the slipstream of students, pulled up the wide stone staircase that narrows towards the top, shoaling them all towards a pair of doors that seem mean for such a place. Reaching for the brass door-plate, he notices it's etched with one word: ART. He's about to push when an arm reaches over his shoulder. As the door swings open, Bobby turns to thank whoever did him the favour, if it was a favour.

'You!' says Bobby, as the last students hurry past.

'Me?' says him off the train.

'I saw you on the train.' Bobby offers a hand. 'You got on at Kilmarnock.'

'Did I?' He nods down at Bobby's hand. 'Observant. I can see why they let you in.'

'MacBryde!' says Bobby, pocketing his suddenly huge hand. 'Bobby MacBryde.'

'Colquhoun,' nods the other, ducking past. 'Robert Colquhoun.'

'Not Bobby?' The din recedes with any chance of them being on time.

'Not Bobby,' Robert insists, placing one hand over his heart, a gesture he's made without noticing since he was a boy. 'Robert.'

'Robert!' laughs Bobby. 'Alright!'

Bobby is just standing there. This close, he sees he did get this Robert's hair wrong, failed to capture how it holds the light – the same as the polish his mother lavishes on their range.

Robert curses the clock placed thoughtfully in the foyer above their heads – the rose-wreathed numerals they will soon learn are by Margaret, not Charles, Mackintosh. They are summoned by the sound of a lectern being thumped. Robert rushes ahead. Bobby follows.

Chapter 3

Robert and Bobby tumble into the hall together, coming to an embarrassed halt as quickly as they can, as a neat coppery man in a heather corduroy jacket steadies his lectern. Their chances of going unnoticed are now doomed. Robert side-steps away from Bobby.

'Glad you could join us,' says their teacher, in syllables as rich and long as the Byres Road. He looks too young to be a lecturer – only a bit older than them. He tilts his head, as if waiting for an answer, and peers to the back of the room. His light blue eyes are tiny fairground fishbowls. Relieved not to be the focus of his attention, the whole class turns as one. Robert takes a sudden interest in the floorboards. Bobby smiles as best he can and says, 'Sorry sir, we were workin.'

'Work-*ing*?' The whole year giggles. 'Such enthusiasm! Well, you both better come and see me at lunch and show me exactly what you were working on that kept you from arriving on time. Names?'

'MacBryde sir, Bobby.'

Fleming looks down at the register on his lectern: 'From Maybole, I see. And your friend?'

Robert is stunned. *Friend?* If it wasn't for this loon, he wouldn't be going through this public cross-examination. Bobby's boot taps the side of his shoe.

'Colquhoun, sir. Robert Colquhoun. From Kilmarnock.'

'Well,' says Fleming. 'Two Roberts! Or a Robert and a Bobby.

Ayrshire's finest. I'm Mr Fleming, your Head of Year. For those of you who make it to the Upper School, I teach in the School of Painting, but we're getting ahead. Today is the first day of your General Course which will ground you in Lettering, Historic Ornament, Sculpture, Metalwork, Ceramics, Design and, of course, Painting, among other options. After these two years you will specialise, if you're still here.'

He delivers this information in a tone that suggests he might quite like some of them to make it. 'I look forward to seeing you both after induction. Guides?'

At this, several older students enter the hall and split up their year. Robert tries to join a different group but finds himself stuck in the same lot as this Bobby. He walks ahead of him as they're led down a long narrow corridor lit by cathedral windows. Built-in benches fill the space between each one, perfect for sitting opposite, toes touching. The walls are lined by reproductions of famous sculptures: heroic figures, all male and naked as the day they were cast. Robert spots Apollo, Samson and emperors (*sundry*). They stand like guards. Each is miraculously white, almost glowing.

Robert eyes them with the appraising look of Mr Lyle, his art master from Kilmarnock Academy. He shudders remembering the row when his father had taken him out of school. After Robert didn't show at art class, Mr Lyle had turned up at the Glen, where Colquhoun Senior was an engine fitter – a highly competent draughtsman, lines stayed where he put them. Mr Lyle had protested over the lathes and presses about Robert's talent, brandished his drawing of a storm lantern – *See!* Robert had stood there cringing as Mr Lyle offered help, a scholarship from a local minister (not a Catholic, thank God) and one of the Johnnie Walker whisky lot (atoning no doubt). That night was the only time he ever heard his mother raise her voice. Next morning he was back at school and now he's here. Thank you, Mr Lyle.

Robert looks up: nowhere do the ceilings come anywhere near his head. His shoulders drop a little. He thinks he could spend his whole life just here. But how could he ever capture such forms on paper? Painting suddenly feels flat, pointless. Maybe his father is right.

Warm September sun streams in from all the windows, more light than Glasgow has ever let on she has. Bobby notices too and wonders where it's all coming from. It was raining not two minutes ago. Are palm trees popping up on Sauchiehall Street? Are the stone lions in George Square yawning and stretching awake? Is the whole dirty city turning tropical?

Their guide is a second year with an entirely unsculptable auburn halo. Bobby recognises her as the girl who wheeched him into his interview. She pauses in front of a lavishly pierced St Sebastian, his sinuous arms raised in protest, ribcage heaving. Robert marvels at the cruel delicacy of the arrows. He can hear them whistling through the air, feel them finding their mark. The saint's face is frozen between agony and something else, obscurely embarrassing. Robert's shoulders inch towards his ears again as Bobby reaches for the tortured saint.

'Oh, you can touch him,' laughs their guide. 'See?' And she skelps St Sebastian's impossibly smooth arse. Everybody laughs. So, Bobby skelps him too, the marble even colder than it looks – his hand stings, so he makes a show of blowing on his fingers. They all laugh even harder. Robert doesn't know where to look.

'We all do it. They get white-washed again every summer. Just don't let the jannies catch you. If they do, say it's *material research*. I'm Moira, by the way. Second year Painting.'

'We've met,' says Bobby, extending his hand.

Moira peers at him. 'Oh yes, you were late! They let you in then.'

Bobby beams. A second year knows who he is.

As they head off again Robert hisses, 'You'll get yourself a name!'

'Will I now?' Bobby shrugs, rushing on, flattering Moira with questions.

Robert remembers long lonely years at Kilmarnock Academy,

knows first days have a way of lasting. It took him finally asking out a girl and taking her to the pictures on several Saturdays to buy some peace. That and keeping all his drawing and painting and noticing to E8, Mr Lyle's art room. His inky-fingered sanctuary. Drawing calmed him, stopped other thoughts – thoughts he knew he shouldn't have, thoughts other boys somehow knew he had.

Chatter echoes up the stairwell ahead. 'Right to the top,' shouts Moira, as they reach the final flight. Bobby steps forward first – he wheezes then gasps.

'This is the Hen Run,' Moira announces, as if she'd built it herself.

They are floating over Glasgow. The outer wall is all glass. Hundreds of panes stretch from the floor to the roof, which is also, amazingly, see-through. The whole corridor somehow hangs out over the top of Sauchiehall Street. Each pane, the size of a gramophone record cover, holds a square of the city. Tenements crowd together like men at the end of a shift. Slate acres roll away, rooftops still silvered with morning rain. A million chimneys smudge the sky all the way to the shockingly green horizon. Giant cranes lining the Clyde turn to one another in conversation. Roped masts and smoking funnels signal the run of the river that is an estuary, an industry, a religion.

'Every week you have to pick one pane and draw everything in it,' says Moira. *'Every single thing!'*

They are all already absorbed in imagining this task – each was top of their class, each believes that this place might be the making of them, that it could lead to a gallery in Edinburgh or even London. Bobby and Robert still can't believe they're here.

'Is that . . . ?' Bobby squints at the view then turns to Moira who is busy, so walks over to Robert who is gazing up at the sky, marvelling that the glass roof doesn't leak – his father will be impressed by this at least.

'Is that . . . Kildoon Hill?' Bobby asks, almost pressing his face against the glass.

'Well, it's no Glasgow,' Robert concedes, leaning in. 'It's higher than Kildoon. It's maybe the Craigie. D'you know it?'

'Aye,' fibs Bobby. 'Am from Maybole.'

'I know,' says Robert. 'Kilmarnock.'

'I know,' says Bobby. 'Townie.'

Bobby is already committing the view to memory in case he never gets to come back up here again, in case Fleming tells him there's been a mistake or the whole school burns down overnight or something. Nobody from Maybole has seen Glasgow like this, endless and smoking but green where it greets the sky, framing the world.

'Right,' says Moira, clapping her hands. 'That's it for now. Don't worry – you'll definitely get lost and we've not even done the Life Drawing Room or the Library but it's lunchtime.'

They tear themselves from the view and turn back to the stairs, heading for the refectory.

'Wait,' she says, stopping Bobby and Robert. 'You've got Mr Fleming, remember?'

Robert sighs: he's not forgot.

Fleming is standing behind his desk with his back to the door when a secretary shows them in. Faculty offices are dim – all light is reserved for the studios. Bookshelves line every wall and Bobby tilts his head, surprised to recognise a title from Maybole Library. Everything is dark-stained wood, inlaid with roses which seem to grow towards the old gas lamps. There's not enough wall to hang a picture so frames are propped up all over.

When the door clicks closed, Fleming turns, smiles and rubs his hands over an invisible fire. He looks from one to the other.

'So, you were working, eh?'

Robert has no idea what to say. Lying is not an option. Will his first day be his last?

Bobby steps forward, unshouldering his satchel.

'Can I, sir?'

'You may,' says Fleming, sweeping some type-written papers to the far reaches of his desk.

Bobby lays down his bag and unbuckles it, removing the brown-paper parcel of cheese and bread pieces made by his mother, his new charcoals and finally the pad of paper christened on the train.

'Come on,' says Fleming, waving a delicate hand. 'We all want our lunch.' He eyes the wrapped bundle, catches a whiff of cheddar and hopes it won't blotch his papers. Robert has been embarrassed by many things but never by a piece.

'It's just a wee sketch,' says Bobby, gently lifting the cover of the pad, taking care not to smudge.

Robert is sure they can hear his heart racing the clock on the desk.

Fleming looks down. Lunch is forgotten. 'May I?' Not waiting, he eases Bobby's sandwiches to one side with the back of his hand then picks up the pad and holds it in front of himself with both hands. He glances to Robert then Bobby then back before turning the pad around, like something at an auction.

'What do you think, Colquhoun?'

Robert stares at himself staring back. How? When? He turns to Bobby who stammers, 'It was on the train this morning, I just wanted to get my eye in, in case we had to do something and—'

'—Mr Colquhoun suggested himself as a subject?'

'Aye, sir,' says Bobby, remembering the imagined feel of curls tightening around his fingers. 'Yes, sir. He did.'

'Well,' says Fleming, carefully closing the pad and returning it to Bobby. 'There's a lot to be done, and undone, but I can see why we let *you* in.'

Fleming picks up the sandwiches. Robert prays for death.

'Brown paper . . .' says Fleming, a smile visiting his lips. 'You're the boy who sent in a portfolio on brown paper?'

Bobby doesn't know what to say. He thinks again of the baldy one in his interview who'd picked up his work like he was lifting a wet teabag.

'Aye, yes, sir,' he mumbles. 'That's me.'

Robert looks down.

'Ingenious!' says Fleming. 'We must make do! More and more we must do more with less. Van Gogh was a great painter-overer – not a technical term. But there's plenty of time for *pentimenti* and the like.'

He tosses the sandwiches to Bobby who manages to catch them. Fleming steps out from behind his desk. Robert retreats.

'Well, Colquhoun, might I suggest you make good use of the train journey back to Kilmarnock?' Fleming nods to Bobby. As if Fleming willed it, his office door opens behind them, letting in a draught. 'You can show me the results tomorrow.'

They shuffle backwards into the hall, like courtiers. Fleming closes the door gently in their faces then stands there for a moment, one hand on the handle, the other remembering the feel of brown paper.

Chapter 4

'Sit still,' says Robert, his eyes darting from Bobby to the pad wobbling on his knees.

'I am,' says Bobby, tucking his hair behind his ears – his hands rest briefly in his lap before taking flight again.

Bobby feels porous where the world hits his skin. It's one of the qualities that keeps his Auntie Maggie awake: the boy has never been able to hide his feelings and, worse still, seems to have stopped trying – twice she's seen him at the pictures after a Garbo. Bobby doesn't understand why not everybody feels the way he does at any given moment. This is another reason he prefers drawing things to people: flowers on a hill, a cup, fruit (if there is any) – things are happy where and how they are, things can never see themselves or feel the hot pang of not-recognition.

'Stop movin,' warns Robert, jabbing towards him with the top of a fine Faber pencil.

Bobby and Robert are sitting on opposing benches at the front entrance to the Mitchell Library. Above them a dome greened by Glasgow rain crowns this people's palace of stories. According to a plaque out front, this is the largest public library in Europe. More miles of shelves than Venice has canals.

'Can we no just go in?' asks Bobby, nodding to the revolving door, which has not stopped birling since they sat down. Some of the books he got at Maybole were stamped from here. Up close, the Mitchell is even grander than he'd imagined. Two perfectly symmetrical wings, lined with fluted pillars, frame the central curve – even its smallest window is bigger than the back door Bobby left by this morning. All for books. He rubs the back of his neck – all this awe is tiring.

'Quit fouterin!' says Robert. 'And no, you cannot just march into a library with a bag full of paints. Anyway, the light's better out here.'

Robert hauled him down here right after Fleming dismissed them. He wants to get this over and done with, doesn't want them lumped together.

'You said it was cos folk on the train would watch,' says Bobby, gesturing at the citizens spinning in and out the doors. He folds his feet under the bench and immediately regrets the gesture. 'But what about all them?'

'They're not stoppin,' says Robert, narrowing his eyes. 'Folk on the train would stare because they've nothin better to do.'

Bobby nods. 'Some old wifie watched me the whole way up.' He smiles at the memory of her chaotic hat. 'Didnae bother me.'

'Well,' says Robert, making a few bold marks. 'Good for you.'

'What are you supposed to do wi your hands?' asks Bobby, knitting his fingers in his lap for a moment then shaking them free, fretting that he looks like a Bonnard lady at a chamber music recital.

'I'm not doin your hands,' says Robert. 'Just keep them off your face.'

Bobby sits on his hands and tries to look around without turning his head: all the drama of Glasgow's busiest crossroads playing out, more people passing in a moment than in all of Maybole. At the foot of Charing Cross Road, a one-legged beggar in ragged khakis balances on a padded crutch, shaking a cap. No stripes on his shoulders. One of the last of the old black hackney carriages, pulled by a matching pair of faded black horses, pulls up, probably picking up from the Grand Hotel. Two lines of brass buttons march down the cab driver's coat and he wears his battered top hat as proudly as the library does its dome.

He leans over from his perch and looks down his nose at them. Bobby begins to suspect Glasgow might secretly have money.

'Alright pal,' Bobby shouts up. 'Havin a good look?'

The cabbie gives Bobby two fingers then sets off with a crack of his whip, just missing a tram going the other way. Bobby laughs and claps his hands.

'Do you never stop?' Robert asks, laying down his pencil in surrender.

As Bobby considers this, his belly rumbles. 'I'm just hungry. First day and that.' He opens his bag, unwraps his piece and takes a huge bite. Hard cheddar, his favourite. He'll thank his mother later. 'Have you not got anything?' Bobby asks, scattering crumbs towards Robert.

Robert shrugs. 'I don't really eat much in the day.' He wonders why he's telling this stranger anything. Something about the face he's trying to capture invites confidences. Maybe it's the mouth, lips parting like they're about to tell you a secret. They're much fuller than Robert's own, which are fine as the rest of him. Robert's eyebrows flick away like a child's drawing of a seagull, whereas Bobby's are equally thick from beginning to end, strong enough to hold up his surprisingly low brow. Bobby's hair is nearly as dark as his but falls straight as a fishing line, down round his face – Robert's hair rolls away from a perfect widow's peak, which makes him look older than he is. Bobby's face is the sun; Robert's a half-moon.

Bobby is relatively still while demolishing his lunch so Robert picks up his pencil again. He's drawn hundreds of faces. It was his portraits that won him the attention of Mr Lyle. When it became clear from school reports that drawing really was homework, Robert's mother allowed him to sketch her but only when his father was out – a wordless agreement. Robert cannot capture the dynamic he observed in the rare moments they sat on the couch together, the space that opened and closed between them. After his wee brother John there was a baby, Janet. Named for his mother as he is for his father. Janet never saw her first birthday.

A blue baby. His mother was never the same. Loss etches her face, stoops her shoulders. Now there is just silence, blue silence. Before his mother would let him draw her, she insisted on brushing out her curls then taking off the apron she wore until just before his father got in. He's only drawn his father once — when he was out the back in his aviary. It's one of Robert's portfolio pieces — his father holding his best wee singer with both hands, cooing into its bright yellow face. Canaries seem more air than matter, more colour than substance, yet each one has a personality: some fluff shyly, others push their shoulders back and beak up. Robert was reluctant to include the cage bars, putting them in last.

'How am I lookin?' Bobby asks, licking his fingers. Nobody in Robert's house would get away with that. Or try it. Since his father got promoted at the engineering works, and his mother was able to give up work, they've taken to serviettes on a Sunday. Bobby carefully folds the wax paper into a square and puts it back in his bag.

'Nearly done,' says Robert, shaking his head. He shades Bobby's hair in with the side of his pencil.

'Lookin good?'

'Wait and see.'

Bobby is affronted. 'What do you mean?'

Robert takes one final look then leans down and blows the page. 'You can see it tomorrow. As instructed.'

'Aww, c'mon,' says Bobby, darting over.

'Nope,' says Robert, disappearing the pad into his bag.

'Just a wee peek,' pleads Bobby — Bobby who did his one and only self-portrait because Mrs Kennedy said he'd fail if he didn't and because disappointing her seemed even worse than seeing himself looking back, the brow that made other boys call him Caveman till they found better names. Bobby who avoids the mirror tile in the scullery. Now this very same Bobby is suddenly desperate to see himself — to see how this Robert sees him.

Bobby grabs for the bag, but Robert is faster. Defeated, Bobby plonks down next to Robert, who leaps to his feet.

'Tomorrow!'

'Fine,' nods Bobby, sliding himself along the bench like a whisky swiped down a bar in one of the Westerns he endures at the pictures. He stops exactly where Robert had sat. 'So, what now?'

Chapter 5

Next morning, Bobby is there before the train and this time the porters think twice. He gets on and the same seat is free – a sign! He waits for Kilmarnock. The Ayrshire Express is even slower today.

Ignoring mutters, Bobby saves the seat next to him. His head is a bit furry from the beer Auntie Maggie brought over last night. His second drink ever: when he'd turned eighteen his father had dragged him to the Maybole Arms for his first pint. They'd all looked at him when he walked in, he'd felt it and, worse still, felt his father try to ignore it. It was like when his father had made him go fishing with the boys from the factory and Bobby had caught a proud brown trout first time, then let it go. But last night was a celebration, his Auntie Maggie had insisted. Already, his first day at the art school has taken on the legendary quality only burnished by repeating: he nearly missed his train, he was hauled in front of the high head of the whole place, a lassie with hair by Millais took a shine to him, and he's already made a pal, from just up the road in Kilmarnock, what are the chances?

The doors open at Kilmarnock. Bobby watches. And watches. As the last doors slam, Robert's head appears, then his shoulders, then the rest of him. He looks up and down the carriage for a seat. Bobby waves. There's nowhere else to sit.

'Mornin,' says Bobby, shifting his bag onto his lap. 'I saved your seat.'

'So I see,' says Robert, folding his knees in, then balancing his bag on top.

Robert says nothing, hoping Bobby will get the message. His head rings with grief from his father for being late yesterday.

'So?' says Bobby. 'What'll we get in trouble for the day?'

'Nothin,' says Robert, his voice rising. 'I nearly got tanned.'

'Tanned? How come? Who off?'

Robert leans into the aisle.

Bobby goes on. 'Bit old for that are you not?'

Robert looks down.

'Well, ma Auntie Maggie came over with some beer and her wee harmonica and gave us all a song and that.'

'Harmonica?' says Robert. 'Sounds criminal.'

'She's good!' insists Bobby, lifting an invisible instrument to his lips. 'And my father can sing – Mother says it's the Irish.'

'MacBryde,' says Robert, dawning. 'You Catholics then?'

Bobby considers the fading Virgin by their back door. 'I never did my first communion. I suppose we're lapsed. My father says we're socialists.'

'That's not a religion.'

'It is in our house,' says Bobby. 'When I was wee, he took me to see the Hunger Marchers go past on their way to Glasgow.'

'Aye?' asks Robert.

'Like a massive funeral. Hundreds of skinny folk, all bundled up in coats – you could hardly tell men from women. My mother baked a loaf and my dad gave it to one of them and they took it and ripped a wee bit off then passed it back and they all did the same. The weans looked like wee ghosts. I'd forgot that. What about you? What kind of name is Colquhoun?'

'Protestant.'

'So, we can't be pals then?' Bobby says, half-joking, knowing that for half the folk on this train such a difference would indeed be a chasm.

Robert is about to speak but remembers his father's dire warning: *fly wi the craws and get shot wi the craws*. He subsides into silence and trusts this troublemaker will be put off.

Bobby turns towards the window, trying not to look how he

feels. He glimpses some ruins in a field, the base of a mossy stone wall and a broken turret and wonders what will be left of the world he knows. The ruins vanish. Were they ever really there?

Robert can't bear even momentary awkwardness, so gives in, risking a joke. 'Forgive me, father.'

Bobby laughs so loudly that folk turn. He's just so relieved. Robert is surprised – at Kilmarnock Academy he was always the quiet one, sat as far as possible from the class clowns. But now here he is making somebody laugh – not just anybody but the somebody who talked back in front of their whole year on their first day. Away from school, and his mother and father and the space between them, who might Robert become?

'That's us,' says Bobby, half-standing as their train slows into Glasgow Central. 'C'mon!'

By some mysterious process, initiated at a handful of schools they've never heard of and continued in the nearest pub last night, groups are forming. Each coalesces around one of the very few girls in their year. Bobby and Robert stand there the only pair. Fleming hands out timetables – classes start at 9 a.m. and finish at 4.30 p.m. with a break for lunch in the refectory.

'I've got Life Drawing,' says Bobby, holding out his timetable.

'Me as well,' says Robert, not looking. 'Then History of Decorative Arts.'

'Same!' says Bobby, waving the paper then realising they're identical. He pockets it quietly.

The bell rings and Robert follows the crowd and Bobby follows Robert and they all find the Life Modelling Room. Here is the promise of nudity, or as close as is legal. The boys nudge each other. Robert remembers to join their nervous laughter. They crush into an airy room bereft of bodies, clothed or otherwise. There are no windows at street level, for modesty. Light streams in from above. Robert admires the cleverness – the room is diffuse with light but none of it glaring. Renfrew Street rumbles outside but this room is quiet enough for thoughts, the ceiling high enough for them all to drift up. It creates a natural hush. Easels wait around in a lozenge. The doors open and in glides Hercules, pushed by two puffing jannies. Every muscle strains.

'Next week it will be Apollo,' says Fleming, processing behind the demi-god. Bobby wonders when St Sebastian will get his turn.

The students cluster around the edge of the room as if waiting for music. Robert cringes at the memory of school dances.

'You expected a bacchanal?' says Fleming. 'Not today, I'm afraid.'

The walls are papered with sketches.

'Each of these was the best of their day,' says Fleming, walking around. Robert immediately searches them for secrets. The models in the drawings are draped in Greco-Roman robes and stand on a dais in the centre of the room, leaning on an antique pillar. 'Ancient Greece by way of our wood shop,' says Fleming. 'The pillar ingeniously heated from beneath so our models don't shiver – shiverers are tricky. But you're all a long way from live models yet. There will be no nudity – unless you take yourselves to Paris where such practices are not prohibited.' A general groan. 'This morning, you will try to capture Hercules. You will draw him from the same position every day. Exactly as you see him. You may make any marks you wish but you are not permitted to remove a single mark and you have only one piece of paper for the week.'

Gasps.

'It will do you all good to be confronted by your mistakes. Glasgow School of Art is not made of money, Mr Fyffe,' says Fleming, to a conker-haired lad in an inky three-piece suit, out to be noticed. 'This is not Fettes!' Fyffe blushes and the boys that are already always all around him laugh.

Bobby doesn't know what Fettes is. Neither does Robert. Bobby is absorbing the luxury of a piece of paper this size that isn't brown and pilfered. Robert is wondering whether to use pencil or charcoal. There are no paints to be seen.

Fleming continues. 'Right then!' He circles Hercules. 'What are you waiting for?'

As the groups break up, Robert heads for the nearest empty easel. Bobby follows but the easels either side are taken. Robert's triumph is short lived as Bobby stands right in his eye-line. The few girls sit. Everybody else stands.

'Good,' says Fleming. 'Now, it's your own work you are here to observe and improve, not your neighbour's. Each of you was the best in your class – you would not be here otherwise. But you cannot all be the best in my class.'

Robert bristles. Bobby thinks of Mrs Kennedy.

'So, keep your eyes on your own work. Remember, you are not here merely to observe but to learn how to see.'

Bobby steals a glance at Robert, who is looking at Hercules like he's challenged him to a square go after the bell.

'There is, of course, no painting this year,' Fleming goes on, his back recklessly to the giant.

More groans. Fleming lifts a silencing finger.

'I really am not interested in whatever tricks you've picked up from private tutors or painting summers in the Adriatic,' says Fleming, raising an eyebrow at a girl he guesses could correctly pour champagne but not boil a kettle.

Bobby sniggers. Painting summers! The Adriatic!

Fleming pauses. 'Ah, Mr MacBryde! Something funny?'

'Nothing,' Bobby smiles. 'It's just . . .' And here he attempts Fleming's Byres Road burr, tried out on his Auntie Maggie last night: *'Painting summers in the Adriatic.'*

He gets close enough. Giggles ripple around. Robert regrets his earlier kindness, braces himself for further mortification, decides to catch an earlier train tomorrow.

Buoyed by the mirth of approval, Bobby goes on: 'What about the Ayrshire Riviera, sir? Largs, Fairlie, Maidens?'

Proper laughter breaks out and Fleming only just manages not to join in. Robert keeps his eyes on Hercules.

'Turner did paint the sands at Troon,' says Fleming, walking over to Bobby who had no idea Turner knew Troon from Trieste. 'It's among the many hundreds of pictures he bequeathed to the nation. You can see them at the National Gallery. And some of you shall! At the end of your General Course, the top two students are awarded a trip to London to see the great works and write a report. So,' he says, turning from Bobby and walking over to the last free easel and picking up a baton of charcoal. 'Let us begin!'

As that first class files out, Fleming calls their names. Fyffe looks back and rolls his eyes at them as he pulls the door shut.

'Your homework?'

'Here?' Robert asks, gesturing around the Life Modelling Room as if he's been asked to strip. 'Now, sir?'

'Yes now,' says Fleming. 'No need for sir. This is not the army.'

'He wouldn't sit still, sir,' says Robert, unpacking his bag. He pegs a page to his easel then turns away.

'I can imagine,' says Fleming, glancing to Bobby. 'Your line . . .' he says, tracing Bobby's brow. As if commanded by a spell, Bobby's hand reaches for his face. He longs to see the portrait.

Robert braces.

Fleming turns. 'You've captured something of Mr MacBryde's restless self. And all with this . . . economical line. Very fine, for a first year.'

Fleming unpegs the paper from the easel then walks over to the wall and tacks it up. Robert can't believe this. Neither can Bobby — there he is, on the wall, as this Robert sees him. He is not hideous. And it is better than his effort from the train. Panic washes over Robert as he recalls Fyffe's dirty look — he feels like Fleming has just pinned up a target. Bobby tries to dismiss the unworthy thought that Fleming didn't pin *his* drawing on the wall and instead be chuffed for his fellow Ayrshireman, especially as he looks so far from happy. Bobby decides to bask in reflected glory, for now. Robert already fears a fall.

Chapter 6

This is how a day goes by at the Glasgow School of Art.

Every morning, before anybody else arrives, the bent-double coalman is in, feeding the furnaces that roar like dragons deep beneath the school. Then in wash the charwomen all on the same tram from Dennistoun, clanking their bright tin buckets and scrubbing every floor, from the Hen Run at the top, all the way down to the doors of the boiler room, because there's no point lifting a brush in there. The front steps are still wet when the first teacher mounts them. Every arriving student is ticked off a register at the door before hanging up their coats. There's maybe time for a glass of milk in the ref before the first bell goes at 9 a.m. Then it's Life Drawing then lunch in the ref or, for Bobby, his piece in brown paper. Afternoons are more material than mornings – in Ceramics, clay is moulded into maquettes; the big north-facing windows bustle with needleworkers, including one boy from the islands stitching some kind of shimmering shroud; sawdust rolls out from underneath the doors to Woodwork, where chisels and polish and time grant new life to elm and ash and lime. At precisely 4.45 p.m. a green-jacketed jannie will bring that day's life model a warm robe then guide them off the stand and the students will say, as one, 'thank you'. Damp muslin cloths will be draped tenderly over drowsy clay charges. Blades will be cleaned then rolled in a bundle until the next day, when everything will start again, only this time they will all know more, work harder, do better. At 5 p.m. the last bell rings and the school empties like a sink, with only the final years permitted to stay in their studios, spiralling towards their Final Show.

And, for Robert and Bobby, at the beginning and end of every day, the impatient expensive train. Robert gets on last and off first so arrives home that bit earlier but still late – his mother leaves him a cold plate. As soon as he walks in the door, his father heads out the back with his birds. Bobby notices Robert open slowly through each day, like the flowers on the side of Kildoon Hill, then close as the day draws done, almost silent by the time he gets off. Bobby finds Maybole smaller every day – you could fit the whole place in Glasgow Central. Only his Auntie Maggie asks how it's going now – clocks every mention of his classmate from Kilmarnock.

There is already feverish talk of specialising – metalworkers shake rough hands, needleworkers form tight seams and the other painters talk of outings to houses and gardens, places Bobby and Robert have never heard of: Traquair, Haddo, Hospitalfield. They all seem so confident of *their* country – a few even have motor-cars. But the train is always about to go. Bobby and Robert never have a spare coin or minute. They begin to dread specialising, not for fear of hard work, but because it will mark the beginning of the end. Their whole lives have been getting here. Now they've pushed open the door marked ART. All too soon it will swing shut. What then?

Their first weeks fly by like this: Bobby with his foot in the door, Robert worrying it's closing already . . .

It's a Monday lunchtime halfway through their first term and Robert is on his own in the Hen Run. He sits cross-legged looking out over the city, wondering if the sun will show. The groups that formed on day one are now impenetrable – they sit together, laugh together, turn their backs if he walks over, which he dared once and will never try again. He resents being lumped in with Bobby. He doesn't hate him. But . . . he sits up straight recalling Bobby giving Fleming lip, reaching for St Sebastian's arse, all the attention he attracts. Bobby and Robert are becoming a pair by default and Robert isn't happy about it but also doesn't want to be hiding on his own in Mr Lyle's art room again.

Robert stands up. There it is again, the hill Bobby pointed out their first morning. It's not Kildoon. Is it? He wonders at all the lives between here and the horizon, all the tenements and townhouses, offices and factories, picture houses and dance halls. Hundreds of thousands of faces, each with a secret for him to decipher. The sun appears and reflects his face back. He rakes his fingers through his waves then blinks and the sun goes, taking him with it. Then it reappears. With another face. Robert turns.

'Found you,' says Bobby, catching his breath from the stairs.

Robert sits down again.

'Getting ahead?' says Bobby, nodding at his work.

'Trying,' says Robert. He notices he's not as annoyed as he thought he would be. It is cold up here. Maybe there's enough view to share?

'Keen,' says Bobby. Robert nods. Bobby opens his pad to show him the page he filled the day before. A busy square of city.

'Already?' says Robert, poking at the world outside with his pencil. 'It's not due till tomorrow.'

'Keen,' says Bobby. 'I've nothin else to do at lunch – nothin free anyway.' He walks over to Robert and sits down next to him. Robert shuffles along. Bobby ignores this and glances over at the emerging sketch. Robert is decisive.

'Very Vorticist,' says Bobby, pointing to a hectically jutting chimney.

'You know your stuff,' says Robert.

'So do you.'

Robert tries not to let the compliment settle.

'We've got an early Wyndham Lewis in our dining room,' says Bobby. Robert stops and turns to look at him.

'Have we fuck?' Bobby laughs. 'Dining room!'

Robert laughs then points to the stairs. 'I bet one of them has.'

'Oh aye,' says Bobby. 'Fyffe'll have Turners in every room and a Peploe in the pantry!'

Bobby starts to say something else but Robert shhhs him. 'I need to get on.'

Bobby mimes zipping his lips. Robert picks up his pencil and continues. Robert looks out at Glasgow. Bobby glances over at Robert. Moira, standing quietly at the top of the stairs, sees them both.

Chapter 7

Bobby is lost in a forest of words and pictures. Mackintosh's Library is as tall and narrow as the books stacked on the coffee-dark shelves. It's hard to tell where architecture ends and design begins. A gallery branches round three sides, sheltering the desks below. One whole wall is windows, but the sun never reaches the books so their pictures never fade. Silver lights pierced with repeating rectangles hang low over desks in the centre – so low Bobby thinks he could almost reach up and pick one.

Nothing in here looks like a tree, not directly, but it all has the feel of deep woods – Bobby scribbles 'Caledonia' on his pad. He doodles one branch then another and sees that they are really hands reaching and missing. The library is glade peaceful. It's lunchtime and Robert is nowhere to be found, again. He's learning not to approach him. To just nod, not smile. It's all an effort and Bobby's not sure he's got much left. Just keeping up here is tiring. They all seem to know each other, talking about their weekends, their old schools. Sometimes he nods off on the train home then resents missing the minutes when it's just him and Robert. Only the library lets him rest. He finds the older students a bit easier, especially the girls. Moira is his favourite and as skilled at painting as she is at winching. After five minutes talking to her he'd said, 'You will be a great artist or a great lover.' She'd replied, '*Or* is such an ugly word.' They'd laughed in agreement and heads turned – folk could think what they wanted. He could go and find her now. But no, not today because she might ask him what's really going on and he might tell and that would be that.

Bobby walks over to 'M'. His fingers travel the spines until they find what he needs. He takes the book over to the nearest empty desk and sits down. As he opens it, he remembers his first visit to Maybole Library – how it changed everything.

Bobby loiters across from the library, which anchors the bottom corner of the high street. He's waiting for it to be almost closing. Then, he figures, the staff will be too busy thinking about their tea to notice him. He's forged his mother's signature on the form. He could have asked her but sensed, as with his drawing, this would somehow let her down. For all she loves stories, he's never seen her reading, not even one of the penny sheets, whose screaming headlines she rushes back repeating from the steamie. The only book in the MacBryde house is the scab-brown Bible his father claims came over from Ireland. That and the Burns, which Auntie Maggie regales them from on Saturday nights, reminding them over and over that the bard's mother was local. *O my Luve's like a red, red rose,* Bobby hums as he waits for the town clock to strike 4.30 p.m.

Other boys have found love, or at least willing girls round the back of the pictures. Bobby tries not to think about Cary Grant or Gary Cooper as he stands flat against the gates to Maybole Castle, each post topped with a perfect pyramid, the symmetry echoing the remnants of the two towers above. For such a wee place, Maybole has many big buildings. This is because, as they heard over and over at school, Maybole is the ancient capital of Carrick, fiefdom of Robert the Bruce. Now Carrick only exists in imagination, like Hardy's Wessex, which Bobby tried and failed to find on the class map after crying over *Tess of the D'Urbervilles*. As castles go, Maybole's has almost gone. Once upon a time, a countess was imprisoned there by her jealous husband. She was locked in a room with only one window, the inside frame decorated with the faces of all the men her husband accused her of gallivanting with. Bobby looked up at it now: the oriel window leaning out like Rapunzel.

Oriel is one of the words Bobby has saved up. He longs for a life where he might drop them into conversation: surfeit, chiaroscuro, badinage, words he'd met in the back row at the pictures. Garbo words. The oriel window stares back. Through it, he can see the sky darken where the castle's roof stood for centuries until the fire, the most exciting thing to happen round here since the castle was built. His mother had rushed him round to watch with all the other Minniebolers – he remembered the groan as the beams finally gave and the applause-like clatter of the falling slates. Bobby puts a hand to his face remembering the heat. Bobby understands the countess at her window. He wonders why she'd never jumped.

Finally, the clock strikes, giving Bobby half an hour to get in, join up, find some books and get out before being witnessed by the tide coursing down the hill at the end of the day shift.

Bobby crosses over and pushes the surprisingly heavy double doors. Beeswax wafts up from the polished floor. The doors swing shut. He freezes, waiting to be chucked out. He considers kicking off his boots, then takes a deep breath and pushes through more doors. He steps into paper quiet. White shelves hug every wall and here and there are cosy armchairs and not one is empty but nobody looks up – they're all cramming in as many words as they can before the sign on the door is flipped to CLOSED. All Bobby can hear is the occasional rustle of a newspaper and the luxurious hiss of gaslights. Where to start? Maybe he should come back. Sensing his hesitancy, a young woman appears from behind the nearest shelf.

'Can I help you?' she asks, her voice kinder than her face. With his mother's eye, Bobby knows her pinafore has been made for her, albeit in an ugly shade of brown. He's never met her before. She definitely does not live in the village.

'Have you a ticket?'

'Aye,' says Bobby, who has been clutching his form the whole time.

'Thank you,' she says, uncrumpling it. 'We can get you a ticket with this. As you're only twelve, you're entitled to two books at a time for up to two weeks.'

Bobby's heard you can take the books home, seen people coming and going with them, but didn't really believe it until now.

'I'm Miss Masterson,' she says, gesturing around. 'One of the librarians here. My position is endowed by the kindness of Mr Carnegie.' She points to a brass plaque over the door.

Everybody knows the name of the home-grown millionaire who shook America like a piggy bank then showered some of its riches on the people he'd left so very far behind. If Bobby ever asked for extra tatties on a Sunday, his mother would reply with 'Who d'you think I am? Carnegie?!' In this moment, he feels profoundly grateful to the man with his name over the doors he's finally worked up the courage to open.

'Pictures,' Bobby whispers, trying not to break the library quiet. 'I'm interested in pictures.'

'You mean, the pictures?' asks Miss Masterson. 'Cinema?'

'No, I like them. But—'

'Picture books?' Miss Masterson says. 'To help you learn to . . .?' She lets the sentence hang. She will not hurt his pride by assuming what his worn boots and frayed sleeves suggest.

'Oh no,' says Bobby. 'I can read!' His eagerness to impress solicits light rustling from the nearest reader. 'I'm after books about pictures – about paintings.'

'Oh,' she smiles. 'You want Art.'

'Art,' Bobby nods. 'I'm after Art.'

It takes Bobby the next eight years to work through all of Art – Section 24 in Mr Carnegie's Library. He starts at book Number 1 and reads all the way through to Number 325, two titles at a time, taking the full two weeks over each because he only has Sunday afternoons free. *The Hundred Best Paintings* was twenty-four whole volumes filled with sepia reproductions. Was *The Knight Errant* by someone called Millais really one of the best? Why was there only one Cézanne? What could the person picking the pictures see that Bobby can't? They must be better in colour. He makes faster progress in summer than winter because candlelight is still all they have and he worries about scorching even a picture of a painting. Rembrandt would not be best pleased. He somehow also makes time for all of Dickens, having never recovered from *Oliver Twist* at the pictures. Miss Masterson calls him her *appreciating machine*.

On Sundays, Bobby takes his books up Kildoon Hill. In breaks from drawing, he stares at the black and white illustrations spread over two pages and curses the binding that deprives him of whatever mystery is lost in the middle. Bobby thirsts for colour. He longs to visit the important pictures – imagines walking into the Louvre and asking to be taken, not to the *Mona Lisa*, but to *The Raft of the Medusa*, a vast rendition of a shipwreck, the desperate survivors storm-tossed and fighting for life. Nothing melodramatic about it – he knows how they feel. Naturally, he won't be alone in the Louvre but he will stand there longest, as amateur lookers come and go noting his deep appreciation and wondering at his erudition. He will try to arrange his features seriously but, as always, his eyes will be darting, his lips never far from a smile. His mouth is too wide, it will get him into trouble, his mother warns – hers has.

One such Sunday, Bobby is walking back from Kildoon Hill, his head full of pictures and flowers.

'What've you got?'

It's Albert Clark, the biggest lad in Maybole. Bobby didn't notice him approach – curses himself. He tries to side-step him and the two boys flanking him, one tall and thin, the other short and round – they look like the number 10. He doesn't know them from school.

'You deaf?' laughs Clark, darting to Bobby and knocking off his cap. It lands in the gutter.

'Fuck you!' Bobby shouts.

'You wish,' says Clark. As Bobby grabs at his cap, Clark steps forward. Bobby freezes. Slowly, almost gently, Clark places his boot on the top of Bobby's right hand, heel first but with nothing like his full weight.

'No,' Bobby pleads, trying to turn to see if somebody is coming down the street. But it's a Sunday. It's just him and them. Maybe it's better this way – spared the shame of witnesses. His parents will, inevitably, hear about it – everybody hears everything here.

'Deaf?' Clark shouts. 'Dumb?' He bears down. Bobby falls forward on his knees. Cold tacks push into the back of his hand – he splays his fingers to spread the pressure, share the pain. His cap sinks into the gutter, soaking up filth. What will his mother say?

At a nod from Clark, the other boys pull Bobby's satchel off his shoulder. He can't stop them.

'What's this?' the tall one says, pulling out the book Bobby was on his way to return. It is Michelangelo.

'Oooh!' says the short one, flicking through. 'Dirty pictures!'

Before Bobby can really register what's happening, the boy rips out a page. 'For later,' he winks, stuffing it in his pocket and licking his cracked lips.

'Please,' says Bobby, trying not to sound desperate. 'Stop?'

'D'you hear that, boys?' Clark asks. 'He wants us to stop.'

Bobby's knees throb. His fingers turn white.

'I'll let you pick,' says Clark. 'Cos I need to get home for my dinner.'

Bobby nods. Guesses what's coming.

'Hand? Or book?'

'But it's not mine. It's the library's!'

'Ooh-hoo-hoo, the librar-eee,' Clark sings. The other two laugh along. Clark nods and they pull the book between them, like a tug of war, their hands slipping as it tears until the bigger one gets it and stands there ripping out page after page, which the smaller one runs about catching and shredding, throwing strips in the air like confetti, shouting, 'He wants to marry us all!'

'Stop!' Bobby shouts, trying desperately not to cry because only that could make this worse.

Clark grinds his heel on Bobby's hand. The tacks bite. Was today his last day holding a pencil? Are the drawings in his bag his last?

'Alright,' says Clark, lifting his boot fractionally. Bobby gasps as blood rushes back in. Then down it comes, again and again. Bobby screams because it doesn't matter now – it can't get any worse.

Suddenly Bobby's hand is free. He opens his eyes. The wounded book lands in front of him, half in the gutter. Clark stands over him and points to the last pages. 'Your turn.'

'I can't,' says Bobby, shaking his head, trying to move his fingers. 'I won't.'

'Won't you?' says Clark, raising his foot. With his other hand, Bobby grabs the book then, without looking, rips out the first page he finds.

'Again,' says Clark.

Bobby tears that page in half.

'Properly,' says Clark, hunkering down to Bobby's level.

Bobby looks down at his hand, watches pinpricks of blood rise up and spill. He flexes his fingers but the pain makes him fall forward on to the book. Clark ducks in so close that Bobby can feel the heat of his breath on his face and hisses the one word Bobby fears the most, because he knows it is true. He hugs the book close and waits for what's next. Three boys. Three pairs of boots. He takes a deep breath and holds it.

Nothing.

He peeks one eye open – Clark and the others are nearly at the end of the road already.

'Bobby?' calls a voice from behind. Bobby tries to get himself up on one elbow. It's Miss Masterson, hurrying down the high street, her dress hitched up. What did she hear? What did she see?

'They made me,' he says, pointing to the book as she got closer. 'I'm sorry.'

'You've nothing to be sorry for,' she says, gently closing the book. 'Bullies. Philistines!'

Bobby nods. Tears fall fast and hot as shame. Snotters blind him. He covers his face with his sleeve.

'Can you move it?' Miss Masterson asks, wincing at his bloody hand.

Bobby remembers holding a pencil then commands his fingers – yes, he can, agony, but yes.

'Boys like that,' says Miss Masterson. 'The world is full of them.' She pulls a white lace hankie from her sleeve and crouches down. She dabs at his hand and he winces. That lace will never be bright again. 'We must get you seen to,' she says, turning to the library. 'Help is coming, Master MacBryde.' She places a gentle hand on his shoulder – she has never touched him. Bobby feels his face flush with relief and something else. Miss Masterson realises he's fainting and leans over, cradling him, not sure he can still hear, and whispers urgently in his ear.

Mackintosh's Library glows with September sun. Books are clapping closed, dust dances into the air. Lunchtime is over any minute. Bobby lays his right hand flat on the desk – only he can navigate the constellation of tiny silver dots there. He flexes his fingers and presses hard against the dark wood, fancies he can feel it pulse. Right on time, the bell. Bobby closes his book carefully and walks back over to 'M' where a gap waits. Tenderly, Bobby puts Michelangelo back. He apologises to the book. As the bell fades, he decides he will write to Miss Masterson – send her a new white hankie and tell her that he did hear her that day.

Chapter 8

A fleet of ships greets them as they spin out of the revolving doors and into the museum at Kelvingrove. Every ship faces the same way and each sails for ever in a glass case, never to be bothered by storms again.

'There's hundreds,' says Bobby, peering into the nearest one – half expecting a navy of tiny sailors jigging on deck.

'From sails to steam,' says Robert, admiring some rigging. 'What next?'

'Destroyers,' says Bobby, looking through from the other side.

'We'll never get round all this,' says Robert, his voice swallowed by the vast entrance hall, words disappearing up into the chandeliers, each one taller than him. The famed organ sits high on the wall at the far end, its gilt pipes glinting. A sign advertises a concert at 2 p.m. They're here on their lunch hour so will just miss it.

'Never mind,' says Bobby, reading Robert's face. 'I'll whistle for you on the train home.' Robert can't shake his disappointment. 'We'll come back,' Bobby reminds him. 'We've got five years, remember.' They're here on a recce before the official class visit next week because they don't want anybody to see them seeing this place for the first time. 'We just want to look like we know what we're doing.'

Bobby heads left, hoping Robert will follow. He walks straight into an elephant.

'*Sir Roger*,' says Bobby, reading the label.

'What's that mark?' Robert says, pointing at the elephant's head.

Bobby reads on: '*From 1885 to 1897 Sir Roger toured the country with Bostock & Wombwell's Menagerie, often pulling a small wagon from town to town.*'

'Poor bugger,' says Robert. 'Probably died of exhaustion.'

'*In 1897 he went to a Zoo in New City Road, Glasgow owned by E.H. Bostock and lived quite happily enjoying walks in the countryside with his keeper. Imagine running into him on a Sunday! But by October 1900 he was becoming unruly.*'

'Unruly?'

'*At the age of 27, Sir Roger developed musth – a dangerous condition that can happen to older male elephants in heat.*'

Robert coughs.

'*He became so aggressive that he broke the arm and several ribs of his zookeeper. Bostock decided enough was enough and ordered the animal to be shot—*'

'That's the bullet hole,' says Robert, pointing up. 'Right between his eyes.'

'They shot him while he was eating his breakfast,' says Bobby. 'They sold tickets to watch. Bastards!'

Bobby wipes his eyes. Robert wonders what it must be like to just feel like that, the way Bobby does. The last person he saw cry was his mother, after his wee sister; that was all she did for months. She cried for them all. His father never.

Bobby leans over the display, gently strokes the back of Sir Roger's trunk. 'I'm sorry,' he whispers. Robert doesn't stop him. A museum guard watches from behind a case of stuffed birds but says nothing, as he does whenever somebody does this, which is most days. Sir Roger stands tall and looks straight ahead – he can never forgive what he can never forget.

Glasgow is a city of firsts. Their first day, their first term, even their first coffee – served in tiny cups at the University Café on Byres Road and even frothier than the gossip about them: *they don't mix, they're really brothers, they think they're better than everybody else.* Bobby is unafraid of firsts, a quality Robert admires. Along with his use of colour, his ability to make him laugh and the unlimited attention he seems happy to give him. Each is fast becoming the other's first proper friend.

Today, now, this saltire-sky October afternoon, is their first visit to the Botanics. They've been sent out to find something green and told to be back in three hours with three full pages.

'It's packed,' says Robert, over his shoulder as they pick their way through the Friday crowd.

'Hoaching,' laughs Bobby, only just avoiding being mown down by a blue-cloaked nanny piloting a pram back to the mansions on Kirklees Crescent, which boasts a private gate into the gardens so residents can smell the flowers and not the hoi polloi – a wee bit of Edinburgh in Glasgow.

Blackened brick pillars guard the gates. Peeking through the trees up ahead are two chimneys topped by black and white onion-shaped turrets, like something from the Kremlin.

'That's the old Botanics station,' says Bobby, catching up.

'How do you know all this?' Robert wonders.

'Have you not got libraries in Kilmarnock? Or curiosity?'

Here and there, glass glints through the trees. Robert follows the sign for 'Kibble Palace'. Bobby hastens after.

'Some greenhouse, eh?' Robert nudges Bobby, banking this as a thing he can safely tell his father. It is all glass and air. Every single one of the how-many-panes is framed by finely iced iron, white despite the soot that drizzles even the West End. The whole confection is crowned by a broad dome topped by a cheeky peak that catches the autumn sun just as they arrive.

'That would have yer eye out,' says Bobby, pointing. 'That nipple!'

Robert coughs dismissively, out of habit now, but can see it. They linger by the glass doors, can't quite believe it's really free to go in. Robert looks about for a ticket man. Bobby dives in. Hot wet air envelops them as the doors open and they step from one world to another. A fig tree spreads in the entrance, immodest in its last leaves. Bobby loosens his scarf. Robert whips off his cap.

The thick air plashes with water from a pond up ahead. Bobby hurries over and pushes his way to the front between some wee ones who've been brought into town especially, judging from their excitement. The coin-round pond boils with carp of all sizes and colours, whiskers waggling as they snout after the bread the weans are scattering right by a sign that says, 'Do not feed the fish, by order of Glasgow Corporation.' The carp love lawbreakers.

A big one breaks the surface, scattering the others. 'The fish that never swam,' Bobby says, by way of hello. It takes him a minute to notice the baby ones because they're black as tar, made for survival. He watches them compete for what's left. Then, up from the deep, rises the mother of them all – red and brown and pink, almost tortoiseshell. Bobby gasps. The wee girl next to him laughs. 'Oooh!' she says, bouncing on her toes. 'Oooooooh!' he says, laughing with her. She puts out her sticky paw, offering him the last of her crumbs, the way Jessie would. As he puts out his hand the girl is pulled away by a biddy who gives him a look like she might feed him to the fishes. The girl tosses her crumbs at him, scattering them over his boots and into the water's edge, and the fish teem over, glittering as one.

'What was all that about?' asks Robert, arriving by his side. He'd gone on ahead, as always.

'Ocht nothin,' says Bobby, kicking in the last crumbs. 'Some old fishwife.'

'C'mon,' says Robert, already turning. 'You won't believe this!'

The circle of people around the pond opens to let them leave, then closes as if they were never there. Bobby scuffs crumbs off his boots as he follows Robert, who is being swallowed by a frondy forest.

'Look!' says Robert, twirling on the spot. Bobby has never seen him so excited. They're under the dome, which is somehow even bigger than it looks from outside. All they can see is impossible greens. It is an Eden.

'Tree ferns,' says Robert, reading a label. 'Have you ever seen the like?' Bobby recalls the ferns on the shadow side of Kildoon Hill, shy wee things, not like these fireworks sparking from tall furry stems. He brushes against one and Robert does too, just for a moment, surprised at their coolness. Towering over these are palm trees — some straight as allotment leeks, others arched and swaying in an invisible breeze.

'Maybe there's bananas!' Robert laughs. He has a holiday air. Bobby can see the boy he was not so very long ago — imagines him on Troon beach poking a jellyfish with a stick or chasing his wee brother with seaweed — they both have younger brothers called John, another similarity Bobby savours. Or maybe Robert's always been like this? Quieter, held back, so the world can't touch him. Robert is a shell Bobby wants to prise open and live inside.

The place echoes with the whoops of weans going wild in the jungle and with the chatter of adults freed of their scarves and everyday selves. Even so, it's a shock to bump into another person in among all the foliage, to be forced back into civilisation. Robert finds himself resenting everybody else.

'Could you not just live here?' Robert says, following his nose to a slender trunk clad in deep orange bark. He sniffs in disbelief. 'Cinnamon!' Bobby dashes over and, before Robert can stop him, Bobby rubs the bark.

'What are you doing?' Robert pulls his hand away.

'I was just looking,' Bobby says, wrinkling his nose by way of explanation and thinking, *Robert touched me, Robert touched my hand.*

'You look with your eyes,' snaps Robert.

'Not your hands,' says Bobby. 'I know. I'm not five.'

'You act it,' says Robert, wiping his hands on his trousers. 'You always go too far.'

Bobby ignores this and lifts his fingers to his face. 'Smells like

Auntie Maggie's Christmas cake.' He offers a hand to Robert, who ignores it, turning towards the benches lining the glass walls. They're filled with people reading. One very small old woman sits next to a huge stack of richly bound volumes of Proust. She must have started them when she was twenty. He imagines sitting in here sketching all day, tropical birdsong sparkling from all the impossible greens, wonders how he might capture these infinite differences.

'Want to go to the other one now?' says Bobby, desperate to get happy Robert back.

Robert nods and leads the way past the still-crowded pond and out through the doors. The light is leaving. It's not cold for October but the change in air halts Bobby, his lungs protest, hacking.

'You alright?' Robert asks.

'Aye,' Bobby coughs, not wanting to appear weak but enjoying the healing attention. 'It's just—' he pats his chest. But Robert doesn't know about his stays at the sanatorium, about the two dreaded letters his mother warned him never to mention. 'It's just . . . the cold,' he says, pointing back to the dome. 'After that.'

Robert waits for Bobby to catch his breath, then they walk on together.

'Civilisation,' says Robert, jabbing a finger at the beds of hot-pink wallflowers hanging on till the first frost. Bobby admires the blast of colour, two fingers up to dourness. It reminds him of the picture in Kelvingrove of the horsey woman wearing a glorious red hat and he resolves to visit her again soon. But, after their wild jungle, he gets what Robert dislikes: uniformity and control. An unexpected revelation.

The main glasshouse is even bigger than the Kibble Palace – a procession of pagodas made of dark teak wood, each housing a different corner of the world. They go in and make their way through all the empire and dominions – cooling under the conifers of Canada, sweating in South America and nearly missing the living stones of South Africa. They cross deserts of cacti,

· 55 ·

wrestle with strange vines that can kill or cure, find a thousand things to draw.

'I can't take it all in.' Bobby finally surrenders in the jewel-room of orchids. All this going from hot to cold and wet to dry is not helping his chest. In a panic, he rushes for the exit. They sit on the nearest bench. The sun is going. A haar rolls in, quiet as cotton wool.

'Will we get you a wee tea?' Robert asks, noting Bobby's pallor.

Bobby nods, catching his breath in the heavier air, watching Robert go over to the tea stand. He walks like a movie star. A young woman gives Robert the glad-eye but he doesn't notice. Bobby closes his eyes and recalls the perfect roundness of the pond, counts all the coins in the bottom.

'Here you go,' says Robert, returning. He hands Bobby a mug then sits down a bit closer than usual. They face the Kibble Palace and sip their tea.

'You go back in,' says Bobby.

Robert shakes his head. 'Plants are patient. But we better get going,' he nods over Garnethill way. 'We've no work.'

'Pffft,' Bobby says. 'We can fill some pages.'

Robert nods. It's true. Neither of them has ever had the luxury of pausing for thought – they just do, start to finish, racing each other, already leaving the rest of their year behind. It's getting dark but the thickening haar holds the leaving light. All around them autumn is packing up. The mugs warm their hands.

'What if we didn't have to leave?' Bobby wonders, looking down into his tea. 'What if we weren't always running for the train. What if we really could just live here, like you said?'

Robert laughs. 'It might be a bit hot and it's no good for your . . .' He pats his chest as Bobby had.

'No,' Bobby smiles. 'Glasgow, I mean.'

'Live here? Leave home?'

'Well,' says Bobby, trying not to sound like he's been thinking about this since Robert got on that train. Robert is his way out. Robert is also a destination. 'It would be cheaper, for a start.'

'How?'

'We'd save a fortune on train fares and you'd not have to buy lunch in the ref – I can cook.'

'Is that right?' asks Robert, nodding along.

'Aye,' says Bobby. 'Stews and soups and soda bread and all that. My Auntie Maggie showed me – she says the man that can feed his wife will keep his wife.'

Robert nearly spits his tea out.

'I only mean . . .' Bobby turns to Robert. 'It's better here.'

'It is.'

'I'm happier here.'

'Me as well,' says Robert, the first time he's admitted it out loud.

Wife. Robert tries to imagine Bobby married – he's always surrounded by girls, cackling down the corridors with him. In his fantasies Robert is always alone in a studio somewhere high up, a bare room filled with paints and possibilities. Stews don't excite him. But Bobby does have other virtues – he works hard too, takes it seriously, even when he's not very serious. He doesn't take it all for granted, not like the others. Bobby gets what Robert is trying to do, stands behind him making annoyingly helpful suggestions. Robert imagines them working late into the night, making better pictures for being together. The door to the studio in his head swings open – suddenly there are two easels.

'It could be brilliant,' Robert says, gesturing around, the gas lights flickering on right then as if commanded. 'To just come to places like this, any time we want.'

'So . . .?' says Bobby, putting his mug down on the bench and rubbing his hands together.

'But what about the rent?' Robert asks, sounding like his father, he realises, the words drying in his mouth.

'You pay digs?'

Robert nods. 'But there's gas, food . . . all of it.'

'Gas?' says Bobby. 'Posh.' He pauses for effect. 'I've got my whole five years saved up.'

'That's loads!'

'A load of old boots,' says Bobby. 'I worked five years at Lees so I could just paint when I got here.'

'If you got here.'

'When,' says Bobby. 'So, I could shell out our deposit and that.' As he talks he realises he's depriving his mother of his dig money, practically robbing her purse, but he carries on, promising himself he'll try to send something back.

'And you've got your parents,' says Bobby, trying not to sound envious.

Robert peers into his tea. 'My father took me out of school.'

'But you said you finished.'

'Only cos of my art teacher, Mr Lyle.'

'How?'

'When I didn't turn up one day he came down to the factory and asked for me and it all went off . . . my mother actually said something.'

'Good for her!'

'First time for everything. My father said he wouldn't be paying.'

'Bastard.' Bobby picks up his mug.

'That's my father,' says Robert, as if from a script.

Bobby shrugs and gulps the last of his tea.

'So, Mr Lyle spoke to a local minister who took on my fees and then Mr Walker of Johnnie Walker.'

'Bet Presbyterian pater loved that.'

'Mr Walker is my benefactor.'

'Like Pip from *Great Expectations*!' Bobby sits back. 'So, if they're not paying, your parents have no say, not really?'

'No . . . I suppose not.' Robert imagines no longer having to tip-toe around his father, darkening the weather. His wee brother will be away to the army soon. Maybe his mother can come and visit. Robert finishes his tea. 'It's still too much . . .'

'Not if we do it together.' Bobby puts out his hand.

Robert pauses. The whistle goes for the Botanics to shut. He holds out his mug and Bobby takes it, two handles in one hand clinking together. And for just that moment the whole world fills with the smell of cinnamon.

Chapter 9

'We should make a wish,' says Bobby not a week later. He pauses halfway across the half-penny bridge linking the back of the gardens with Botanic Crescent and the rest of the West End.

'What for?' Robert asks, checking his watch. They're due to meet their potential landlady at noon and they're already pushing it. They'd found the advert in the *Evening Times* that Bobby had picked up as they'd left the Botanics last week.

'We should wish that she likes us,' says Bobby, closing his eyes.

'She just needs to like our money,' says Robert.

'What if somebody else has already got it?' says Bobby. 'Or what if she doesn't take artists?'

Robert pauses. 'When you telephoned, was the room still available and did you tell her we were at the art school?'

'Aye and she didn't ask so I didn't tell her,' says Bobby, worrying the cast-iron railing of the bridge, observing his shadow already standing on the other side.

'Come on,' says Robert, sweeping his hand along the railing towards Bobby. 'It's nigh on twelve and if we're late she'll think we'll be late with the rent and that'll be that. Come on. Or somebody'll get there first.'

Bobby makes a wish that leaps into the water rushing under the bridge and is already halfway to the Clyde as they nip up the steps and cross the cobbles of Botanic Crescent.

Number Three is right there waiting, sitting near the end on a long gentle curve just where it meets Kelvin Drive: a teardrop in the corner of an actor's eye. Each of the grand terraced houses is four storeys tall, five if you count the maid's quarters up in the slated mansard. The stucco fronts — some a rich double cream, others gravestone grey — look down over gated gardens and across the tops of the trees lining the River Kelvin, which is always rushing to catch the shops before they close.

Bobby steps forward and pulls the doorbell. Nothing. They assume it must be ringing somewhere deep inside the house so stand back from the tall black storm doors and wait. The paint is lifting. The lace curtains in the drawing room, fashionable when Belgium was last invaded, don't so much as twitch. For something to do, Bobby wipes his feet on the well-worn mat.

'Are we late?' Robert whispers, shaking his watch hoping answers will fall out.

Bobby steps forward and pulls the doorbell again, this time holding it. Just as he lets go, one of the storm doors creaks inwards, as if the person behind is unsure. They step back as one, each noting the other's care for whoever is there. A woman about their mothers' age steps out, obviously not a maid. Behind her they glimpse a faded black front door and beyond that a long dark hall.

'Well, come in,' she says, waving a book, her fingers holding her page. 'I'm not heating the street.'

She opens the door behind and steps back into the hall. They wipe their feet again as they go in. Outside it's a dreich October day in 1933 but in the hallway it feels like a cosy midwinter evening in 1918. The walls are arsenic and the heavy furniture looks tea-stained. A grandfather clock stands like a coffin. Coving ices the ceilings. Bobby thinks of Miss Havisham. A telephone on the wall is the one concession to modernity, though it was probably fitted by Alexander Graham Bell. Bobby has never set foot in a house like this. Neither has Robert. Their eyes adjust.

'Mrs Cranston,' she announces, standing by a full-length wall mirror at the end of the hall so there appear to be two of her. 'Like the tearooms, though I've never been.'

'MacBryde,' says Bobby, glad he wiped his feet twice.

'Colquhoun,' says Robert, bobbing his head.

'A noble name,' says Mrs Cranston, donning the round tortoiseshell spectacles hanging on a fine gold chain down to her waist. She makes no attempt to hide her appraising and doesn't have to – rooms in Glasgow have never been scarcer. The whole country is emptying into the city in search of work. The Depression visits the rich too but the residents of Botanic Crescent have this thing called capital, silver to sell or even (at a pinch) rooms to let. Robert and Bobby stand still as a pair of vases. Robert looks past Mrs Cranston towards the stairs then back to the hall floor in case he seems presumptuous. Bobby looks right back at her – she's tall for a woman and slight, the front of her black shift dress flat, from when that was the fashion. The only jewellery she wears is a simple gold wedding band. All this simplicity throws her extraordinary hair into relief – it leaps back from her face as if she's shoved her fingers in a plug socket. It's the exact white of the bark of a weeping birch. Yet her skin, such as the gloomy hall reveals, is that of a much younger woman.

'The war,' she says, reading Bobby's mind. 'The last one. Or the first one. The one after the Boers.' She pushes her hair from her face and walks down the hall towards them. 'I used to be your colour,' she says, stopping an arm's length away. 'Then I got the telegram. Captain Cranston was not much older than you then. Neither was I. The next morning I woke up a white-haired widow.'

For once even Bobby is stuck for words.

'Needlessly dramatic,' says Mrs Cranston. She pauses and peers at them. 'So, you are artists?'

'Students,' says Robert. 'First years.'

'How did you know?' Bobby asks.

Mrs Cranston reaches out and takes his hands in hers, turning them over: hers spotless, his flecked with India ink and paint, fingerprints smudged.

'That or a pair of forgers,' she says.

'No,' says Robert. 'Nothing like that.'

'Good,' she says, letting go of Bobby's hands. 'You'll be my first tenants and I'll have no criminality under my roof, so . . .'

Mrs Cranston fishes in an invisible pocket and produces a small brass key, more suited to winding a clock.

She offers it to Robert. He daren't put his hand out, fears it will betray him by trembling – he feels the word 'criminality' hang in the air. It blooms around him like ink in water, threatening to stain him and everything he touches. He needs to get away from it, to turn back down the hall and run out through the doors into the air, maybe into the river. Bobby takes the key.

'You'll have the whole attic,' says Mrs Cranston. 'There are two sides – one for working and another for sleeping. There's a gas stove and a lavatory and a tin bath, which you may fill every Sunday. The rate is as advertised. Come and go as you please but the front door will be double locked every night at 10 p.m.'

Bobby steps forward. 'Can we . . . ?'

'Of course,' says Mrs Cranston, stepping aside. 'I won't come up, I've not been up there for years.'

Bobby catches lily of the valley as they pass. A dark-red runner leads the way up the stairs, growing thicker underfoot as they get higher. It's brighter up here, thanks to a skylight, its edges wreathed with plaster leaves and flowers. 'Baroque,' Robert nods, recalling a class. Every door they pass is closed. After the last carpeted landing, the stairs are narrower and bare. At the very top, on the very last stair, Bobby puts the little key in the lock, then, as if he's done it a thousand times, turns the handle, easing the door from its frame. It swings inwards. Decades of dust dance up in shafts of sun from a trio of skylights.

It's huge, it's theirs, its . . . home. Well, nearly.

'I'm telling mine the night,' says Bobby, as soon as they're sat on the train, which they nearly missed.

'The night?'

'Aye. I cannae wait. Fuckity-bye-Maybole!'

As Bobby says this his heart aches with Kildoon Hill, Auntie Maggie's laugh, the warmth and light of the library. But, no, he needs to get out, to become an artist, to become himself. He tells himself he'll be one less mouth to feed. Robert knows moving out will be taken as an affront. He will have to make his case watertight. He rehearses his lines in his head and Bobby leaves him be because, from tomorrow, Bobby will be with Robert every day – and night.

Robert's mother is laying the table as he walks in. She's felt Robert drift since he started at the art school. *He's just growing up*, she tells herself. She supported him staying on at school and keeping at his drawing but now curses herself for it. His brother will be away with the army eventually, if the news keeps getting worse. Robert Senior has added an extra wing to his aviary out the back. She envies his canaries the tenderness they elicit just by virtue of being. That was her, once. They've got colour and song. What does she have now her boys are going? A surprise, that's what. She lays a hand over her belly.

Over pork chops, Robert introduces the idea. 'Bobby says they're putting up the train fares again,' he says, marshalling a fact he knows his father can't argue with.

'Does he?' says his father, trimming his chop.

Robert's mother chews, regrets giving the chops that extra minute. But she'd wanted to wait for Robert. Chops were special – a special dinner for special news.

'Aye,' says Robert.

His mother swallows. 'Yes,' she says. 'Don't be saying "aye" at the art school – they'll think you were dragged up.'

'Yes,' says Robert, patting her on the arm. 'Sorry.'

'Don't be giving your mother lip,' says his father, spearing a finger of fat.

'I never—' Robert starts.

'So,' his father lifts his fork. 'What else does this Bobby have to say?'

'Nothing—' Robert starts.

'It's Bobby this and Bobby that.' His father chews the fat as he talks. 'Have you not a thought of your own?'

'It was Bobby's idea.'

'What was?' his mother asks, abandoning her own news, along with her dinner.

'He's flitting,' says his father, sitting back, pleased at having got there first. 'Aren't you?'

'It'll be cheaper,' says Robert. 'And I won't be late for class anymore and I can come back and visit and—'

His mother wrings the serviette in her lap. 'What? Where? When?'

'Glasgow,' says his father.

'We found a room—'

'A room?' his mother asks.

'It's a big attic in this posh house.'

'It would be,' smirks his father. 'How can you afford that?'

Robert has nothing to lose. 'It'll be cheaper. We're at college most of the time anyway and we won't even need tram fare because it's only up the hill.'

Robert's mother has no fight left. But her boy does, she sees that. As much as she never wants him to leave, she needs part of herself to be free. She's noted every mention of this Bobby she has yet to lay eyes on. Robert didn't have pals at school. This Bobby has filled the vacancy and then some: *He was top of his class. He's that funny. He works hard.* A proper pal, at last.

'And what do this Bobby's parents think?' she asks, standing up, her chop never to be finished.

Robert shrugs.

'You'll get a crick in that shoulder,' warns his father, rounding up his last tatty.

'Sorry,' says Robert, laying down his knife and fork.

'Is there something wrong with that?' his mother asks, channelling her worry into the chops. 'I'll tell the butcher.'

'Bit tough,' says his father, pushing back his seat from the table.

'So?' his mother persists. 'What do these MacBrydes say?'

Robert banks the expression for Bobby: *these MacBrydes*. Like the MacBrydes of Maybole are a Fettes-sort of family – Robert knows all the private schools now.

'They're fine,' says Robert.

'Weather is fine, Robert,' says his father. 'People are not. You've got your scholarships. What does he have? What does his father do?'

'He works at Lees.'

'A cobbler?'

'A tanner.'

His father sniffs. 'What about the mother?'

'What about her?' Robert asks.

'Temper,' his father's voice gets dangerously low.

'She's a . . .' Robert notices he's lowering his own voice too. He tries to think of a nice way of saying *buys and sells clothes round doors*. 'She's a seamstress.'

His mother believes him. 'And do they help him out?'

'Bobby's got it all saved up,' says Robert, proudly, standing up. 'The chops were lovely, Mother, thank you.'

He's flattering my food, she thinks, *he's sparing my feelings*. Robert never notices a thing she puts down in front of him. Suddenly she cannot bear it. Her oldest boy. She turns to the sink and runs the hot tap.

'I've got some news of my own,' she says, her back to the pair of them.

His father stands up then kicks his chair under the table. 'If his lot are happy then your mother and I can't stop you but you're to split every expense – you're not to be a penny in debt to him or anybody else.'

Robert nods then walks over to his mother. 'What did you say, Mum?'

'I said I'd like to see this place first,' says his mother, over the tap. 'I'm sure Mrs MacBryde will as well.'

Robert pauses. 'We got the keys today.'

'Oh,' his mother gasps, plunging her hands into the scalding water, eyes brimming. 'Then I better help you pack.'

Next morning, Bobby arrives with one bag and Robert with three, including some kitchen bits his mother made him take. Mrs Cranston gives them a second key, explains the rules again, then asks them to leave the rent, weekly, by the telephone. As she disappears into her drawing room, Bobby glimpses a book-lined wedge of it. They go up the first flight of stairs like they're sneaking into a lecture that's already started then get faster as they go higher before shouldering through the attic door as one. It's even bigger and emptier and brighter than the day before.

'So, your lot really didn't bother?' says Robert, laying down his bags.

The attic is divided by a simple stud wall down the middle with an arched opening between. Three evenly spaced, perfectly square sash windows look down on to the crescent below.

'Look,' says Bobby, darting to the windows, leaving boot-prints on the dusty boards.

'Bobby!' Robert hisses, pointing to the floors below.

Bobby tiptoes theatrically over to the door, then kicks off his boots without unlacing them. Robert gives him a look until he stands them side by side then heads back to the nearest window. 'You can see the top of the Botanics! The nipple!'

Robert takes off his boots then goes to the next window.

'They were a bit bothered,' says Bobby, still looking out. 'My Auntie Maggie cried and that set Jessie off, so my mother made a pot of tea. My father shook my hand. So that's that. What about yours?'

Robert opens his mouth to speak but says nothing.

'What?' Bobby asks.

Robert has the nagging feeling his mother was trying to tell him something and that if she had then maybe he wouldn't be standing here now.

Bobby starts unpacking in case Robert changes his mind.

Robert follows suit, for the same reason. They commandeer a drawer each in a tallboy pushed into the eaves at the gable end. Next to this they find a low rocking chair with a high back and a pale lemon cushion and, shrouded under a paint sheet, a cot.

'Oh,' Bobby sighs, as he uncovers it. 'It's new.'

'It's not new,' says Robert, running his hand along the carved ducklings waddling round the sides. 'It's old. Just . . . not used.' He remembers his baby sister bundled up in a Moses basket.

Bobby clocks his face. 'Homesick already?'

'Dusty up here,' says Robert, wiping his eyes.

Bobby covers the cot. Behind it he finds a brass studded trunk stamped with M.O.D. and CRANSTON. Bobby throws a sheet over that too.

'He's not in there,' says Robert.

'He might be,' says Bobby, crossing himself.

'So Catholic,' says Robert, walking over to the only door in the whole space. He pushes it open.

'A lavvy!' says Bobby, dashing in and enthroning himself. 'Royal wee?' he asks, pulling the chain. 'I bet your lot had one.'

'Up,' Robert says, hauling him out and stepping in, shutting the door behind him. He unbuttons himself and stands there ready to go but can't. He is acutely, agonisingly, aware of Bobby on the other side of the door.

'Am no listenin,' says Bobby, right through the door.

'Fuck off,' says Robert, laughing and squeezing.

Bobby is busy trying not to listen, trying not to think of Robert unbuttoned on the other side of the door. Bobby gets hard. Adjusting his trousers in a panic, he rushes noisily about the attic. He finds two navy-striped mattresses propped one against the other, the straw inside them long gone to dust. Bobby wonders about mice, then surmises they wouldn't dare cross Mrs Cranston's door. Rats haunted the close at Maybole so mice seem almost quaint.

'It works then,' Robert announces, emerging as the flush thunders behind him.

'We need to get some straw,' says Bobby.

'We getting a horse as well?' Robert asks, rinsing his hands in the little sink.

'No.' Bobby kicks a mattress then coughs as it wheezes into the air.

'Oh,' Robert says, waving the dust away.

'Are we used to fine feathers in Kilmarnock? The deepest eider down? Feathers plucked from the King's swans?'

'No, we had, I don't know . . . horsehair?'

'Well, we had straw,' admits Bobby. 'Or the floor.'

'I wasn't saying anything. I'm sure they'll do the job.'

Bobby pauses. 'So, which side?' he asks, looking up through a skylight, trying to make the question sound as ordinary as possible.

'What do you mean?' Robert asks.

'Or will we keep one side for working and the other side for sleeping?'

Robert tries to look like he hasn't already thought about it.

Bobby is regretting his words, wishing he could take back this obvious scheming, but he can't stop himself. 'So . . . we'll sleep this side and work that side?'

'Aye,' Robert says, noting the way the sun is hitting Bobby and delighted to have a reason he can say out loud, 'We'll get the north light on that side!'

Bobby tries not to sing out loud: *We, we'll. We, we'll. We.* Not you and me. But *we*.

'Great,' says Bobby, not turning in case his face shows him up. 'We better go out and get some bits, get this place sorted.'

'Where?'

Bobby knows from his Auntie Maggie there's one place in Glasgow where you can find everything you'll ever need.

'C'mon,' he says, turning, hoping his excitement just looks like busy acquisitiveness, toy-shop delight. 'We're going to the Barras!'

The tram from the West End to the Barras trundles from deep pockets to penniless. It is a moving metaphor for the Depression gripping Glasgow, Scotland, the world. The endless strikes, the soup kitchens on every corner and the growing sense that something is going to have to happen lends a simultaneous urgency and torpor to everything and everyone. Even the trees look tired. The world does not need artists – has no work for them, and yet Bobby and Robert paint night and day. The School of Art sits on top of Garnethill but is not above the concerns of the world. A house for refugees has opened over the road, taking in arrivals from Poland and Germany and other places with accents even beyond Glasgow. The grand old synagogue a street away has queues when their kitchen opens. Jews are new to them. Bobby is seduced by the smell of a soup he later learns is *borscht* and quickly works out how to make it.

This tram route is their story in reverse. Maybole can't keep Bobby. Robert feels no kinship with Kilmarnock. They each leave easily, like a tooth that was ready to fall out. But can Glasgow really be home? Even as students, they're richer than they've ever been. They get off at the Gallowgate and surge towards the Barras with the rest of the city.

'It's teeming,' says Robert. Bobby is already distracted by a barrow piled high with rugs of every shape and colour.

'Look,' says Bobby, folding his arms and hopping into the air. 'Am Aladdin!'

'You're insane,' says Robert, looking about them. But nobody bats an eyelid because nobody is paying attention because everybody is out getting their messages. It's Saturday morning and there are bargains to be had. The carpet man plants his hands so deep in his trouser pockets they might take root. He clocks them as down from the art school, which doesn't mean they can't buy – far from it – but they're more likely to drive a harder bargain and less likely to get it.

Everything worth having is here – from every corner of the Empire shipped right up the Clyde, for every room in your home, be it a single end in Dennistoun or a West End mansion flat. Big wooden barrows jostle along every inch of the narrow cobbled streets, each announcing the name of the vendor. The air is filled with promise and promises: THE FINEST MEAT YE'LL EVER EAT! STRONG BOOTS FOR SURE FOOTS! THE SWEETEST SWEETIES OR YER TEETH BACK! Cavernous warehouses stretch off every street, tempting in the flush with row upon row of covered stalls, some boasting electric light. For those with the thickest pay packets, there are actual shops with big windows so everybody else can see what they can't afford. You can buy yourself a dozen eggs or a twenty-four-carat-gold necklace thick as your thumb, half a side of Galloway lamb or a whole horse to ride home on. This is no mere market – it's a grand bazaar. The biggest in all Britain – worlds bigger than the weekly affairs at Maybole and Kilmarnock.

As usual, Robert strides on ahead. If he lets Bobby walk by his side folk sometimes mistake them for brothers. But Bobby has a tendency to stand too close and close in the wrong way. So, Robert goes on ahead and Bobby follows, and neither question it.

Bobby dawdles through the crowd distracted by this and that and by his belly, which rumbles, as usual. He's stuck by a tray piled high with crumbly squares of tablet guarded by a granny done up like a highland wifie. She has a starched white mutch round her head and silk-grey hair pulled back in a bun that tight she barely looks thirty, never mind seventy. It's never too early for tablet, thinks Bobby, making a note to come back. It's also never too early for chips. Or too late for square sausage. Fried onions season the air.

'Watch yer step,' Robert shouts over his shoulder, skidding on a half oyster.

'Check for a pearl!' Bobby shouts back, shuddering at the mucous mess. Vinegary whelk shells crunch underfoot.

'Can we not get a wee roll?' Bobby asks, as he catches up with Robert who has paused in front of the doll stall. A row of tiny girls in Victorian dresses stand in front of him, all eyes wide and arms out. Robert leans in to peer at a ringletted redhead.

'You gi'n me the glad eye?' the doll asks. Robert gawps. The doll laughs without blinking and a young woman steps out from behind. 'Every time.'

'I was just—' Robert stutters, and a blush creeps over his collar.

Bobby laughs along, hopes it will soften Robert who still doesn't get that every single citizen of Glasgow sincerely believes they're treading the boards at the King's Theatre. It is a city of stars in search of an audience.

'Bit of a doll yersell,' says the young woman, winking. She's about their age. Her deeply unfashionable ringlets match the doll; her eyelashes are even longer. 'Ye dancin?'

'Ye askin?' says Bobby, stepping forward, between the two.

'Oh, I see,' she says, standing back and folding her arms, but with no trace of anything else. 'Everybody's out for their messages this morning.' To Bobby: 'You're too big for dollies.'

Robert doesn't know what to say or where to look, so ducks into the nearest warehouse. Bobby nods at the girl then flashes a smile. It doesn't do to make enemies, not even in a city.

Robert pushes on ahead, trying to lose himself in the crush. 'She was only joking,' Bobby whines, his entreaty lost beneath a cry of BURNT ROLLS! 'Don't be like that!'

Robert comes to a halt, the crowd parting either side of him, like the Clyde round the pilings on the Jamaica Bridge. Folk tut.

'You saying she didn't want me to take her dancin?'

'No,' says Bobby, catching up. What he wants to say is *I didn't want her taking you dancing, I don't want anybody taking you dancing.* 'She was just having a laugh. Come on, we've plenty to get.'

Robert's eye is caught by a platoon of old military clothes. He goes over and lifts a heavy grey greatcoat.

'Get it on,' Bobby says, stepping over.

Instinctively, Robert refuses attention, pushing Bobby's arm away.

'Oh, c'mon,' says Bobby, popping it over his own shoulders. It's way too big. Robert surrenders, whipping it off and slipping his arms in the sleeves. He has to admit it looks good.

'You'll be needing that soon enough, son,' says the stallholder, the only woman in the ranks. 'This weather won't hold.' She sticks her finger through a hole in one of the sleeves and laughs. 'Hope you've better luck!'

Robert gasps.

'Och it's only moths,' she says then names a price he can't refuse.

Robert keeps the coat on and off they go. Within minutes he's too hot but taking it off would feel like admitting some kind of failure. Next, they buy two surprisingly heavy sacks of straw. There's more to get – Bobby made a list. Soon, their pockets are empty and their arms full: a pair of navy woollen blankets, two plates, bowls and mugs marked with the stamp of a big hotel that shut down and, best of all, a silver-plated coffee pot in search of a lid. Bobby will boil the blankets – they look loupin. He wonders where Mrs Cranston gets her clothes washed, because even posh people need clean knickers, then imagines the looks he'd get if he walked into a steamie here. They'd scour him alive. He'll make do with their tin bath. He will be washing Robert's clothes, all of them.

'Our own coffee pot,' says Bobby, eyeing their haul.

'All we need now is a plant,' says Robert, swept up in comforts.

'I'll take a wee cutting at the Botanics.'

'You dare!' says Robert, wondering if he'd spurn a geranium, should one appear.

As they pass the carpets Bobby has an idea and runs over.

'What scraps have you got?'

The carpet man snorts in the end-of-day cold then ambles over to the lock-up behind his barrow. He tugs the damp door open and beckons Bobby over. Inside is a nest of oddments: corners cut from bay windows, strips of wildly varying lengths and widths and even, to Bobby's delight, an oriel triangle.

'One man's rubbish, eh?' says the man, rubbing thumb and forefinger.

Bobby thinks how proud his mother would be. Robert still doesn't really get it.

'For our floor,' said Bobby, turning to Robert. 'It's draughty and I worry she'll hear us walking about and that.'

Robert nods. *Our floor?* He's had the same worry.

'It'll be like a collage,' Bobby says. 'I'll make a big rug.'

The carpet man names a figure. Bobby halves it. Robert tries to walk away. This goes on for five minutes before the carpet man makes a show of caving in, thrilled to have his rubbish carted and be paid for the privilege.

'Can we come back for it next week?' Bobby asks, making a show of not having a spare hand.

'Aye, but any longer and I'm charging rent.'

'Deal,' Bobby says, turning to Robert.

Our floor.

They gather their things and head for the tram, arms full of home.

Chapter 10

Bobby doesn't know where he is. He rolls over, feels the crunch of fresh straw then sees Robert's sleeping face.

As quietly as he can, he gets up – the floorboards are freezing, but he'll soon have them covered. He considers making toast over the gas ring but won't risk waking Robert. He taps the frigid block of butter – a moving-in treat – then pads over to the nearest window to let in their first day. That's Glasgow out there! The net curtain flutters into his face. It tickles. He half-sneezes. Robert rolls over. A deep sleeper? Bobby adds this information to his growing collection of things he knows about Robert.

Bobby returns to his mattress and lies down, willing the straw to shush. He looks over to Robert then back to the net, shaking itself awake in the breeze. He remembers the curtains flapping at the sanatorium – the nurses were murder for fresh air, no matter the season. The windows were wide open unless there was actual snow coming through. He'd lain still in the high hospital bed, sheets tucked up to his chin on his worst days. Eventually, they got him up and sat him in a yellow-striped deckchair, like he was on his holidays. His second stay was the longest – three whole weeks. He wasn't as scared that time, knew the layout, the rhythms, knew he'd get better sooner here. He needed 'building up', according to the big Irish nurse who always gave him an extra slice of bread and butter. He knew his parents would be presented with a bill for his stay, as if he'd been at a grand hotel, so he tried to get better as fast as he could, strained every atom towards vitality. But also loved having his own bed and three square meals.

From then to now, thinks Bobby, looking over to Robert barely an arm's length away. From there to here: lying on *our floor*, waiting for Robert to wake.

But Robert is not sleeping. The window creaking had woken him and he'd caught half-sight of Bobby, silhouetted against the morning sun in his pants, his legs surprisingly strong and thick with hairs springing up in the chill. Robert rolled on to his side to hide the tent in his drawers. His body is giving him away again. So, he pretends to be asleep.

It's Saturday morning in Kilmarnock too. Robert's father will be up and about already, fettling his birds, sliding fresh sheets of newspaper into the long row of cages lining the back wall of his aviary. Robert used to help his father with the birds – he had about twenty, mainly canaries but some budgies too, blues and greens, Robert's favourites. It's one of the few things he and his father did together. Other boys had football but, mercifully, his father never went in for that. Robert Senior blames himself for his son's lack of knowledge of such things. As they flattened out the papers Robert read the headlines. More lay-offs at Ferguson, because Americans don't need tractors in the dustbowl. Empire Bonds promised healthy returns. Fife Yachts, 'fast and bonny', were sponsoring a tall ships regatta out from Bute around Ailsa Craig and back – the Marquis himself would present the cup. But they talked only of the birds – Robert had learned from his mother how not to darken his father's mood. What happened in the world was not their concern. The Colquhouns had made it to their new council flat in a clean, quiet close on New Mill Road. Mrs Colquhoun no longer had to take in washing. His brother was going to the army. Robert was not to be a disappointment.

For years, Robert was top of his art class – he gave the few drawings he was proud of to his mother, who hid them all in the bottom of her sewing box under her chair. He imagined this might lead to being a draughtsman like his father, delineating cogs and wheels in the machines that made money for men they'd never meet. Sometimes they sketched the birds together, his father always starting with the bars on the cage. So, of course, his father had taken him out of school to do an apprenticeship. Five minutes into the din and filth of his one and only day on the factory floor he'd been seized by a coughing fit, which caused his new colleagues to collapse in laughter. It had given Robert some respect for his father. Within hours, his art master, Mr Lyle, had turned up at the gates and got him out. Back in school he'd said, 'You must continue to excel, you must never prove them right.' From then on, Robert spent every spare hour in the art room. From then on, his father was alone with his birds.

Robert rolls over and opens his eyes.

'At last!' Bobby says, getting up and heading over to the corner he grandly calls the kitchen. 'I thought we'd lost you.'

Robert nods. He sketches the scene in his head and imagines sending it to his mother. What would she see? Maybe he'll send her a drawing of something she can show the neighbours, maybe he'll even deliver it to her and bring Bobby along like she asked. Bobby is loud, but almost always funny, and frequently a lightning rod for mortification. But he's never boring. He attracts people, he invites possibility. Obviously, she would like him.

'Coffee?' says Bobby, holding up their lidless pot.

This lays down a template for their Sundays. Bobby wakes first and makes coffee. Then they lie on their separate mattresses and drink it together and talk about the work they plan until they achieve sufficient momentum to get up and make it to the work side of the attic, Robert ducking through the arch. Bobby has yet to recover from Fleming not putting his sketch of Robert on the Life Modelling Room wall – after all those years doing caricatures at the factory he knows faces. He could compete, he thinks, but doesn't want to overshadow Robert. So, that first Sunday in their attic, Bobby decides to draw his favourite thing – he takes their coffee pot off the gas ring and puts it on the table. Fleming likes Bobby's still life work so Bobby does more of it. Bobby becomes a master of objects. Sometimes he finds their obstinate thingness frustrating – Robert threw a dirty sock at him for this pretentiousness. Bobby prefers objects that are imperfect – cracked cups, tired flowers and over-ripe vegetables (which he magicks into the various delicious soups they live off). Flaws speak of their past, which suggests to Bobby the possibility of changes to come. So, Bobby draws broken things. And Robert draws Bobby. And Bobby lets him.

Chapter 11

The rest of their first term flies by in a blur of classes, exploring and exhibitions. Now they're practically round the corner, they're first in and last out. After class, there's always something new. No event gets past Bobby: an apologetic show from Germany in one of the posh galleries by Blythswood Square, some watercolours in one of the old trades halls and they're never away from Kelvingrove. One exhibition changes everything.

'*Modern French Painting*,' says Bobby. 'We'll see.'

As always, Bobby makes Robert salute Sir Roger, then they head upstairs. The gallery is mobbed.

'*Seated Woman*,' says Robert, reading the label on the first picture. 'Pablo Picasso. How come he's in it? He's not French.'

'He's Picasso, that's how come,' says Bobby, thrilled by the woman's triangular face.

'Imagine trying to get that by Fleming,' says Robert.

'You must learn the rules before you can break them,' says Bobby, his Fleming impression now perfect, the burr rrrolling.

'If it's good enough for Picasso,' says Robert.

'Look at this *Still Life*,' says Bobby, turning to the next picture. 'It's no very still!'

A jaunty vase, an overflowing fruit bowl and a tiny guitar bicker on top of a table that looks like it's trying to find the door. Bobby considers Braque's brushwork. 'It's like a print,' he says. 'Flat but not and the colours are all autumn but it's so alive.'

'Ma wee lassie could do that,' says a man next to them, pointing at the Picasso.

'Could she aye?' says Bobby. The man's contempt tips him into defending the choices of the faraway Spaniard.

'Never mind,' says Robert, smiling at the man then leading Bobby to another Picasso that looks like it's vibrating.

Somehow, they're already halfway through the first term of their first year. Two students have left quietly, him for 'family reasons' and her in the family way, Bobby speculates. Trusted to stay on, they are allocated studio space. It's no surprise to anybody when Fleming assigns them to share.

'MacBryde and Colquhoun,' says Fleming, reading from a clipboard, with an air of surprise as if he'd not assigned them. 'And that's everybody. Off you all go!' Their year scatters. *Favourites*, somebody mutters. *Married*, laughs another. Fyffe looks fit to spit.

'Thank you, sir,' says Bobby, hanging back.

'Just down from my old studio,' says Fleming, ticking them off his list.

Fleming is only a few years older than them but has already graduated, exhibited in Edinburgh and London, and returned wreathed in recognition from the imperial capital, his way undoubtedly smoothed by his adopted Kelvinside ways and means. But he does not look down on these two. He admires their industry, the way each pushes the other, and their quaint determination to bring honour on Ayrshire. The only subjects they do not excel in are Embroidery (to be expected, of Colquhoun at least) and Metalwork (the workshop fumes sent both into coughing fits). It will be interesting to see which of them comes top of their year. And to see how the other takes it.

'You'd only spend all your time visiting each other anyway,' says Fleming. 'And nobody else could work with either of you. This way you've no excuse for not getting on.' Not that they're lazy, far from it. They're last out every day but more than simply being here they give the impression of not wanting to be anywhere else. Every student here was top of their class, but Fleming knows these two have grafted – will never forget the greasy feel of the brown paper MacBryde submitted his extraordinary drawings on, covered in tiny morning-blue flowers from a hill above his home, frail yet quivering, more animal than plant. Colquhoun carries himself more quietly but no less determinedly and is an even finer draughtsman, his eye for line seeing long past mere verisimilitude – his figures in Life Drawing hold the paper as if they had always been there, just waiting to be revealed, as if Colquhoun had taken something away, rather than added.

The studios are all north facing and each is messier than the last, immediately betraying the ambitions of past occupants – porcupines of needlework, corners full of sawdust, paint on the door-handles.

'Is this not great?' says Bobby, closing the door behind them. 'It's even got a heater!' He peels off his fingerless gloves and warms his hands over a huge cast-iron radiator hulking in the corner.

Robert says nothing.

'I'll knit you a pair if you want,' says Bobby, laying down his gloves. 'What, do you not like it?' Bobby paces out the room wondering if they could secretly sleep here on really cold nights. He could put a spirit cooker in the corner, maybe invite Moira over for tea, tempt Robert out of his shyness.

'It's fine,' says Robert. 'It's just . . . it's just us two?'

'Aye,' says Bobby. 'Did you want one of the Hugos or Henrys? Or maybe . . . Moira?'

Robert doesn't want to share a studio with anybody else. But also doesn't want Fleming to have realised this.

'Don't be daft,' says Robert, claiming the half of the room furthest from the door by placing his still-new black jacket on the chair.

'What then?' Bobby asks. Robert's proprietary gesture annoys him so much he steps over, lifts the jacket off and drops it on the floor.

'Haw!' says Robert, swooping to pick it up and brushing the sleeves. 'There could be anythin on that floor.'

Tension blooms between them, rising with the heat from the radiator, filling the small room. Bobby never shuts up. Getting a word out of Robert is like getting blood out a stone. Bobby fusses like a housewife. Robert never lifts a finger. Bobby slurps his coffee. Robert never finishes a thing Bobby cooks.

'Fine,' Bobby snaps. 'Share with somebody else if you want. I see you night and day as it is.'

'Maybe I will,' says Robert, laying his jacket down again, keeping one hand on it, daring Bobby.

'Aye, will you?' Bobby stomps over to the studio door and pulls it open with such force it gusts all the old papers off their shared desk. He leans out into the hall so everybody can hear. 'Out you fucking go then!' Doors open up and down and heads peep out.

Robert stands there for a moment and considers sharing with somebody else, sharing his minutes and hours with anybody else. Nobody knows him like Bobby, nobody sees the world the same way, even if they move through it so differently. Nobody else believes he can become an actual artist. Bobby's certainty about Robert's talent mirrors his own anxiety. Bobby can see a world for him.

Robert shakes his head.

'Thought not,' says Bobby, slamming the door then opening it again and shouting, 'Show's over!' He closes the door calmly and casts his eye over what is now undoubtedly their studio. 'Aye, a wee spirit cooker would be just the thing.'

Robert notices how people are drawn to Bobby, especially girls. Like fish towards food. They can't help themselves. Bobby listens, Bobby is funny, Bobby knows it. As soon as Bobby steps out their studio he's swooped on and carried to one of the sitooteries lining the ground floor corridor, little booths of intrigue. Robert is harder to approach, does not smile so readily.

For one or two dedicated girls, this makes him all the more attractive.

'Moira fancies you,' says Bobby, when their studio door is safely closed. 'I've just come from lunch with a group that she was in, so speak with total authority.'

'Why are you talking like yer on the radio?'

'I don't know,' Bobby laughs. 'But I'm right.'

'Your Moira?' Robert asks, lost in a study of the stone lions guarding the war memorial in George Square.

'She's not my Moira, not like that,' says Bobby, knowing Robert is barely half-listening. 'So, I told her you'd take her to the Hogmanay Dance.'

'You . . .' Robert screws his eyes shut – he's failed to capture the lion's nobility, made it look like a sulky cat. 'You what?'

'She asked me if you were a good dancer and I said "Aye".'

Robert blinks disbelievingly.

'I'm guessing yer not,' Bobby continues. 'But anyway, that's that.'

'How do you know I can't dance?' says Robert, his feet refusing the memory of Highland dancing class.

'Can you?' Bobby twirls.

'No, but—'

'But nothing.'

'You don't know everything about me.'

'No, but I do know you're going to the Hogmanay Dance with Moira,' says Bobby, jigging around him.

Robert stands up. 'I'm not going anywhere with your Moira.'

'She's not my Moira!'

'You better tell her that.'

'I've told her you're taking her so that's that,' says Bobby. 'You're going to Hell!'

'What?'

'Helll!' Bobby says, flapping like a bat, swooping round Robert and bumping into him. 'It's the theme for the Hogmanay Dance, it's on all the posters, if you ever took your head out your arse.

She asked me if I was going and I said I doubt it and she looked disappointed and I asked how and she said that meant you wouldnae be coming cos we're two peas in a pod so I told her you're yer own man.'

'I am,' says Robert, trying to convince himself.

'You are.'

'So that means you're taking her. Or standing her up?'

Bobby thinks he knows what he wants – he doesn't know about Robert, maybe it is only pals and art, not that art isn't everything. Bobby hates waiting – even when what he's waiting for seems impossible. Moira might force the issue. And what then? There can be no real future, no life together. But Bobby can see no future, no life at all, without Robert.

Bobby looks down at the lions. 'The paws are wrong.'

Robert nods, a peace gesture.

'Don't wear your blue shirt,' says Bobby.

'I'm not going. I can't afford to take a girl out. She'll be wanting dinner and dancing and god knows what.'

'True,' muses Bobby.

'You take her if you like her so much.' As soon as he's said this, Robert feels a flicker of, what . . . jealousy?

'Maybe I will,' says Bobby, offering his hand to Robert as if at a dance. Robert knocks it away then turns back to his lion, traps it under the heel of his hand then walks his fingers across the paper, furrowing it as he goes. He scrunches it into a ball, which he drops at Bobby's feet.

'Fine,' says Robert. 'I'll take her.'

Next morning is Saturday and they're planning another day in the library. But first, Robert fancies a second cup of coffee.

'You've drunk it all,' says Bobby, not looking up from his book.

Robert walks over to the kitchen searching for the tin.

'We can't afford it,' says Bobby, raising *Death in Venice* to his face like a mask.

'Another cup of coffee will bankrupt us?'

'No, but another cup means another pot and we've run out so I'd need to go out.'

'So, let's go.'

'Go? What am I?'

'I said let us go — I'll come with you.'

Bobby turns a page as noisily as he can.

Robert finds the coffee tin and peers into it, muttering.

Bobby abandons Aschenbach and Tadzio and looks over the top of his book. 'What was that? What did you say?'

'Nothing.'

'Aye, nothing. We've spent our money for the week.'

'*Our* money?'

'Aye, *our* money.'

Robert shakes his head. 'You're like an old wifie with a purse.'

'Nae wifie would put up with you!'

Robert lowers his voice. 'Keep it down.'

'Or what?'

And they're off. Three floors down Mrs Cranston covers her ears. She gets up and turns on the radio — the news from Europe is more peaceful. Finally, something clatters into a corner then there's thunder on the stairs before the front door slams. She catches sight of Robert raging down the front steps.

For hours, Bobby paces the attic, counting every floorboard again and again. Where did all that anger come from? Where has it gone? Why did he not just go out and get more coffee? Did Mrs Cranston hear them? Where is Robert? Should he go out and look for him? Will he ever come back? What will happen if he does? What will happen if he doesn't? Where will Bobby go? He can't afford to stay on his own. What will his mother say when he lands back on her doorstep? Bobby hears the clang of a fire engine and runs to the window just as Robert's key turns in the door.

'Coffee?' Robert asks, shaking a tin that sounds like sorry.

★

Their ancient mattresses already need more straw. As ever, Bobby plans this domestic mission. Robert agrees easily, aware the peace between them is delicate.

They are greeted at the Barras by a cry of *TOFF-EEE AIP-PLES!* Bobby's belly heeds the call. Robert runs over and gets one then hands it to Bobby who accepts it like a trophy. It's a sticky red he'll struggle to recreate the next day. They head into the big green warehouse and the dear indoor stalls. Bobby takes a bite, cracking into the red, not worried for his teeth. He watches the man and woman behind Robert, struggling to hold hands in the crowd, him lifting his arm to let her go in front, as if they're at the dancing. What must that be like?

One stall outshines all the others. It's lit by an extravagant chandelier and backed by a deep-green velvet curtain – the same plushness lines a counter strewn with treasures. Bobby is pulled in.

'Robert.' Bobby waves his half-chewed candy apple. 'Look!'

Robert appears by his shoulder. Here is beauty. A white rabbit's foot is ready to dance, adorned with a multi-faceted orange stone crackling with fire. Impossibly dainty cups jostle with gilded saucers. A lonely majolica candlestick waits for its better half. A brass toasting fork promises plenty. Stacks of spectacularly mismatched dinner plates transport Bobby to dining rooms no ancestor has ever set foot in. Deep within a perfectly round clear glass paperweight, a red rose unfurls, permanently perfect. Next to it another orb, seemingly filled with rain that's still falling. Another swirls grey like the depths of the Clyde. Arranged around all three, and radiating out, sit highly polished silver spoons. Here and there are tiny carved boxes depicting scenes from places they'd struggle to find on a map: Lichtenstein, Carpathia, Abernethy. In the middle of it all glows what looks like a big white spiral shell, poised on a delicate mount of silver seaweed. Robert marvels.

'That's a nautilus,' says the stallholder, appearing from behind the curtain. He completely fills the space behind his stall. Gold buttons strain down the front of his waistcoat, also green velvet.

He's wearing a startlingly obvious toupée – a dead black cat asleep on the ashes of his heyday. Each of his forearms bulges with a tattoo of a crossed pair of hammers. You wouldn't steal from his stall. Bobby notices a gold Claddagh where a wedding band would go, two hands crossed over a heart with a crown atop. The man offers the nautilus to Robert. 'This marks you out as a man of refined tastes.'

Robert hesitates, then takes it with both hands. It's as light as one of his father's birds but not fragile – he can tell without pressing that there's no way he could crack it. Here is beauty made from strength. Carefully, he holds it up to the electric light and watches it glow pinkly. How to capture a form that's no longer living but holds such life?

'You cannae afford it,' says the stallholder, not unkindly, as he gently takes it back. 'But it's nice to look, eh?'

Robert stares at it. 'It's like the corals in the Hunterian.'

The man raises a strong black eyebrow as he puts the nautilus back in pride of place. 'It is. But better.'

'It's beautiful,' Bobby says, wishing he'd got to hold it.

Robert shuffles. They can't afford a thing on this man's stall but he's not hunted them. 'We should go,' he says, tugging Bobby's sleeve.

'Without introducing yourselves?'

'This is Robert,' says Bobby, stepping forward. 'Ma pal. Am Bobby.'

'Twa Boabs,' the man laughs. 'A matching pair!' He bends down then reappears with a sign which he hangs above his stall. It's an oval mirror painted with a name, bottle-green letters outlined with actual gold leaf. The man gestures to the sign like a magician: 'Morris.'

'Morris,' Bobby nods. 'How come yer opening late?'

'Because nobody appreciates beauty before midday,' says Morris. 'And I do not appreciate mornings.' With one finger he flicks a switch under the stall and the chandelier fairly sparkles.

Robert realises with devastating certainty that Bobby is going nowhere – it's pointless trying to extract him from a conversation once he's off. Sometimes he likes watching Bobby with people, enjoys his ease. But this Morris is different.

'You look like you could blow away,' says Morris to Robert. Then, to Bobby, 'You need to feed him up.'

Robert gawps.

Morris waves over to the woman running the wool stall at the end: 'Hiya Janey hen!' She waves back: 'Hiya Morris hen!' Robert gawps. Even Bobby just stands there.

'Yous catching flies?' Morris asks, closing his mouth slowly then pursing his lips. 'I've been here since before you were born. This lot are my family. They're not blind or daft.'

Right enough, thinks Robert, trying not to look at Morris's wig. He turns to go.

Morris pauses then leans over to them and says, 'I tell yous what, come back next week and I'll show yous something really special.' Then he stands back and coughs lightly, returning to character. 'Look with your eyes, boys, not your hands.' With a wave of his ringed fingers he dismisses them then flashes gold molars as his first real customer approaches. 'Mrs Grantham,' he intones, with the seriousness of a funeral director. 'You're looking awfy lovely.'

'We're not going back,' says Robert, before they're even out the market.

'He seems . . .' Bobby searches for the right word. 'Nice.'

'Nice?!' Robert shakes his head. 'He's . . .'

'He's what?'

'We need to get our messages somewhere else.'

Bobby puts his hand out for the tram.

Robert lowers his voice. 'We can't be seen with a man like . . .'

'Like what?' says Bobby, readying their change. The tram stops and they cram on, only resuming their conversation as the attic door closes.

'What are you worried about?' says Bobby, carefully unwrapping the cow's head he plans to sketch before turning into a soup.

'He's . . .' Robert drops his bags. 'You know?'

Bobby stands there. 'I don't know. Shit!'

'What?'

'We forgot the straw. We'll have to go back.'

'I'm not going near that man, he's—'

'What? Say it.'

Robert looks up through a skylight and out into space. He closes his eyes as he says it. 'Queer.'

The word hangs between them.

Bobby turns away and thinks fast. Is this an accusation? An admission?

'So?' shrugs Bobby, his back to Robert. 'It's not catching.'

Robert replays their every move. What did this Morris see in them, in him? What does he think he knows? If a total stranger can leap to such a conclusion then surely the police can't be far behind? How long until there's a knock at the door?

'How are you not bothered?' Robert asks, walking over to the sink and splashing his face with cold water. 'What if somebody saw us with him and followed us home, saw where we live – what if they blackmail us?'

'Blackmail?' Bobby says, walking over to a window and gesturing to the empty street below. 'Us?'

'I live here with you.'

'So?' says Bobby. 'We're just two students on the same course saving on rent. Right?'

Robert pauses. There is a space in the question Bobby asked. Not so anybody else would notice. He is afraid to fill it. 'Right.'

Six days and nights go by and nothing. Robert barely sleeps, sure this Morris will be the end of everything. Not even the daily rhythm of classes pushes the fears from his head. People are looking at him all the time – he walks further and further ahead of Bobby. He's sure he'll be expelled, sent home in disgrace, if not to jail. Do they still ship men like Morris to Australia?

It's not that Bobby isn't worried – far from it. He can read the papers as well as anybody else: INDECENT BEHAVIOUR, LEWD CONDUCT, PUBLIC CONVENIENCE. But to Bobby there's only one greater danger and that's not going back. Bobby glimpsed whole worlds in Morris's paperweights, saw new vistas on those carved wooden boxes, heard whispers from the nautilus. This Morris knows things. Bobby needs to know them too. Whatever the price.

The next Sunday, Bobby arrives at the Barras as the place is emptying – a new naval frigate is being launched later and a launch is something you don't want to miss these days.

Bobby forges past the carpet man, who nods over, and into the warehouse.

TOFF-EEE AIP-PLES!

The stalls are shutting up. Bobby worries Morris has gone already – he can't see all the way down to the end. Did he imagine the whole thing?

'You made it then,' says Morris, closing his cash tin but not before Bobby clocks the notes. 'I was gonnae send out a search party.' He pauses. 'On yer tod?'

'Just me,' nods Bobby.

Morris picks back up where they left off. 'So, the Hunterian eh? Tat!' He pops below his counter then reappears holding some kind of dome under a square of black silk. 'Well?' he asks, whipping the silk away.

Bobby's mind immediately goes to Leonardo's anatomical drawings. He leans in. Morris switches his chandelier back on.

'What is it?' Bobby asks. 'A brain?'

'Bingo,' says Morris. 'It's a brain coral – a perfect specimen. All the way from Australia.'

Convicts. Bobby shivers at the thought of the law. He looks into the dome, at all the tiny twists and turns, the swirling lobes of calcium, each hemisphere identical. He's never seen such a thing, not even in a museum.

'Where did you get it?' Bobby asks.

'Not Australia,' says Morris, covering it up again. 'A lady never tells,' he winks, turning off the chandelier again. 'Glad you like it. You can tell your pal about it.'

'I will,' says Bobby. Morris stands there, arms folded, his tattoos flexing.

'What else can you show me?' Bobby asks.

Morris tilts his head. 'What else? Grab this.' Bobby helps Morris pull a cloth over his wares then, with one hand, Morris pulls a heavy steel shutter down over the front and padlocks the lot.

Bobby wonders if Morris has forgot his question and is working up the courage to ask again. Morris steps out from behind his stall. 'Everything else,' he says, pocketing the padlock key. 'C'mon.'

Morris leads. Bobby follows. Ten minutes on a tram and they're in Dennistoun. Morris reaches into his pocket and produces another set of keys as they round the corner to his street. Two scabby wee girls run by, chasing a red rubber ball – Bobby thinks of Jessie back in Maybole, her sticky wee hand in his.

Morris ducks as he disappears into the tenement close. 'Coming?' asks the voice from the dark.

Morris jingles his keys. Bobby steps in. There's no going back.

They stop on the first floor. It takes Morris a minute to open each of the four locks on his door.

'Preferred first floor,' says Morris, opening the door. Bobby hesitates. 'Don't worry, I'll let you out!'

Morris goes in first as if to prove it's safe and Bobby follows. 'Wait till I tell Robert,' he says, not sure where to look first. Morris's flat is a grotto. There can't be a shell left in all the seven seas. Every table, every shelf, is a reef. Every size and shape and colour, they cover every surface – even the ceiling has a nacreous glow.

'One from every sailor I know,' winks Morris. 'I've never been further than Troon.'

Morris's flat is one big room – a conspicuous double bed lies in the corner, draped with a pink blanket patterned with starfish.

A round table sits in the window – it's completely encrusted with what can't be real pearls and in the middle stands the nautilus. Two scalloped chairs sit round the table. The far corner is curtained off with a shimmery silvery sheet. Shells of every shape and colour.

'That's the sink and the po,' says Morris, nodding to the corner and freeing himself from his waistcoat. 'All mod cons. Shoes off.'

Bobby pauses again.

Morris points to the round cream rug covering the floorboards. 'I'm not going to jump you. Or did you want me to?' Morris laughs. He holds up his hand and points to his Claddagh ring. 'I am a married woman and I don't like chicken.'

'Married?' Bobby stammers. 'Chicken?'

'Are you just gonnae repeat everythin I say?'

Morris remembers what it's like to be Bobby. Long ago, he'd stood in a room much grander than this with a man called Hamish.

'Are you alright?' Bobby asks.

'Am fine, says Morris, wiping his eyes and shaking his head free of the past. 'Just a long day, a long life!'

'So, married?' says Bobby, not wanting to miss a thing.

'Aye,' Morris says, walking over to the table and opening a drawer. 'To Tam and he'll be in off his shift in a couple of hours and wanting his dinner. I was gonnae show yous this.'

Bobby walks over, relishing the deep pile of the rug, thinking maybe he'll give up art for antiques.

Morris holds out a flat blue-pink shell. It looks like something you'd skim across the water at Troon.

'Look properly,' says Morris, moving into the light from the window.

'Oh,' says Bobby, blushing. There are men cut into the shell. Sailors. All naked, except for their caps, and all with massive . . .

'Is that a ring?' says Bobby, squinting. 'In his . . .?'

Morris nods.

'Is that not sore?'

'Not at first.' Morris laughs then puts it back in the drawer.

Morris subsides into one of the scallop chairs – sturdier than it looks. 'Now sit down,' he says. 'You need an education then I need to get some stovies on.'

Sunday morning November frost etches the skylights over Robert. The coffee pot on the gas ring is a million miles away across the vast frozen tundra of the attic. The water in their toilet will be frozen. Overnight his blanket has somehow grown thinner. He rolls over and looks at Bobby, snoring soundly, face down under the next skylight along. How does he do that? Every night he's out like a light, sometimes mid-sentence as they talk between their two beds – about their latest library book, the pictures they will paint, about everything but the things they can't say.

Despite their promise to sleep on one side and work on the other, the whole attic is a nest of paper and pencils, charcoal stubs and paint tubes salvaged from the bins of richer students. Without shifting his gaze, Robert fumbles to his left and finds what he needs. Trying to sit up without letting the heat out from under his covers, he sketches sleeping Bobby – face down, blankets rising round him like waves, his left arm by his side, his right folded under his pillow. Robert's sole focus is the world of the bed, its contours a map, delineating hills and valleys, his eyes lingering on *terra incognita*. They've seen one another in their pants, of course. But not naked – they take care to avoid this and this care only draws attention to what they're avoiding. The air in the attic is thick with not looking. Sunday baths are taken in shifts, they take it in turns to get the water first. Robert sketches on. With no warning, Bobby is awake.

'You're drawing,' he yawns.

Robert holds his pencil over paper.

'I heard your pencil.'

'Oh aye?' Robert asks, inserting a skylight with one swift diagonal stroke. 'What am I drawing?'

'Me,' says Bobby, pushing himself up on his front. 'Unless you've snuck a model in.' He finishes yawning. 'It's your turn for the coffee.'

Robert shivers theatrically.

'I'll do it,' says Bobby jumping up, his blanket over his shoulders. 'Your coffee's shite anyway.'

Bobby fills the kettle. This normal noise gives Robert the cover for the questions he's been afraid to ask since Bobby got back last night. 'So, what was he like then, this Morris?'

'Oh, so you do want to know,' says Bobby, twisting off the tap and bursting to tell him. 'Well . . .'

A Sunday morning with nowhere to be.

'We might as well go out for a walk,' says Robert. After the talk they've just had, movement feels necessary.

'It might actually be warmer outside,' says Bobby.

They bundle on every stitch so they look like snowmen and head out into the bright white. A parcel greets them on the doorstep.

'Don't be nosy,' Robert says, as Bobby picks it up.

'More books,' he says, judging the weight. Bobby notes the label: 'The Socialist Bookshop, 31 Lothian Street, Edinburgh. Glasgow socialists not good enough for her?' Such boxes arrive a few days after they leave their rent by the phone in the hall. They rarely see their landlady – occasionally catch her in the hall after a 'meeting'. Robert opens the front door again and shoves the box in so it doesn't get wet. As they set off again, Bobby looks back at the house as they round the corner to make sure it's still real, still there. Mrs Cranston has placed a large peace lily in the front room window, the flower even whiter than the snow settling all round them.

Glasgow's never looked cleaner. Every rooftop is freshly iced. Every twig on every tree sparkles. Carefully, they cross the crescent and pick their way down the steps to the Kelvin, half expecting icebergs to float past.

'We could go sledging!' says Bobby, who never dared join in when he was growing up.

'We've no sledge,' says Robert, stating the obvious.

'Somebody'll gie us a go,' says Bobby, with customary certainty. He points along the path towards Kelvingrove Park.

They slip and slide along the Kelvin, racing to crack the perfect icy puddles. The trick is to just tap with your toes – no knowing how deep they are. Every now and then some snow slides off the branches overhanging the water, slipping silently in, like a boat launching itself. Bobby wonders how long it takes for snow to turn back to water and if this snow will ever pass them again – maybe it already has. All the sounds of the city are muffled like a funeral horse's hooves. Even Bobby is quieter.

They pause at the fancy cast-iron gates to the park. Bobby tilts back his head and opens his mouth. There aren't many folk about but his behaviour makes Robert shuffle, although it's nothing compared to the revelations he's still getting his head around.

'What are you doing?'

'Getting a drink,' says Bobby, without closing his mouth so the words are mangled. He makes a show of swallowing then talks normally. 'Cleanest water in Glasgow.'

Robert looks around then sticks his tongue out – heat draws the cold, sparkle evanesces in his mouth.

'See?' Bobby says, pretending to gulp.

'Race you!' Robert says, emboldened by the taste of snow. He bolts up the path towards the statue of Field Marshal Roberts atop his horse. Bobby takes off after him, huffing and puffing up the hill. Frost silvers the shadows. Briefly, Bobby worries about the cost of a doctor, should one of them fall and break an arm.

Kelvingrove Park slopes from the grand sweep of mansions at the top all the way down to the river. More than once, Bobby has felt eyes linger on him here, near the bushes. Now, thanks to Morris, he knows why. The park has four tiers like a fancy cake. From wherever you look you can see the gothic spire of the university flanked by noble sandstone attendants glowing orange even at night. The paths are littered with statues Glasgow City Corporation can't find better room for. There's a lion, or maybe a tiger, with a peacock twitching in its jaws. There's Lord Kelvin looking pleased in academic robes. Conquering all is Field Marshal Lord Roberts. Robert reaches him first, reads the statue's inscription aloud: '*I seem to see the gleam in the near distance / of the weapons and accoutrements of this army / of the future, this Citizen Army.* Pish.'

Bobby loves it when Robert swears. 'Imperialist pish!'

Robert reads on. 'From a speech he gave in Glasgow on the 6th of May 1913.'

'The year I was born. Surprised Glasgow let him in.'

'The year before I was born. Says he died in France the next year.'

'We should do something for our birthdays,' says Bobby. 'We're only a couple of weeks apart.'

'Like what?' Robert asks.

'I don't know,' shrugs Bobby, worrying he's pushed too far.

Robert changes the subject. 'Did your father go?'

'To France?' says Bobby. 'Fight for the Empire? Did he hell. Did yours?'

Robert shakes his head. The war was just another thing his father resented. 'He did his bit, at the engineering works.'

They look out over Glasgow, spread before them like a crisp tearoom tablecloth. Behind the city rolls the Campsies and beyond them the peak of Ben Lomond, all so white they're almost pink and distinguishable from the sky only by their mass. How much of seeing is knowing what is already there?

'We should go up there for a walk one day,' says Bobby. He can't stop thinking about Morris – about what he told him, the secret places for men like them, how not to get caught. The world looks different today – he sees one city superimposed over the other, like tracing paper that's slipped. 'There's a tram that goes right out.'

Robert mumbles noncommittally. He's still not used to making plans. Bobby is so very alive that he is permanently alert to the pleasure in even the smallest thing. He is always being swept up in new excitements – an urgent need to check on the holly berries at the back gate of the Botanics, a mission to find duck eggs because they make the best omelettes, another trip to the Mitchell to look – again – at the table-sized Titian book, slowly giving up its secrets. All adventures he would never have considered before.

The park is filling up. The cold air echoing with steamy curls of laughter as bin lids and tea trays and anything that can skite is redeployed as a sledge. In this cold, everybody has the cheeks of a child from a picture book.

Bobby makes a beeline for two lads with red shop-bought sledges. After a moment he waves Robert over, handing him a string.

'How?' Robert asks.

'We've got one go.' Bobby says, holding his sledge with one foot and lowering himself, trying not to wet his arse.

Robert looks to the boys for permission and they look down.

Bobby is in and ready to go. 'I told them you'd chuck them in the river if they didnae.'

Robert gawps.

'Posh boys," says Bobby, leaning forward. 'Race you!'

Bobby is away. The string burns his hands as he pulls at it. The world is coming at him faster than the pictures – there's no way he can stop before the first path, teeming with wrapped-up walkers, so he shouts 'MIND' and they all get out the way as he flies through to a bit of the park steeper than bookshelves, then 'MIND' again as he soars over the next path and now, somehow, Robert is beside him then pushing ahead, snow spraying back as they head straight for the bushes and the river beyond and Bobby's last, very Catholic thought, is *This is what I get*.

An audience gathers, as it always does in Glasgow. Bobby staggers out the bushes, blinking. 'Ma heid,' he moans, rubbing his scalp. The spectators applaud. Bobby takes a bow then turns to see Robert emerge, shaky as a foal. They've both got wet arses from where they landed and have just become a story to be told in a steamy café later that day and forgotten by breakfast the next, two students from the art school who stole some sledges then nearly ended up in the river.

Their crowd wanders off, warmed by witnessing near disaster, already in search of another show.

'We better take these back,' says Robert, retrieving his sledge.

'No need,' says Bobby, as the owners slide down the path towards them, pointing and laughing and then BOOM!

They freeze. An explosion echoes around the park. The only thing still moving is a dog in pursuit of an old tennis ball – its owner silently begging it to stop. Smoke drifts over from the university. Over the settling silence a bugle announces the Last Post. Robert remembers the date and takes off his cap; Bobby follows. The statue of the General is now pooled black by mourners. Many hold rings of poppies, even redder in the snow. Frost rimes the faces of those who survived the war that Bobby and Robert were born into. That war made Glasgow rich – kept the shipyards and steelworks busy. Peace held little profit, as the Depression proved, but now, whisper it, the shipyards are taking orders again.

BOOM. The gun goes again. Life resumes. The dog brings back its ball. Sledges take to the skies. Bobby cannot feel his feet.

When they get back to Number Three, the peace lily has gone from the window – Mrs Cranston has made her point. Bobby can't imagine her lifting a pot like that by herself but they never see any staff in the house, not even a char. When he'd told his mother his new address she'd asked if there was any cleaning work and he'd felt ashamed of her and then himself.

By the time they get back up into the attic they're shivering. Bobby fills the kettle.

'Good idea,' says Robert, thinking it's coffee time again.

'A bath?' Bobby chitters, not waiting for an answer.

'But it's not Sunday,' Robert frets, ever alert to any infraction, not wanting to give Mrs Cranston any excuse to chuck them out.

Bobby lights the gas ring then fills every pot he can find. Soon steam plumes the air. Robert worries about the gas meter spinning down in the cellar as Bobby drags the tin bath out from the eaves. They toss a coin over who goes first. Bobby wins and kicks off his socks. Robert retreats to the other side of the attic. The arched wall between muffles the sound. Bobby's belt buckle strikes the floor with surprising force.

'We so nearly came a cropper,' says Bobby, folding his trousers, projecting his voice across the attic.

'Aye,' says Robert pacing. 'Did you see their faces?'

Robert hears the smallest splash – Bobby must be testing the water with a toe, which means he must be naked right now, just a few paces away. This conversation is now a wire linking the two of them. Robert tries not to transmit. Can't stop himself receiving.

Bobby groans as he eases himself in. 'What?' he wonders out loud, hoping to tempt Robert out from the other side, not sure exactly what he'll do if he succeeds.

Robert closes his eyes but this only makes it easier to see Bobby in the bath. He slides a hand down his pants.

'What?' shouts Bobby. 'Come through, so I can hear you. It's like talking to my auntie.'

Robert can't go through to the other side, especially not like this. He picks up a towel and, holding it in front of himself, steps over to the archway dividing their attic. He pointedly faces their easels and talks over his shoulder.

'Better?'

'A bit,' says Bobby, his skin pinking below the tideline. His cock and balls bob up and he doesn't bother to push them down. He lifts his hips and his pubic hair rises like an island then returns to the warm depths. In his haste he forgot the soap.

'Robert?'

'Aye?'

'Gonnae get me the soap please?'

Robert, willing away the bulge in his trousers, cannot.

Bobby twists awkwardly, water sploshing, pointing to the sink. 'Robert?'

Robert side-steps in with his back to Bobby. This side of the attic is warmer now. The pink cube of soap sits on the sink, the soap they use for brushes and pants and socks and everything. It sticks to his fingers as he picks it up. What now? How to hand it over without glancing down? It's not like he's not seen Bobby in his pants, they've lived together two months now. But this is different. Today is different. Maybe it's the snow. Maybe it's what Bobby told him.

'This water's going to freeze,' says Bobby, 'I'll become an Eskimo. Or Ophelia!' He sinks below the surface and blows bubbles loudly. As he resurfaces he sees an upside-down Robert approach the head of the bath. Bobby swings his arm backwards, grasping for the soap and their fingers touch, for only as long as it takes snow to melt on your tongue but that's enough. Bobby rushing his hands between his legs but Robert has already seen and bolts back to the other side of the attic.

'Not divin in?' Bobby shouts after him, laughing, trying to make this a joke so he's not risking everything – their friendship, their freedom, their home.

Robert sits on the floor in the arch, his back pressed against the dividing wall. With one hand he worries their kaleidoscopic rug, the centre sun-bright, and wonders who would want a room of that, who could live with that? *Yes, Bobby, I want to dive in that bath with you and I don't know what happens after but yes I want in.*

'It's getting cold,' Bobby warns, easing himself up.

Robert can't reply. His mind is full of the possibility of what he knows is wrong – what he's been imagining since he was a boy, what presented itself in Bobby's lips that first time he sketched him, what he dreams about every night in their attic, what he pictures when Bobby is out getting the messages and he locks himself in their toilet, one hand braced against the wall, the other busy with *Bobby, Bobby, Bobby*. Of everything he glimpsed in the bath just now.

'I'll boil you an extra pot,' Bobby says, standing up. Robert hears the water run off him. Drip, drip, drip.

'Thanks,' Robert stammers but it's Bobby's bathwater he wants, would swim in it if he could.

It's their first Christmas already and they've each made their own excuses for not going back; Robert claims 'studies' and Bobby blames 'money'. Mrs Cranston has invited them down to lunch. Her neat little note waits on a windowsill.

'We can't kid on we're out,' says Bobby. 'Anyway, it smells nice. I think she's got a turkey.'

'We've not spent five minutes with her,' says Robert, unfankling the tie Bobby knitted for his birthday.

'Would you rather hide up here?' Bobby says. 'Or break into our studio – finish that ballet study you're overworking?'

Robert shakes his head.

'Right then,' says Bobby, knotting the bow tie – he has knitted one each for him and Robert. 'We better not be late.'

As they head downstairs the grandfather clock in the hall strikes noon.

'You're early,' says Mrs Cranston, poking her head out of the drawing room door. The chimes are still fading.

Robert blushes red as a berry on the Botanics' holly. 'Sorry.'

'You will be,' says Mrs Cranston. 'If that bird's still raw.'

She waves them in. They've never been in any of her rooms. The drawing room is more like a library – busy shelves cover every wall. Side tables stagger under teetering tomes. Bobby tries to check out the titles without being too obvious. Newspapers slip off the sofa but the antimacassars are immaculate and the rug is faded in that way Bobby is recognising as posh. Double doors open into a dining room at the back of the house.

'Come through,' says Mrs Cranston.

Bobby notices the table is set for four.

'Mind,' she says, wrestling with a champagne bottle. 'Nobody wants a one-eyed artist. One ear, aye, but . . .' The cork flies past them and out into the other room. 'It'll turn up,' says Mrs Cranston, proffering the bottle. 'Glass then,' she says, pointing to the department store of crockery and cutlery on the table. Robert hesitates. Bobby grabs the biggest glass.

Mrs Cranston fills Bobby's glass then turns to her own – a tall thin one, Robert notes, searching for the same. 'I really don't mind which you choose,' says Mrs Cranston. 'I grew up in a house with jam jars for glasses – Mr Cranston bought all this – but this bottle is getting heavy.'

Bobby waits for more story but Mrs Cranston rattles on, filling their glasses, then plonking the bottle down: 'A toast!'

'To what?' Bobby asks, reappraising their landlady. He spies an empty bottle on a table by the door.

'To the future,' she says, nodding to Bobby then Robert. 'A future without war.' Then she raises her glass to the head of the table, where a silver-framed photograph sits cornered with black ribbon. Turning back to them both, eyes brimming, she raises her glass again: 'And to love.'

They spend all Boxing Day keeping warm in their beds and talking about Christmas, Mrs Cranston's revelations, the joy of champagne, the wickedness of their first proper hangover. They don't have breath to spare for Maybole or Kilmarnock.

1933 is about to be over: the year they got in to the art school, found this place, found each other.

Hogmanay beckons and with it the pressure to have a historically good night. Bobby and Robert don't have the time or money for pubs – their seeming refusal to mix is another source of gossip about them. There is also the small matter of Hell – the Hogmanay Ball that Bobby made Robert promise to attend with Moira. But that was before Morris told him where he should be going. How to get Robert to go with him?

'I've got to take her now,' Robert says, sweeping his hair from his face with Brilliantine so it shines like a magpie's wing. 'Folk will talk.'

'Folk talk already,' shrugs Bobby, waiting for the comb. 'I'll get you out of it – she's my pal, remember? And anyway, I've found us a better place.'

'Where? Do I want to know? I should at least tell her in person,' says Robert.

'That would be the gentlemanly thing to do,' says Bobby, taming his fringe. Satisfied with what the mirror says, they head out to Hell.

A huge dark angel leers over them, his horns nearly touching at the top. Orange and red flames flicker up from a pit that conceals the Glasgow School of Art band but sadly not their jazz.

'Make it quick,' Robert says, spotting Moira. She is fending off Fyffe, who is sporting a pair of red horns.

Moira looks over and their faces tell her everything. The cheek. She was the one doing Robert a favour, being seen with him here, and she thought he had the sense to know it. It was Bobby she was doing this for – him she was protecting, not that they'd discussed it. Now here they are, the pair of them, looking sheepish. She decides she's not going over to get a knockback on a winch she didn't want – he can come to her, that's what a real man would do. As much as it pains her, she smiles at Fyffe who is wittering on about some country house dance.

'Maybe I should just take her?' says Robert, half-meaning it.

'It's her or me,' says Bobby, his words half-lost in the music.

'What?' Robert turns to him. 'What do you mean?'

'I'm not staying here to be a gooseberry,' says Bobby, turning.

Robert has been worried for weeks by the prospect of Moira – the dancing, the after. Bobby knows he can't end the night, the term or the year without Robert.

'You're always saying she's lovely,' says Robert, grabbing Bobby's arm to stop him leaving.

'She is,' Bobby says, not shaking his arm off. 'A light heartbreak will only make her even more lovely. I'll think of something, don't worry. I'll make it my fault.'

'Will you?' says Robert, relieved. 'Promise?'

Moira dodges a kiss from Fyffe and starts to come over.

'Promise,' says Bobby, pulling Robert towards the door. 'C'mon, before all hell lets loose.'

'What is this place?' asks Robert.

'Morris told me about it,' says Bobby, stepping towards the door, which swings open, releasing a roar of patter and smoke and two men in white hats clamped over Greta Garbo wigs.

'Don't mind her,' says the nearest, winking a well-mascaraed eye. 'She just needs some air.'

Robert turns on his heel.

'Oh, come on,' pleads Bobby. 'Just five minutes?'

Bobby has convinced Robert to mark the new year with him – he just didn't say where. Now the bells are nearly here. The Napoleon looks like any other pub from the outside. Except for the blacked-out windows. And the Garbos.

Robert storms across the road to the river. 'I'll wait,' he shouts. Bobby can't wait – he pushes the doors open again and steps in. Of course it's fancy dress. His bow tie won't cut it among assorted animals, machines and queens.

Just inside the door, should muscle be needed, stands a man with the same tattoos as Morris. 'Tam,' he says, extending a shovel-sized hand. 'She told me to watch for you.' Bobby follows Tam's adoring gaze to a tiny stage behind the bar.

It's Morris. But it's also, according to the sign on the bar, *Doris!* Shimmering in a sea-green sequinned gown and easily seven foot in a high blonde wig studded with pink seashells, she waves over, the tattoos on her arms disappearing under bangles. Bobby gawps back. Doris steps up to a microphone and the music starts: 'Stormyyyy weatherrrr . . .' She teeters on the edge of her stage. Should she topple, any of the hundreds packed into the Napoleon in their fancy dress would happily be crushed by her gloriousness. What a way to go!

The crowd pulls Bobby in. A friendly dragon buys him a pint, which tastes nothing like the one his father took him for when he was eighteen. Doris sings on. Hit after hit. Pint after pint, one from Tam, another from a big silver fish. Then the cat working behind the bar hands Bobby a dainty glass and fills it with his first ever gin 'from Doris'. He makes a face as he sips. The Garbos come back in and ask after his 'friend' and he wonders what Robert would make of it all. The gin burns as Doris begins the countdown.

'Ten,' Doris booms, now perched on a perilous stool.

'Nine!' Bobby turns to Robert but no, he's still not there. Maybe they should have gone to Hell. He feels guilty about Moira. The space where Robert should be has already been filled by a five-foot dog with a big collar round its neck.

'Eight!' Panic grips Bobby. He must be with Robert for the bells.

'Seven!' A pair of identical girls with tiny charcoal moustaches bump into Bobby as he turns on the spot. Are they Charlie Chaplins or Hitlers? They waggle their 'taches but he's not got time. Ignoring him, they risk a quick kiss, under cover of the nearly here new year.

'Six!' Doris signals to Tam to open the front door. Out with the old, in with the new. The draught from the street reaches Bobby and he swims towards it.

'Five!' Doris holds up one hand, her golden Claddagh catching the light.

'Four!' Bobby must get to Robert but the door seems to be getting further away. He stumbles and is helped up by a six-foot-tall banana.

'Three!' Doris is speeding up. Or is it the year? Bobby finds the door.

'Watch it, hen,' says Queen Elizabeth, his dress a rot of old doilies, his wig a joke, his teeth possibly not. 'You'll no see next year!'

'Two!' Bobby is through the door. Outside the road is empty because everybody's got somewhere to be and somebody to be with. But the river is mobbed with ships of all shapes and sizes – you could walk across it without wetting your feet.

'ONE!'

The Napoleon erupts. Doris starts on Auld Lang Syne.

That's it! That was 1933! The first person Bobby sees in 1934 is Robert – standing on his own, leaning over the railings, looking down into the midnight river like he's lost something. He's popped up the collar on his coat. Bobby has already committed to memory all the ways Robert occupies space, how he ducks slightly when he walks through a door, the fine apse between his long arms and slender body. But the broken leaning form he sees now is new.

'Robert!' Bobby shouts, suddenly desperate. His voice is carried away by the horns and bells of all the boats and ships as they welcome the new year.

Robert puts one foot on the railing.

Bobby steps into the road.

'Robert!'

But Robert doesn't hear him. The boats have too much to say. And Bobby doesn't hear the motor-car swing around the corner, only the roar of its horn.

Robert turns.

The driver doesn't even slow down, just races on.

The Bobby-shaped bundle in the middle of the road is not moving. In seven – eight – steps Robert is there. He closes his eyes. Can't bear to look. Can't bear not to. All the thoughts he was having, the thing he was considering, all are banished by a surge of terror he now understands is love. Robert wishes he knew how to pray. He opens his eyes and looks down. Bobby's eyes flutter open. Slowly, carefully, Robert lifts Bobby to his feet and leads him out the road.

'He missed!' Bobby sways. Robert only just catches him. This time he doesn't let go.

Robert looks over Bobby's shoulders to the Napoleon where Doris leads her worshippers in Auld Lang Syne. It looks like any other pub, maybe a bit brighter. The road is empty again. The boats finish hailing 1934.

'Happy new year,' says Bobby, muffled in the folds of Robert's coat. Becalmed in private warmth, ensconced in a dark woollen world he can never imagine leaving, Bobby gives up trying to stop the thought that all he wants is for Robert to lean down and kiss him.

'Daftie,' whispers Robert, pulling him even closer, buttoning him into his coat and holding him there for a moment, for ever.

It is 1934. A new year. Their future is now.

Next morning, they lie awake. On the same mattress. Each looking up at the same frosted skylight, focusing so hard on the same patch of sky they might crack the glass. Each breathes carefully, pretending to be asleep. The matter of who will speak first seems vital. Robert can't believe what he's done, feels pinned to the floor by the weight of it. Bobby can't wait to do it again.

Bobby breaks first. 'Coffee?' he asks, rolling over then immediately regretting it. This must be what seasickness feels like. *The Raft of the Medusa* drifts into his head.

Robert has no idea how Bobby can be so casual but is determined to be as normal as possible. 'Aye,' he croaks from his side of the mattress. At no point do their bodies touch. A strict frontier is observed. Robert spots his pants on the floor. Or are they Bobby's? He pokes his foot out the bottom of the covers and tries to hook them with his toe.

Robert's blindly crabbing foot is so ludicrous it gives Bobby the giggles and that's what finally cracks Robert.

Bobby jumps out of bed, balls swinging, and grabs the pants, popping them on his head like a party hat.

'Happy new year!' he cheers, launching himself at Robert who considers daring himself to wonder if it might just be.

Chapter 12

After this, everything is different. And everything is still the same. Their new secret knowledge is thrilling and terrifying. It changes everything and nothing.

They spend the rest of that winter in a strict rotation between studio and attic, working and fucking then working some more. They're learning lots. Mrs Cranston has never come up to the attic but they never push their mattresses together just in case. They are as careful as scared people should be. Soon, it's March 1934. Winter shows no signs of leaving.

'The spring that never sprung,' says Bobby, peeking out the window at the still-sleeping branches of the trees in the Botanics. He near garrottes himself with the scarf his Auntie Maggie knitted him for Christmas, which feels years ago already. The only word he's had from Maybole. It's made of every bit of wool she had spare – every colour under the sun. It hangs down over his bum, which is on display along with the rest of him.

Robert is lost in the intricacies of the cornice, fancy even in the attic. *How long can this last? How long before we're caught? What then?* He has taken to getting up in the night and checking the lock on their door.

Bobby dives back under the covers, throwing himself over him like a blanket.

'Can you believe this?' Bobby asks, stroking Robert's still-sticky chest, conjuring the statues they sketch in Life Drawing, trying to decide which of them his private god most resembles.

'No,' says Robert. *Is that door locked?*

'Me neither,' Bobby replies. Scarf flying, he dances across the attic. 'Our own sink, our own lavvy, our own gas ring'. He points to each thing and won't move on until Robert applauds. 'Our own coffee pot, our own plates, our own cups.' He burrows back into bed. 'My own you!'

'Imagine having to get up there to clean that,' Robert says, pointing to the cornice.

'You cleaning anything would be a start,' says Bobby, noticing a spider has moved in with them.

'Don't start on domestics,' says Robert.

'I keep a clean hoose,' Bobby insists.

'You'll make a fine wife.'

'I already am,' says Bobby, worrying he's gone too far but hoping not because Robert said *wife* first. He reads him with as much success as Auntie Maggie and her tea-leaves.

Robert rolls away. 'How's about that coffee?'

Bobby gets up again and goes over to the ring where the coffee pot is warming – he'd put it on earlier, anticipating this moment, always alert to the next pleasure. Robert holds out his mug, picks up the book he's finishing.

Bobby savours the scene. Their own coffee pot, their own books, their own jokes. Neither of them had even tried coffee until they got to Glasgow. Now, like so much else that's new, life seems unimaginable without it.

'How's old Virginia?' Bobby asks, filling Robert's cup.

'Not as good as the coffee,' says Robert, putting his book down and thinking *Not as good as it is to have you make coffee for me*. But his joy in this comfort only points up the potential for disaster. *Two men. It's not right.*

'Oh,' winces Bobby, reading the title upside down. 'Why are you bothering then?'

'Because it's Virginia bloody Woolf!'

'I know,' laughs Bobby. 'Mrs Dalloway said she would go to the Barras herself.'

'You liked that one!'

'I did! But you've been wading through this one for weeks.'

Bobby downs his coffee, calculating how long until they need to put on their clothes and coats and outdoor faces.

'You're still on MacDiarmid?' Robert asks, hunting around for the slender volume. He finds it face down on Bobby's side of the bed and reads from the open page. 'Oh, this is cheery.'

'Finish it!' says Bobby. 'Then we'll go.'

Robert snaps the book shut and gently bops Bobby on the head with it. 'Now come on! Fleming will have us if we're late.'

Robert is dressed in minutes and donning his tweed cap. Bobby is reknotting his scarf, the colours spooling past him.

'Are you wearing that out?' Robert asks.

Bobby considers the colours. Remembers the looks he got last time and, worse still, the way Robert shifted away from him on the tram. He lets the scarf fall to the floor. They nod at one another then head out and down the steps of Number Three Botanic Crescent into the waiting world. Without trying to, they have begun to dress a wee bit the same – never without a tie and always immaculate. To save money, Bobby cuts their hair – giving them both the same short back and sides. They can't afford an iron and it feels incriminating to ask Mrs Cranston so Bobby heats a ladle over their gas ring and uses it to smooth out their shirts. The first time Robert saw him do this he laughed, thinking it was another joke until Bobby chased him with it.

'Look,' says Bobby, pausing as they round the corner.

Bobby points to the grass in the crescent-shaped Residents' Garden that sets their street back from the road – Mrs Cranston has not given them a key for it. Robert follows his gaze. There, through the wet green, peeps a lighter shade, the merest glint, so that it might simply be dew disappearing in the morning sun.

'A daffodil!' says Bobby, turning and running ahead, leaving Robert to follow for once. 'It's sprung!'

Chapter 13

The Napoleon is just the start of Glasgow's second city.
'Morris says it's really fancy,' says Bobby.
'So, you go then,' says Robert.
'And you'll do what? Just sit here, on your own?' Bobby asks, sniffing the air. 'You could actually do with a bath.'
'Cheek,' says Robert, lifting an arm. 'If I do, it's your fault.'
'The stench of sin!' laughs Bobby. 'Poor wee Presbyterians cannae wash it off with Confession . . . so you might as well come to these baths with me.'

Robert's alternative is an afternoon on his own, which wouldn't be so bad if he could share it with Bobby. He could have another go at the picture he's been working on, of the one-legged beggar at the cross. He looks over to the beggar, who stares back accusingly. Robert shrugs and Bobby smiles and that's enough for now.

They pull their jackets over their heads, run down the crescent and over the bridge round the Botanics and down to Great Western Road then sneak on the first tram to town. It's packed. Everybody smells of wet wool. The windows are steaming. It's like they're underwater already. As the conductor fights his way downstairs, the tram stops right where they need it to and they hop off, landing in a puddle.

'We deserved that,' says Robert, shaking his feet.
Bobby ignores him, clinking the saved coins in his pocket. 'C'mon, it must be just round here.'

The Arlington Baths was founded in 1871, according to the

sign out front. Bobby and Robert admire the arches framing the door and recall their architecture lessons.

'Are those pediments Doric or Corinthian?' Robert asks.

'Just posh,' says Bobby. They shelter there and wait for Morris. The rain is determined.

'It looks expensive,' Robert frets, nodding at the velvet curtains in the window. He shakes a wet foot.

'It does,' Bobby says, excitedly.

'Can we afford it?'

'No.'

Robert turns to go but Bobby catches his arm.

'It's free, ya dafty!'

Robert shakes him off.

'How?'

'Morris is a member and we're his guests so it's free. And don't be funny about Morris, I don't hear you complaining when he gets us discounts at the Barras.'

With that, Morris rolls round the corner, a ruby-red umbrella held aloft. With his bottle-green coat, he looks like a walking test for colour blindness.

'Touting for business?' he laughs.

Robert cringes.

'This one definitely needs to relax,' says Morris, leading the way, shaking off his brolly then pushing open the heavy double doors.

The Arlington is still lit with gas lamps, so has that wet coal smell – Robert sniffs in recognition. Bobby's lot were still on candles. There's also something new, acrid.

'Chlorine,' says Morris, wrinkling his nose.

The man on reception looks like he's on shore leave – anchors covering his massive arms. He smiles at Morris then sizes up Robert and Bobby before opening a drawer and handing over two pairs of blue-striped guest trunks. Morris signs them in then lifts his trunks from a hook on the wall, which has his membership number on it. Arrival at the Arlington is a process of gradual disrobement. In the next room, Morris kicks off his shoes so Bobby then Robert follow, leaving them side by side under a plain wooden changing bench. Bobby notes his are the best polished – Robert's too, since he's got hold of them. Bobby spots some holes in Robert's socks and makes a mental note to tackle this shame later. They go through to an adjoining room. Robert nearly turns back. It is wall-to-wall naked men: old, young, fat, thin, more naked men than Robert knew there were in the whole world. He'd endured cold showers after rugby, but this is something else. Most are just standing around in pairs or threes chatting away. There's talk of the rain, as ever, whether or not the *Queen Mary* will be finished on time and some general cursing of Ramsay MacDonald, who is somehow hanging on. One or two are sat reading the evening papers, their towels hiding nothing. This is all even more embarrassing because Robert is standing there fully dressed – he's brought the outside world in, conspicuously cold air on his clothes.

This final changing room is painted a kidney red – like the Regency dining rooms they studied in Interiors. Surprisingly plain slatted benches line the perimeter. Morris heads for an empty spot. Bobby copies him. Robert does too. Nobody looks over as they strip, which faintly offends Bobby.

'Right,' says Morris, turning his broad hairy back as he bends down and pulls off his drawers, kicking them onto the carpet then pulling his trunks on and up in one fluid motion. 'Shower time!'

Bobby has never had a shower. His chest meant he always got out of sports at school and it was a tin bath every second Sunday in Maybole. He steps under the hot water and feels distinct jets push through his thick black mop, pasting it down over the hedge of his eyebrows and onto his eyelids where it tickles. He knows that admitting the gloriousness of this would mean admitting this was his first time so, for once, he says nothing and just savours this new sensation. Droplets dangle off his lashes as he opens his eyes and turns to see Robert, his curls straight with the weight of water but already snapping back up.

'Right,' says Morris, shaking himself like a bear.

They walk out to the pool – it almost fills the room and is lit by skylights running above. The tiles are the blue of faraway waters.

Bobby can swim – his father had made sure of that on their first visit to Troon when he was five or six. One minute he'd been in his father's arms, the next he was gasping in the salty cold, his mother held back by his father who said it was *for his own good*.

'Can you swim?' Bobby asks Robert.

By way of answer, Robert dives in, cleaving the water as cleanly as the gannets off Ailsa Craig. He surfaces halfway along the pool and is nearly at the other side by the time Bobby and Morris have shimmied down the ladder into the shallow end.

Bobby starts on his back: these skylights are even bigger than the ones in their attic. He catches up with Robert kicking his feet idly at the other side. They puzzle over a strange arrangement of wooden rings dangling over the water, tantalisingly out of reach.

'The travelling rings,' huffs Morris, from the next lane. 'You swing across. I've never seen anybody get all the way. I'd bring the roof down!'

'How do you get up?' Robert asks.

Morris points to a ladder that leads up to a platform.

'Right,' says Robert, launching himself backwards up out of the water and onto the side in one move, the lean muscles in his arms doing more than they let on.

'There's always one,' says Morris. 'On you go then, show us up.'

Out of the water, Robert silvers with goosebumps. Tiles suck loudly at his feet as he slips over to the ladder. From up on the platform, the water looks very far away. The men either side of the lanes below swim out into the middle then, to his horror, turn and watch. Any hesitation now will, he calculates, detract from any success. The platform is fitted with a long, hooked pole, like for catching ducks at the shows. He takes it and pulls over the first ring. No going back. He grabs the ring with both hands, stepping back then leaping out into the air, both feet kicking. As the sky rushes to meet him he feels sure that the moment for the next ring is now so lets go with his right hand and there it is! Triumphant, he lets go of the past with his left hand swinging towards the third ring, lifting up his feet in front like he's punting on a swing.

'On yerself!' Bobby shouts as Robert reaches the fourth ring.

How many more, how many till the other side? Robert is still flying, flying but now his legs are heavy and his arms are burning and then he's falling, falling. His feet push him up off the bottom. As he heads for the surface he wishes he could just stay down here because only shame waits at the top, but then he's up already and the first face he sees is Bobby, his smile wider and brighter than Fair Fortnight sunshine. Worth it.

'That's the furthest I've seen anybody get!' says Morris.

'Really?' says Robert, catching his breath.

'Aye,' laughs Morris, hauling himself up on to the side. 'C'mon, we've earned a wee relax.'

The Turkish Suite is another room that does not look like it belongs in Glasgow. The four walls slope up to a point, like a pyramid. It makes Bobby think of Carter's discovery of the tomb of Tutankhamun. Each side is pierced by star-shaped windows, alternating red and blue. The floor is miraculously warm underfoot and a fountain burbles in the octagonal centre. Radiating out from this, like petals, are wooden recliners. Heavy teak benches lie evenly around the walls and each one has a wooden block for a pillow. Morris heads to his favourite corner, facing the door so he can check everybody coming and going. Bobby and Robert take the only other two empty spots, on opposite sides of the room – if they turn they can see each other but it's not exactly comfy. Nobody says a word. The air is full of steam and glances. Robert tries to follow Bobby's gaze but each look is so fleeting, so deniable, he can't keep up. Instead, he focuses on the stars above. It's only when Morris passes, following a man twice his age and half his size into the sauna, that Robert remembers he's in Glasgow, not Istanbul or Constantinople. Sitting up, he looks over to Bobby, who is smiling, but not at him. He turns to his left and sees the beneficiary of Bobby's smile – his soldier's chest a pillow of spun gold, his moustache somehow pert in the wet heat. The man gets up and rewraps his towel, allowing half a flash in Bobby's direction, then heads for the sauna. Bobby looks over to Robert but they're forbidden from speaking and anyway he doesn't know what to say. Bobby gets up and follows the man. A discreet moment later, Robert follows.

Stars of red and blue pierce the steam, the colours chasing each other round the hot wet walls as day slips into evening. When they finally leave the Arlington it's dark outside.

Spring gives way to warmer days. Their fellow students moan about going back to their big houses or hectic trips to Europe, always with a capital E. Mrs Cranston has mentioned holidaying in Bute. Just to be sure, Bobby checks their lease on the attic: it very clearly says 'for the academic year'. With the art school closed they have no official reason to stay together – their families will be expecting them home. Summer is splitting them up.

Suddenly Bobby is back at Lees – can feel the tacks between his teeth. Robert's stomach sinks at the thought of his father's face and he feels guilty at how happy his mother will be to see him.

'Even if she did extend the lease, we couldn't afford it,' Bobby says. But just in case she does, he tries desperately to stretch their funds – cooking huge pots of soup that Robert can't face. No amount of economising makes a difference. As the days get longer, Glasgow slips away.

They're working in the Hen Run when Bobby has an idea.

'Let's go and find that hill,' he says, pointing to the horizon – to the hill he spotted on their first day.

'Why?' Robert asks, sunk in despair, his drawing heavy with it.

'We've not actually been home together—'

'I can't take you back to Kilmarnock,' Robert starts.

'No,' says Bobby, not even he would try that. 'I mean, if we go back . . .' – he points towards Ayrshire – '. . . we can make a shared memory, something we can think back to, that'll help us get by until we're together again. What do you think?'

Robert looks over to the hill then back to Bobby.

They set out on the longest day, back on board the cruelly fast Ayrshire Express.

Bobby marches Robert up Kildoon Hill. They have their endless impossible afternoon. The pair of them lie panting together, curled like commas, naked in the nest they've rolled in the high golden grass. Tomorrow is happening. But not today.

'What do you mean, leaving?' asks Mrs Cranston, stepping out into the hall.

'Our lease is up,' says Robert.

'Already?' Mrs Cranston enquires, her finger keeping her place in a book. Bobby cranes his neck and curses the curiosity that will not leave him even now. 'Is it your families?'

'In a way,' says Bobby, pushing his hands into empty pockets. To have found Robert when he didn't even know it was possible to look and to now be split up by a lease, by the holiday plans of a rich lady, by pounds, shillings and pence.

'Money?' Mrs Cranston continues, her thoughts wandering in search of a solution.

Robert blushes.

'Finding new tenants will be an inconvenience, as will finding new accommodation, I'm sure.'

Bobby and Robert haven't been able to face thinking beyond the cliff-edge of summer but, of course, their attic will have new tenants in the new academic year. Bobby tries not to cry.

Mrs Cranston can't bear it. 'How about this? There are a number of jobs that need doing around the house. The window frames at the front rattle like a tram in the lightest breeze and there's painting to be done indoors.'

'Painting?' Robert asks.

'Skirting, cornicing and the like,' Mrs Cranston continues, warming to her theme. 'Not portraits. Nothing beyond your skills, I'm sure.'

'And you want us to do it?' Bobby asks.

'In lieu of rent,' says Mrs Cranston, looking pleased with herself. 'You can write to your parents and tell them you have summer work here. You can start with this hall. I think we can all agree the green should go.'

'So, we can stay?' Bobby asks. 'Really?'

'Really,' she nods, retreating into her drawing room, already back in her book.

They start the very same day, washing down paintwork that's older than them. It's slow and dirty work but they're together – every night they return to their attic, tired but happy. It's the same all summer. And the next summer. When they're not dragging Number Three Botanic Crescent into the twentieth century, they're taking extra classes. By the time their General Course is over, the house looks better than when it was built. After two years of putting in the hours, they now get to specialise in painting with Mr Fleming – he is doing them the honour of painting their portrait. In it, they're wearing matching bow ties and their hands are almost touching, but not quite. Bobby wonders if Fleming notices – how could he not? Their portrait scandalises the school but they shrug it off as more envy. All they really care about is this: which of them will be top of their year? The top two will win a trip to what Fleming insists on calling 'the imperial capital' and must return with a written report on its galleries and museums.

Robert is finishing his painting *The Hat Shop*. Inspired by the green of the hallway at Number Three, he's imagined a trio of women fussing over millinery. The customer stands, arms folded uncertainly, as she waits to be crowned by the shopkeeper, while a pair of white-gloved friends look on, hoping for disaster or success, the potential for both lighting their faces. Bobby is painting their coffee pot alongside a gilt cup and saucer and sugar bowl he's borrowed from Morris. There's still no lid for the pot but Bobby manages to bring out an unpolished patina that speaks of years of pleasure and more to come. *Still Life with Coffee Pot* contains all his memories of the Dutch pictures he first saw in those big books in Maybole Library. It glows with his hopes.

Mrs Cranston has accepted her invitation to their General Course Show, saying, 'I'd be delighted to finally see what you've been up to.' Morris has said he wouldn't miss it for the world and casually mentioned he was one of the school's life models until 'the incident'.

Mrs Cranston is one of the first to arrive. She is majestic in a new red silk shift dress that makes her white hair glow. The room fills quickly with mothers in furs and fathers in unborrowed suits, keen to see where their money is going. The air fills with darlings and perfume and cigar smoke. Mrs Cranston seems to know everybody and does the rounds, reaching Bobby and Robert last.

'So, you are artists after all,' she says, leaning into Robert's hat shop. 'She looks a wee bit like . . .?'

Robert smiles. 'Maybe a wee bit.'

'I'd not realised I was a model,' says Mrs Cranston, blushing despite herself. 'I would have added a fee to the rent.' She turns to Bobby's picture. 'And since when could you afford silver service?'

'We wish,' Bobby laughs. 'I borrowed it from a pal at the Barras.'

'Pals at the Barras? So much to learn,' says Mrs Cranston. 'Where is the lid?'

'I don't know,' says Bobby. 'I don't think it matters.'

'It doesn't,' says Mr Fleming, arriving to congratulate his star students and hoping to meet their parents – this woman is not what he expected.

'Mrs . . . Colquhoun?'

'Not at all,' their landlady laughs, looking from one tenant to the other, noting how they keep glancing at the door. 'I'm Mrs Cranston.'

'Our landlady,' says Bobby.

'A classic example of the capitalist greed that is dividing our society and pushing our world, once more, to the brink of war,' she says, extending her hand to Mr Fleming. 'Have I not seen you at a meeting?'

Mr Fleming shakes his head.

'The Workers' Guild?'

'Not me,' says Mr Fleming.

'The Labour Party?'

'Politics is not my thing.'

'Politics is everyone's thing,' says Mrs Cranston. 'Whether we like it or not. As I fear this generation is about to discover.'

Bobby watches for Morris. He has also sent invitations to Maybole and to Kilmarnock, without asking Robert. Tonight is proof that they are working hard and that other people take their art seriously and he wants their families to see – he wants their fathers to see, especially Robert's. Over at the door, a dark-haired woman peeks in – his heart leaps with home. She's in a rabbit-fur coat but it could be her, it could be one she was repairing. The crowd shifts and the woman is lost.

Mr Fleming dings a fork on a glass and a hush settles. 'Every single student who has made it to the end of the General Course is a winner,' he says, not bothering with niceties. He's embarrassed speaking in front of parents, Bobby realises. 'But each year we award three prizes to the students who have demonstrated the deepest commitment to their practice.' An intake of breath. 'I won't embarrass them by announcing their names.' Fyffe's parents ooze with anticipation. 'Instead, I would ask you to raise a glass to the General Course class of 1933.'

Mrs Cranston nods her glass to them. Bobby looks over to the door for the woman. But she's gone. Was that his mother? Robert wonders what's distracting Bobby.

'I've pinned our winners on the noticeboard,' says Fleming, winking at Mrs Cranston. He stops Bobby and Robert.

'So?' he says, handing them each a fresh glass of wine. 'London? Just don't forget to come back.'

Bobby feels stupid for sending invitations home – a feeling that grows as proud parents make a show of their offspring announcing fancy dinner plans. He shudders at the thought of a borrowed fur coat in here. Then feels disgust at his shame. Suddenly he needs to get away – he nudges Robert and they sneak out, heading to the Napoleon to toast their success and find Morris. They are, of course, the top two. They will now proceed to Painting. They have won three more years together.

'Maybe we should have brought Mrs C,' says Bobby.

'Imagine!' says Robert.

'I can,' says Bobby. 'I actually can – what was all that about capitalism?'

'All her little red books,' says Robert.

But Morris is not at the Napoleon. Neither is Tam. Nobody's seen them. It's nine o'clock on a Friday night. Doris is supposed to be on at midnight.

'He'll be at the flat getting ready for tonight,' says Bobby, heading for the tram. 'Maybe he's doing us a surprise party.'

'Hey Bobby,' says Robert. 'We won – top of our year!'

'You won,' says Bobby, his thoughts racing ahead of him.

'Only the General Course,' says Robert, making his achievement smaller and easier for Bobby to carry. 'You're second.'

'Don't remind me,' says Bobby, then sees Robert's hurt face. 'Second to a genius! Might as well be first. Come on,' he says, heading to the tram. 'We need to tell Morris his crockery got second prize.'

All the way to Dennistoun Robert is thinking about London.

'Wait till you see their place,' says Bobby, turning into Morris's close. 'Honestly, it's like Aladdin's cave, if Aladdin lived under the sea.'

They reach the first-floor landing. The door is not shut.

'The locks,' says Robert, pointing to the splintered frame.

Bobby peeks up and down the stairwell – there's nobody about but there's always somebody here, a wean at least. On the floor, just inside the door, sits the nautilus shell – its silver mount gone.

'We should go,' says Robert, pulling Bobby's sleeve.

Bobby knocks the door, barely brushing it with his knuckles, and it yawns open. 'Morris?' Nothing. 'Tam?' Nothing. 'It's us. We won.'

Bobby tries to sound normal, in case anybody hears but also because he thinks if he says normal things in a normal voice then he will find something normal in the flat. He reaches in past the door frame for the light switch and flicks it on. Darkness. Taking a quick deep breath, as if diving into water, Bobby rushes in. Robert goes in after him.

The floor crunches underfoot. 'His shells,' Bobby sighs, trying to step lightly. He remembers his Auntie Maggie warning him never to walk across a grave.

The curtains are only open a crack but it's enough. The pearly table lies on its side. Both chairs are broken. The bed looks dark, wet, the sheets strewn.

'We should go,' whispers Robert, pulling Bobby's sleeve. 'Get help.'

Bobby doesn't want to look into the room's darkest corner. But forces himself. It's like trying to decipher a smoke-stained altarpiece. He can make out details – dark on dark, half-wrapped in a sheet, a silhouette he knows but twisted in a position he has never seen, one arm escaping, tattooed with a pair of crossed hammers.

'Don't look,' says Robert, but it's too late for that.

Bobby remembers what Morris told him about the police, about what to do when something bad happens, about who they believe. He crosses himself then walks slowly towards the door, followed by Robert, shells crunching accusingly beneath their feet. Just as they're about to leave Bobby turns back, bends down and picks up the nautilus, the shell no longer perfect white.

Chapter 14

'Is it ever gonnae fuckin stop?' Bobby wonders aloud, pressing his face against the smeary window.

'We'll get there,' says Robert, counting their bags again, all two of them. The khaki bag Bobby's mum stitched for him is now pleasingly scuffed.

Bobby flings himself back against their third-class seats. He'd spotted them after standing all the way to Crewe – a pair of reserved seats claimed by nobody – then plonked himself down. After five anguished minutes wondering if you could actually get the jail for such a thing, Robert sat down opposite and they felt the train gathering speed, devouring the miles between them and the next stop on their way.

As Scotland turns into England, Bobby tries to imagine the glories of the National Gallery on Trafalgar Square, where so little is from this nation but everything is for it; about all the Turners lighting up the Tate, where they look forward to despising the Pre-Raphaelites; and Fitzrovia, everything about Fitzrovia. Fleming has cautioned them against it, with a lecture about Sickert and dark hints of alleyways, even naming some particularly debauched pubs to avoid at all costs: the Fitzroy Tavern, the Wheatsheaf and the Bricklayer's Arms. Bobby has memorised them all.

They've got just two days to see all the pictures they've only glimpsed in books before heading back to Glasgow with their reports. Neither has lifted so much as a pencil on the train.

Instead of working, they just talk and talk, faster and faster, Robert almost as much as Bobby, as he does when it's just them. Nobody else understands him like Bobby does, so he doesn't waste words on them. The roar of the engine gives them cover to say what they want and, anyway, it's mainly English folk who wouldn't understand them. Mostly they talk about Morris.

'We should have gone to the police,' says Robert.

'Morris said not to. They hated him – they hate everybody like him, everybody like—'

'Don't say it,' says Robert. 'We're not like him.'

Part of him agrees with Robert – he doesn't feel the urge to put on a dress and get on a stage. But he loves that Morris does, did. They've seen no reports in the paper, nothing about a murder in Dennistoun.

'Will there be a funeral?' Robert asks.

Bobby sees an open grave with no mourners, no headstone. It is unbearable. He lets the argument go.

'What about Tam?' Robert wonders. 'Whose flat was it?'

Bobby hadn't thought about this. He remembers the lessons Morris told him that first time he went to his flat: 'Don't shit on your own doorstep; Never write anything down; Don't ever go to the police.' Don't, never, ever. He hopes never to have to follow his wisdom about VD.

Light dims in the carriage as the train finally enters the belly of Euston and slowly, slowly comes to a halt. It takes even longer than at Glasgow Central. As it gives one final lurch forward, whistles wheen from all around and their fellow passengers burst into life, each desperate to be off first. Cigarettes are stubbed out and bags, boxes and parcels retrieved in a knot of busy limbs. A conductor comes towards them and watches as Bobby nips up to fish his bag from the overhead rack. This is it, Robert thinks, we stole the seats and now it'll be the jail. 'Got it,' says Bobby as his bag breaks free and he falls back, right into the conductor. Robert doesn't know where to look.

'In a rush?' the conductor asks, brushing himself down.

'Sorry,' says Bobby. 'I, we, my bag was stuck, I couldn't get it down.'

'You should have let your friend help,' says the conductor, looking Robert up and down. 'He's taller.'

Social smiles do not come easy for Robert – each one exacts a personal price he will have to pay later, but he tries one on.

'Not to worry,' says the conductor, slamming down the window of the nearest door then reaching out to open it, letting it swing, all of London just beyond.

Robert stands there. Is this a trick? Are they missing their last chance to confess?

'First time?' asks the conductor, removing his cap and pushing a lick of dirty blond hair away from his face before putting it back on. He must just have missed the last war.

'Aye,' says Bobby, pulling his bag over one shoulder and nodding to Robert. 'Our first time.'

'Well,' says the conductor, gesturing to the platform, now full of nothing but smoke. 'You better not keep her waiting.'

Bobby is straight out and down onto the platform. Robert nods at the conductor for letting them go and as he reaches the door the conductor brushes by so close he feels the rough grain of his serge trousers. 'Mind how you go,' he shouts, leaning out and pulling the door shut. He winks, actually winks: 'Don't do anything I wouldn't.'

Bobby and Robert run-laugh the length of the empty platform before being pulled into the dance of the ticket hall. It's busier than the Barras on a Saturday. Stunned, they stand still as it turns around them.

'It's like a cathedral,' says Robert, shouting to be heard. He points to soaring columns leading the eye up to clerestory windows no cathedral would be ashamed of.

'A noisy one!' says Bobby, lighting a cigarette and taking a deep draw before shoving two fingers between his collar and his neck, trying to get some air. 'Did you hear him? *Don't do anything I wouldn't.* Disnae leave much, I bet!'

'Don't be daft,' says Robert, looking for the exit. After that, they need to find a Tottenham Court Road, which supposedly goes all the way down to Trafalgar Square and their first stop: the National Gallery. The map Fleming gave them is folded carefully in his hand. 'He was just being . . . English.'

'Tryin it on, more like!'

'Bobby, shhh—'

'They don't care. Nobody cares. Nobody knows us here. See?'

Bobby spins on the spot, his arms out and the crowd parts around him. This is London: nobody cares what he is, only that he's blocking their way. 'Anyway,' says Bobby. 'The ticket man's not your type.'

A pigeon skims their heads, flying across the ticket hall and out through the vaulted arches into the city.

'This way,' says Robert, tapping Bobby's arm, pointing towards the arches, already gas-lit even in the afternoon. 'And I've not got a type.'

'You so have,' smiles Bobby, nipping out his fag and pocketing it for later, grateful Robert knows where they're going.

Robert steps out into the street first and is nearly hit by a messenger boy on a bike who turns around, without slowing, and shouts 'watch it' before disappearing into the smog. Nobody here is standing still. Robert tries to unfold his map but he's bumped from all sides and can't see any street signs anyway. The familiar tang of horse dung cuts through the smog. It's hot here – spring in London feels like summer in Glasgow.

Robert gives up on the map, carefully folding it to return to Fleming. He shrugs at Bobby. They let the crowd carry them along, wondering how they'll get across this road of trams, horses and honking belching motorcars.

'There!' Bobby points over the way and Robert sees a street sign high up on a shop called Heal's: Tottenham Court Road. A policeman's whistle peals, parting the traffic like Moses, and they all surge across. They manage to walk side by side past all the shops, the huge windows depicting scenes from clean-lined lives, all with electric light. Then it's bookshop after bookshop, Bobby desperate to stop and browse but painfully aware of the pennies in his pocket. Finally, they fall into Trafalgar Square and onto a bench where they pause; the lions remind Robert of his failed George Square drawing. Bobby starts to cough. They've barely been sat five minutes and are considering braving the National Gallery when a bus marked TATE GALLERY (MILLBANK) stops right by them.

'Let's go,' says Bobby, suddenly seized by a desire to see one particular painting right this very minute, as if it might disappear without him standing in front of it. He runs for the bus and Robert follows and they make it just in time.

Soon they're standing on the steps of the Tate, trying not to gawp provincially. The woman behind the till at the door takes their money. She holds their pound note up to the light.

'Scotch?' she asks, her accent easily able to sharpen pencils.

'Scot*tish*,' says Bobby, holding his hand out for change, which the woman passes over with two pink tickets.

A guard checks their tickets as they pass and finally they're in. 'We're closing soon, you know,' he says, looking at Bobby's boots.

'Thank you,' says Bobby, pocketing the stubs, saving them to look back at one day.

An hour off the train, here they are, sitting in front of Van Gogh's *Sunflowers*, the picture Bobby had to see.

'The cheek,' Bobby goes on, still talking as he pulls his jumper over his head. '*Scotch?* And him on the train – cracking on to you like that. You thought he was going to huckle us and there he just wanted a bit.'

'No, he didnae,' whispers Robert. 'Keep yer voice down.'

Bobby stuffs his jumper in his bag. Now is not the time for a fight. 'Well he didnae get the door for me.'

'He didnae need to,' Robert laughs. 'You were out like a polecat down a hole!'

Bobby shrugs. 'Fair enough.' He looks around then budges up on the two-seater bench so their shoulders almost brush. Robert doesn't move away.

The gallery is starting to think about closing for the day but the sunflowers don't care if they've got an audience or not – they blaze off the wall, somehow lit from behind or within.

'Do you think they're real?' Robert wonders, his eyes roving from petal to petal like a bee, unpicking every brush stroke, every decision. He sticks the tip of his tongue out between his lips, the way he only does when he's lost in something. He remembers the sunflowers his father grew up the side of his aviary, so tall they peeked out over the top – the one and only non-edible plant he permitted. 'I mean, do you think he drew them from life or do you think he just made them up?'

Bobby thinks for a moment, recalls their long afternoons in the Life Room and Fleming's endless command not merely to look but to *see*. He shrugs. 'Aye, no. I don't know. But they're here now.'

'I think he was looking right at them like we are now,' says Robert, leaning forward and pointing to a big tufty one in the middle. 'They look hot, like the sun's still in them.'

'Aye,' ponders Bobby, leaning forward too, suddenly desperate to run his hand across the rough salt glaze of the jug. 'And the yellows. I want to find a screaming kind of yellow. And see that green? Round the jug, on the table? That's the bones, it's nothing without that.'

Robert sits back and nods. 'The green!' he says, surprised. 'I see it!'

'Can you believe we're really here?' Bobby asks, nudging almost imperceptibly along the bench – he looks about and spots a guard slipping into the room to stand sentry by the arch to the next room. Bobby shifts back to his side of the bench, not suddenly, not so anybody would notice. 'A long way from Maybole eh?'

Robert turns to him and smiles. In Bobby's eyes, he can see all the sunflowers, the yellows, the oranges and that green. His smile evaporates as he spots the guard over Bobby's shoulder.

'What?' asks Bobby, ever sensitive to any change in the weather around his beloved. Robert flicks his eyes over his shoulder and Bobby gets it. They sit in observed quiet facing the picture until the guard's shoes squeak out the room. When they're sure he's gone, Bobby lets out a sigh and points to the picture, doing his best Fleming impression. 'You must not simply look – you must *seeeeee*!' They giggle before resuming gallery manners. They sit on the bench as the light falls from late afternoon to early evening and watch the sunflowers turn with it. The two of them are here. All the flowers are here. And now they will always carry these flowers within themselves; they can call upon them to bloom whenever they need. The guard squeaks back in, gives a polite cough and taps his watch as the last of the light goes.

It's a guidebook stroll from the Tate along the Thames, which, they concede, competes with the Clyde. Bobby is, as always, starving. Robert is, as always, not bothered. Because they've been warned to avoid Soho they head straight for it, vaguely sure it's somewhere beyond Trafalgar Square. Their feet have never felt heavier. Finally reaching Leicester Square, they're stopped by a woman standing under a streetlight.

'Got a light, love?' she asks Robert. While he's fumbling for a match Bobby gets a good look. The old gas light is kind, flickering just enough; electricity will be the end of mystery. She could have been standing right here at any point in the past hundred years. She's curved like an armoire, a sort of furniture he knows from Interiors, her burgundy velvet dress is cinched by a thin black patent leather belt that's doing a lot of work.

'Company?' she offers, blowing a perfect smoke ring at Robert, giving him a fleeting halo. He coughs, too politely.

'I see,' she says, gesturing to Bobby with her cigarette.

'Thanks,' says Bobby. He likes working women.

'We're going to Soho,' says Robert. 'Or Fitzrovia.'

'Oh yeah?' asks the woman, drawing hard on her cigarette, her lipstick marking the end like a starlet giving an autograph. Bobby goes to say something but the woman raises a hand to silence him while she takes another, even deeper draw. The cigarette is disappearing fast. She blows smoke out, picking up where she left off. 'What you after? Eh? I can give you some tips.'

'Just dinner,' says Bobby.

'Well,' the woman dredges her lungs, laughing and spitting at the same time. 'Somebody's hungry.' She sucks the last life from her cigarette and flicks it on the pavement, grinding it under the heel of a high-laced boot, which has seen many better days. Bobby wonders if her boots were made in Maybole and what the women who cut and sewed and tacked would make of the present wearer. Without warning she grabs Robert's face and kisses him rapid-fire on each cheek.

Bobby bursts out laughing and the woman joins in, hacking and cackling. Robert touches his cheeks in disbelief.

Spotting a potential customer, she hoiks up her chest and throws back her shoulders. 'Go enjoy your dinner, boys,' she says, pointing north across the square. 'Stop at the Golden Cock on Old Compton, tell them Elsie sent you. And don't have the liver!'

She waves them off while blowing a kiss to a manly shadow emerging from the gloom.

'Fancy!' says Bobby, when they're out of earshot. 'She didn't bat an eyelid!'

'She's in no position to judge,' says Robert.

'Neither are we,' says Bobby, coughing again. 'Robert, your legs. Gimme a minute.'

Bobby staggers to the nearest lamppost and leans against it, trying to catch his breath. Every rattle takes him back to when he was a boy, laid up in that clean white hospital bed. That cough got better but it never really left – he feels it running for a tram, on bitter days when the cold of the Clyde sweeps through the city, or when the factory chimneys are busy. London air makes Glasgow seem clean – it's so close even in spring, what must summer be like? He tugs at his collar then pats his pockets.

'They won't help,' says Robert, holding up their cigarettes. 'It's your dinner you're needing and a sit down.'

'Aww, c'mon,' whines Bobby, making a grab for the packet. Robert lifts it up out his reach then pockets it before offering him a rare shoulder to lean on. Every other person seems pissed, and he'll never see any of them again, so Bobby takes advantage and leans right into Robert, the two arriving as one on the southern border of Soho.

The Golden Cock is not hard to find even if the cockerel over the door has seen shinier days. But the embossed bird on the hand-written menu in the window is enough to make Bobby wonder if they can afford it. Spaghetti, Chicken Forestier, Spam Fritters and hamburgers – straight out the pictures! Bobby can still remember every meal he's ever eaten out. He can't stand the tweeness of Glasgow's tearooms but him and Robert get no bother in those delicate houses of women and talk. He dreams of restaurants – plates of faraway tastes, ingredients from the crates that come off the big boats that go all round the world then right up the Clyde.

'It's full,' groans Bobby, noting the steamy windows.

Robert, with his better vantage point, spies an empty table at the back. 'C'mon,' he says, pushing the door. He's determined to be bolder for London.

They step in and none of the other diners so much as looks up. They stand there unsure if they should just go to the empty table or wait. They feel heavy and provincial. Robert is turning to leave when a waiter appears asking, 'Two?' Bobby nods and they're whisked to the last table.

'Wine?' the waiter asks, his pen poised over a pad, while they're still sitting down. He's only about their age but the pen and pad give him total authority. Somebody shouts something not in English from the kitchen behind him then there's the smash of a dish and some rich cursing followed by a whoosh of steam. 'Red or white?'

They've only had wine once – the night of the General Course show, when they won this trip. Drink is a distraction they've not been able to afford.

The waiter taps his pen on his pad.

'Red,' says Robert.

'Bottle or glass?'

'Glass,' says Bobby, mindful of their money and the need for an early start.

They avoid the liver, as cautioned. Bobby decides a hamburger is too pricey so opts for Chicken Forestier while Robert orders cod à la crème.

The waiter disappears into the kitchen and Robert admires his arse as he goes.

Having congratulated themselves on getting the last table in all Soho they realise why nobody else wants it – the restaurant's only toilet yawns right by their table. Soon they know their fellow diners too well.

Their food arrives before their wine.

Bobby attacks his dinner. Robert picks at his fish, pale as a priest but hopefully tastier.

'You need to try,' says Bobby, mouth half full. 'You've had nothing fae the train.'

Robert dimly remembers a sandwich somewhere around Carlisle. To appease Bobby, he has a few more pokes at the cod before pushing his plate across the table – he'd rather watch Bobby eat.

The restaurant starts to empty and the kitchen quietens – it's getting on for 11 p.m. They need a place to sleep. Fleming warned them against the B&Bs around Euston because they extort anybody with an accent north of Watford.

'Bill?' asks the waiter, his pad down to the last page.

'Yes,' says Bobby, picking up the local lingo. 'Do you know . . . is there a place near here where we can get a room?'

The waiter laughs. 'I don't doubt it. How long for?'

'Just the night,' says Robert. 'We're down from Glasgow.'

'I'm round the corner on Berwick Street,' says the waiter, looking from one to the other. 'I've got a couch.'

Robert blushes. Bobby considers the waiter again: Italian,

maybe, and about their age but somehow he already has his own flat in Soho and in this flat he has a couch – a spare couch!

'You've got good table manners,' the waiter goes on, writing up their bill. 'You can have the couch for the price of dinner. It's up to you.' He leans in. 'I won't watch or anything.'

Robert telegraphs a message to Bobby with his eyes but Bobby can't quite work it out: yes, no, run?

The waiter lays their bill on the table and Bobby reaches for it – with the wine, it's more than their budget for the whole night! They need money for the galleries tomorrow. Also, it might be nice to eat another meal or two. Even the waiter's couch now seems beyond them.

'Sorry,' says Bobby, patting his pockets and shrugging.

'Shame,' says the waiter, counting out their change. 'It's a nice couch, comfier than a bench in St James's. Mind how you go, then.'

Robert and Bobby gather their bags and put on their coats. The waiter flips the sign on the door to CLOSED as they step onto Old Compton Street. It's even busier than before. Soho is just waking up. The night is so bright the moon struggles to make herself noticed. There are half a dozen people per paving slab – Robert counts them, mentally sketches a pane of glass of this place. A boy their age swishes past, his hair fully hennaed and his nails shocking pink and nobody seems to notice. A pair of sailors sway towards them, their uniforms shining in the smog, arms linked, anchors well away. Just as they're about to ram them they part and pass either side before linking arms again and rolling on their way.

'I love Soho!' says Bobby, turning to check them out before turning back to Robert who is pretending not to have noticed.

'Right,' says Bobby. 'That park then?'

Robert gets out their map again.

London, like Glasgow, is filling up with soldiers. The barracks by St James's Park are packed tighter than a guardsman's trousers. As they step under the first tree, a voice from the shadows asks them for a light. Robert pats his pockets. Bobby produces a box of matches and rattles it.

'Much obliged,' says the owner of the voice, stepping into the moonlight. He's too young for the last war.

'Nae worries,' says Bobby, putting his hand out for the matches.

'Scotch eh?' If he was less handsome, Bobby would pull him up for this. He takes a deep draw on his cigarette then blows smoke out one corner of his mouth and over his shoulder without turning his head.

'Aye,' says Robert. 'Down from Glasgow.'

'I've met a lot of gents from Edinburgh,' says the soldier, straying into an awful Scotch accent. 'But not from Glasgow.' He eyes their bags. 'You working?'

'No,' says Robert, earnestly. 'Well, a bit.'

'We've come down to see the art,' says Bobby.

'Well, you found it,' says the soldier, knotting his tie higher. The brass buttons on his jacket glint in the glow from his cigarette. He advances. Bobby and Robert stand their ground. The next sound is a fancy brass buckle jankling. 'Standing to attention,' says the soldier. 'Who's first then?'

The National Anthem wakes Bobby and Robert. They nearly fall off the bench they're balanced on, bags for pillows, when the regimental band strikes up. The conductor allows himself a smile at the state of them.

Bobby rubs his eyes – he's still in last night. Was the soldier a dream? Robert stretches and feels his back crack but not in a good way. They're still in London and still alive. It's their last day already. Glinting on the bench between them is a single brass button. Bobby picks it up and hands it to Robert, who pockets it while the band plays on.

PART TWO

Sketches from Europe

1938–1939

The Glasgow School of Art wishes to award the 1938 Travelling Scholarship to Mr Robert Colquhoun. The Award is £120. On Behalf of the GSA, Mr Ian Fleming.

Dear Mr MacBryde,

I wish to congratulate you on your performance here at the GSA. At every turn you have impressed your tutors with your dedication and commitment to learning. It is clear you will 'do us proud'. Furthermore, it is clear that your companion Mr Colquhoun will doubtless share his award with you as you have hitherto shared your studio and student lives. You have each developed a standard of work not inferior to professional artists. Difficulty was found in deciding which of you was to receive the Travelling Scholarship. However, as it can only be awarded to an individual, I have seen fit to make a further personal award to you of the same sum – this should fund six months' travel in Europe, all being well. I do not wish for Mr Colquhoun to miss out on opportunities foregone should he halve his award and it is my belief that you will each continue to be more successful in the creative company of the other. I look forward to reading your Reports and to seeing the faith this school has put in you repaid.

Sir John Richmond, Chairman of Governors.
12 June 1938.

Paris

Leith to Dunkirk is one endless briny boak. October sailing is not kind.

'No seascapes,' says Bobby, heaving again, head hanging over the side.

'Ever,' retches Robert, knuckles whiter than his face as he grips the railings.

Their *couchettes* are far less comfortable than the term suggests – a bunk would be luxury beyond the dreams of avarice. So, they tangle together in whatever combination of limbs sleep allows. They don't worry too much about how this looks because everybody else is in the same position. Still, Robert is watchful. After what feels like years at sea, they finally arrive in France as a foggy dawn breaks.

'This is the furthest any of my family have ever been,' Bobby realises, gathering their rucksacks. *Never forget where you come fae.*

Robert is too weak to point out the MacBrydes supposedly came over from Ireland, whose west coast is probably just as distant. He banks the thought. The Colquhouns have certainly never been further, although his wee brother John might be coming here. He tries not to think about that.

They stagger down the gangplank, each holding the rail with one hand, like the last drinkers leaving the Napoleon. Boots clattering the gangplank remind Bobby of running over the railway bridge at Maybole to catch the train that first day; him and his boots have come far. A tri-coloured official steps forward and, without looking up from his list, asks in English 'Purpose of your visit?'

Bobby is disappointed not to hear French. But he's rehearsed his answer. 'Art,' he hiccups. It sounded better in his head. Robert sways, wondering if there's anything left to come up. France won't stay still. The official takes their passports, then looks up at them for the first time – this pair are something like brothers but do not share the same name. He shrugs, in a thrillingly Gallic gesture, then steps aside. Immediately, a man in khaki rechecks their passports and only when he's happy do two other soldiers slide open a gate made from barbed wire – the kind that snags sheep on Kildoon Hill. Finally, they are here. Bobby spots their first real café and plonks himself down outside, patting the empty chair next to him. It's not Toulouse-Lautrec but it'll do.

'Deux café au lait, s'il vous plaît,' says Bobby, to a silvered waiter, who whisks their coffee over in moments.

To calm his nerves, Robert tries sketching the hectic harbour scene but it doesn't work.

'Santé,' says Bobby, clinking the comically dainty cups, the sophisticated froth swelling up and almost over the brim. 'Beats the University Café!'

Robert regrets his one sip. He does not look or feel good. A silver-haired gentleman breezes up to the next table and leans down to kiss the waiting lady on each powdered cheek. Bobby is spellbound. Robert braces, knows what's coming – he closes his eyes as Bobby leans across their table going left, then right, his lips sticky with foam. Robert feels the kisses burn on his face – even his Protestant brain remembers Jesus and Judas in the garden. But there is no ambush, no arrest, the soldiers stroll by talking and smoking, ready for the next boat.

'Santé,' Robert croaks, hoping it comes true.

Despite their excitement, and the coffee, they sleep all the way to Paris on the relatively smooth train.

'Bienvenue à Gare du Nord,' says Bobby as they disembark so far down the platform they're not even under the station roof.

'Are you going to keep at this?'

'Mais oui,' says Bobby, counting their bags again.

Robert is even shakier. Bobby tries to remember the last time he saw him eat. Not since Mrs Cranston's farewell breakfast. 'To the first ever joint winners of the Travelling Scholarship!' she'd said, toasting them with actual champagne.

'Let's get you a wee petit-déjeuner,' says Bobby.

'I just want my bed,' says Robert.

'Oh aye,' winks Bobby, though even he is too travel-worn for antics. How glamorous to feel travel-worn. How Garbo-ish.

'B-e-d,' Robert spells it out, his bag slipping from his shoulder.

Bed is where Robert spends their first two days in Paris. Apart from frequent trips to the shared toilet on their floor of the smallest hotel in Montparnasse. Each morning, Bobby brings him charming little bottles of freshly squeezed orange juice from the café opposite and day-old croissants got for cheap. Robert sleeps through. On the third day, he rises.

'It's a miracle!' says Bobby, perching at the bottom of Robert's bed.

'Bonjour,' croaks Robert.

'Come on,' says Bobby, tickling the soles of Robert's feet, discharging his electric excitement. Robert, more ticklish than he lets on, pulls his knees up to his chin.

'It was touch and go,' says Bobby, placing his hand against his own forehead. 'I nearly had to find a handsome doctor.'

'No surprise there,' says Robert, sitting up and looking round their tiny, shared room.

'Somebody's feelin better!'

Their two single beds are barely arm's length apart. Between them stands a spindly little table topped with a big pink water jug. Their sole window stretches from floor to ceiling and has pale yellow shutters. The floor is bare but for a deer-skin rug that looks like it's still trying to escape. Their hotel takes bookings by the hour, day and week. Robert has no memory of arriving here, of getting into this bed. 'It's got springs,' he says, the mattress dinging.

'The luxury!' says Bobby, bouncing up and down, desperate for Robert to get up. 'Come on! We're wasting time!'

'Paris can wait one more minute.'

'Non,' says Bobby. 'Jamais!'

'Jesus,' says Robert, stretching. 'How long was I out?'

'Days,' said Bobby. 'I tucked you in.'

Robert feels more rested than he knew was possible. He's in Paris. They are in Paris. Him and Bobby. They've made it. Pooling their prize monies will turn six months of travel into eight – maybe more, if Bobby can work his usual magic.

'I've not stolen all the joy,' Bobby says, throwing an arm around the brass bedstead. Robert watches late morning light slide in through the shutters and hit the wall where it animates some egregious floral wallpaper.

'Promise?' says Robert, hugging his knees. He can hear it all outside. It's all right outside: the Louvre, Notre-Dame, everything they need to see.

'Promise,' says Bobby, wondering when to tell him about the waiter at the café opposite. Maybe just let them meet. 'Now, petit-déjeuner?'

'Sasha!' The waiter kisses Bobby on both cheeks as they arrive, flashing his shiny silver tray.

'Bonjour,' says Bobby, returning kisses then gesturing to Robert like a magician who has just restored two halves of their assistant.

The waiter applauds with one hand on his tray, holding it like a cymbal. Robert, flush with novelty, does a courtly bow, which he immediately regrets.

'He lives?' the waiter asks, rubbing down a tiny table then stepping back. Bobby slides in, as if it's something he's done every morning for his whole life.

'Oui,' says Bobby.

'Welcome, friend of Sasha,' says the waiter.

'Robert,' says Bobby.

The waiter smiles then turns and shouts 'Deux café au lait!'

'Sasha?' Robert asks, savouring the cool metal café chair pressing on his back. Paris does not feel like October.

'I fancied a new name,' says Bobby. 'For new horizons.'

That's not all you fancied, thinks Robert. Bobby reads his mind but says nothing – souring their first morning could endanger their whole trip and one hour with Robert in a dark mood can feel like a month. He learned how to bring him around in the attic, but here? They are unmoored. The waiter nips back with their coffees and Robert gets a good look: his luxurious moustache veers from gold at the edges to copper where it meets his lips, his mathematically perfect side-parting is pure blond and his tightly trousered arse is like something from the sculpture hall, only, Robert guesses, warmer to the touch. Wasted on Bobby, who will be much more interested in whatever's in the front.

'Fair play, Sasha,' Robert says, tearing open two sachets of sugar and tipping them into his coffee to the horror of a poodle-wielding lady two tables along, who thinks to herself, truly, it is the end of times.

It takes Robert nearly a week of eating, sleeping and gentle wandering before braving their first gallery. Bobby tries to be patient. *The whole city is an artwork*, Robert says and Bobby seriously considers leaving him. They discuss investing in a map but don't know how long they'll be here. *It's chic to look lost*, Bobby insists and Robert is relieved not to be the only one guilty of triteness today. All the cafés serve wine and after a few days it seems rude not to. Vin rouge takes the edge off all the headlines, all the conversations overheard in every café . . . all suggesting they are wise to see what they can while they can. It seems the rest of Europe has the same idea – Paris is filling up; their hotel bill doubles in a week. The city has an increasingly frantic air. Bakers crown their windows with ever more fantastical cakes but run out of flour for bread. Jewellers are exhausted by wedding rings. The Seine runs faster and higher. But perhaps Paris is always like this?

'It is all a fuss,' insists Pascal – their waiter now has a first name. 'I am in the reserves so would have been called up if something real was happening.'

Robert is both relieved and disappointed.

Pascal goes on. 'But the city *is* full.' He flicks croissant crumbs off their table with the corner of his cloth and a pigeon wastes no time. 'Foreigners.'

Bobby sips his coffee pointedly.

'Oh Sasha, not you. I mean from the east. You know?'

Relieved not to be the outsiders for once, Bobby shrugs, hoping his shrug is getting more local. Pascal leans in and whispers, 'Jews.'

Bobby thinks about the refugees at the centre that's opened down from the Art School – they serve soup every day to anybody that needs it; he recalls the Polish granny who showed him how to make borscht. Robert realises Pascal will probably not be marching alongside his wee brother John. Rain patters the café awning. Breakfast is over.

Back in Glasgow they sat together in the library compiling a list of the pictures they needed to see, then carefully consulted the atlas and ordered their trip accordingly. Mrs Cranston promised them the attic would always be waiting. Expectations that they would go back to Maybole or Kilmarnock had stopped after neither of them went 'home' that first Christmas. Nobody had come to their final show, so Bobby resolved never to send another invitation. But he does send the odd postcard to Auntie Maggie. Bobby is, as ever, keeper of the purse and plans. The Vatican is top of Robert's list, with the promise of Raphael and Leonardo and Michelangelo in one heavenly morning. Bobby enjoys teasing him about this, telling him its doors were closed to Presbyterians. The picture at the top of Bobby's itinerary was in the very first book he got out of Maybole Library: today, finally, he will take his place on the *Raft of the Medusa*.

The queue for the Louvre is still growing by the time they arrive mid-morning.

'We should have got here sooner,' says Robert.

Bobby takes a deep breath, does not regret stopping for breakfast. 'We'll be in soon,' he says, admiring the mirroring of the vast wings of the museum as they shuffle along, wondering what treasures lie beneath the courtyard between the two.

'No wonder they had a revolution,' says Robert, ticking off Baroque, Neoclassical, Neo-Baroque, watching their Architecture classes come to life. He has enough time to sketch more than a few columns, starting and stopping as they shuffle along.

'Alright, Robespierre,' says Bobby, counting the necessary francs. 'We're next.'

'Where are you going?' Robert half-shouts as Bobby disappears into the crowd. The Louvre is more like a train station than a gallery.

'Room 700,' Bobby shouts over his shoulder without looking back. He needs to see it now. He needs to see it first. Pushing through the crowd, he feels like one of the survivors on the doomed ship, rushing for one of the too-few lifeboats. He passes paintings and statues he knows he should stop for and begs their forgiveness, knowing it will be given because his mission is in good faith.

And then he's there. Bobby's shoulders barely kiss the bottom of the huge frame, which is thicker than his thighs. Instantly he is on board, clinging to the roped-together raft. He can now see the ragged sail is actually the colour of dried ox blood – a stain his mother struggled to get out of his father's shirts after he'd done some work on the side at the slaughterhouse. What's left of the sail sags with hot wind somewhere off the coast of

Mauritania. Clouds and waves are closing in. There are now only fifteen survivors left of the 147 who'd hauled themselves from the waves two desperate weeks before. Maddened with thirst and hope, they reach for a ship that may or may not be coming.

'Is that . . . a body?' asks Robert, walking up to Bobby.

Bobby nods.

Robert reads aloud from the caption, which is in English, French and, he's surprised to see, German: '*The only hero in this poignant story is humanity.*' He stands back to try and take it all in.

'That's Delacroix,' says Bobby, pointing to a brooding figure in the foreground with an arm stretched over a corpse.

'Is he the hero?'

'No,' Bobby shakes his head. 'There's no hero.' He remembers seeing this picture shrunk into a book in the library in Maybole but still feeling all this drama, the drive to survive and being amazed a painter could capture all that. 'It took Gericault a whole year. Imagine?'

'Imagine being that rich you could spend a whole year on one picture,' says Robert.

'It wasn't even a commission. He was just obsessed.'

'You're only making my point,' says Robert, admiring the twist in the torso of the man waving a rag at the horizon.

'What happened to all the rest of them?'

'Custom of the sea,' says Bobby, in his storytelling voice. 'See that half a man?'

Robert nods.

'Where do you think the other half went?'

Robert notices some survivors are not as thin as others.

'Perfectly legal,' says Bobby. 'Until 1900 or something. They called it "the delicate question". In case of disaster, when there was not enough food for the survivors, bodies could be eaten. If there were no bodies—'

'They made some.'

'Yer catching on.'

'How?'

'They drew lots. It was luck.'
'And what about Gericault?'
'He went mad, I think.'
'Maybe he was mad to start,' says Robert, reading the caption. '*Dead at thirty-two.*'

Bobby recounts details gleaned from the librarian one lunchtime. 'He borrowed a human head from one of the asylums and drew it every day for two weeks, kept it out on his studio roof to slow the decay.'

'Did he return it?'

'Would you want it back?'

They drift for what's left of the morning, sketching studies of faces, hands and feet in their journals. At lunchtime the crowd gets hungry, so they chance the *Mona Lisa*. Even on his tiptoes Bobby can really only see heads and hats. Robert is better placed but less patient. The picture is smaller than they imagined and the gallery busier. The experience of half-seeing the *Mona Lisa* will stay with them longer than her expression. They head off in search of *Saint John the Baptist* then agree that Leonardo obviously fancied his model. As they leave in search of a cheap lunch, Robert splashes on a postcard for Bobby.

Tired from all the looking, and already fearful of forgetting what they've seen and letting homework pile up, they head back to their room to update the journals they must present to Fleming after their travels to secure their final grant instalment. Wordlessly, they take a route that avoids Pascal's café. Later that night, long after they've fallen asleep with their heads full of Room 700 and the heroes of the Greek sculpture hall, a lorry pulls up at the Louvre, as close as possible to the doors they used earlier. It is circus red and so long the driver has to plot a route out of the city that avoids many streets. On the side it says *Comédie-Française*. Inside are six strong men all sworn to secrecy. They are led through darkened galleries by a curator flashing a heavy electric torch; every now and then a glint of marble or gilding reminds them they are not alone. They work in silence. It takes all six men most of that night just to get the picture off the wall where it has been for over a century. Somehow ignoring the pacing curator, they wheel *The Raft of the Medusa* through room after room then out into the midnight courtyard. For a moment, the survivors feel a fresh breeze upon them. Once again, they are caught on the tide.

The Miracle of Saint Irene, South of France

The nun glides on ahead of them, the frayed hem of her habit whispering across the nut-dark floors like dry autumn leaves blown in through an open door. She does not look back to make sure the young men are following. She walks assuredly through bare white room after bare white room, each clean as a baby's first tooth. One unvarnished wooden door opens on to another, as if in a dream. She is the only person they have seen here and for all they know she is the lone inhabitant of the vast convent hanging on the hillside above the terracotta-roofed town.

'Get thee to a nunnery,' Robert had whispered, as the tall iron gates squealed closed behind them, the only sound the place made.

Bobby hushed him. 'Shhh. Or she'll not show us.'

'Yous Catholics,' said Robert. 'So sensitive.'

After four, or is it five, such rooms, the nun finally stops. With her back to them still, she dips to her knees as well as she can now and crosses herself before rising again. Bobby follows. Robert just stands there. Bobby nudges him. She knows, without turning, that both young men will show the proper respect. They had arrived the day before but been refused, as was customary. Nobody gets in first time. Surprisingly few try twice. This morning, at first light, they had turned up again and been refused – this time she caught their accents and thought them Flemish. One said his name was Sasha. This afternoon they had chanced it one more time, seemingly on their way to the station, from their bags. This time she'd let them pass, nodding just once then standing aside. The painting was in their eyes already. She could see it. She has not left this place since the gates closed on her when she was fourteen but even after all these years she knows there is still so much more to know about the picture; perhaps, she thinks, these two can help open her eyes, even just a little. Certainly, she knows the convent's greatest treasure will show them much.

They stop in a room with no windows and, seemingly, no further door. It is lit only by the lozenge of light from the doorway they stand in. The nun reaches into her pocket, a worldly piece of tailoring allowed only to her and to the Mother Abbess, and retrieves a small golden key, which she takes to a matching padlock hanging on a chain linking the long thin doors that conceal the painting from the world. The chain slides through her fingers like a rosary, coiling satisfyingly into her palm. She pockets it then reaches up to the handles on the frames and opens them in one movement, like a pair of shutters, standing back quickly as if something might fall from above. As the doors settle either side of the painting, she crosses herself again.

Bobby gasps.

'It's so bright,' says Robert, stepping forward and pointing up to the canvas, which is as tall as him.

'That blue,' says Bobby. 'It must have cost a fortune. Pure lapis.'

'Can we . . .?' Bobby gropes in the battered canvas bag over his shoulder and fishes out a palm-sized notebook then fumbles for a pencil, as if the painting might vanish.

The nun nods – she doubts they mean her charge any harm.

Saint Sebastian is pinned against a giant twisted oak, his surprisingly dainty feet bound at the ankles. His skin is paler than porcelain but somehow shines from within. His face is contorted between agony and ecstasy, his whole body pierced with arrows, each sunk to a different depth, the one in his right thigh fixing him to the tree. He looks up and out of the heavy gold frame to whoever he sees descending from above, his free arm pleading. The painting is unsigned.

Bobby and Robert sketch at speed. They don't know how long they have. There is also, always, a train to catch. Bobby says, 'The arrows didn't kill him.'

'How not?' Robert counts and winces: this Sebastian has a dozen arrows. Some have only three or four, as if the artist couldn't bear it. There's no way this one would see another dawn. Robert remembers the statue of Sebastian from their first day – how embarrassed he was when Bobby tried to touch it.

'Aye,' says Bobby, warming to his story but wishing for just one window as he peers into the gloom. 'The Romans left him for dead then this old woman came along to cut him down but he was still breathing so she took him home and tended his wounds. When he got better, he went back to confront the Emperor who had ordered him killed. At first, the guy thinks he's a ghost but then realises he's actual flesh and blood so has him clubbed to death right there and then, to make sure he can't come back again, then chucks his body in the sewers.'

'Your lot are brutal,' says Robert, adjusting Sebastian's nose with the side of his pencil, casting a shadow down.

'My lot?'

'Catholics. Bloody.'

'True. But anyway, *Saint Sebastian in the Sewer* wouldn't be a pretty picture, would it?' Bobby steps forward so he is next to their guide. 'God saved him,' he says, peering into the bushes behind the fatal tree. 'God and . . .'

Bobby points up with his pencil. Their host waves frantically and Bobby turns his pencil round so the tip isn't aiming.

'Sorry,' he says. 'Sorry. Désolé. Can you see . . .?'

Robert steps forwards and shakes his head.

'Is that . . .?' says Bobby, standing on his tiptoes. 'Can you not see? There, peeking through the leaves.'

The nun follows Bobby's gaze. Her eyes are not so young and yet . . . Surely not? Not after looking her whole life long? She swallows a gasp.

Bobby pulls a clean white hankie from his back pocket and silently thanks his mother for never letting him out without one.

He shakes it out. 'S'il vous plaît?'

Even on his tiptoes, Bobby can only just reach the canvas. The nun presses the tiny key into the palm of her hand. She yelps, the sound a stranger to her after all these silent years. It was a mistake letting them so close. But now she has to see – she darts into the other room and brings through a tiny stool even older than her and sets it before the picture like an offering.

Robert steps forward and takes the hankie from Bobby.

'Wet it,' says Bobby. 'Just a wee bit'.

As Robert passes a corner of the hankie between his lips he feels the private heat from Bobby's pocket.

'Just there,' says Bobby, pointing urgently to a spot just over Sebastian's right shoulder.

Robert wobbles onto the stool then stands as tall as he can and reaches up, delicately dabbing one corner of the hankie on the canvas, as if drying a crying eye. He steadies himself for another pass. Bobby gasps. The nun crosses herself. Robert wants to hop down and see but hopping doesn't feel right here, so he steps off carefully.

'It's her!' says Bobby. 'It has to be.'

'Who?' asks Robert.

'The woman that saved him,' says Bobby, beaming. 'See?' He points to the face that has appeared in the bushes. 'C'est Saint Irène?'

The nun is weeping. She does not bother to hide her tears. There is no shame in divine revelation. She has not heard her name uttered since the closing of the gates all those years ago, has not even said it to herself: Irène.

Marseilles

The port is supposed to be just changing trains on the way to conquer Rome – there are no pictures here, no statues worth a visit. But the bar full of sailors that Bobby and Robert try to teach Highland dancing would make very fine statues. Not even a Parisian gallery would dare hang the pictures of what they get up to on their one night in the city, not even in France, where nudity is basically mandatory. They miss their train. They miss the next train. They leave the next day, happy to have renewed historic bonds between Scotland and France and forged new ones with Morocco. Or was it Algeria? Or both?

Modena

Punch, or whatever he's called here, is kicking three shades of shite out of the carabinieri, who are wearing a uniform not unlike the brownshirts multiplying wherever they stop in Italy.

'Are we not a bit old for puppets?' Bobby asks, carefully placing the teaspoon by the side of his now-empty coffee cup. They are sat at the Caffè Concerto in the Piazza Grande, colonnaded arches all around them and all watched over by Ghirlandina Tower. The square is full of stalls and the cries of peddlers – it's like the Barras, only warm. There is a closing-down air to the city even though it's only late morning – the sun has not yet reached the legendary steeple.

Robert sketches in his travel notebook. Punch menaces the policeman – Robert makes his club comically large. He places them both in a tiny theatre but leaves out the fringing because it looks too merry. The harder Punch hits, the louder the children laugh, the queasier Robert feels and he puts all this on the page – has to get it out of himself. It was not, he knew, strictly representative, which would raise an eyebrow back in Glasgow but they're not there anymore. He lifts his pencil from the page briefly and Bobby peers over and lets out a small whistle.

'Something's missing,' he says, wondering if their budget could take one of the wee plates of fried pasta pillows the caffè specialises in. His head buzzes with last night's vino. In Paris they'd identified being drunk as a definitive feature of Bohemia, the mapless region they longed to be citizens of. It was the done thing. And it was quite something to sit by the Seine and cloud a glass of pastis with water from a carafe. As it is to travel by train from city to city splitting a carafe of whatever is red and cheap and wet. Wine in Europe is more elegant than beer in Glasgow, and cheaper. Bobby didn't need loosening up but Robert did, and the combination of wine and travel worked magic so Bobby keeps his glass topped up.

Robert's pencil hovers over the page. Bobby is, as ever, right. As Robert ponders, he feels someone step behind him. He turns to find a pair of men in uniform. Quickly, he draws an arrow towards them, knowing Bobby will still be looking at his page. Sure enough, Bobby turns just enough to gauge the threat but that's excuse enough for the uniforms.

'Documenti!'

Bobby shrugs and waves towards their empty cups. They look to Robert then jab at his notebook. Without asking, the taller of the two snatches it up, flicking through the pages, accidentally animating every sketch Robert has made along the way: the harbour at Dieppe, with barbed wire coiling along the water's edge; square after square of Paris; a longing Saint Sebastian; the Duomo in Milan, impossible to see anew. And faces, so many faces: the sailors of Marseilles, arms roped with muscle; a bent-double flower-seller outside the Louvre and a young priest in Florence they gave plenty to confess – human architecture never glimpsed in Maybole or Kilmarnock or even Glasgow, faces that open to another sun.

'Cosa?' the younger uniform spat.

'We're artists,' Robert tries to explain. People are looking over now, noticing their faces, faces not from here. The carabinieri puppet lands a blow against Punch, who falls back and the children roar.

'Che?' the older one demands, pointing to Robert's notes, to dates and times. 'What?'

Bobby gathers their cigarettes and matches. He's glad he left his sketchbook at the pensione. He knows what's coming – remembers the fate of Michelangelo in Maybole. As Bobby stands, the younger guard kicks away his chair.

'Don't,' warns Robert.

'Don't what?' Bobby asks.

This is every nightmare they've ever had but in fine Italian tailoring. Everyone around them is busy pretending not to notice.

A priest rushes over from the cathedral, drawn by the commotion. Bobby crosses himself and the priest nods a brief benediction. This slows the uniforms who show the priest Robert's sketchbook. He leafs through it, respectfully, recognising the square arranged around them, the arches and shops and the puppet show.

'Ah,' he says. Then, in English, 'Artists.' He translates for the uniforms, who shake their heads. 'No,' the priest says, shooting Bobby a look. 'Not spies.'

'Artists,' says Bobby. 'Michelangelo.'

The uniform holding the book rips it neatly along its spine, then hands both parts to Robert, all the while speaking slowly to the priest, who translates. Robert puts both halves in his inside pocket.

'You must go now,' the priest says, not taking his eyes off the carabinieri. 'Leave the city today.'

'But we just got here,' Bobby protests.

'If you are still here tomorrow it will be in a prison cell,' says the priest. 'Or worse.'

They grab their things and rush back to the pensione where they haven't even unpacked. Bobby gets their passports. Robert holds both halves of his sketchbook.

'Not now,' says Bobby.

Robert finds the page with the puppet show. He gets his pencil out and puts in a giant naked figure, its hands hidden, no pupils in the eyes, watching the brawling puppets.

'Done?' Bobby asks, shouldering a bag.

'Done,' says Robert, heading for the door.

They run to the station and don't look back, won't give any excuse to whoever might be watching. Bobby remembers Morris saying – if you're running, run, and never look back.

Rome

Rome doesn't notice their early arrival.

'You do look a wee bit Italian,' says Robert, as they search the cheap streets round the station for a hotel. 'The sun suits you.'

Bobby is used to Robert's attention but actual compliments, unsolicited, remain a rare thing.

'Grazie,' says Bobby, trying to work out which hotel is least likely to harbour pests, based only on the signs. Il Palazzo is not looking palatial.

'I'm not joking,' says Robert.

'We've only been in Italy five minutes,' said Bobby. 'What's got you? Have you been at the Chianti already?'

'I don't know,' says Robert. 'You've always had that . . .' He touches his own face in lieu of Bobby's.

'Well, it's the only face I've got,' says Bobby, thinking about his Auntie Maggie and how one of the worst things she could say about somebody was that they had *mair faces than the toon clock*. To be more than one thing is a crime he cannot help. Suddenly he feels very far from Maybole and, for once, this gives no comfort – they're both still jangled by Modena.

'Come on,' says Robert. 'Let's find a room.'

They can afford three nights in Rome at Il Principe. Their room looks out on to a courtyard strung with laundry, which reminds Bobby of the steamie where he'd often gone to look for his mother. Robert pronounces it 'picturesque' in the manner of their former fellow students, the painting holiday people, but he's only half joking. Bobby has picked right up where Mrs Colquhoun left off. Robert wouldn't know a mangle if you shoved him in it and sometimes Bobby finds this endearing. Sometimes. After a quick splash in the sink they head out into the cool spring evening.

Scarlet flowers bleed from the branches of the trees lining the streets.

'Judas trees,' says Bobby, who admired the one in the Botanics.

Robert loves that Bobby knows about nature — the stories of fruits and flowers and trees helps him capture them on paper. No wonder still life is Bobby's thing.

'After betraying Jesus, Judas strung himself up from one of these.' The branches don't seem very sturdy to Robert. 'They used to have white flowers but after Judas all their flowers turned red for ever.'

They walk as Bobby talks and stumble on the Pantheon.

'It's the love child of the Albert Hall and the British Museum,' Bobby pronounces.

Two students walk by taking turns licking a coffee-coloured ice; one looks at Robert as he licks his cone. Robert smiles back and the other grabs the cone and sticks his tongue right in. The pair walk on, one drops a paper napkin — Robert picks it up. It's decorated with a print of antlers: Sant'Eustachio il Caffè.

'We should get a coffee,' says Robert, handing it to Bobby.

'At the very least,' says Bobby, forgetting the Pantheon as the students turn round and whistle.

It takes them ages to find the caffè and then it's closed but the hole in the wall next door is open and has no shortage of Chianti and olives big as eyes. After an hour or three they try to find their way back.

'Left,' Bobby insists.

'Right,' Robert maintains.

They bicker like this until they fall into a small square, completely shaded by tall buildings on all four sides. Sun warms only the top floors. There is no obvious way out. Robert shivers. While they're working out where to turn next, a young woman runs into the square, frantic. Her blouse is torn off her shoulder and a red scarf spools from her long black hair. She's missing a sandal.

Bobby walks over to her slowly, carefully, his hands where she can see them. Saint Eustace. The stag. Up close he can see she's only a girl. Running from men. He knows the look. 'Where are they?'

The girl throws herself on him, looking over her shoulder, babbling, unable to catch her breath. Robert rushes over and the girl turns this way and that. She kicks her surviving sandal off – she knows how to run.

The square begins to fill with the shouts of approaching men, young ones, a football team of them maybe. 'Zingara!' Their tone is that of a parent trying to tempt a naughty child out of hiding. They are in no rush. Bobby looks at Robert who looks to the girl – recognition passes between them. Fear is a shared language.

'Zingara!' They're getting closer. The last few shutters close on the windows above them.

'Hide,' Bobby says, picking up her sandal and putting it in his satchel. He holds his hands up in front of his face. The girl nods then darts across the square and through the only open door, dragging it shut. 'Hotel,' says Bobby, hoisting his bag and heading straight for the voices. 'Go,' he says to Robert and points in the opposite direction. Two young male foreigners together will be a problem. As they walk their separate ways, resisting the impulse to run, they hear the square fill behind them, echo with shouting and laughing and then, when they're still not far enough, the breaking of a door then screaming.

Venice

'All this way for a bunch of English sailors,' huffs Bobby, pointing to the bottom of St Mark's Square where HMS *Sussex* is anchored. She floats side on, guns pointing politely out to the lagoon, her funnels towering over the winged lions atop the pillars, which mark the beginning and end of this empire of the sea. The deck is lined with saluting sailors, their whites signalling against the gunmetal grey.

'You'll not be complaining later,' says Robert. 'You or your porthole.'

'Any port in a storm was the better joke,' Bobby laughs, pretending to elbow Robert off the plank they're walking. It bounces with every step, slapping in and out of the water.

'Watch it,' says Robert. 'These are the only shoes we've got.'

'Canaletto, Canaletto, Canafuckingletto,' says Bobby to Robert's back, as they plod along in single file. 'That perspective would do your nut in.'

Robert nods, not wanting to turn in case he causes a pedestrian pile-up. The people on their plank speak every language but Italian. Locals in black wellingtons splosh across the square, stopping in the middle to gossip. Hunched wet pigeons wait around on the colonnades.

The Vatican had delivered Raphael, Leonardo and Michelangelo to Robert who, Bobby joked, got as close to God as was possible for a Presbyterian. The impossibly young Mary cradling the broken body of her only son reminded them of the girl they'd left behind

– they'd searched the papers but found no mention of the crime they'd heard committed. Venice is their last stop in Italy.

The line of tourists halts outside St Mark's, which somehow looks like it is rising and sinking. 'No going in,' says a tour guide, pointing to the sandbags.

Bobby nods up at the four horses over the doors, each with a hoof raised hello. 'Napoleon nicked them.'

'Who got them back?' Robert asks.

Bobby shrugs. 'Wonder if Hitler will want them.'

'Shhh,' says Robert, glancing about. He changes the subject. 'Who was St Mark? What's he famous for? Raising dead donkeys, walking on wine . . . what?'

'I don't know allllll the saints,' Bobby says. 'I'm a Catholic, Robert, not an encyclopaedia.'

Robert laughs. 'Load of old bones.'

'That's exactly what you won't make if you keep this patter up.'

'Does somebody need their lunch?' Robert asks.

'Possibilmente,' says Bobby, counting coins in his head. If they don't eat for the rest of the day they can share one hot chocolate at Caffè Florian, where a platform has been built over the flood because nothing stops money. A mongrel tears through the water, chased by a bare-kneed boy with a stick, shouting something foreign. Sticks must be precious here, Bobby thinks, there are so few trees.

As they turn away from St Mark's the whole of the lagoon stretches before them, lapping right from their feet all the way to the horizon, doubling every dome and bringing down the sky. HMS *Sussex* has vanished – slipped away as if she was never there. Bobby resists the urge to reach for Robert's hand, but only just.

Paris, Again

Paris boils over in surprising moments: a bitter row between a baker and a customer who have greeted each other every morning for twenty years ends in a stabbing; the hanging on, too far into the season, of the heart-shaped leaves on the clipped linden trees that guard the Place des Vosges and once sheltered Victor Hugo; the double drowning, one Sunday afternoon, of a noted lady and her beloved bichon, her stepping silently into the Seine cradling him. Poland, Belgium, Holland. This is just the beginning. There's nothing to worry about. It will all be over soon.

Bobby enrols them at the Académie in Montparnasse. The school specialises in life drawing and is famous for naked models – men and women. There are no coy togas here, no modest vestments. The classes are strictly timed, and criticism comes from classmates and tutors. Bare flesh quickly seems ordinary. They've unclothed plenty of men on their travels – collected a button from each, since their soldier in London. But they still feel they've got some making up to do. Robert thinks of the sketches he made of Bobby in the attic – Bobby in the bath, Bobby smiling across a pillow at him, Bobby with his arse out magicking up an omelette on a Sunday morning. Robert had fed each one into the fire before they left, along with the silly wee notes they used to leave lying around for each other. Morris's advice.

Robert nods approvingly at Bobby's work as the tutor signals to them to lay down their charcoals. He's captured the weight shifting between the right and left foot of the ballet dancer earning extra francs.

'At this rate I might give up the fruit and veg,' says Bobby.

Robert nods in a way that could mean anything.

Objects for Bobby, subjects for Robert – this is how they will divide the art world between them in order to conquer it. What started out as a joke is becoming a contract that Bobby doesn't remember signing.

After the Académie, the rest of the day is free for private pursuits. They are drawing one another as a thank you to Fleming. A very Bobby idea. He's doing a three-quarter length of Robert sitting with his hands and lips pressed together, looking away and over his shoulder. Robert is drawing Bobby in profile, eyes down with his lips parted, about to say something funny. They will post the portraits on ahead, along with some other work and a book on surrealism from Shakespeare and Company for Mackintosh's library.

'I should never have put in your hands,' says Bobby, wondering if Robert really does have only ten fingers. He considers his own hands – which are really his mother's hands – and tries to imagine them holding a gun. Sandbags are appearing all over the city. All across Europe, fates and envelopes are being sealed. Auntie Maggie writes to say that Bobby's brother has joined up – Mrs Cranston forwards the letter. Robert wonders if their brothers might meet, imagine that.

'I will not kill,' says Bobby.

'What?' says Robert. 'What have I done now?'

'Don't move,' says Bobby, trying to finish Robert's hands. 'I mean, I won't fire a gun. The work of an artist is to immortalise – to extend life, not extinguish it.'

'Try that at your medical,' says Robert.

'I'm serious,' says Bobby, lifting his head.

'I know,' says Robert. 'Now put your head back where it was so I can get this finished.'

'I look like I've been smacked in the mouth,' says Bobby, glancing over and sucking in his lower lip.

'Call it clairvoyant,' Robert laughs.

Bobby and Robert work on, not noticing what time is doing, alone in their world of two. Saving their world with their work. When they're finally done, they head out to find that first café they went to – the one in Montparnasse. The streets round the station are mobbed – half of Europe is coming, the other half going. They bag the last table outside. Their waiter arrives. It is not, thankfully, Pascal. The other waiter, the butch bald one, is also missing. In fact, all the male staff have gone.

Bobby puts his hands over his ears. He can hear the picture. *Guernica*. It's too much. Robert steps back to escape the blast.

'It's terrible,' Bobby shakes his head. 'In the true sense.'

They are barely a day back from Holland where they saw trenches being dug all along the coast as their ferry docked. Day and night their hotel shook to the march of soldiers, most even younger than them. They visited the Rijksmuseum and venerated *The Night Watch* then went in search of *The Milkmaid* only to find she'd already been removed 'for her safety'. After Amsterdam their next stop was to have been the high gothic of Munich but nobody was headed to Germany – Germany was coming for them. Now they are back in Paris, standing in a cavernous temporary space filled with *Guernica*. It is returning to the city where Picasso painted it before heading somewhere safer and anywhere but Spain.

'It's like a photo from a newspaper in hell,' says Robert.

'There's not even the possibility of colour,' says Bobby, willing himself closer but hanging back to try and get the scale. 'It's so matte, it sucks all the light in.'

The gallery is mobbed. But nobody is talking.

Bobby squints at a rearing horse and a skull leers out of its head, its flaring nostrils forming dead eye-sockets. A wailing mother cradles a baby that will never cry again. In the square a bull charges on, unaware it's already dead. Giant heads scream towards the skies as death and terror rain down on the Basque town. Bobby and Robert and the rest of the world had read the papers on Monday, 26 April 1937. Guernica was miles from enemy lines. The planes had come at 4.30 p.m. on market day. Hour after hour the bombs fell, heavy and slow as ripe fruit. Generations huddled in cellars. Some fled into the surrounding fields, emerging after the bombers, only to be strafed by fighters flying so low survivors said they could see the swastikas on their wings. Not even Franco believed his lie that the Republicans had done this to themselves to win the war for sympathy. Bobby and Robert had sat in the University Café in Glasgow reading the news and feeling glad to be safely far away. Now, here, they are faced with *Guernica*.

Bobby wonders how many brushes and assistants Picasso went through. It felt indecent to view the work as the product of an artist with a process but he couldn't not. Robert is lost in the derangement of it all – eyes where mouths should be, everything askew and nothing whole. What had it cost Picasso? What had it given him?

Neither sleeps that night.

Next morning, 10 August, all the café newspapers carry a full-page appeal in English: 'In response to the international crisis and the deteriorating political situation all British nationals at present abroad in Europe are advised to return to Britain as quickly as possible.'

'I will not kill,' says Bobby, reaching for Robert's hand under the newspaper. 'I refuse to let them make me into a monster. Or you.'

Robert nods.

They hurry back to their hotel.

A letter has come. For Robert. An official letter.

PART THREE

Scotland, Again

1939–1941

FAO Robert MacBryde DOB 5/12/1913

Subsequent to your examination, you have been found medically unfit and are hereby exempted from active service. Retain this letter in the event it is required. You have been advised to attend hospital for a chest X-ray as soon as possible due to your tubercular lungs.

    God Save the King.
    District Commander Hynde.

•

FAO Robert Colquhoun DOB 20/12/1914

You are hereby called up to service in the Royal Army Medical Corps. You are ordered to attend basic training at Dalkeith barracks in Edinburgh for a period of three months after which you will see active service. Family members can write to you care of the barracks and, after such time, letters will be forwarded if and when possible. Visits may be possible.

    God Save the King.
    District Commander Taylor.

Despite their best efforts, Bobby and Robert cannot stop the war.
    It is their last night together. Bobby cuts Robert's hair because he can't bear the thought of anybody else doing it. As he places the flat of the scissors on the back of Robert's neck, Bobby tells

him about that first glimpse on the train, of dark curls flirting with a fresh white collar. Unreal that he can just touch him now, unreal that from tomorrow he cannot. Might never touch him again. He dismisses the thought as ridiculous. But so much that seemed impossible is happening.

'Nearly done,' he says, stepping back, realising this is a movement only barbers and artists share. Robert's scalp is even paler than the rest of him, a private white not meant to be seen. Like the inside of the nautilus shell he rescued from Morris's flat. Bobby hates to see it.

With only a few curls to go, and his head still bowed, tears fall onto the back of Robert's neck, rolling round to his collarbone.

'Stop it, Bobby,' Robert sighs. 'Please.'

Robert can't join in with this display – he's hardly ever cried, not even on his own. He pushes his feelings down, swallows them – maybe it's why he never really gets hungry. But he can't add Bobby's feelings on top; it's like Aesop's crow and the pebbles. As Bobby's tears dry on his skin he feels himself threaten to spill over.

'Stop! Will you!'

Robert stands up, sending his curls drifting along the floor, the autumn of his youth.

'It's me that's going, not you,' he says, running his hands over his scalp, pulling at the last of his own hair until it hurts. It feels good.

'Stop that,' says Bobby, stepping towards him.

Robert snatches the scissors from Bobby and attacks what's left.

'Do you think I don't know that? sobs Bobby, picking up one of Robert's loose curls and twirling it round his wedding finger then slipping it off carefully in his pocket. 'I would go if I could.'

'Would you?' says Robert. 'That's not what you said in Paris: *I will not kill*, you said.'

Robert never forgets a word. Bobby never forgets a feeling.

'I can't help the state of my lungs,' says Bobby, beating his chest so hard he starts to cough. 'I'm sorry, I'm sorry.'

'And I can't help the state of the world,' says Robert, firing the scissors into a far corner of the attic.

'I'll die without you,' says Bobby, falling to his knees, racked by coughing and crying. 'I'll die.'

'You won't,' says Robert, his anger subsiding as quickly as it erupted. 'C'mon. I'm sorry. I know. I'm sorry.'

'You're not allowed to die, Robert Colquhoun,' says Bobby. 'Do you hear me? You have to promise.'

'I promise,' says Robert, joining Bobby on the floor. 'I promise.'

They do not sleep. The next morning won't wait.

'You don't have to stay with me,' says Robert. He's watching for the train to the barracks and then god knows where. Glasgow Central is a Pathé newsreel of tearful sweethearts.

'I know,' says Bobby. 'No more tears.'

Bobby is already writing a letter he knows he can never send. They are getting good at living between the lines. But they've not spent a night apart since they moved into the attic — Bobby considers this their anniversary and celebrates each year with a breakfast in bed of toast cut into love hearts or whatever he can get his hands on. They've had nights with others, of course (never in the attic). But not a single night without each other. Once or twice, Robert has wished for a quiet night in by himself and now he regrets it.

The train is here. It is for soldiers only. Goodbyes must be said on the platform. Robert hauls his bag over his shoulder and joins the khaki surge. Bobby waves — everybody is waving so he thinks he can get away with this; he could be waving to a brother. Bobby bites his lip — no tears. Robert didn't want him to come but he demanded every last second. The train is here. Robert is already on it. The whistle is blowing. The wheels of history are turning. The train is leaving. Bobby keeps waving, has no clue if Robert can still see him or not. He keeps his other hand in his pocket and wrapped tight around his wedding finger is the last of Robert's curls. No tears. Bobby digs his nails into his palm. He steps towards the train as it leaves the station for the barracks and then and then ... and then.

Bobby falls to his knees.

No tears.

Robert appears on every corner as Bobby wanders dazed back to Number Three Botanic Crescent. When he finally drags himself up the stairs he is stopped by a note on the attic door — the first and last. It will be an eviction notice, he thinks. Or worse. *Dear Bobby, Robert is away now but he will be back. Until he returns there is only one of you up there, so I am halving the rent. This is a temporary measure. Mrs Cranston.*

That night Bobby mixes a black wash with what's fast becoming the last of the paints they brought back from Paris. They spent their last few francs in Sennelier: the venerable shelves filled with everything but inspiration itself. The ghosts of Degas and Cézanne shuffled impatiently waiting for them to choose between *Bleu Anglais* or *Bleu Azur* and *Laque Alizarine Cramoisie* or *Laque d'Alizarine Rouge*.

Bobby finishes mixing the wash then fetches a chair and clambers on it. Reaching up, he starts painting over their skylights. That night everybody in Glasgow — everybody lucky enough to have a window — is doing the same. For this new thing called 'the blackout'. It suits Bobby's mood — he doesn't want to see the stars tonight. On a chair in the attic of a house on a hill, he is as close as it's possible to be to any German flying over Glasgow. They could hear him breathe in bed. He recalls *Guernica*. In that very moment he would welcome a bomb.

Bobby finishes one skylight and moves on to the next. The stars don't only shine at night. They blaze all the way through every day but we just can't see them. Not until it's dark. Until Bobby spotted him on the train that day, Robert had always been there, just waiting for Bobby to see him. Where is he now? Bobby paints on and the stars go out. One by one.

Robert folds the sheets on his camp bed, trying to do the corners the way Bobby showed him. The other nine men in his bunk room have finished and await inspection. Each of them has pinned up a sweetheart, or starlet, by their bed. Robert keeps catching sight of himself reflected in the window by the bare bulb hanging from the middle of the freezing cold room. He does not recognise the face looking back. He's been in barracks less than six hours, showered, inspected and then the stubble on his head cut to the wood with what felt like sheep shears. Gone is the good shirt Bobby made for him and the smart black jacket his mother saved for. On is a regulation boiled simmet and over that a khaki shirt with brass buttons hidden in a flap that marches straight down the front. He tries not to think about why a soldier might not want buttons glinting. Epaulettes – a word he memorises for Bobby – wait on his shoulders for stripes he feels honour-bound to earn: his wee brother only just made it out of Dunkirk, was on one of the last boats, the talk of the street.

'Shat yourself already?' laughs the lad on the next bed, lounging across it like a nightclub singer on a piano. Robert's trousers are so stiff he can barely sit.

'No plans to,' says Robert, fiddling with the final sheet.

'That's no gonnae pass,' says his neighbour, nodding over. 'Ma maw wid batter you fur that.'

'Aberdeen?' asks Robert, trying to work out the accent.

'Fife!' his neighbour protests, putting out his hand. 'Taylor.'

'Ayrshire,' says Robert, putting out his hand. 'Colquhoun.'

'Not a worker then,' says Taylor, dropping Robert's hand. 'Smooth paws you've got.'

'Gies a feel,' says another lad, bouncing over and taking Robert's hands. He whistles. 'Gie it a week and you can sort me out after lights out.' He grabs his crotch and thrusts and the others copy him and they're roaring. 'Milly! Darlin! Keep going!' Then come the other names: *Betty! Sandra! Mary! Mary! Mary!*

Robert can't very well shout *Bobby!* But he thinks Bobby might very well shout *Robert* if he was here. He feels like a coward. So, he laughs along instead. Does he laugh too hard? Not quickly enough? Taylor jumps on his bed with both feet, the thin springs protesting, then kicks his sheets up before dashing underneath, running about like a child's idea of a ghost. The breeze panics the pin-ups on the wall, causing the women to flap, and for a moment they look alive. It's minutes till inspection. But it's already too late. Robert will not pass muster.

Next morning, Bobby wakes alone. He's not sad or mournful – he's furious. He storms around the attic in his pants, tripping over his mosaic rug and raging at his stupid fucking chest because if he wasn't so weak he could be with Robert, could take a bullet for Robert, but if he wasn't so weak he would have to be there with Robert, have to take that bullet for Robert. Guilt asks his anger for a light.

Bobby counts and recounts what's left of their travelling scholarship and tries to budget for paint and paper, rent, cigarettes, gas and something to eat. There's just him to feed now, not that Robert ever ate as much as Bobby encouraged him to. He throws on his clothes and goes out in search of work. He hurries over the half-penny bridge to the back of the Botanics but the gate is closed. 'War Works,' says a newly posted sign printed in the hateful font of officialdom. Bobby storms back over the bridge and round to the front.

A crowd gathers at the gates.

'What's going on?' he asks the woman next to him.

'They're clearing it,' she says, turning away, dabbing at her eyes with a dainty lace hankie. 'For the war effort.'

Bobby pushes up to the gates and peeks through. A storm rages inside the Kibble Palace: unseen winds push and pull the palm trees, their tops lashing this way and that before eventually toppling. He is close enough to hear them topple, all the fine fronds snapping like fingers. Minutes later the glasshouse doors open and a pair of gardeners file out carrying a tree fern on their shoulders like a coffin. One of them tries to rub his eyes without dropping it. The crowd surges against the gate. Then a wean cries 'Horsey' and they all turn as one to watch the lumbering arrival of a Clydesdale horse, guided along by a lad in country clothes. Bobby wonders where they've come in from. The lad hitches the horse to a harrow; he remembers them turning the dark-brown fields round Maybole, ready for the prized tatties. It is so quiet, despite the crowd, that he can hear the brass badges tinkle on the horse's bridle as it sets off. Its eyes are blinkered, its head lowered. The flowerbeds disappear. The sign on the gates says, 'Henceforth the Botanics must grow only what Glasgow needs.' But their city needs beauty too, Bobby thinks. Bread and roses. He remembers the words he heard the Hunger Marchers sing: 'Hearts starve as well as bodies: Give us Bread but give us Roses.' As he turns to leave, he remembers the fish in the pond then wishes he'd not.

Town is mobbed. The Clyde is busier than it has been in years – the yards bustle with ships at all stages of construction, all the same grey. War is good business, the Depression yesterday's news. Bobby guesses models of these boats won't end up in Kelvingrove. All the talk on every tram is of spies, firebombs and typhus-infected lice raining from the sky.

All over Glasgow, official orders are arriving and with each letter a nobody becomes a somebody: a fire marshal, a territorial guard, an air raid warden. Fleming has organised a rota of observers to sit on the roof of the art school night and day, ready with buckets and sand. The one-legged beggar outside the Mitchell has taken to wearing his medals from the last war and the one before that and takes in enough in one week to feed him and his dog for a month. Bobby waits for the War Art Committee to write to him – joint top of the class at Scotland's top art school. He expects to be invited to document events for the nation. But no letter comes for Bobby. He is useless to the war, useless to Robert. Not that he can paint right now, even if he did have supplies. *If I can't join Robert*, he thinks, *I must get him out.* The nation needs Robert's art to show the faces we hold dear, to reflect back the way of life we are fighting for. He begins to write letters pleading Robert's case; Fleming provides references. He must keep a roof over his head for when Robert gets out. He must have bread, yes, but also roses.

So, every morning, Bobby lines up at the Labour Exchange. Every time he reaches the front of the queue he is asked why he's not serving his country and he passes them his medical dispensation, which they slide back, reluctant to touch. He's never going for that X-ray, can't afford it. Every day, they tell him the same thing: there are no jobs for artists, except teaching. He gives them the same reply: *I trained as an artist, not as a teacher.* Bobby has so much to say to the world and needs a gallery for it, not a classroom. Eventually he's called for an interview at, of all places, the Labour Exchange. When asked what regiment he would choose, Bobby says 'none' and is told 'work is only available for loyal subjects'.

As lads his age disappear from the streets, he gets dirty looks, especially from some of the young women he envies for being able to broadcast their broken hearts. His dark complexion, even deeper from their year in Europe, does not help. Even the Napoleon is full of whispers of spies – the clientele there know it is possible to seem one thing and be another.

Bobby is losing weight; Mrs Cranston comments whenever she catches him in the hall. He's saving for stamps – he can afford to write to Robert every day if he has just one meal. A big pot of cow's head stew with bits from the Barras can get him through a week. Bobby spares Robert news of the Botanics. In none of his letters can he write what he really feels – such queer sentiment would get Robert out the army but straight into jail and Bobby along with him. At least then they'd be together. Bobby can see it: four walls and bars, yes, but to keep the world out. All he wants is Robert back. Bobby signed up for Fleming's fire-watch but feels unable to serve, writing a note to his old teacher, which is as close to confession as he dares: 'I have become seriously afraid for Robert, for both of us. All his feelings on the matter will be deep down inside him until there's an explosion. Such a close bond was, I am afraid to say, a great mistake up to a point, since our mental attachment has a terrific root. The breaking off of a friendship on these lines between members of the same sex produces chaos for quite a time.' Fleming keeps Bobby's note, but not where anybody might find it.

As per military rules, Robert is confined to barracks for the first month and not permitted to write or receive letters. There are no rules against drawing. The barracks are never empty but he has never needed a quiet place to work, not like Bobby, a difference that surprises him. So he does his best to ignore the insults as he attempts a self-portrait. *Ponce, Picasso, Queer.* His drawing says everything he cannot write.

Robert's first letter greets Bobby after yet another day failing to find work. 'My darling,' he cries out loud, covering then uncovering his mouth, not caring if Mrs Cranston hears.

Bobby caresses the envelope, holds it up to his face. It's daft, he knows. Melodramatic even. He'd roll his eyes at this in the pictures. Up in their attic, he opens the letter carefully. Inside is folded a delicate pencil sketch. The verticality of it pains Bobby: Robert's cheekbones pierce the page, the skin on his temples is thin enough to see a heartbeat, his lips disappear and he is being choked by the top button of his shirt. But already his curls are furring back in. The accompanying note is all peeling potatoes, washing dishes, cleaning out lavatories and scrubbing floors from six-thirty in the morning until late at night. It closes with 'please don't visit.'

The next morning Bobby heads to Edinburgh.

Robert is dying. Bobby is sure of it. The army will kill him before Hitler gets the chance. With every visit he gets thinner, weaker, quieter. Even he admits he's hungry. Bobby has got to get him out. Day after day Bobby writes letter after letter to the War Artists' Advisory Committee: 'We were top of our class at the Glasgow School of Art. I am not pleading for artistic boys who are pale and interesting, but for two young men who must contribute to a real culture after the storm has passed and while the storm is raging.' No response. 'For a little food, a battle dress and a private's pay I would work night and day to make useful historical and artistic records of this thing that threatens to change the face of the world.' Nothing.

Bobby goes to the barracks every Sunday. While he's waiting for official visiting hours he stands by a quiet stretch of the chain-link fence hoping for a glimpse – the first time he spotted Robert he hardly recognised him. Despite having a visitor's pass for his 'family friend', the guards always keep him at the gate – make him stand while the official sweethearts traipse past in their painted-on stockings. Some of the girls are alright. Only one ever stops to talk – Sadie. She never asks him who he's here for, just talks about her Alfred and how glad she is he's not made pilot, because that's a recipe for widowhood. Sadie had shown Bobby a wee photo of the two of them, their official engagement portrait. She looked weirdly old in it, blonde curls piled on her head like cakes on a plate. Her Alfred stood head and shoulders over her, his cap under his left arm, his right arm in hers. He had a face you'd want to come home to. The next time Bobby sees Sadie he gives her a present – a sketch of the photo.

'What a thing,' she says, holding it carefully. 'You did this?'

Bobby nods. He hopes she never has to treasure it too much.

Bobby is waiting by the gates, again. He turned up earlier than usual so the guards couldn't claim all the permits were gone. Every now and then a khaki-coloured van trundles up then pauses before heading off, the back doors open and filled with recruits facing each other, kitbags between their feet, cigarettes glowing semaphore. Who will make it back?

Bobby wonders when Sadie will show. He leaves the gate and paces the perimeter to pass the time. He stops and gets out his sketchbook, tries to make sense of the rows of tents, the procession of triangles reminding him of the roof of Glasgow Central, the crocodile ridges. He loses himself quickly.

'What you doin?' A woman's voice, accusing.

'Nothing,' he says, pocketing his pencil before looking up. There are three women, all just a bit older than him, on a good day. All primped to visit their men. They are the grown-up versions of the girls he'd avoided at Lees. One of them models a new pillbox hat – they share that, he'd take bets on it.

'What's that accent?' asks the nearest one, a bottle blonde.

'Maybole.'

'Where?' says a redhead, folding her arms.

'Maybole,' Bobby says again, closing his sketchbook. As he does, the blonde grabs it.

'Give that back!'

'Or what?' she says. The other girls take a look.

'Maybole in Bavaria?' laughs the redhead.

'In Ayrshire,' says Bobby, looking for a way out. They're not going to hurt him. But they will know men who can. He must give them no excuse. But he can't lose his sketchbook. Paper is impossible to come by nowadays.

'So how come you're drawing this place?' asks the redhead, pointing to the barracks.

'Making plans?' asks the blonde.

'I'm not a spy,' says Bobby.

'We never said you were,' says the redhead. 'Did we?'

'Give me that back and I'll be away.'

'Or what?' The blonde flicks through. She stops at a nude, a memory of Robert.

'Oooh! Look V!'

'I'm not a fucking spy,' Bobby insists, grabbing for the book, fearing it will go the way of Michelangelo in Maybole, of Robert's journal in Modena. Art makes certain people afraid.

'Why else would you be here? We're all visiting our men.'

'Listen . . . is it Vera?' says Bobby, trying to calm everything.

'I never told you my name,' says Vera.

'This is getting ridiculous.'

'I'm going to get somebody,' says the redhead, stepping away.

'Don't,' says Bobby, touching her arm. Then they're on him.

Instinctively he cups his balls. Nails claw at his face so he puts his hands up but that gives one of them an in. He keels forward, retching.

'Stop!'

They stop.

'You with this . . . whatever he is?' the redhead asks.

'Aye,' says Sadie, extending a hand to Bobby. 'I am.'

'Good luck,' says Vera, flapping her wrist at them both. 'C'mon girls. War effort.'

And off they go.

With its blackout makeup on, Waverley Station is even darker than the long tunnel leading into it. Bombers are rumoured to be circling the capital. As he waits for his train, Bobby reassembles *Guernica* in his head: the charging bull, the screaming horse, the grieving mother. Edinburgh is too posh to bomb – the city has a self-assured indestructibility . . . they don't like to talk about how the castle was nearly taken by the Jacobites – there are probably still biddies in Morningside who recall that fateful day.

Bobby's train is not where it's meant to be but he's in no rush to get back to Glasgow and the empty attic. He stands with his portfolio under his arm – he takes drawings to show to Robert, to remind him of who he is. Bobby watches what's left of the world go by. There are fewer and fewer children about and very few lads his own age.

Bobby clocks him first. Another man of soldiering age also with a portfolio under his arm. He's shorter than Bobby and his navy overcoat was made to last several winters, even Edinburgh ones. A railway guard flashes his half-light and the platform fills with steam. Under cover of this moment the man glances over. Bobby nods back in a way he could argue in court was just politeness. The man walks over but Bobby stands his ground – if he is a policeman it will not do to run. Bobby hoists his portfolio up into his armpit as if to say, *I have business here*. The man does the same, then pushes a pair of gold-framed glasses up his nose. He passes – not too close, not too far. Bobby turns. The man glances over his shoulder then heads to Left Luggage. Bobby follows. There's nobody else in the queue and nobody at the counter.

'What have you lost?' the man asks, his accent expensive, maybe English.

'Everything,' Bobby laughs.

'A real artist's response,' says the man, laying his portfolio on the counter.

'Aye,' says Bobby. 'Maybe. What have you lost?'

'Not sure yet.' The man holds Bobby's gaze. 'So, you're an artist?' he asks, tapping Bobby's portfolio.

Bobby nods. 'You're not?'

'No. I merely traffic in them. I'm a journalist and a writer and keep an eye out for some of the London galleries.'

'London?'

'Yes,' says the man. 'London.'

'I'm John,' the man says, afterwards.

They're lying naked across his bed on the top floor of a house on Rankeillor Street, in the orbit of the university.

'So am I,' says Bobby, hoping he's not missed the last train for this.

The man laughs and reaches for the stiff towel waiting in peaks on the floor by his bed.

'What's funny? Bobby asks.

The man points to his portfolio, which very clearly says R. MacBryde.

'Well, I clocked your post when we came in the door,' says Bobby. 'Mr Tonge.'

'You really do have an eye,' says Tonge.

'And an arse,' says Bobby, shaking his hips before throwing himself back on the bed.

'So,' says Tonge, pointing to Bobby's portfolio on the floor. 'Are you going to show me your etchings?'

'Thought you'd never ask.'

· 181 ·

Tonge braces himself and prepares his 'good effort' face. He feels even more naked as he puts on his glasses. Bobby opens the folder.

'Oh,' says Tonge.

'Is that a good oh?'

'A very good oh,' says Tonge, reaching for the drawings. 'It's been a day of finds. May I?'

Twice Bobby has to ask directions to the Café Royal from Waverley Station. Tonge has told him to bring all their best drawings – he was taken with Robert's severe self-portrait. Bobby has polished his boots and emptied the coffee pot of their savings. He's borrowed Robert's good black jacket and rolled the sleeves a bit, can smell him on the collar. The restaurant takes up a whole corner. The double doors are open and inside he glimpses golden pillars, sparkling hand-blown lamps and a white-aproned waiter who looks a bit like Pascal. The place is full and smells like money. Bobby jinks the coins in his pocket and steps in.

'MacBryde,' says Tonge, standing up awkwardly behind a table for four in the middle of the room. He sloshes a glass of red wine towards Bobby. Nobody looks twice.

'Mr Tonge,' says Bobby, walking over, resisting the impulse to say, 'nice to see you with your clothes on.' The other two guests don't get up, don't even pause their conversation.

'It will be the bomb to end all bombs,' says a bull-headed wee man – he turns to Bobby, sucks his cigarette then says, 'Connolly' on a rush of smoke.

'MacBryde,' says Bobby, seating himself opposite Tonge.

'So, I hear,' says Connolly. 'Wine?'

Connolly reaches for the nearest bottle – their table has more bottles than the bar.

'Tragedy,' says the other man at their table as Connolly holds the bottle upside down. A waiter appears. 'Another of the '20? Last good year for Claret.'

'This is Peter Watson,' says Connolly. 'Proprietor of *Horizon* and our resident margarine millionaire.' Connolly emphasises the hard *g* in margarine.

'Don't worry,' says Watson, wafting for another waiter. 'I won't make you eat any.' He pauses. 'I also choose all the pictures for our little magazine.'

'You shall be reunited with your Picassos,' says Connolly, patting Watson's hand.

'Only if we get Paris back,' says Watson.

'Back to this bomb,' says Tonge, who has procured many paintings, and also the occasional painter, for Watson.

'Yes, some new kind of bomb,' says Connolly as the first of their food arrives. 'Or something to do with cosmic rays.'

Bobby does not know what to do with the tiny bird placed in front of him. It's the saddest chicken he has ever seen.

'First grouse,' says Tonge, rescuing him, lingering over the correct cutlery. Bobby copies.

'So . . .' says Watson, pushing his plate aside. He's about to ask Bobby something when a waiter appears, concerned by his lack of interest. 'Oysters, I think.' He looks around the table. 'Two dozen.'

'Our next issue has lots of food in it,' says Connolly. 'Dreams of beef.'

'*Horizon* is not a recipe book,' says Watson, archly. 'It is not for ration-mad housewives.'

'My wife would like to hear a lot less about *Horizon*,' says Connolly. 'But it is my calling – to keep the arts alive while all else burns. We are more than simply . . .' Here he dances his fingers across the table as if typing. '. . . *A Review of Literature and Art.*'

The grouse is unexpectedly delicious – Bobby tries not to eat too fast. The wine has already gone to his head. It tastes of Paris, only better. Oysters appear. Watson polishes off one, two, three, like the sailors in Marseilles downing shots of grappa. Champagne arrives.

'Vulgar, I know,' says Watson. 'But the oysters demand it. They demand it!' He gets to his feet and toasts the oysters and the others follow so Bobby does too. Lunch never stops here, Bobby realises. There's no rationing, no shortage of anything. He's never seen a millionaire before. Or eaten an oyster, despite growing up so near the sea.

Watson polishes off a dozen then sits back. A tray of roast potatoes arrives, heralding a haunch of beef so hefty two waiters strain to carry it. Course after course, plate after plate. Bobby frets about the bill, feels foolish for bringing his portfolio to what is clearly not a place of work.

'Where are you from?' Watson wonders. Bobby has never felt so full or so foolish.

'Ayrshire,' says Bobby, wondering how to explain Maybole.

'Do you know Duncan MacDonald? At Lefevre? He's from there, I think. Or mentioned it.'

Bobby has barely read about the Lefevre Gallery. Before he can say anything Connolly pipes up, 'The Scottish Bard!'

'Or, just the Bard,' Bobby says, emboldened by drink. 'When you're on his turf.'

Watson roars then Connolly follows and Tonge tips a glass to Bobby.

'That's the spirit,' Watson slurs.

'Burns! Burns! Burns!' Connolly chants as he gets up on his chair.

Bobby thinks of Auntie Maggie doing her party piece then climbs up on his chair, glass in hand. Suddenly the whole place is watching.

'Fair fa' your honest, sonsie face,' he rummages for the words. 'Great Chieftain o' the Puddin-race.'

'No more food,' burps Connolly. 'Another!'

Bobby thinks frantically. Somehow everything hinges on this. Yes, he remembers one that Robert found, one they never got in school. He has no fork to ding his glass so taps it against his teeth then takes a deep breath and begins. 'Come rede me dame, come tell me dame, My dame come tell me truly . . .' He pauses to make sure the English are following and to remember the next bit. 'What length o' graith when weel ca'd hame, Will sair a woman duly?' He winks and slurps his wine in a manner Tonge recognises then bucks his hips. 'I learn't a sang in Annandale, Nine inch will please a lady!'

Gasps and then guffaws with just enough outrage. Watson tumbles off his chair and twirls with Tonge and the waiters don't say a word, just move the chairs. When the cheering and dancing finally stops, a bottle of brandy appears on their table.

'So,' says Watson, lighting another cigarette. 'Tonge says you have some talent?'

PART FOUR

London, At Last

1941–1947

'What if they've sold out?' Bobby beetles along the pavement towards the newsagent at the corner of Bedford Gardens. The idea that their *Horizon* debut could cause a rush is both fantasy and fear. Nevertheless, he picks up speed, sharpening his elbows for the last copy.

'It's Notting Hill,' says Robert, gesturing at the stucco streets, still grand even where the odd house is missing. 'Not Soho. There'll be plenty.'

Sure enough, there it is, in the half-boarded window, *Horizon*: Volume V, Number 29, May 1942. Red ink on cheap grey war paper.

'*Horizon: A Review of Literature and Art*,' Bobby reads the words he learned at the lunch that changed everything. He scans the front: 'Something about Hart Crane then Flaubert, some fruity Gide, and then it's us, look!'

'*Scottish Paintings* by yer man Tonge.'

'He's not my man,' Bobby insists for the umpteenth time.

'You better tell him that,' says Robert.

'He was a man of a moment. I can't help he's got a wee bit attached.'

'Only natural I suppose,' Robert pouts like Bobby.

'Anyways,' says Bobby, keen to avoid any fractiousness on this day of days. 'All he bloody talks about is you: McPicasso!'

'MacBraque!' Robert replies, as is now their routine. 'Wheesht. We've not even read it yet.'

'It'll be good – you saw his face at opening night,' says Bobby. 'Red dots on every picture! Thank you *Lefevre!*'

Robert presses a finger against the glass, tracing their names:

'*Reproductions of paintings by John Maxwell, Robert MacBryde, Edward Baird and Robert Colquhoun!*'

'Say it again,' Bobby hops from foot to foot.

'*Reproductions of paintings by John Maxwell, Robert—*'

Bobby hooks Robert's arm and birls him round, a cèilidh for two on the pavement as the newsagent peers out. The world really has gone mad.

Hundreds of miles and a world away Mr Justin Theodas sets aside the one and only copy of *Horizon* he's ever got in. He's been asked by a customer to look out for any mention of her oldest boy and to save any paper he appears in, however briefly. She'll pay when she can. He's been asked not to reveal this arrangement to her man, who collects their evening paper. So, the newsagent pops the magazine in a discreet brown envelope and lightly writes her name: Mrs Colquhoun.

They rush back to 77 Bedford Gardens resisting the temptation to read as they go. Banging the front door behind them, Robert shouts up the stairwell. 'Adler! Master! We've got it!'

Jankel Adler's head cuckoo-clocks over the banister. 'Kettle or bottle?' he asks, holding up a mug and a jar.

'Whisky,' shouts Bobby, throwing open the door to their studio.

'So, what does it say?' asks Adler, arriving. Bobby fishes down the back of the clock for the emergency Bell's and notes it feels emptier than when he last stashed it. He passes round jars for glasses then pours them each a finger before plonking himself on their couch for two and flicking to Tonge's article.

'Sláinte!' Robert cheers and they clink.

Bobby aherms theatrically. '*Above all, the Scottish painters have excelled by their brushwork and colour* . . . That's the first line.'

'Not wrong,' says Adler.

'Good start,' says Robert. 'Get to us.'

'Yes,' says Adler. 'Let us hear what the English critics have to say.'

'Shhhsht, I'm reading as fast as I can,' says Bobby, scanning the tight print, sardined to save ink. 'Oh, this is not good: *Only a* handful of them, as anywhere, show a critical awareness of the times and make a contribution, however, slightly, to the movements that have produced Picasso and Max Ernst.'

'Ernst,' Adler spits, though not actually wasting booze, because that would be sacrilege, even if it is only Bell's. He misses the taste of Armagnac and thinks only true Scots would drink such cheap whisky. 'German Surrealism – why?'

'But he said Picasso,' says Robert. 'We're on the same page as Picasso, Bobby. Wait till I write to Fleming. Crack on!'

'He's talking about Maxwell and says *Like so many Scots, two countries compete for his affection.*'

'You must not run from your Celtic heritage,' says Adler. 'I have said this: be here in London to do business but the work must come from here.' Adler beats his chest and declines another pour. 'This is something the English can never have.'

Bobby pauses dramatically. 'It's us,' he gulps. '*Colquhoun and MacBryde, both products of the Glasgow College and much influenced by each other—*'

Bobby jumps up and throws his arms around Robert and tries to kiss him but Robert turns away.

Adler has heard a lot from downstairs but not witnessed anything, until now.

Bobby steps back, still holding the magazine. Robert can't believe Adler is still standing there – isn't walking out in disgust.

Adler steps forward, placing a hand on their shoulders, stitching them and the moment back together, and says, 'This is what you have to paint – this passion!'

'We can't paint two men, we'd be in the jail,' Bobby falls back onto the couch.

'Who says show?' Adler protests. 'Symbolise, abstract, reimagine!'

Bobby reads on. '*They are the youngest of the six Scottish painters in the show at Le Fevre and the only two at present working, as they say, "furth of Scotland". Sharing the experiences of English artists during the past two years, it is not surprising that they have found subjects in some of the same places.*'

'Bombs,' sighs Adler, gesturing to the ceiling. 'Martyred architecture.'

'And refuge as well,' says Robert, correcting him as a way of rejoining the conversation — suddenly desperate to be back in that place of excitement, wanting to show Bobby he can just be happy too. 'My picture is from that week we got out to the countryside and saw everything still growing, the marrows and tomatoes all rampaging.'

Bobby pushes on. '*But their affinities with, say, Sutherland or Moore in their paintings of tree-forms and ruined buildings are only superficial* . . . then it says you've moved on from Wyndham Lewis.'

'Which you are doing,' says Adler. 'Thank god.'

'And,' Bobby stands up again. 'It says I've got *the tactile beauty of the Glasgow School* and then that's it.' He shakes the magazine, hoping more words will fall out and they do. He spots their names, the way you can always find your own even on the longest list. '*Colquhoun and MacBryde's portraits are VERY FINE INDEED* dah de dah de da *adding richness and diversity to the somewhat myopic and insular English tradition . . . they are young artists of promise!*' He bounces on the couch. 'YOUNG ARTISTS OF PROMISE!'

Robert grabs the magazine and opens it to the next page. There, in black and white, is Bobby's *Ave Maria Lane*, looking like a Roman ruin. On the next page are his own *Tomato Plants*, leaves curling so he can almost smell their tang. He feels a pang for his father's vegetable patch, the ashes from the fire silvering ridges of rich brown Ayrshire soil.

Adler examines the pictures. 'But these are your past. To fulfil this promise you must go deeper.' He waves his empty jar but declines another. 'Deeper!' His voice catches — suddenly he can see the faces of all eleven of the brothers and sisters he was forced to leave behind.

Robert knows Adler is right. Seeing Adler's grief, and wishing to thank him for witnessing their triumph, Bobby kisses Adler right on the lips, a great big smacker. The older man blushes. 'Away with you both,' he smiles, walking towards the door, sensing he is now surplus to requirements. 'Celebrate now. Work later. Always work.'

Robert's trousers are round his ankles before Adler's foot is on the first stair.

Here they are, at last: together again in their own studio with their own coffee pot (still missing its lid), their own plants turned to the kind north light, their own shelf for their own books – books they love, books they're illustrating, books they keep on show because so many writers come to their Sunday Salons (and nothing pleases a writer more). Morris's nautilus shell gleams in the middle of the mantel. There are two easels, each facing the other. One bed. Their own world.

Number 77 Bedford Gardens is an island of bohemia between the twinset smartnesses of Kensington and Notting Hill, a late nineteenth-century purpose-built block of dried-claret brick housing seventeen studios. Robert and Bobby occupy the first floor, peeking out through a glossy-leaved magnolia tree to the street. The neighbourhood's other residents had long since decamped to their country houses to avoid the inconvenience of bombs when Bobby and Robert arrived in February 1941. All except the beetroot colonel across the way who threatens them with lawyers first thing every Monday. *Fuck him!* says Bobby. *There's a war on. A wee party's not the end of the world.*

They still can't believe their luck.

Their saviour is Peter Watson – he invited Bobby to contribute to *Horizon* and introduced him to Duncan Macdonald at Lefevre. One minute Bobby was alone in their attic and the next he was living in luxury as Watson's houseguest at 10 Palace Gate. Mrs Cranston refused his last month's rent and, when Bobby handed her his new address, said she hoped he wasn't being seduced by capitalism. Now Bobby had London but still no Robert. He'd written hundreds of letters but nobody cared – the country was all special cases. But now Watson had a Colquhoun over his fireplace and wanted more. So, he suggested to an old pal from

Eton that this rare Scottish talent be saved for the nation – they wrote to an acquaintance of T.E. Lawrence, who wrote to the War Office and suddenly Robert was out: 'heart weakness', officially. When Robert arrived at Watson's flat Bobby barely recognised him – his skull poked out of his face like rocks from a field in drought. Robert envied Bobby's well-fed glow, couldn't believe the deep cream carpets he stood on, gasped at a picture of his on Watson's wall, between a Nicholson and an Ernst (there was a MacBryde in the kitchen Watson rarely ventured to). Staying with Watson was like living inside an orchid from the Botanics. Full cupboards, hot water on tap, more wine than in all of Europe. Even the bombs were quieter here. They were shown off as discoveries at drinks parties, Watson urging them to wear kilts. Given enough whisky, Bobby would give them his Burns. Robert was glad of supper but soon grew tired of singing for it. And a year of them was enough for Watson, who pulled another gilded string to find them their studio before throwing a small (possibly too eager) leaving party. 'It's been a pleasure,' he said, toasting them with champagne and oysters, savouring how deliciously empty and quiet his flat would be by morning. John Craxton and Lucian Freud, not yet twenty and an ever-present pair if not an actual couple, lounged either side of the fireplace, instant new interest. They all raised their glasses, looked down upon by the Colquhoun, Nicholson, Ernst, a new Moore and a socially acceptable Grant. 'What a year!' Watson said, eyeing the clock and handing Bobby and Robert a hastily wrapped present: a Graham Sutherland of a twisting tree. What a year indeed.

Number 77 is a single square room, twenty by twenty and almost as high. The whole front is north-facing windows – it reminds them of the Hen Run. There is a kitchenette near the front and a sort of sleeping nook at the back. The Sutherland print is propped on their mantel behind the nautilus, tree reaching for shell. Next to that a pencil drawing of Robert by Lucian, one of several. It's all perfect, except for the colonel across the road who makes no secret of being able to see in from his net-curtained fortress.

On their second day at Number 77, they meet Jankel Adler – a disciple of Klee who had fought the Nazis then had been condemned as a 'degenerate' before fleeing to Britain where his heart was slowly breaking for all to see. They'd read all about him in *Horizon* and were astonished by his dark urgent style. It is not an auspicious introduction.

Each landing at Number 77 shares a lavatory. Bobby keeps theirs spotless and well supplied with squares of improvised toilet paper weighted by a big stone. Ever the magpie, Bobby glimpsed some sheets of gilding screwed up in a skip – only in London – and dived in to retrieve them, not caring what the neighbours said. He was trying to flatten them out with the stone in the lavatory. Nobody had told Adler. So, the first they heard of the great man was when he stormed out, buckling up his trousers, bellowing in thickest Mitteleuropean, 'Who has gilded my arse?'

Despite this, or maybe because of it, Adler takes instantly to these other outsiders. He can't believe Bobby knows how to make borscht, although it needs more salt. Adler is the same age as their fathers but couldn't be more different. He shows Robert the clever bit of trickery with the pin pushed into the wrong end of the brush, the way to speedily and cheaply make a one-off print, the secret of the monotype – Klee's own technique. From Klee to Adler to Robert, connecting them and their work to Europe even as it breaks into a million mourning pieces. Often Adler paints rabbis, gatherings of his scattered family – he likens his Jewishness to their Celticness, warning them against too much drink, too much London and losing contact with their roots. Adler rails against mere observing and simple prettiness. 'There is nothing left out there to see,' he said the morning after yet another bomb had blocked their road; already Bobby couldn't remember the building that had watched the corner the night before. 'Nothing,' Adler said, sweeping away a still life of wooden fruit Bobby had arranged, knocking it all to the floor. Closing his eyes, he stood to his full, short, height and announced, 'Memory is all we have now. But you must stop trying to show what is no longer there. You must render the feeling of what is no longer – the pain, the fear, the grief.'

This freed something in Robert he dimly senses was trapped – sad figures begin to populate his pictures, lonely even when they're not alone: young girls with the faces of old women, leaping cats scared by something humans cannot see, weeping wives holding each other for comfort so they begin to seem like one long sobbing form. Hunger Marchers. Robert catches his mother's tears, the blue tears he wasn't allowed to cry for the wee sister who would never grow up. His figures bear the losses of all. They often have his own long face or Bobby's full lips but nobody sees what they don't want to.

Critics love them. 'There is a grave dug behind all his canvases,' one writes – Bobby sticks that one on the wall. Collectors come knocking too.

With every new picture, Adler's approval grows and Robert's sales with it – Bobby isn't sure which Robert values more. Adler arches his big bushy brows when Robert insists on calling him 'Master'. Bobby appreciates all the extra housekeeping, soon stops looking at prices. They can afford an iron now, but Bobby keeps up the show of heating a ladle over the gas ring and smoothing out their clothes, especially when they have visitors hungry for artistic poverty. Bobby paints away at his fruit, often imaginary as there is scarcely an orange to be found in all London – he depicts gaping gourds, wet insides, pips pouring from gouged flesh, apples ripening in the dark and all in colours that vibrate at the frequency of his feelings. More and more he is using green. Robert eventually notices and makes a peace offering of their latest review: '*MacBryde's use of colour is unsurpassed!*'

Bobby sees Robert making an effort but is embarrassed that he feels the need. They were joint top of their year, Europe was theirs, this is supposed to be their success.

Robert goes on. 'See, they love your way with colour.'

Bobby sighs. 'It's like somebody saying *You've got nice eyes,*' he says. 'Instead of saying *You're beautiful.*'

For the next four years, they work and work: show after show, endless commissions, praise upon praise. London is happening wherever they are – holding court at the Fitzroy, trawling the all-night Turkish baths on Jermyn Street (close cousin of the Arlington), bouncing about in the back of a taxi birling through Soho. Bobby buys drinks for whoever's next to him and then whoever's next to them. They're the talk of the town. One Saturday-nearly-Sunday a spiv fronts up to Robert after giving him and Bobby dirty looks all night. He spits on Robert's shoes. Bobby stands up to go. The bar stops to stare. Robert stays put. The man spits again and says, 'Queer.' Robert finishes his whisky and turns to the man and says, 'Sir, I am as God made me and so, unfortunately, are you.' The place erupts and Robert stands up to his full height and the man pockets his punch. Bobby can't wait to drag Robert back to the studio so stops them in an empty bomb shelter to show his thanks.

Colquhoun and MacBryde. McPicasso and MacBraque. The Two Roberts – twin stars, burning ever brighter, certain observers determined that one must outshine the other.

'All hail these cunts!' Muriel Belcher claps slowly as they stagger into her Colony Room. They've already wet their beaks at the Fitzroy. Or was it the Wheatsheaf? A few regulars cheer, most are already deep in gin.

'The Golden Boys of Bond Street!'

Another sobriquet for their growing list of legends. Robert's latest show has sold out.

Muriel reigns supreme on a leopard-skin stool in front of her bar, in the club she has made the epicentre of all Soho, the source of all art, the confluence of all the culture that's left in London. Somewhere an air-raid siren sounds but Muriel just turns up the music. She takes a long draw on her cigarette, jammed firmly in a slender black Bakelite holder. 'Now clear your fucking tab before I cut off your tartan balls.'

Muriel's favourite spreads across her black silk lap — tonight Francis is showing a bit of fishnet where his socks should be. He lays his head on Muriel's shoulder and purrs. Muriel pets him and whispers 'Daughter'. Behind the bar, Muriel's girlfriend Henrietta polishes coupe glasses. Francis smiles at Robert — makes no secret of admiring his picture-house looks, his talked-about talent. Robert is on his second, or maybe even third, show at Lefevre. Meanwhile, Francis is hoping people have forgotten his foray into interior design — making beautiful rooms for rich queers after months being used and useful in the leather-lined salons of Paris and Berlin. He shudders to think of the rugs he designed, has asked his darling Nanny to track them down and burn them. But Robert and Bobby are making proper art from nothing — it is noble, Francis has decided, there's the potential for suffering, and this he can never resist.

'D'you want some jam?' says Bobby, reaching into the Fortnum's bag he's carrying. 'Sorry, *preserrrve*,' he says, reading the label. He lifts out jar after jar, handing them to Muriel who passes them around the bar like some mad game of pass-the parcel. 'Strawberry, Rose Petal, Rrrrrraspberry Delight!'

'He couldnae stop himself,' Robert smiles.

'The first time I went in there that wee queen looked at me like I was shit on his shoe,' says Bobby. 'Not the day!'

Bobby liberates an open bottle of Dom Pérignon from a bowl of ice on the counter and takes a foaming swig.

'Filthy little bitch,' says Muriel, her painted-on brows marching towards her kohl hairline. She does nothing to stop him.

At this the exquisitely tailored arms and legs of Johnny Minton windmill over, dancing to jazz only he can hear. He can never resist Robert, has bought several of his oils but not said so. 'Darlings,' he zig-zags over in his handmade shoes. 'What more do I need to do?' He sports a weathered sailor on each arm, splendid in their whites — they glow against the gold and emerald walls. Minton's flailing threatens to take them all out and Muriel swats him away but Francis catches one arm and holds him while snatching the Dom Pérignon from Bobby, who watches as Francis tips the last of it over Johnny's long sad beautiful face. Johnny doesn't struggle, doesn't even close his big brown eyes – just lets the dregs run down his chin then crazily licks at it, his tongue roving everywhere. The sailors gawp, unsure about their port for the night.

'Champagne for my real friends,' drawls Francis, kissing Johnny before pushing him back into the arms of his sailors. 'Real pain for my sham friends.'

Henrietta takes the bottle, wonders quite whose bill to put it on, tilts her head at Bobby.

'Drinks for all!' says Bobby, drunk enough to sound like home. He produces a brown envelope from his jacket and pulls out note after note – suddenly he is his father handing his pay-packet over to his mother back in Maybole. In his hand is more money than they will see in a year. 'That's us paid, hen,' he slurs to Henrietta, who takes it without counting then bangs the till closed, startling the goldfish in the bowl above, causing it to realise, yet again, that it's going nowhere.

Bobby leans over to Robert and kisses him with lips that taste of champagne.

'Hold that pose while I fetch Lily Law,' says Muriel. 'Indecent, I call it! It'll be buggery next!'

Only now does Johnny feel something.

Johnny wakes up in a Bobby and Robert sandwich. He looks left then right and tries to remember last night.

'Coffee?' asks Bobby, rolling out from under the thin cotton sheet.

'Yes please,' says Johnny, begrudgingly admiring Bobby's high tight arse, although it holds no interest for him.

'Keep it down,' growls Robert, pulling the sheets with him as he rolls onto his side.

Bobby dances back from the gas ring as it lights in a puff of blue.

'If you fry so much as a fucking egg I will kill you,' says Robert, from the depths of his pillow.

Bobby cracks an egg into a tiny cast-iron pan. 'Robert, we've got guests!'

Johnny panics briefly, looks around for others, prays not Francis, before Bobby corrects himself. 'Guest, singular.'

Johnny sinks back against the pillow in relief. Who else has seen these two like this? Private them. Not the celebrated artists or party stars. So close he can count pores, Johnny examines the nape of Robert's neck, the perfect taper of curls. Robert rolls back towards him, pulling the sheets away. Johnny is suddenly naked. Again. Robert surveys him.

'So,' says Bobby. 'Fried or scrambled?'

After that, Johnny more or less moves in. He spends his nights between them and his days in the big window scratching away at small pen drawings.

'What do you think?' he asks Bobby, who is darning Robert's socks and wondering what to make for tomorrow's party.

'Sexy sailors,' says Bobby, looking over.

'Good,' says Johnny. 'I think housewives should have a thrill.'

'What's this for?' Bobby asks.

'A cookbook,' says Johnny. 'Elizabeth David. I'm doing the whole thing.'

'Rations à la mode?' Bobby laughs.

'No,' says Johnny, shading a crotch. '*Mediterranean Cooking*, hence sailors.'

'And you complain when critics call you an illustrator,' growls Robert, standing at his easel, facing down a stern Hebridean woman.

'He's right,' says Bobby. 'And it's not like you need the money.'

'You did that book jacket for Fred what's-his-face!' Johnny protests.

'Short stories,' says Bobby. 'Literature. Not *Six Ways with Spaghetti.*'

'He's right, Johnny,' says Robert, wondering if a blue might be better for this woman's skin than any real hue. He'll ask Adler later. He likes having Johnny around – he's endearing, that way he pouts to cover his buck teeth. *Gies my arse a break*, Bobby thinks, although he does enjoy the sight of Robert with an even taller man. *And if the work dries up we've got a rich man living in and in love with him.*

Johnny wonders if anybody will notice that all his sailors are variations on a theme and that the theme is Robert, Robert, Robert.

Later that day Bobby takes a couple of Johnny's sailors to the Lefevre and gets them into the upcoming MacBryde & Colquhoun joint show. 'You should call the big one *Robert*,' says Bobby, raising a glass.

You are cordially invited to our Sunday Salon at Number 77 Bedford Gardens. Bring a bottle. Don't be boring.

'This'll make a big salad,' says Bobby, pulling apart the still life he's carefully arranged: a cucumber, some apples, a pungent mackerel. He always starts party preparations a day before so he doesn't miss anything. Bobby stands ready to feed the five thousand – he is to ration coupons what Jesus was to loaves and fishes. Auntie Maggie showed him how to stretch a pot of anything. 'Johnny, can you splurge some of your pennies on some stewing steak?'

'Of course,' says Johnny, who doesn't actually know how much money he has, only that dear old Granny ensured he never had to count. He looks up from another sailor.

'A particularly fine specimen,' says Bobby.

'The man or the drawing?' asks Johnny.

'Both,' says Bobby. 'He can pressgang me any time. Four the merrier! And get us some bubbles?'

'Not until we beat Miss Hitler,' says Johnny, fetching his coat. 'Beer, whisky, whatever else I can find.'

'Mind you don't get in trouble,' says Bobby, as Johnny heads for the door. 'I'm far too busy to be visiting you in the jail!'

Robert stands at his easel, a cigarette dangling from his lip while he tries to work out why these two figures just won't connect. Something to do with the way they're standing. They need to be closer. He is undisturbed by the preparations taking place around him, could work with bombs dropping – actually has done. He dimly registers peace between Bobby and Johnny, which is good – one war is enough.

'I'll do us a stew, Robert,' says Bobby, fetching out his big pot. 'Air this place out,' he says, throwing open a window. The colonel is stationed across the way, like a sniper. 'Fuck you,' says Bobby, making sure to mouth the words slowly then flicking two fingers. The old man turns puce, firing back the words furnishing his latest complaint to their landlord: *Drunks. Queers. Orgies.*

Within a couple of hours, the studio is artfully dishevelled. The big table has been mostly cleared of books and papers to make way for plates and bowls and, crucially, bottles and glasses. Bobby has gone up the road and rescued some flowers from the gates of Kensington Palace – loyal subjects regularly leave tributes there, Athenians hoping their gods will bring them peace. Robert has almost solved his picture problem. Bobby is raring to go.

They head out to gather guests. First to Fitzrovia: Augustus John – looking like a figure from another century, which he is – rots next to Nina Hamnett in their corner at the Fitzroy, which is where they leave them but not before Anthony Cronin joins them and then they roll along to the Wheatsheaf in search of Dylan, who accompanies them to deepest Soho and Muriel's where Francis continues his worship of Robert and heads out with them via the French, nodding to the hennaed magnificence of Quentin Crisp on the corner before finally rescuing Elizabeth Smart who has again been stood up by her tortured and torturing poet and then Bobby leads all, and sundries, back to Number 77.

Names, names, names. Names they read about in *Horizon*, *New*

Writing, even the *Evening Standard*. Names that are now their friends. Well, mostly.

'Let me begin at the beginning,' intones Dylan, somewhere after midnight.

'What?' shouts Bobby, over the laughing and swearing and dancing and clanking.

'The beginning,' says Dylan, swaying towards him.

'Is he . . .?' Elizabeth asks Bobby. 'Please, no more verse,' she shudders. She necks another whisky and curses the already married George Barker, who has already given her one child and more heartbreak.

'It is spring,' Dylan continues, raising his voice to a level that might actually make spring happen.

'Welsh it up a bit,' says Bobby, over the din. 'The BBC will love that.'

Dylan shouts now. 'IT IS SPRING! The night is moonless.'

'Good, no bombs!' shouts somebody from the back of the room where the mattress is already busy. The party takes a quick gulp of air then carries on. Adler nods off in a corner.

'So, Sir Kenneth fucking Clark turns to me and Robert,' says Bobby to Dylan, who is grieving his poem. 'This is at the National Gallery, and he says to us, we're standing right there, and he says *One reads about Communists and homosexuals in all the papers but one never actually encounters any.* Can you believe it?!'

Tonge is still making eyes at Bobby who is avoiding him but not so obviously that it might get him a bad review. Johnny is looking adoringly at Robert who is back at his easel drawing Cronin who can't stop thanking him for the introduction to Connolly who has finally printed one of his poems. 'Be grateful and still,' says Robert. 'It can be a wee present.'

'Why don't you work during the day like everybody else?' asks Francis, at Robert's other shoulder. 'I do enjoy your bourgeois maison.'

'Bobby keeps a tidy house,' says Robert.

Francis revels in appalling visitors to his studio, knee-high squalor, layer upon layer of torn-up magazines and naked photographs he gambles might chance an idea. A mad nest. Francis throws his arms round Robert's neck and proclaims, 'You are one for whom the night has come before the evening!'

Robert raises a hand to slap him so Francis bends over and peeps back shouting, 'Arrest me, constable!'

Bobby starts singing, 'Water, water wallflower, growing up so high! We are all children and we all must die!' Johnny hops into the middle of the room and spins like a mill in a gale.

Robert finishes the song, 'Except Johnny Minton, the fairest of them all!' Applause from all but Bobby.

Johnny spins on the spot with his eyes closed, smiling like a saint and murmuring over and over 'money, money, money, they only love you for your money' and everybody ignores him except Francis, who leans over to say, 'you better hope it never runs out' before turning back to Robert.

The party roars, the room spins, the building lifts.

'Francis, did you want some salad?' yells Bobby, waving half a cucumber.

'Where's that been?' says Francis.

'Where's it no been?' says Bobby, suddenly a sword swallower – Robert paints them and clowns and puppets.

'It's the colour of VD,' Francis says, accusingly.

'You'd know!' says Bobby, muffled by cucumber.

Elizabeth nudges him and he nearly chokes on it then tosses it over his shoulder and tells her, 'You're a better writer than that shite man of yours.'

Elizabeth shakes her head. 'Sadly, he is a genius.' Then she leans her head on Bobby's shoulder. The studio door is open, as always, and in wanders a man Bobby doesn't recognise but one who is clearly used to being recognised. Elizabeth lifts her head. Dylan makes daggers. 'Is that the bastard?' Bobby asks. Elizabeth nods while fixing her hair. Bobby drains his vin rouge then very neatly taps his glass on the side of their table, snapping it at the neck.

Sliding the smooth foot of the glass against his palm, Bobby extends his hand in greeting. Elizabeth couldn't stop him even if she wanted to and she's not sure she does, after George's latest paternal revelation. Dylan watches with pleasure.

'Mr Barker, finally,' says Bobby, nice as you like, pressing his hand into George's. 'Welcome to our wee party.'

One Monday afternoon – many Sundays later – Elizabeth is sitting for Bobby.

'You should leave him,' says Elizabeth, trying not to move her lips. 'Or maybe live apart?'

'Easy for you to say,' says Bobby. 'Keep still.'

'Let Johnny have him,' says Elizabeth, regretting her decision to be a model. She will submit to being admired but this is much less comfortable.

'Watch it,' says Bobby, snapping a stick of charcoal in two.

Elizabeth takes this rare opportunity to look around their studio in daylight and minus a hundred fashionable bodies. She admires the nautilus on the mantel, notes how it holds the north light. This is her favourite room in all London.

'You're thinking about writing,' says Bobby.

'I am not,' says Elizabeth, indignant. 'Well, I am now, obviously.'

'I can tell,' says Bobby, laying down his charcoal. 'It gives you a wee v between the eyes.'

Elizabeth is wondering if she really can write something about George: chasing him, loving him, hating him. It would have to be a fiction, of course, like so much of their life. She'd met him in a bookshop on Charing Cross Road – well, in the pages of one of his books there – 'Daedalus' was the poem that did it.

'Sit still,' says Bobby. He is attempting a portrait of Dear Elizabeth because he wants her face around even when she's not and also to stick two fingers up to the critics who think he's only good for fruit (Robert included). So far he's managed one eye and a lip.

Elizabeth wanders over to take a look. 'Very Dalí.'

They laugh and Bobby pours them a morning sharpener.

'Cheers,' says Elizabeth, casting her eye to the clock where Bobby keeps the good whisky. No more Bell's. Not since the success of *Scottish Painters*, half a war ago.

'You should leave him,' says Bobby, clinking glasses. He has graduated from jam jars to cut crystal from Fortnum's – bought without checking the price.

'Who?' says Elizabeth, walking over to the window.

'Your lover, the King.' Bobby laughs. 'George Barker, who do you think?!'

'I can hardly leave a man that's never around,' says Elizabeth.

'Fair,' says Bobby. 'But he is charming. No wonder you never wanted me to meet him.'

'Look what happened when you did!'

Barker had boxed Bobby's ears before rushing his bleeding hand under the tap, his red joining all the others in the bottom of their oily sink. They'd made their peace over a long lunch at the French – their shared love of Elizabeth an excellent starter. The story still doing the rounds is that Bobby pressed a broken whisky bottle or a razor blade into Barker's palm. Neither corrects it.

'At least your man doesn't leave a trail of offspring.'

'Not yet,' says Bobby. 'Not for want of some women trying.'

'Robert can't help looking like a film star,' says Elizabeth.

'Aye look but don't touch,' says Bobby, inwardly cursing the two or three very rich, very unmarried lady collectors who are always making eyes at Robert. He sips thoughtfully then tops up their glasses. 'Robert is welcome to do whoever he wants, we've always given each other our freedom—'

'You did move Johnny in for him—'

'I moved Johnny in for us—'

'Why?' Elizabeth asks. 'He's not your type.'

'He's not bad company,' says Bobby. 'And if he's here then Robert's here more as well. Plus, you know . . .'

Elizabeth necks her whisky as insurance against the subject looming. Sometimes she wishes Bobby would have just a little shame, then she hates herself – she loves him for saying what so many others wouldn't even admit to thinking.

'We don't all own half of Canada, or America, or wherever it is,' says Bobby.

Elizabeth rolls her eyes luxuriously and for a moment Bobby wonders if that's what she looks like under George. He dismisses the image. Pictures of sex, like stories about dreams, should never be shared.

'You've got it made,' says Elizabeth, gesturing around the studio, at pictures parcelled up in brown paper and ready to go, at matching plates, at full kitchen shelves.

'No,' says Bobby. 'We've made it – I've made this place. That's different. The money goes out as fast as it comes in—'

'You will insist on feeding half of London every weekend and buying drinks for all of Soho—' says Elizabeth, gesturing around at the invisible party.

'I don't see you spurning my hospitality!'

'I could never spurn you,' says Elizabeth, blowing him a kiss.

'But so long as Johnny's here we've always got the rent and light covered.'

'That's very cynical,' says Elizabeth, holding out her empty glass.

'That's very easy for a rich person to say,' says Bobby, walking back over to the bottle.

'I'm not rich.'

'You live in a country house—'

'Rented!'

'In Suffolk.'

'Essex, actually.'

'And you rhyme house with nice,' says Bobby, pouring her another glass. He hates it when the rich plead poverty.

'Tilty is rented!'

'Oh, are you down to the last thread on your last Aubusson rug, hen?' Bobby laughs. 'Are you having to sell the family silver?'

'You know you're always welcome.'

'I can barely survive ten minutes from Piccadilly,' says Bobby. 'It would be like taking the penguins out the Zoo and plonking them down in a desert. And, further to your earlier suggestion, I will not be leaving him.'

'Who? Your lover, the King?' Elizabeth asks, resuming her pose.

'Robert!' says Bobby, smiling – Elizabeth is as close as he gets to patter down south. 'I do seriously think I might murder him – he never lifts a finger, his moods, his big long face despite everybody loving him and everything he puts his hand to. I might definitely kill him. Or myself.'

'Bobby, don't!' Elizabeth has heard too many stories of accidental overdoses, faulty gas ovens, midnight swimmers who never made it home. All the happy bachelors made unhappy by a world whose cruelty Bobby helps her grasp.

'I'm only being dramatic,' says Bobby, sketching furiously now. 'I'm not killing myself for any cunt. And I could never leave Robert – I knew that the minute I set eyes on him. We both did, sadly.'

Elizabeth believes him. Elizabeth knows love. Bobby occupies the bits of her heart not taken up by her children, George or writing. 'Where is he anyway?' she asks, making a show of looking around as if he might crawl out from under their big table, as stragglers have been known to. 'Out saving his conscience again?'

Bobby shakes his head. 'His brother nearly died in France – it's not a principle, it's family.'

'And guilt.'

'Yes guilt, I got him out. I think he resents me for depriving him of the chance to be a hero. Now he's driving ambulances with Francis fucking Bacon. Imagine . . . you've been bombed and then they turn up, half-pissed?'

Elizabeth shakes her head.

Bobby finishes his whisky. 'I'd rather have him angry and alive.' He holds his drawing up for Elizabeth. 'What do you think?'

★

Robert signed up the morning after he got the letter from his brother, on thin army hospital paper. The only unit that will take him is the ambulance corps. The young woman who enrols him is surprised a man wants to do this work.

Robert can't drive. But Francis can. So that's that. Every day, they meet for their shift by the market at Smithfield, no longer the bloodiest bit of the city. Francis idles in front of the butchers, windows filled with pigs and cows, their ribs open to the world, their organs arranged neatly on steel trays in front of them.

'I think we all deserve to die,' says Francis.

'No doubt,' says Robert. 'But maybe not just yet.'

The meat will all be gone in hours, once word gets out. The only thing scarcer now is fish. Next time he'll get Bobby some liver.

Their ambulance waits outside the depot – it's really just a Bedford van with a big red cross painted on the side, which Robert tries not to see as a target. Francis opens it and they get in. Robert unfolds the map marked SECRET – it shows the field hospitals and emergency clinics as well as all the morgues.

'There's a morgue in Soho,' says Robert.

'You mean Muriel's on a Sunday morning?' laughs Francis, revving the van into life.

Almost instantly their radio crackles into life: *Firebomb, Shoreditch.* The other side of the city and then some. Francis waits for another, closer, emergency.

'C'mon,' says Robert, reaching over and tapping the steering wheel. 'Let's go!'

Francis heads east and Robert peers up through the windscreen half-expecting Hitler. Barrage balloons bob above the city. He's grown used to them, everybody has, some have names. It's the steel cables they hold aloft that threaten enemy aircraft – he longs to see the wings clipped off a bomber but knows it would probably be the last thing he saw. He remembers looking up into the blue with Bobby, lying on top of Kildoon Hill, the skies harmless.

'No traffic,' Francis marvels as they cross what should be Gray's Inn Road.

'Left, left,' says Robert, peering at the map.

'Do they honestly think taking down the street signs will stop the fucking Nazis?'

'Nearly stopped us!'

Robert hasn't been this far east for years; it's far outside the holy triangle of their studio, Soho and Fitzrovia. Suddenly the ambulance cab is awash with light that shouldn't be there. He peers out: the whole of Cripplegate is gone, bombed back to before the Middle Ages. Even the Romans would recognise it.

'Now I can look the East End in the face,' says Francis, doing a fancy radio-lady voice, fluttering one hand off the wheel.

'She didn't say that, you know.'

'I know,' says Francis. 'I was there when Backstairs Billy said it and what's-her-face from the *Mirror* scribbled it down and, hey presto, the Queen's got a sense of humour. Backstairs Billy is the real queen!'

'He should get the credit,' says Robert.

'Won't happen,' says Francis. 'That's not how history works. Look, smoke.' He points to the only building still just about standing. St Giles, a Great Fire of London survivor, has not quite made it through the Blitz.

'We better stop,' says Robert.

'It's not our address,' says Francis.

'But there's a fire,' says Robert. He can't fight, he can't do what his brother has, but he can do this and do it right.

Robert thumps the wheel so Francis slows. Robert is out before the handbrake clunks on. Francis follows.

The church is upside down and inside out: charred pews crash at crazy angles, broken gravestones make new names, a breeze whistles through jagged organ pipes. The sky is framed perfectly by the missing roof. A wisp of grey drifts up from a neat little fire burning in a bucket on the exact spot where Daniel Defoe was baptised.

'Hello?' Francis calls out.

A moment and then a voice from beyond. 'Hello?'

'C'mon,' says Robert, turning. 'There's no emergency here.'

The voice goes on. 'Don't get many visitors.'

It sounds as old and broken as the beams around them. Francis steps forward and peers at whatever is cooking over the fire – a rabbit on a stick. Hopefully a rabbit.

'Get yer own!' shouts the owner of the voice, a bony old man, heaving himself up from a lidless stone sarcophagus. 'Back off!'

Francis staggers back. The man braces his elbows on the sides and pushes himself up. He is as grey as the stone encasing him. Newspaper sticks out his sleeves like straw from a scarecrow and his eyes are streaked red, like the threads of blood in an egg white, when eggs weren't powdered.

'Sorry to disturb you,' says Robert, realising they've walked into this man's house. Had he not seen it with his own eyes he wouldn't believe it – it's beyond even a Bobby story. He can't wait to tell him.

'We'll leave you be,' says Robert. But Francis just stands there. He is staring past the man at something even more extraordinary: Christ's arms broken, his body thrusting forward and up as if something is trying to get out – the Crucifixion rendered as reality-splitting as it must have been. Robert turns away and walks back to the ambulance. Francis arrives a full minute later, his eyes wet, his head filling with meat and blood and bone and paint. Chance was a fine thing.

Robert is in the ambulance all day and their studio all night. Bobby is always out – touting for commissions, attention, trade. The harder Robert works, the harder Bobby drinks. Sometimes Johnny stays in but not often because he knows word of him being alone with Robert will get back to Bobby and that won't end well, it never does. They are to be a three, never a two. Bobby is the price of admission, which Johnny increasingly resents paying. Number 77 gets smaller every day. Johnny has suggested the three of them visit Scotland – he thinks he might finally crack their code if he can see where it was laid down. If not, well, it gets him out of London. Robert and Bobby can't decide if this trip is the best or worst idea.

Two figures stand in the picture Robert is painting. A man on the left, with his hand held out to a woman on the right. She is holding a small birdcage, and he grips a penny. They seem to be agreeing a price. Or maybe he's working up to asking her something, something he already knows but doesn't want to hear yet must. The background is split vertically between past and present. The man is foregrounded by mustard yellow – rumours of gas bombs still swirl. The woman stands in front of a darker shade, like the phlegm that stands up in the sink when Bobby coughs first thing.

Robert peers. Even this candle is too much but let the wardens come. Robert sees every day what the bombs do and knows it's instant – only buildings are strong enough to be broken; bodies mostly just disappear. Robert likes his night colours, sees in them his absence from the day, his doing something good, what Bobby mocks as his Presbyterianism. Just the thought of Bobby takes Robert out the room. Where is he? Who is he with? What if, even now, a pilot is dropping his last bomb before buzzing back to Berlin in time for breakfast and what if that bomb falls on the Fitzroy and Bobby is, as always, ignoring the sirens? What if? Robert drags his brush through a rag and drops it in a jar of turps then pulls on his jacket before blowing out the candle and heading out the door.

'What do you intend your work to mean?' the young reporter asks, pad balanced on his knee, poised to capture the truth for his millions of readers.

It means we can pay the bills. It means I can stay here with Robert. It means everybody in Maybole was wrong, except Auntie Maggie. Bobby says none of this. Instead, after seeming to think for a serious amount of time, he says: 'I set out to make statements, in visual terms, concerning the things I see, and to make clear the order that exists between objects which sometimes seem opposed.'

Robert nods in the way laypeople expect artists to nod.

'Could one of you maybe take off your jumper?' the photographer asks, looking up from his camera.

'Good idea,' says the reporter, tugging at his own collar as if he's warm. 'It's a bit . . .'

Bobby refuses to fill in the blank, then says, 'I knitted them.'

'Yes,' the reporter says, scribbling that down.

'Not for publication,' says Bobby.

'I thought this was just supposed to be a short interview?' says Robert, putting one hand behind his back and straightening himself. 'You've been here all morning.'

'I'm sure the young man's nearly done, aren't you?' Bobby nods, lighting another cigarette. 'Have you got his picture in?'

The photographer nods. He is astonished by the canvas in front of him. 'What is it called again?'

'*Two Scottish Women*,' says Robert, proudly. He's pleased with the way one woman holds the other – stops her from falling into her sadness but also from rushing into her rage.

'Mine is *Woman in a Red Hat*,' says Bobby, leaning on the top of the frame, which is turned from the viewer.

'Perfect! Hold it there.' The camera clicks away.

'Make sure you mention that,' says Bobby.

The reporter remembers the opening night for one of Colquhoun's solo shows – that night he'd vomited all over a major critic who'd suggested in print that MacBryde was merely his 'follower'. He wonders how far he can push the pair without having to get his jacket cleaned.

'Mr Colquhoun, you were described in *The Listener* as "the most promising young painter England has produced for a considerable time". How do you feel about that?'

'I am not English,' growls Robert.

'It is only right that Robert's talent is recognised,' says Bobby, as if raising a point of order in the House of Commons.

'Mr Francis Bacon, who is being described as Britain's most radical young painter, is reported to have said "All I know about art I learned from Robert Colquhoun".'

Bobby rolls his eyes.

'Mr Wyndham Lewis wrote that your work is so very similar you must "be regarded almost as one artistic organism". Is he right?'

'Shite,' says Robert, breaking pose. The camera quiets. 'Now you listen to me. I've written this to Michael Ayrton and other purveyors of the insidious notion that we are indistinguishable or that Bobby is somehow merely my follower.'

I would follow you anywhere, Bobby thinks.

'Let me be clear.' Robert kicks his easel so the photographer will have to shift it back. 'I have known Robert MacBryde too long and admire his endeavours too much to let you or anybody else label him as *merely* anything – he is his own man and the very best of men.'

Anywhere.

'One last question,' says the reporter, licking his pencil as he'd once seen a reporter do in a film.

'It very well might be,' Bobby mutters.

'Our readers wonder why so many modern pictures feature figures that are . . . well . . . not as they appear in the real world. Often violent. Why do you and artists like Mr Bacon do this?'

Robert shakes his head and smiles. 'Figures and objects in many modern paintings may appear distorted. They will be so to those who seek a factual resemblance, or a mirror-like reflection.'

Bobby finishes his thought. 'The special forms, evolved from the relation of colour masses, line and composition, to express the painter's reaction to objects, will be the reason for a painting's existence.'

'Thank you,' says the reporter, closing his notebook and nodding to the photographer to stop.

'Who are we in with again?' Bobby asks.

'You are in with Keith Vaughan, Prunella Clough and John Minton.'

'We know them all and dear old Johnny,' says Bobby. 'He practically lives here.'

Robert shoots him a look.

'Well,' says Bobby. 'He did. We hardly ever see him now. Everybody is so busy these days, forgetting and rebuilding. What will our headline be?'

'I don't actually write them,' says the reporter, noting that the studio has just one mattress and imagining headlines that can never be printed. 'But it will be something like *Robert MacBryde and Robert Colquhoun: Two Scottish Painters Who Live, Travel, Work and . . . Exhibit Together.*'

'Sounds about right,' says Robert.

'We can't wait to see it,' says Bobby. 'We'll frame it next to our wee bit in *Vogue.*'

'To Alfred Barr!' says Robert, grabbing the champagne bottle from Bobby. 'Curator of the – wait for it, wait for it – Museum of Modern Fucking Art in New Fucking York!'

'He's bought Robert's *Two Scottish Women,*' says Bobby.

'Not more of your miserable widows,' sighs Muriel, who prides herself on knowing everything about painting and pretending not to. 'Henrietta, darling, will you mourn me?'

Henrietta leans over the bar and takes Muriel's hand, pecking the finger where a wedding ring might go. 'I mourn every second I am not with you.'

'So your husband tells me,' says Muriel, blowing smoke and kisses to Henrietta, who wafts them towards herself.

Francis rouses his head from Muriel's shoulder where he's left a wet patch. 'What did he buy from you?' He nods to Bobby. 'Let me guess: *Still Life with Cock-like Cucumber?*'

Bobby bristles. '*Woman in a Red Hat!*'

'Not a banana?'

'If it's a banana you want,' says Bobby, unbuckling his belt.

'Girls,' says Muriel, flicking ash into Francis's waiting hand. 'Play nice.'

'Well, I'm glad Mr Barr and his chequebook visited you too,' says Francis, wincing pleasurably at the hot cigarette ash. 'Really I am. I know things have been slowing down. We are now officially the five Best of Britain! Francis Bacon, Robert Colquhoun, Robert MacBryde and . . .'

'Who are the other two?' Robert asks. 'Sutherland? Piper? Nash?'

'Which Nash?' says Muriel.

'Take yer pick,' says Bobby.

'Who else then?' says Muriel. 'For New Fucking York!'

'Dear old Burra,' says Francis. 'And darling Lucian, obviously. Not a Nash, no Sutherland, no Piper and—' He shouts to the back of the bar where Johnny likes to sit. 'Noooooo sailor boys!'

'That's not nice,' says Bobby, only partly because he knows Robert will want to hear him say it. 'Now, who wants a drink!?'

From Your Most Beloved Minty, train back from Scotland to London (thank God). December, 1946.

Darling Keith,

Stop gawping at the boys around the Men's Pond and read this missive. IMMEDIATELY! You will NOT believe! No sooner were we off the train at Kilmarnock than here we are back on it. Scribbling quietly as I can. They're finally sleeping – Bobby is drooling against the window and Robert leaning out into the aisle, a very clear V between them. This is their WORST yet – I know I say this every time and I know you think it's because I want each fight to be the last so I can scoop up Robert and give him what he actually needs . . . and I do, despite everything, I would, but honestly, this was new.

I splashed out and got us Second Class all the way up, which put Bobby in a good mood. I sat opposite Robert, which put me in a good mood, my feet resting between his for hundreds of miles. Bobby noticed but was mollified by my outlay. I would go First for Robert.

We played Snap for a bit but cards were abandoned due to Definite Tension the further north we got. Extraordinary thing – as we passed Carlisle, their accents thickened, the way they do when they're really drunk.

Slight stirring then but back to sleep again. Onwards. I'll be quick. They haven't been back since before the war and now Robert's brother is injured and recovering at home. Their hope is he won't be sent back. If it all keeps going they'll be taking cripples. I would rather die than go back in. Robert obviously continues to be gripped by guilt despite having been legally invalided out so insists on doing his ambulance work with Francis B who I do think gets a kick out of all the horror.

So, we get off at Kilmarnock and there is Robert's mother – petite, tight like a pin and with the air of a housekeeper. He leaps off the train and sweeps her up like a sweetheart and as he kisses her their cheekbones touch and it's clear where he gets his looks, if not his height. Then this girl comes running and honestly I've never seen Robert look so happy.

'This is yer wee sister, Sheila,' says his mother.

I had no idea there was a sister! Only found out about the brother when he was injured in action and Robert signed up. Turns out she was born when they were at art school in Glasgow and, for some reason, he didn't want to see her until she'd turned one and then he was doing his exams and then they were abroad and then he was in the army but he always wrote to her and sent her drawings. Bobby told me all about it – I knew nothing. It's like they didn't exist until they got to London.

'Bobby,' she says, shaking Bobby's hand and he takes her hand right there and kisses it. I thought Robert was going to kill him. All this before they've even introduced me.

'This is Mr Minton,' says Robert. 'He's an artist too.'

I said, 'Johnny to my friends.'

'Then ah hope you'll be Johnny to me,' she says, sweetly pleased with herself. You can hear Robert in her long looping vowels. He makes more sense to me now. Anyway, I kissed her hand hello and Robert just went dark, the way he does, but said nothing.

There's no car, just a packed bus to 'the scheme' where the Colquhouns live. Sheila sat on Robert's knee. Every time I opened my mouth people turned to stare – I don't think anyone English has been here since Cromwell. I suppose Robert's family home is like a Peabody Estate or similar – grey pebble-dashed two-storey dwellings that look like a house but are actually two flats, one on top of the other, with a shared hall they call a close. It's all immaculately clean with doilies and such all over but it's very much not 77 Bedford Gardens. The only picture up is a pencil sketch of Robert's from school, a ship's lamp so round I nearly mistook it for the real thing. No, not so – there was one painting – *European Street scene with Stone Archway, 1938*. A midday street in Florence maybe, with a tower shading a street and a peasant woman with a cloth over her head walking by an arch. He'd given it to her as present to celebrate getting his scholarship. Painted by Bobby! His lover hiding in plain sight in the old family home!

Robert then goes out the back to see his father who is, apparently, 'with his birds'. Extraordinary that he didn't come in. First sign, I suppose.

While we're sitting there Mrs Colquhoun leans under her sewing chair and gets out this old chocolate box with a blue kitten on. I thought Bobby was going to cry. Inside are years of clippings about Robert and him – reviews, interviews, photographs of them looking painterly at their easels.

'Mr Theodas saves them for me,' she whispers, as if I know who that is. 'This is my favourite,' she says, carefully unfolding the *Kilmarnock Standard* and reading quietly. 'The headline says *London "Discovers" An Artist. When a London West End gallery presents a one-man show it usually and quite definitely means the artist has "arrived". Very many considerable Scottish (and English) artists have never achieved that through their lengthy careers. And yet here is a young Kilmarnock man, still on the sunny side of thirty, exhibiting in the West-End getting favourable notices from the critics and – not less remarkable – finding a ready sale for his pictures.*'

Bobby turned red.

'I'm sure your mother has her own wee trove,' says Mrs Colquhoun, folding it carefully. 'I've got *Vogue* and liked the *Picture Post* bit too. How is your mother? I would very much like to meet her one day. I still can't believe I've not.'

Bobby didn't have time to answer. In comes Robert Senior. You know that feeling after a bomb? When the air is sucked out into space? That's him walking into a room. Mrs Colquhoun slid that box right back under her chair and was on her feet and heading for the kettle before her husband was one step in. Sheila smoothed her sundress.

'That's the birds done', he announced, drying his hands on a rag – just as Robert does.

Bobby shook the father's hand and I swear the father nearly broke it. Robert was nowhere to be seen, maybe out with the birds? The father announces he's going to the pub and leaves, which lightens the room. Mrs Colquhoun serves some curious bread rolls – lightly burnt on top and absolutely delicious, smeared with a butter that's almost double cream and enough ham to make a showing. Bobby ate two. Mrs Colquhoun took one out the back for Robert and when she was gone Bobby turned to me and said this would 'end in murder'.

After our food, we went out and Robert showed us his father's aviary. It's full of formative images, birds in cages and birds fleeing cages. He's so delicate with the little things but firm, holding them tight so they can't hurt themselves. Their whole back garden is an allotment and again I see the origins of his early marrow patches and the jagged tendrils he uses still. This place is the source. More than anything, I see his mother alone and on edge. I see a town full of people with no idea who Robert really is. Robert has lived with loneliness and danger all his days. The Blitz holds nothing new to him. He carries it all within and resents it for being there and so ends up hating himself.

Robert's mother insisted we go to the pub in search of Robert Senior. Bobby suggested she joins us and she actually blushed. So out we headed, trailing Sheila to the door. It was like a Western walking down that road. Every single person stared at the three of us. Like we were from the moon. Robert paused at the door of this tiny pub called the Burns Inn and took a visible breath before pushing in. There was no music but all the talk stopped. Robert's father was sat in the fug at the bar, a pint nearly done.

'My oldest,' he says to the barman, who barely nods and starts pulling pints. I probably shouldn't have asked for a gin. Robert took the seat next to his father and then Bobby and then me so I was almost at the door, relief. Bobby asked the father question after question getting only one-word answers. Robert said nothing then less and less. On pint four Colquhoun Senior said to Bobby, 'Will you gie me a minute's peace?' To which Robert said, 'I've given you peace for years.' Father and son leaped up and Bobby tried to pull Robert back as he swiped at his father. I just sat there. The father necked his pint then stormed out followed by Robert, followed by Bobby followed by me.

Robert shouted down the street after his father, who kept his head down until he was back in the close and then he grabbed Robert as he came in and the two of them rolled along the close walls slapping and punching until Mrs Colquhoun appeared from upstairs with Sheila bawling. The whole street watched. Bobby tried to get in between Robert and his father and got punched in the process, by who I couldn't tell. I just stood there. Then the father ran into the flat and Robert caught the door with his foot and I don't know what was said because Robert was out in a minute. As we left the close the window above was thrown open and out came the blue kitten and the sky was filled with all Mrs Colquhoun's treasures – I caught sight of Bobby and Robert leaning on their easels for the *Picture Post*. Robert's mother leaned out grasping for them but was pulled back in and the window slammed shut. Robert turned on his heel and went out the back and I knew what he was going to do and Bobby did too, running to help him and they opened all the bird cages and as we ran down the street back to the station canaries flew all around us with children jumping up to catch them.

We're past Carlisle. They're stirring again. Bobby is drooling on Robert's shoulder. I better stop. But I mean, really, can you believe it?

Drop by 77 on Saturday and see which of us still living.

Minty x

Bobby steps on to the platform at Marble Arch – there's nothing doing above ground; it's mid-morning, too late for the last of the night and too early for the first of the day. Plus, it's raining. He admires the efficiency of lunchtime trade – in and out, as it were, and time for a sandwich after then maybe even some time in the studio. But after last night's fight he wants to lose himself, wants a bed and arms around him, not a stand-up at a urinal.

Scotland had not been a good idea and Johnny took the fall for it – that was Bobby's official reason for asking him to leave. Robert blamed Bobby for landing a punch on his father and wrote letter after letter back to Kilmarnock, but it was a waste of stamps. He drew Sheila over and over, taking it all out on everybody, including himself. Bobby never mentioned that he never even got to Maybole.

The platform is dismally empty. The only men on it are employed to be here and railwaymen aren't usually amenable. Same for cabbies. Not like waiters or soldiers. His cock fills with memories. Fewer men wore hats now. Bobby had asked a guardsman about it, a lance corporal he'd gone with a few times, and he said it reminded him of being a target, then he'd rolled over and after that Bobby didn't see him around so much.

A woman steps onto the platform annoyingly close. A provincially be-hatted mother up from Surrey or Sussex, trailing a boy in grey school shorts, his hand in hers. She'd brought him 'up to town' for a new uniform or a trip to the zoo. Bobby liked Regent's Park at night for all kinds of reasons, enjoyed all the animal noises, has heard the wolves howl. Bobby envies the fresh linen ease of the boy's life, his never going without, which leads him inevitably to his own mother – the tickle of her borrowed rabbit-skin coat. What would she think of him now? He realises now he spent most of their Final Show looking at Robert, who was watching the door for his own mother, for anyone from Kilmarnock.

Up bubbles another memory – he is becoming dangerously sober. He suddenly recognises this platform, the particular curve of its walls. It is almost exactly three years – no, more – since he spent a suffocating night trying to sleep down here. At that first long-awaited siren they'd surged down into the underground with everybody else and nobody knowing what to do, only that down here was a chance of making it through the night. Every now and then they felt more than heard a gigantic crump and the grout between the tiles released little puffs of dust so the air soon became heavy with it. Bobby sat up coughing and wheezing and the family lying next to them rolled away. The darkness down here was even deeper than the blackout above because the gas lights revealed its depths. Every now and then you'd hear a sharp cry then a *sorry* as somebody searching for their sliver of safety misjudged their step and stood on a hand or worse. Henry Moore was the only one who'd got this particular hell right – his drawings of people sheltering in the Tube, bodies lining both sides into infinity, a mass grave waiting to happen. After that night, they'd never sought shelter again – Robert refused to leave their studio and Bobby refused to leave him.

Bobby runs his hand along the curve of the Tube wall now lined by Sanatogen sunshine adverts. He feels crushed by the weight of the city above, by all the happy families, by all the futures he and Robert can never have. He shakes his head to clear the memory, which disturbs the mother who takes a tiny step away. Bobby needs a drink and some company. Mentally he scans the streets above: the French will be shut. Nobody worth talking to at the Fitzroy at this hour. He's barred from the Colony until Muriel forgives him for freeing her goldfish (into his mouth). Robert will be at the Wheatsheaf already – their all-night fight today's excuse for not touching a canvas. Bobby knows fine well it's partly the pressure of not painting that led to their fight in the first place. It is Bobby the galleries chase – not for new work from him but late work from Robert. There is a general sense the world would rather have one picture from Robert than three from him. Bobby decides there and then to go back to their studio and use Robert's absence to finish his latest still life. Fuck him.

As he turns to head back up, a man brushes past, running for a train that isn't there. Bobby turned to check him out – the brush past is a time-honoured signal, especially on an empty platform. The man looks his sort of age, inevitably taller and in a smart serge suit – he must be going somewhere, a job interview maybe, his old school tie knotted high. He looks anxiously left and right as if to show Bobby his unusually even profile. A night of sandy stubble grazes his jaw. The man's hands flutter to his collar. His fingers are those of a musician, a flautist maybe.

The tracks rattle to life with the approaching train. A warm breeze arrives on the platform, pushed through the tunnel. The little boy turns towards it and his mother turns towards him. Only Bobby sees the man jump.

A week or so later, Bobby is cutting up newspaper to make stencils. As ever, he can't help but read whatever is in front of him. A headline in the *West London Observer* catches his eye: MUSICIAN DIVED IN FRONT OF TRAIN. It's him. He turns to tell Robert, standing at his easel, but daren't interrupt. Besides, what happened was between the two of them. He's not stopped thinking about the man – he'd run home that morning to find Robert sleeping it off and woke him up saying *sorry, sorry, sorry*, not because it was his fault but because he'd seen what he'd seen and knew how close the platform edge really was. A week of peace ensued and with it work. That morning Bobby felt a stencil was the thing, it would give him the crispness of outline he craved. So, he'd picked up a newspaper to begin snipping then found the man again. He had indeed been a musician. Andrew Morrison, thirty-eight years old, had been arrested the night before by a plain-clothed officer in a public convenience in Mayfair and taken to the station where he was told to appear in court the very next day. Importuning was the charge. He never went home. It went on: 'The jury returned a verdict that the man took his life at a time when the balance of his mind was disturbed by ill-health.' He hadn't looked ill. Bobby cuts out the story tenderly then makes a paste of flour and water and sticks Andrew's story to his canvas, right in the middle, where the flutes are in an orchestra. Then he goes over to their record player, gets out *The Magic Flute* and puts it on. Robert pops his head round his canvas hoping for the kiss that Bobby plants on his cheek as he dances by.

7 May 1945

Sometime around 3 p.m., rumour coalesces into something like certainty. The news reaches the Fitzroy, rushing up Windmill Street all the way from Westminster where crowds gather outside Downing Street. Hitler is dead, maybe. Germany has surrendered, we think. It's over, it's over, it's over.

'There were still Doodlebugs last night,' says Robert, shaking his head.

'Last month!' says Bobby, ever eager to believe good news.

'The month before that,' says Vera, lifting a stubbornly stained pint glass to the light. This has to be the only pub in London where the pint glasses have permanent lipstick marks.

The saloon bar is even busier than usual – the usual faces are rapidly being outnumbered and not happy about it. Augustus John is pushed into a corner and not his usual one. Pathetic Nina Hamnett rattles her little gin tin; she's becoming more and more like a vision of Modigliani – *I was his muse, you know*. 'Business as usual during alterations in Germany,' promises the sign over the bar. The Fitzroy has not fallen. But now the patrons' carefully cultivated state of artificial vitality is being threatened by something like real feeling. It will not do. Vera clears the chairs, as if to make room for the news. The wireless shouts from the top shelf by the whisky but is lost over the growing roar. It has all been over before – false endings, just like the phoney wars before the whole thing. It will not do to celebrate. And yet . . .

'I'm going out to see,' says Bobby, necking his pint and turning to the door. The gap he leaves is filled immediately. Robert sways after him. Together they step out into the unusually heavy spring afternoon.

'It's close,' says Bobby, regretting his jumper.

'Aye,' says Robert.

As they stand deciding which way to go, a young nurse runs by them, her skirt up around her knees. She's followed by two black GIs, one pausing to throw his cap in the air, the other leaping up to catch it for him. They are all headed west.

'Let us go,' says a voice from behind, which they immediately recognise. 'I've waited long enough,' says Adler, who has heard the rumours and come out looking for what family he has.

'Master,' says Robert, bowing his head ever so slightly.

'Enough with the master,' says Adler, waving his hands. 'We owe it to the dead to be among the living.'

Bobby nods.

Adler steps towards them and lowers his voice. 'We must be sure these bastards are finished.'

They make a strange sight – all three men arm in arm, Adler in between the two, leaning heavily on Robert. Progress is slow in the heat and throng. They let themselves be pulled along. That afternoon they are only one sight among many. For every person laughing there's another crying and sometimes it's hard to tell the difference. Children are hoisted up onto shoulders. The traffic gives up trying to get anywhere as the line between pavement and road dissolves. On the corner of Oxford Street they pass a woman, old enough to remember the last war, looking lost, one hand over her heart, the other gripping a string bag full of what looks like scrunched-up newspapers.

'I wish it would rain,' says Bobby.

Adler looks up at the sky: the purple of a fading bruise, the clouds low as a coffin lid. 'Hasn't it rained enough?'

Bobby instantly feels foolish. It's not that they haven't all, somehow, survived the same thing – the same bomb that had blown in the windows of their studio had done the same to

Adler upstairs. They'd helped him sweep up the glass. They'd shared their rations, pooled paints and brushes and paper, precious paper. London has taken them all in and they've watched their new home reduced to rubble then remade in fantastical forms – pyramids of house bricks sprang up on street corners where houses had been, ziggurats of bent steel held up the sky. Many times Robert and Francis would arrive in their ambulance to find only a shoe or two, one memorably still containing a foot, which Francis had wanted to take and sketch. They survived together. But Adler had actually fought. He'd signed up for the Polish army even though he knew it was doomed – gone to the front as a gunner. All this after he was forbidden from being a painter, condemned as a 'Jewish degenerate': two of his pictures were displayed as part of the *Entartete Kunst*, the most popular exhibition in German history, as Adler never tired of saying. Those pictures were missing. As were all eleven of his brothers and sisters.

It's not that they haven't all, somehow, survived the same thing. It's that the war has taken more from Adler than it has from everyone else they know.

And yet, Bobby knows, it has given them something too. Is it over? Could it ever be? What then?

Soho is impossible and impassable. Old Compton Street seethes with tarts roused from their pits.

'Gonnae be a busy shift,' Robert shouts to one venerable lady. She squints at him then blows a smoke ring in his face. He coughs and remembers a lifetime ago but she's lost in the crowd. Quentin Crisp minces by – it's a historic day when he's up before noon.

'Let's go round Leicester Square,' says Adler, steering them. Red, white and blue fills the thick air. A sailor streaks past wearing only the Union Jack; it streams behind him as he soars past two constables, who salute him and laugh. Bobby doesn't recognise the man's tattoos or anything else. Neither does Robert. They catch each other looking and laugh. Adler doesn't even bother pretending to disapprove.

The rain starts as they round the corner into Leicester Square. 'You got your wish,' says Adler.

Bobby looks round for an old paper to pop over their heads but can hardly see his own feet in the crowd. Down the rain comes, perfectly perpendicular, as if drawn by a child. Robert turns his face up towards it and tries to keep his eyes open. It's the sort of thing he only does when it's just the two of them or if they're pissed with people they love very much in that moment. Bobby opens his mouth too, remembers the taste of snow.

An umbrella opens by their heads and is instantly booed. The national anthem plays from a million wireless sets but nobody stops to sing. The cinemas empty and people who'd been sitting in the dark step blinking into another world. The pavements steam and slip so Robert reaches for Adler but there's not enough room for anybody to fall. The three of them move as one, pushing through to Piccadilly Circus where, it seems, the world is headed. Even Bobby doesn't bother trying to talk over the din.

They pass the bombsite on the corner of Haymarket – no point cleaning up until you know you won't have to do it again. Outrageous pink spires of rosebay willowherb bloom in the ruins. They spring up in craters, as if Germans dropped the seeds. Bobby loves these flowers – their colour, their courage. They wouldn't be here without the bombs. Without destruction they cannot thrive.

The trio squeeze between a bus and a lorry as they cross on to Piccadilly – ahead of them hulks the giant jelly mould built around Eros to protect his wings. People clamber up and over it, trying to free him. A sailor shins up a streetlight. Flags, flags, flags. But still no official confirmation. A rumour ripples through that the King and Queen are going to appear on the balcony at Buckingham Palace. A lipsticked Wren twirls past Bobby and he will swear for years after that it was Princess Elizabeth. As the tide turns towards the Palace the rain eases. It's almost dusk – almost blackout.

Without warning, and for the first time since September 1939, the streetlights spark into life, so suddenly the climbing sailor falls off but is caught by the crowd, reappearing instantly to a massive cheer. Above them the giant Bovril sign blazes, its glare catching the water on the pavements.

'Is it over?' Bobby asks.

'It's over,' says Robert.

What now?

PART FIVE

Westgate House, Lewes

1947–1949

'I am not sucking Virginia Woolf's cock,' says Bobby, unpacking the last box – he was sure they had more. Their bowl of buttons glints on a round table in the bay window, which gives them a view right up and down the High Street. He places Morris's nautilus shell on the mantel.

'She's dead,' says Robert. 'She's been dead years.'

'You know what I mean,' says Bobby. 'They're all the same, the Bloomsberries. This is their turf. We shall have to venerate.'

'I know,' says Robert, checking the ceiling height – Georgian but generous. 'But you wouldn't say no to Grant – he's a genius. A Scottish genius.'

'Disnae sound it,' says Bobby, carefully folding the last cardboard box, wondering if it might make a stencil for the ballet they're about to design – it would certainly speed up the work. 'He only likes lads in uniform . . .' He does some maths in his head. 'We're, what, thirty-four . . . are we still lads?'

'Compared to Grant,' says Robert. 'Anyway, we'll see if they invite us over for tea. Do you hear that?'

'Hear what?' says Bobby, alert to anything that might disturb their work – after all, that is why they accepted the invitation of sisters Frances Byng-Stamper and Caroline Lucas to make prints at their new lithography workshop a few doors down. That and the fact they were evicted from Number 77. The sisters, known locally as the Ladies, simply do not mention this fact. All Soho knows: how the old colonel across the road finally got them for 'drunken orgies', how it took two vans two weeks – no, three vans three weeks – just to shift all the empty bottles. Lewes offers respite from Acute Sohoitis.

'I can definitely hear something,' says Robert. 'Ticking.'

Bobby rushes to the timbered wall and presses his ear against it. 'Deathwatch beetle!'

'It's coming from over there,' says Robert, tracking the sound to the sash window, which he pulls up, shoving his head out into air once breathed by various English martyrs. Thomas Paine's house is next door. Anne of Cleves is close enough to borrow sugar. As Bobby sticks his head out next to Robert he feels a chill on his neck. They look left and right.

'There,' says Bobby, ever-keener. He points to a big black clock sticking out the side of a flint-faced church opposite. It has gilt roman numerals and its own little roof and is telling you the time whether you like it or not. It is always five past the last century here. Lightly strangled chimes announce the hour and Bobby slams the window shut. 'Tempus fuckit!'

Bobby finishes settling them in. He takes care to make up a bed in each of the bedrooms in case of nosy visitors – two neighbours have already 'popped by'. Bobby reserves the biggest bed for them – a brass bedstead that sparkles when Robert flicks the light switch, luxury.

'No!' Bobby yelps. He dashes to the switch and flicks it off. 'Not the big light!'

'Fine,' says Robert, sitting on the edge of the feather bed, barely denting it. That first night they both dream of clocks.

'She's awful pleased with herself,' says Bobby, coming back from fetching their messages on the High Street. He's carrying a wicker basket filled with produce from the fields and farms around. Lewes has a better larder than London.

'Who?' Robert asks, absorbed in a costume he's starting for *Donald of the Burthens*, the ballet they've been commissioned for – a project Robert declined until Bobby told him Picasso did the Ballets Russes (and showed him some overdue bills).

'Lewes,' says Bobby, taking his haul through to the kitchen, planning a big pot of soup and no fewer than three meals from the one fat chicken. An apple tree fills their backyard, its branches almost reaching both sides, the fruit just starting. He makes plans for pies.

'Aye well, she's a lot to be pleased about,' says Robert. 'It's like an actual postcard out there.'

'She is beautiful,' Bobby concedes. Last night he crossed the road and sat in the ruins of the castle, imagining battles gone by. As the shadows deepened and joined up he watched glow-worms semaphore to one another deep in the lee of the storied walls – their messages known only to each other and him. *Notice me. Love me.*

'One bomb and it would all have been gone.'

'But does every single fucking one of them have to say HOW VERY LUCKY they are to live somewhere SO VERY, VERY SPECIAL?'

Bobby brings through a half bottle of whisky.

'Bobby,' says Robert, shaking his head. 'We're here to work, you said.'

'It's only a half,' says Bobby, pointing to the sketches. 'I see you've made a start already.'

'Aye,' says Robert. 'It's no good.'

'Not yet,' says Bobby, opening the whisky. 'But it will be.' The neck of the bottle clanks against the glass as he pours.

'Clumsy,' he says, explaining away his shakes.

'Listen,' says Robert, ear towards the window and the clock. It takes several years to strike noon. 'Pour on MacDuff.'

Bobby pours them just a finger each and sets to colouring the King that Robert has conjured. After a bit he looks up at the wall.

'Robert, where's the Sutherland?'

'What Sutherland?'

'We only have the one – the Sutherland tree Watson gave us for our housewarming at 77.'

'Aye, well,' says Robert, pushing himself down into the armchair, trying to get on with reading *The Plague*. 'I don't know.'

Bobby gets up from the table and goes over to Robert, snatching the book from his hands.

'Give it back, Bobby,' says Robert. 'I was reading that.'

'You do so know,' says Bobby, putting the book behind his back. 'In ten years that picture will be a deposit on a house!'

Robert gets up slowly and puts out his hand. 'Book?'

'No,' says Bobby, pointing to the wall. 'Picture!'

Robert tries to get the book from Bobby but he spins away, falls into Robert's chair.

'Bobby, don't come the cunt, I'm not in the mood.'

'What are you in the mood for? While I'm sitting here colouring in for you? Where are all the big new ideas you promised?'

'We've been here a week—'

'So—'

'So, we're not even unpacked.'

'I've unpacked nearly everything,' says Bobby, getting up and gesturing round the room. 'And there's no Sutherland. So where is it? And we're missing half our books.' Bobby steps towards the fire, low for the afternoon. He holds the book over it.

'Fine,' says Robert, sitting back down in his chair, his anger dissipating as quickly as it arrived. 'I didn't want to tell you but—'

'But?'

Robert looks down at the floor, where the rug Bobby made from the Barras fragments has yet to flatten itself. 'You gave it away.'

'I gave what away?' Bobby laughs. 'You're the one always giving your work away.' Then he remembers something, somebody, very late one Sunday night. He tosses Robert's book back to him.

'You gave it to—'

'Who, who the fuck?' Bobby rushes over to the whisky bottle and takes a swig. 'Do you remember?'

Robert shrugs unconvincingly. 'No,' he says, recalling the pneumatic ginger lad with the ballet arse, who he later brought to life in *Lovers*. 'I don't think we ever got his name. He just came to the one party. He danced on the table and you said he was the most beautiful thing you'd ever seen and—'

'—So I gave him my one of my most beautiful things . . .'

Robert opens his book again then looks up and says, 'Don't ask about Lucian's wee sketch of me.'

'Not even dear Vanessa would risk such colours!' exclaims Frances, who is hosting them at one of her interrogatory teas at Millers Press, a few doors down. 'You have achieved so much in just a few months.'

Bobby nods and hopes this is a compliment – if their work goes off the boil they're out of another home and then what?

'I'm very pleased with the yellow,' says Bobby, pointing to a lemon that looks like it's levitating in among other equally excited fruit.

'The outline is so bold,' says Caroline, never first to speak. On the ladies' constant ups and downs the High Street, Caroline always trails behind; it reminds Bobby of Robert always walking ahead of him in Glasgow. In Soho it was safe for them to walk side by side.

'It reminds me of Mr Minton,' says Frances, finishing her sister's thought.

Bobby is about to say something then thinks of the roof over their head. For all he can see that Johnny is not, as he'd often called him, 'a mere illustrator', he does not enjoy the comparison.

'I see what you mean,' says Robert, leaning in, twisting the knife.

'Have you been out to the farmhouse yet?' Frances asks, her accent as fine as the china she serves tea in. She knows the answer very well. Half of Lewes does. They have been for tea. And they won't be back.

'We've just not had a chance,' says Bobby, gesturing at the works covering the table – dozens of designs for costumes for the ballet, three new monotypes and his own still life.

'You mustn't work too hard,' says Frances. 'There's not a pick on you, Mr Colquhoun. I'm told they do a very robust supper at . . .' she makes a show of fumbling for a name. 'The Dorset?'

This is the farmers' pub where Robert and Bobby have taken to spending every Friday, Saturday and Sunday and some Thursdays too.

'We could show you where it is,' says Caroline, over the rim of her teacup. The landlord has sent the ladies their bill and she will pay it, this time.

'Not to worry,' says Bobby. 'I try to cater at home – it's cheaper and more nutritious and there's less likelihood of—'

'Distraction?' says Frances, putting down her cup.

'Have you climbed Mount Caburn yet?' asks Caroline, changing the subject.

'It's hardly a climb, dear, says Frances. 'More a Sunday afternoon stomp.'

'Mount what?' Bobby asks. 'There's not a mountain for miles.' Unless, he thinks, we're talking about your money.

'Our own wee Ben,' says Frances, in that way that makes Robert want to punch all English people.

'A Ben?' says Robert. 'Down here?'

The steepest incline they've faced together is Garnethill, drunk, in a gale. Or the escalator at Oxford Circus. But they make a show of sighing over what the ladies think of as Scotland.

'We should go and take a look,' says Bobby.

'Aye,' says Robert.

'Lovely!' says Frances, clapping her hands. 'You can tell us all about the view!'

1 September 1947

Dear Johnny

Now Robert and I are very settled in our Sussexshire ways you must come and visit. It is all very *Mapp & Lucia* – I won't say who is who. You will not recognise our country glow! It is aggressively pretty here and the air is so fresh I worry it's actually good for us. I can breathe at last and even Robert has some colour. We hope you are well. I hear from Elizabeth that you've not been seen out much. Robert and I are very fond of you, as you know. No, our big trip to Scotland did not go as planned, I think we can all agree that. But it was not your fault, whatever was said. I was under a lot of pressure when we got back and said things I should not have. I shouldn't have thrown you out like that and I know it is not your fault either that our landlord moved us on. I see what you admire in Robert – I admire the same qualities, believe it or not. There's many nice people would share a place with you, if that is what you thought of. I'm glad you're getting on well with Lefevre – so much starts with a sailor or two! When you're next in please ask them to send along any funds we are due. We both think very fondly of you and hope you will come and visit. I'll do your eggs the way you like. The Ladies of Millers will be delighted to meet one of our posh friends and, I bet, keen to take some of your work.

All the very best, Bobby.'

'How much further?' asks Bobby, again.

'It gets further away every time you ask,' says Robert, his eyes on the hill ahead.

It is a cold clear November morning but there's hardly anybody out and about – Lewes is building up to Guy Fawkes night, the whole town meeting in secret societies to plot one night of brimstone and misrule.

'So, is it part of the South Downs?' Bobby asks, thinking about the picnic he packed: beef paste sandwiches, thick local cheese and plums from the tree over the wall behind Westgate House. He's saved a few plums to paint.

'How the fuck am I supposed to know?' Robert asks, turning to face Bobby. 'Nature is your thing.' His irritation vanishes when he sees Bobby huffing and puffing. 'This takes me back to Kildoon Hill. Remember?'

Does Bobby remember? 'We were nineteen, twenty.'

'If that,' Robert says. 'And we had no money.'

'Nothing new there,' says Bobby, catching up.

'We had no money and our lease was up and we thought Mrs Cranston was going to turf us out.'

'I was going to die,' says Bobby. 'I would have topped myself if she did.'

'Don't be daft,' says Robert, nudging Bobby then throwing an arm round his shoulder. He thinks back to being alone in the barracks – being made to empty the latrines, to carry the mail sacks, all of it. He'd imagined going out to the railway line behind barracks and putting one leg on the track. He remembers trying to work out which leg he would give to live.

'Well, we're here now,' says Robert as they start the ascent, the shadowy side of the hill still silver.

'It's not a mountain,' Bobby puffs, his hangover hitting. 'But it fucking feels like one.'

Half an hour later they think they're at the top but they're not.

'What's this?' Robert asks, stepping into a ditch that goes up to his knees.

'A fort,' says Bobby, wishing they'd brought some water. 'Like Kildoon. It'll be Roman or earlier.' He goes on ahead, conquering the top and stands there beckoning to Robert: the frosted blanket of Sussex spread before them, bare fields quilting all the way to the horizon where the sea somehow hangs above it all.

'Some view eh?' says Robert, putting his arm around him.

'Not bad,' says Bobby, checking around. 'For England.'

And they kiss.

February 1948

'Have no fear for your virginity, girls,' says Robert, sweeping his arm in what he hopes is a courtly fashion, music blaring behind him. The two fourteen-year-old girls look distinctly unsure. They have been dared to knock on the door at Westgate House, home of thrilling rumour. They peer past the swaying Scotsman and glimpse men waltzing past and one shrieks, 'Save me, Robert!' The Scots have been the talk of the town since they arrived over a year ago. Every weekend, the train from London brings fresh guests who go through the doors and don't come out till Monday. Few ladies visit.

'We're not heating the street,' says Robert, slamming the door then spinning back in to tonight's party. He stands on an unopened envelope in among the bills, on handmade paper with the legend 'Charleston' calligraphed on the back.

They're celebrating finishing all the designs for *Donald of the Burthens*. Every surface in Westgate House is covered with images of a megalithic Scotland – as far from a shortbread tin as possible. Strictly no tartan. Impassive rocks and knowing mountains slide onto the floor where Donald the woodcutter makes a deal with Death to give him a comfortable, meaningful life as a doctor in exchange for his soul. Robert is dimly aware he's knocked some papers off a table as he fumbles for the banister but is sure Bobby will have made copies.

'Colquhoun,' sing-songs Bobby from a bedroom upstairs,

savouring each syllable. 'Wait till you see the size of this!'

Now who is up there? Is Johnny back? Is that thick-thighed butcher giving Bobby extra again? Are they finally doing Duncan Grant a favour? Or another button for the bowl?

'I'm coming!'

June 1948

Dear Auntie Maggie,

I've had a wee drink. A couple of wee drinks. Was it you that got my mother to my Final Show? Was that your rabbit coat? Was it even her? We're famous, you know? Am I famous in Maybole? Do you remember when you stood on the step and told everybody I was gonnae beat Burns? I've still got the boots you gave me – I resoled them a hundred times. Robert says I'll be buried in them. He's sleeping it off up the stairs. I need to fork this place over before I go up. So long as I'm with him I don't care. I wish you could meet him but I won't ever be coming home, I don't think. We went up to see his folks last year and I was going to come and see you. You were just up the road and I was desperate to see Jessie's grave – God forgive me, I've still not been, I can't. But we had to come back. We live in Lewes now – it's like an English village from a play nobody in Glasgow would go and see. We're 'the talk of the wash-house'. It's nice talking to you like this. I've painted you – not you, I mean I think of you when I'm painting so you're in lots of my pictures. I remember you waiting for me after my big interview. I hope I've not let you down. I miss you, Auntie Maggie.

I love you. Never forget where you come fae, you said. I've not but I can never come back, can I? I'm away to burn this now.

But I will always be, Your Bobby. x

26 December 1949

Dearest Peter,

Merry Christmas! It is very cold here in Lewes and the whole place is snowed in so this letter might never reach you. I'll try and catch a reindeer to wing it to you. We hear you have finally been reunited with your pictures in Paris and hope that you can bring at least one Picasso to show us when we're back in London. We will be up for the ballet – we hope! We have completed all the work but are not to be paid until, and unless, it is put on! I bet Picasso wasn't on sale or return! The music is good and the story timeless and we are lucky Scotland continues to be just about fashionable. Speaking of which, and it is so difficult to ask a friend who has been so generous already, could you advance us another £100? When Covent Garden pay us, we can repay you. Or we can advance you some of the prints we have been working on here? Making the ballet deadline has taken a lot from Robert and it has taken a lot from me to keep him on the page. He is now working on new prints for the Ladies of Millers, drawing these wild-looking horses and fearsome owls, all so immediate and just straight from him. The monotype technique he is developing means he has to work fast – painting onto glass and then making the one and only print before it all dries. So, the images are very instinctual, which I think you will like. I am mostly taken up with supporting Robert but I have got two pictures of my own, big ones, in Lefevre's and they say they are hopeful as people are buying new pictures for all the new houses going up. Yes, still life, but the colour is rare I think and really saying something. We had hoped to visit New York and see our pictures there but nothing more has yet come of Mr Barr's visit, although Francis writes to say he might go under his own steam (easy now since everybody is buying him up). We have been here for nearly two years now – we do wish you had been able to find time to visit. Dicky and Dennis are v fond of Lewes and stop by on the way to the opera at Glyndebourne. Dear Elizabeth has been down a lot on account of how much closer Sussex is than Suffolk – we still cannot imagine the Queen of Bohemia out there in the sticks but maybe it gives her peace from George? We have, as you doubtless know, been to Charleston just the once. As with the stories of our departure from Number 77, that tale is wildly exaggerated – we have enemies, of course, do not think we don't. Our one and only visit to the farmhouse was, like the Bloomsberries, simultaneously more boring and more interesting than you can imagine. Old Grant's work fair lights the place up. And the garden is marvellous. But the kitchen is like a bomb hit the Barras after bouncing through a paintworks (get someone from Glasgow to tell you what the Barras is). My dear old mother would be at it with bleach. I will say this: one bit of the story is true. I did write a 'thank you' to Johnny Minton for securing us the invitation 'to tea with the driest cunts imaginable' and a dry bread and butter note to Vanessa thanking her for her 'warm hospitality'. And I did, in my haste to be polite, confuse the two envelopes. But all the rest is made up. I hope to hear from you about the loan but we will quite understand if you cannot extend further kindness to us, you have already done so much – I would still be freezing in Glasgow if it wasn't for you. It's a lifetime since our lunch at the Café Royal. And Robert would be . . . well, it doesn't bear thinking about. We begin to feel we have maybe had the best of what Lewes has to offer and sense the Ladies of Millers are keen to refresh their printing experiment with new artists. This suits us fine. Lately we find we are exhausted by the exoticism of Sussex village life – I'm even starting to write like one of them! Maybe it is the ballet, but I dream of mountains – real mountains, the kind you can die on. Thank you for all your help. See you in London, if not sooner. Let us hope for a kinder year.

Yours, always, Bobby.

28 December 1949

Dear Johnny,

I hear you're selling well these days! Thank you for the early copy of *A Book of Mediterranean Food*. I'm sure it will do well. It is delicious and your sailors are too – Robert has noted the resemblance, which isn't helping his ego. We have finished our ballet and will take you to go and see it when it's on. I hate to ask, because you've always been so generous to the pair of us, but could you advance us a few pounds against our next money from Lefevre? The ballet won't pay until the first pirouette. I promise to pay you back when next we see you. I'm sorry you never got down to visit us here. Give our love to Lucian and Francis if you see them. Tell Muriel she's an old cunt, from me.

All love, Bobby.

30 December 1949

Dear Johnny,

I hope the arrival of a letter from me doesn't knock you off your perch. Bobby has reminded me that he is not my secretary and that our friends might appreciate a fresh voice. I never write so you'll have to excuse my scrawl. I hope you are looking after yourself. I saw your notices in *Horizon* and you deserve every good word. As artists it is our job to free ourselves from what the world expects of us and to understand who we really are – Adler taught me that. Do you remember how he was always around the place? Almost as much as you. I miss him. This year has been hard in lots of ways but losing him was just cruel. He beat the Nazis and then to just drop dead like that. I looked for you at the funeral. It took us all day to get to Hertfordshire from here. I still don't know who paid for his headstone because he had nobody left but us and we've got nothing. Was it you? It's the kind of thing you would do. I'd never been to a Jewish funeral. Something about it, the bits I didn't understand, made it alright for people to cry. Half of Soho was there – the local pubs will have had a rare day. I didn't see you and I hear you've not been out much lately but you hear all sorts. I hope it's just because you couldn't get away from the College. I wonder, do they need any more lecturers?

I was thinking I could teach printmaking and it would leave me enough time to get on with my own work as well. Do you think you could put in a word for me? We – I – hope to see you in the new year.

All the very best, your Robert.

PART SIX

Tilty Mill, Essex

1950–1954

'Did yous no see the big aeroplane?' Bobby rushes to the kitchen window and points to the distant hill. The Barker children follow – there are four of them now – Georgina and Christopher leading, Bashie and little Rosie trailing.

'No,' says Christopher, old enough to remember planes as a source of terror. 'What was it?'

'It was a cargo plane,' says Bobby. 'It went down just over the hill. And do you know what it had on it?'

Books, thinks Georgina. *Elephants*, thinks Bashie. Rosie pushes four fingers in her mouth. 'What?' Christopher asks.

'Chocolate!' Bobby announces. 'Thousands of rations!'

Bashie and Rosie squeal with delight.

Bobby goes on, 'It said *Cadbury's* all down the side in big purple letters!'

Christopher turns back to the window. He is not so easily taken in. 'But won't all the chocolate have melted, in the crash?'

'Only one way to find out . . .'

As the children dash for the door Bobby hands them each a brown paper bag containing an apple and a cheese sandwich, like the ones his mother used to make for him.

'Save me some!' he says, as they fly out into the yard, scattering some little white hens. 'And don't be late back for your dinner!'

There is not much peace at Tilty Mill. So, some days – like today – Bobby has to manufacture it. Robert can, as ever, work in pandemonium, but Bobby has always needed quiet: no music, no Blitz, no snoring remnants of the night before. Recently, Bobby has seriously considered killing Robert for breathing noisily. He doesn't think he had such thoughts in their attic. That was just one room as well but their room here feels different. Then it was more, now it is less. Maybe his need for peace comes from a deeper time, from when he sat on his hill above Maybole drawing every living thing he could see and the imagined centurions that had once occupied the high ground. If he can recapture that stillness – if – then he might paint all day again, forget the clock, forget money, forget this trendy American pish everybody says is next.

The village of Tilty is England as imagined by somebody from the colonies, which is exactly why Dear Elizabeth pounced on the sublet from the supposedly Scottish poet Ruthven Todd who had originally taken it after his flat in Bloomsbury was bombed only to find New York life more tempting. Tilty isn't so much a village as a handful of houses thrown like dice along the backroad between Dunmow and Stansted. The house is a mile from the nearest road through dark old woods, which lead to the meadow holding the house, a church and an actual water mill. Even on the sunniest days, the post-mistress whistles loudly as she wheels along the long-shaded lane to meet Bobby, who is always dancing by the gate in hopes of a fiver in answer to one of his many missives.

Elizabeth took Tilty Mill despite its distance from the Soho offices of *House & Garden*, where she works while dreaming of proper writing. She's charmed by the absence of electricity. Nobody else is. Antique oil lamps keep the country nights at bay. Quickly, she realised commuting daily was deadly. She needed a nanny. Or two. Bobby said they were tiring of Lewes and needed an even quieter place to work, so that was that.

She has always loved them – especially Bobby. And her children love them – the child in Bobby is always ready for games. It's perfect. It's madness. It just is.

Bobby spends most days sweating over the double-fronted cast-iron stove, which stands on an island of greening copper in the middle of the kitchen – sometimes he catches Dylan on the wireless, his old friend talking to him from another room. Bobby pumps water into the sink from a well beneath the house. Upstairs is a deep enamelled bath, deep enough for all the children at once when they first moved here, what, three years ago? From one window stretches a meadow lit by buttercups in the summers that come late to this corner of Essex, nearly Suffolk. From the other window marches a stretch of ruined abbey wall lending the whole place its ancient air.

The abbey's mill still runs. It's worked by Fred – also here since before the Reformation. He also does the bloody bit of the hen-keeping neither Bobby nor Robert can bear. Fred never comes near the house. His wordless diligence reminds them of the men back home. A church keeps watch over all, as it has done since 1220, according to marks Bobby finds over the door.

Elizabeth gives them food and board – Robert protests that they will only accept money for art, not friendship, which is what Tilty is to them. So, Bobby, already a wife to Robert, becomes mother to Elizabeth's four children with George.

Every Monday morning, Elizabeth leaves long before the children wake. She catches the first train to town, where she works all week, writing a letter or two if she gets time. After dinner Bobby and Robert take turns reading her letters out loud, doing their mother's voice and sometimes Bobby puts on one of her headscarves. After the first two years here, when all the children are at the nearby school, the days are quieter but never free. Bobby is picking up clothes, putting away toys and howking up tatties from the patch he tends behind the mill. All with a hangover. They never touch a drink until the last wee one is down. They are scrupulous about it. Until they're not.

They are supposed to paint in the slumping slatted shed at the bottom of the garden – Elizabeth warned the children they must never go there because artists must never be disturbed. Robert has rigged one whole wall with glass from old greenhouse windows and it's covered by a shutter he lifts with care. Inside is just one easel – a simple square of plywood, the edges a halo of marks that have veered off. Some nights Robert sleeps out here, safe from Bobby's bombs.

Right now, Robert is finishing his monumental *Figures in a Farmyard* – a redhaired woman (very like Elizabeth), a broken old man and a demonic snorting pig. He's spread his sketches everywhere. It's for a new show at the Tate of One Hundred Pictures to mark the coronation of the other Elizabeth. Bobby is, once again, determined to make a break from things, from all his fruits and vegetables and objects – he feels buried alive by them. Domesticity is dragging him down – colanders draining his very essence. So, he's started painting *Two Women* and needs peace to get on.

Bobby has gone big, as if size will make up for the absence of works in recent years. The two women are starting to emerge. As he paints, Bobby thinks about the girls either side of him at Lees, their swift fingers, even faster than their patter. Where are they now? He gives the woman on the left tar hair, dark as his mother's. Before he knows it, he's drawn in a sewing machine. He resents it and thinks about covering it but can't bear to start again. So she stands over her sewing machine and now she's being fed black and blue cloth by the younger blonde on the right. Each woman has black sockets for eyes, like a Greek mask but they are not tragedy or comedy, not mournful or mirthful – they are simply busy helping one another. They are now *Two Women Sewing*.

Bobby is fretting over their hands when the kitchen door bursts open.

'No plane!' says Christopher, furious, screwing up his empty lunch bag and throwing it on the floor. Georgina arrives behind him, trailing Bashie and Rosie, both tearful. Night creeps in the open door.

'Where have yous been?' says Bobby, drying his brush on a rag. He notices the day has gone. 'It's dark.'

'We know,' says Christopher, lip trembling. 'It was getting darker all the way home.' Rosie starts to cry.

'You're late for your—' Bobby is about to say dinner when he realises he's not even started it; he's been lost in his work at last, even resisted checking on Robert.

'This time I'm telling,' says Georgina, lifting Rosie.

'Ah no,' says Bobby. 'Don't bother yer mum. There now, there, there. Did you find the plane?'

'No,' says Christopher, resenting the painting on the table where their dinner should be.

'No?' says Bobby, lifting the lid from the bread bin. 'But, you see, there was a plane, I promise, and it must have had its cargo doors open because I went out in the yard and—'

He pops his hand in the bread bin like it's a magic hat. 'See what I found!'

He flourishes four bars of royal purple and all is forgiven, almost.

12 December 1951

It's their birthday month and Christmas is around the corner but none of this is as exciting as the long-awaited premiere of *their* ballet (and the pay day to follow).

The orchestra is finishing tuning as the Roberts tumble into the Royal Opera House. They almost fall into a real Christmas tree, nearly as big as the ones that have turned Trafalgar Square into a living room for London since the war. Jacketed staff turn to the commotion, having already started to reclaim the place the moment the final audience member made their way through and now here are these two . . . what? Tramps?

'Has it started?' Robert asks the nearest steward, who lifts his wrist so slowly Bobby fears the show will start by the time he's looked at it, before pushing back a white glove, glancing down and announcing, '7.26 p.m.' A pause to look them up and down. 'Sir'.

'Madam to you,' Bobby snaps, straightening Robert's lapels, guessing a gesture like this is safe at a ballet. Bobby knows queens like this, give a wee squirt a uniform and it gives them the authority they lack everywhere else. Little Miss Hitler.

The steward steps in front of them. 'Tickets?' Flutes trill through the glass doors ahead. Chatter soars expectantly – this is a first night of a new ballet with the delicious potential for triumph or catastrophe. *Donald of the Burthens* is about to leap into the world: Choreography by the legendary Massine, Original Score by Ian Whyte, Set & Costumes by Acclaimed Artists Colquhoun

& MacBryde, in crumpled suits and stinking from a brief victory lap at Muriel's.

'Tickets?'

Robert pats the pockets of his borrowed jacket. He produces their tickets back to Tilty. Dancers flutter in the wings.

'Got them!' Bobby shouts, whipping a pair from his inside pocket like a blade. The steward takes them very slowly.

'Hold them up to the light,' says Bobby.

'This is our show, by the way,' says Robert.

'An excellent choice, sir,' says the steward, noting Robert's height then the shadows under his eyes, his trembling hands, decides he can probably throw him out after all.

'No, it's *our* show,' says Bobby. 'We designed it.'

Bobby storms over to the poster and jabs their names. 'I am MacBryde,' he says, flicking his hair from his face, a gesture more effective when his hair was thicker. 'And this is Colquhoun.'

'And I'm the Queen of Sheba,' mutters the steward, opening one door for this pair of Scotch chancers. They pass in a reek of whisky, leaking from their pores with a tang of something else – he's woken up in enough boarding house rooms to detect desperation.

'Enjoy your opening night,' he says, letting the door swing shut.

Nobody turns as they blink into the plush dark.

Disappointingly, the spotlight does not swing on to them. It's too late to find their seats as the lights come up on stage. Their stage. This is not the first time they've seen it – they've been in during rehearsals to make adjustments, the producer's frown deepening with every change. The giant streak of blue running from top right to the peak at the centre of the stage is now the exact shade of the lightest patch you can only glimpse in the sky over Maybole at midnight in late June but try explaining that to somebody who's never been north of Hendon. *It will do*, Robert nods. In the dark, Bobby lays his head on Robert's shoulder and Robert lets it rest there.

'We're geniuses,' says Bobby. 'Pure geniuses.'

They look around for Massine. He is trembling in the cheapest seats, far from where anyone will expect him. He's wedged between students, one already taking notes. Massine will find Whyte after – together they will read between the lines of the responses. 'You've done it!' from his agent means certain death. The only thing worse is: 'I've never seen anything like it!' Massine wonders if the Roberts will turn up in kilts – they're always easy to spot because they're always together and always with people, social satellites pulled into their irresistible orbit. He admits to being charmed – not charmed, because they are direct to the point of rude, especially with each other . . . no, not charmed. Warmed. They are sincere. He has only ever seen them sober.

Donald of the Burthens is based on an old Scottish tale, about a woodcutter who dreams of becoming a doctor and saving people so he makes a pact with Death, who elevates him on the condition he never sings or prays and if he does . . . The sets and costumes in front of them represent over 250 drawings worked on together. They tweaked Adler's carbon transfer technique to save time and paper, recolouring each design over and over until they were happy.

Their first set is a stylised mountain with cottages at its foot. The thatched roofs are fairytale-like and the boards of the cottages at this scale are like big books laid on their sides; the family Bible, thinks Bobby. Their mountain is megalithic. There is not a strip of tartan – there are kilts, of course, but of heather and moss and the forest that will be cleared before the people are too.

Bobby and Robert stand at the back, by the doors, watching the audience wait. The conductor stands up and, after polite applause, turns and taps the stand, once, twice, thrice and up spring the strings and away we go.

There's no interval – the whole thing flies by, costumes whirling, colours flashing . . . all too soon Donald must dance with Death – being played, daringly, by a woman. 'Listen,' says Bobby, as if Robert can do anything else. Strings and flutes blaze a path and then a rumble of brass before an unpromising wheeze swells up and out and then the skirl of pipes, scattering air, summoning Death. Bagpipes have never been heard in the Royal Opera House before. Robert gives Bobby an arm and they whirl, not stopping for tuts or *well I never*s, spinning as the pipes soar, panting for breath, beating Death herself.

'We did it!' Bobby shouts, as the audience rises. 'Encore!' The dancers fly back on and roses bloom between their satin feet. As the conductor takes a bow, Bobby admires the stage – they have made a world and everything in it . . . he reaches for Robert's hand, it's cold.

'You're pale,' says Bobby. 'Peely-wally.'

'Drink,' says Robert, turning to the doors.

They ride the tide into the foyer. Bobby raids an ashtray and again thanks the rich for their wastefulness as he retrieves two smokeable dowts, one smeared with lipstick.

A tray of champagne floats by and Bobby frees a glass. 'To us,' he says toasting Robert then offering it to him.

'Where's Massine?' gasps Robert, waving the glass away then patting his pockets frantically. The wage that's coming has already been spread generously round Soho.

Robert sways.

'When did you last eat?' Bobby props him up. A tray of tiny sandwiches goes by and Bobby grabs a handful.

'That's it,' says their nemesis steward, grabbing at Bobby's hands. The sandwiches smoosh between their fingers and fall to the floor, cucumber rings and egg yolk. Bobby reaches down.

'Out!' the steward hisses. Half of London is already looking.

'Hands off him!' Robert swings a fist, momentum nearly pulling him over. Bobby only just catches him and they make for the revolving door, the steward right behind them.

Mobbed by admirers, Massine turns towards a fuss but it's already receding.

'What was that?' he asks a pleased-looking steward.

'Just some chancers, sir. Apologies.'

★

The bagpipes delight the critics. The ballet is a hit. It's staged again in the spring, but they can't afford to get into London to see it. Then, despite promises to the contrary, Covent Garden tours it no further. No more royalties.

'They've done Scotch now,' Robert rants, ripping up the letter. 'I should never have let you convince me. I could have done umpteen pictures in that time, real pictures!'

'Could!' hisses Bobby. 'And shhh.'

'Or what?'

'You'll wake the wee ones.'

Robert throws the letter in the fire. They are running out of bridges to burn and driving each other mad, madder. He combs his hair to hide the fact it's thinning, tells himself he looks wolfish when he knows fine well he wouldn't turn up on his mother's doorstep looking like this. He lights a cigarette, curses his shaking hand.

Bobby puts on the gramophone, hoping to drown out what he knows is coming. Christopher is listening at the top of the stairs. He loves the Roberts and hates the Roberts but never tells on them. Delia Murphy begins to sing – Bobby's favourite, he croons to 'Three Lovely Lasses from Banyon', performing the final line '. . . and I shall be dressed like a queen.'

Christopher hears a glass smash against a wall.

'It'll be me that cleans it up,' Bobby shouts. 'Muggins!'

'You love it. The only thing you love more is going on a-fucking-bout it.'

'Pres-byt-erian!' Bobby howls. 'You want her. Admit it!'

'Want who?'

'Who wrote this?' Bobby produces a letter from his back pocket.

'That's not for you,' says Robert, snatching at it.

'Oh, I know, says Bobby. *Dearest Robert, I can give you what you need.*' Bobby minces to the music, turns it up, lifts one of Elizabeth's headscarves and does a deranged dance of the seven veils. 'Is this what you want? A wee lady wife, respecta-fucking-bility?'

'A minute's fucking peace!'

'Or do you want me to off myself?' says Bobby, kicking around for a bit of the broken glass. 'Give you all the peace you want, eh?'

Robert sits back and watches. 'You're just jealous.'

'Of what? Of her, whoever she is?'

'Of me.'

'You! Who saw you in the first place? Who got you out the fucking army? Who knocks all the right doors? Who writes all the letters? Who chases the money and keeps the house going while you fuck off to your shed all day with our bottle? Eh? Muggins – that's fucking who!'

'You love it,' Robert roars. 'When did you last pick up a brush?'

'A sweeping brush, this morning.'

'I'm not stopping you working.'

'The ballet was as much me as you.'

'Aye, you did all the colouring in.'

'Ya bastard!'

Christopher flinches as another glass smashes – this one is older than the house and will be missed when the landlord finally returns from New York prompted by rumours.

They pace around the couch, need something to keep them apart.

'They would have been black and white if it was up to you,' says Bobby. 'You were fucked the whole time we were in Lewes.'

Robert stops in his tracks. 'I was grieving.'

'For your talent? For your careeeeeer?'

Robert pauses. 'For Adler.'

'He would be ashamed of you!' says Bobby, brandishing the letter again.

Robert launches himself at Bobby. 'Ya cunt!'

Christopher hears the back door slam twice in quick succession. He runs to his bedroom window and creaks it open, watches Robert run after Bobby who is waving a letter, white in the night.

'End it!' screams Bobby, his words filling the garden and spilling out in the meadow. 'Whoever she is. End it. Or I will!'

'You'll do what?' Robert spits, still trying to get the letter. Ever nimbler, even plastered, Bobby dances away. 'Give me that!'

'A man I could have understood – we've always given each other our freedom, I let you have your thing with Johnny, but some rich bitch? Everybody says I should have left you.'

'Everybody who?'

'Stopped propping you up!'

They face each other a few feet apart, Bobby right by the shed. A match dances to life in front of Bobby briefly, illuminating his face.

'What are you doing?' Robert asks, already knowing.

'Ending it for you,' says Bobby, dropping the burning letter.

The flames find the dried straw insulating the buckling corner of Robert's shed, a trick from his father's aviary. 'My work,' he howls.

Bobby watches the flames take hold: so much unexpected green in fire.

'Bastard!' Robert shouts, dragging the door open.

Now Bobby moves. 'No! Robert, don't!'

Robert disappears into the smoke. Bobby is seized with coughing. He staggers back into the house to call the fire brigade but he started this, it's all his fault. He runs into their room and grabs his coat. The pockets are empty. Money, he'll need money. He grabs the nautilus, sole survivor of all their flits, and runs out the front door, watched by Christopher who is already dialling 999.

'I've killed him,' says Bobby.

'Again?' Muriel sighs, taking down her crisis whisky.

A posh boy who, once upon a time, Bobby would have refused, gets up from the bar and seeks the furthest corner, dripping disdain and Chanel.

Muriel pours three fingers.

Bobby drains the glass.

Muriel pours more in the hopes of a story. It's been a quiet night. Bobby obliges: an unsigned letter from some scarlet woman, a fight, a fire.

'Not a vision of loveliness,' says Muriel, putting back the whisky. Bobby catches himself in the bar mirror, soot kisses his face, white where he's been crying, his eyes red-raw.

'Vada the state of you,' says Muriel, pointing towards the loo. 'Pop and have a touch up.'

'Robert. I've killed Robert.'

'Yes, poppet,' says Muriel, shaking her head. How many times has one killed the other?

The phone rings but Muriel ignores it. More ringing. 'It might be the police,' says Bobby, wondering where to run to next.

'They're too busy with poor old Montague and his castle full of bumboys,' says Muriel. 'Or snaring Sister Gielgud at the cottages.'

Ring, ring, ring.

'Lily fucking Law,' says Muriel, nearly ripping the phone off the wall. 'What?!'

The look on her face tells Bobby he was right. He tries to stand, checks he still has the nautilus; he's going to sell it for ferry fare to France. He won't fuck about at Newhaven like Oscar. He's going. He's got to go.

Muriel lays the receiver down with a gentleness never seen before or since. She lifts a champagne glass and dings it with an olive fork. The bar stops.

'Dylan Thomas has died,' Muriel announces. 'In New fucking York.'

Soho mourns all night. The story of Dylan leaving the manuscript for *Under Milk Wood* in the Admiral Duncan or the Swiss or the French grows wilder with every telling. Muriel Belcher, who was first to hear, had apparently announced it by saying, 'Death has a dominion after all.' She said it in Welsh. No, she definitely said, 'Fuck going gently into that good night!' Bobby hears all the stories on a circuit from the Fitzroy, where a black cloth hangs over the door, to the Wheatsheaf, where an eisteddfod is in full swing. He stands hungry in front of the Golden Cockerel, closed for the night, empty but for two boys sitting at the back. He squints through the glass, presses his face against the window, misting the pane with whisky. The boys are gone.

Bobby wheels down Portobello Road clutching the nautilus. *Where are all our beautiful things? Where is our bowl of buttons – one from each of the beautiful men before we stopped counting? The pictures from pals – Francis and Johnny and Lucian? Our coffee pot without the lid?*

The traders are setting up already, whistling as they push barrows to time-honoured places with no respect for the hour. The not-quite-morning air fills with the smell of bacon and coffee – Bobby's stomach turns. He heads for the nearest stall.

'What can you give me for this? Bobby asks, holding out his one remaining treasure.

The stallholder turns. He pauses. 'I wondered when you'd turn up.'

Bobby stands there, noting the nautilus blush as it catches the new sun.

'Seen a ghost?' the man says.

The memory unspools: shells crunching underfoot, red on white, dark on dark – one arm escaping, tattooed with a pair of crossed hammers.

'Morris?'

'We thought you were dead,' says Bobby, still not sure this isn't a whisky hallucination.

'I nearly was,' says Morris. 'It was Tam you saw, God rest him.'

They're sitting in the market café drinking hot sweet tea, their mugs leaving moon-rings on red Formica. The nautilus glows on the table between them. They slip into the comfortable accents of a shared past.

'Tam,' says Bobby, remembering Morris's man.

'Aye, says Morris. 'What a man.'

Out pours the story – a variation on a theme they've heard a hundred times. No witnesses. No charges. No justice.

'We thought he was you,' says Bobby. 'We just ran.'

'Never look back. I taught you that.'

'Is that what you've done?'

'I landed in London afore yous,' Morris smiles. 'Seen yous in all the papers.'

'How come you didn't tell us?'

Morris pauses. He considers the man slumped opposite, older than his years, so much sadder than the lad he found in the Barras. 'And who would you have told?'

Bobby wishes this was worth arguing with. 'So the polis never caught them?'

'Him. I know who it was. No, course they never. But I will.'

'How?' Bobby asks, then wishes he'd not. He finishes his tea, grateful for the sugars. 'Wait till I tell Robert.'

'Where is he then?' Morris peeks under their table. 'You couldnae see daylight between the pair of yous in Glasgow.'

Bobby tries to answer but can't. The letter, the fight, the fire, all of it.

'How much were you wanting for this then?' Morris asks, pointing to the shell and reaching into his pocket.

'No,' says Bobby. 'Don't. We thought you were – I wasn't stealing. I just grabbed the first thing – something to mind you.'

Morris counts cash onto the table: 'Five pounds? Ten? Fifteen?'

'Morris, no, don't.' Bobby pushes the notes away.

'I need to go and run my stall,' says Morris. 'Or I will end up deid.' He gets up, leaving the shell and the money on the table. 'I'll come and get you when I'm done, make you something to eat and you can tell me all about it. Aye?'

Bobby nods.

Morris knows fine well Bobby won't be there when he gets back. Sure enough, he's not. And neither is his money. But the nautilus is still there. Morris picks up the shell, puts it to his ear and waits for it to whisper what he already knows.

PART SEVEN

No Fixed Abode

30 December 1955

Old times are back at the French. Bobby is up on a table belting out some Burns, as invented as all the rest and just as sincere. As his eyes mist up he falls forward, hoping somebody will catch him and they do and he and this stranger do a mad waltz. Drink flows and talk with it. Johnny makes one of his increasingly rare appearances, reprising his demented jig, like a puppet being electrocuted. Lucian smooths with some blond. Francis out-glows his rouge. Nobody knows the time and why would you care. At one point the whole bar floats up into the night sky. Nobody is leaving. Nobody wants to. But last orders are always called.

Francis frogs into a waiting cab shouting, 'Café de Paris', and birls off before anybody can join him, clearly on a mission.

Johnny sags as if his strings are cut. 'Home,' he says, throwing an arm around Robert.

'No,' slurs Robert, not unkindly. 'You don't stay there any more.'

Johnny sways and squints.

'Neither do we,' says Bobby, producing a precious bottle from inside his jacket. 'Shhh,' he pats it like a baby. 'Fae behind the bar!'

'Where then?' Johnny asks, like a child that's just woken up.

'Home,' says Robert, wondering where home will be tonight.

Johnny hails a taxi and as it pulls up he starts to sing, 'Water, water wildflower, growing up so high!'

Bobby catches the tune – an echo from a party past – and joins in. 'We are all children and we all must—'

'Die!' Johnny shouts, as the taxi stops. He gets in and is gone.

'Except Johnny Minton,' Robert shouts at the fading brake lights, remembering the end of the song. 'Fairest of them all!'

Bobby holds up his bottle. Now it's just him, Robert, Anthony Cronin and his girlfriend Thérèse.

'Fancy a wee party?' Bobby asks.

'Where else are they going to go?' Anthony pleads with Thérèse as they go down into Tottenham Court Road Tube. 'It's nearly New Year. They've not got a roof, they're barred from—'

'—Everywhere. For good reason,' says Thérèse, not bothering to be quiet.

Anthony remembers the day *Horizon* finally bought a poem – opening the note signed by Cyril Connolly himself! All because of a word from MacBryde and a nod from Colquhoun. His success was their success and they'd toasted their fellow Celt at a Sunday Salon – beef, champagne, the works! Everybody was there and they all made him feel like this was always going to happen. Dylan Thomas had actually nodded at him. Now, the Golden Boys of Bond Street are broke, broken. He's watched – they all have – MacBryde's puckishness give way to puffy and Colquhoun's wolfishness to bone. Neither could run for a bus, even if they had the fare. There's a smell, too. Fame to infamy. Supposedly they burned down Elizabeth Smart's house. They're banned from Lewes. No gallery will touch them. They have no canvas now, no paints, no studio, no home that anybody knows. Yet they're still so obviously and completely obsessed with each other that they make you want to see what they see, to sit close around the embers of a love that still burns far brighter than most and certainly more than their prospects.

'Ah want ma hole!' Robert roars, to nobody and everybody, as the escalator pulls them down.

There are no passing Scots to translate but the general thrust is clear. Robert has reached that stage of drunk. Anthony had forgotten the transformation of Robert deep in whisky, complete and total and always completely forgotten next day. But he's said yes now.

Bobby makes sure not to fall – he holds the rest of their night in the bottle stuffed up his jacket, the promise of continued company and a bed for a night or two. Thérèse stands far ahead – Cronin braces for later.

The changing of trains to Wembley is a cold eternity. Bobby cradles their bottle in a brown paper bag carefully unfolded from his pocket, saved since when for who knows what. He sings it a lullaby: 'Three Lovely Lasses from Banyon.' Robert smokes and paces the platform to hurry their train and it works because soon they're staggering out of Wembley Station – the only Soho survivors this far out. Their fellow passengers hurry by and don't look back.

'Fuck yous all!' shouts Robert, giving them two fingers. Bobby does the same. Tragedy strikes. They all watch as the bottle slides out from under Bobby's jacket and straight down between his legs like some miracle birth. The brown paper bag bleeds in the yellow streetlight.

'No!' wails Bobby, hunkering down, reaching for the shards.

Robert staggers over. He kicks the broken glass then helps Bobby up.

It is a long trudge back to Cronin's, a ground floor flat in a Victorian semi, their landlady upstairs. Robert and Bobby bounce into hedges and startle cats. Thérèse turns and says, bright and false as electric light, 'When we get back I'll make some tea. You look like you could do with a sandwich. I've got some ham.'

'Ham?' says Robert, putting his hands around his neck. He looks like he's been offered a choice between hemlock and arsenic.

The rain starts.

Their spirits are even damper than their coats as they finally bundle through the front door and in through the door to Cronin's flat, falling straight into a little living room, which overlooks the front garden. Thérèse shushes them as shoes clatter off – their landlady lives above in Pooterish propriety but thinks herself Bohemian for letting rooms to 'the young poet'. He once read her something and she said, 'why doesn't it rhyme?' It was the poem Bobby had placed at *Horizon* – how long ago? Ten years. Just ten.

The Roberts collapse into each other on the couch and Cronin takes the armchair while Thérèse bothers mugs in the kitchen. The gas meter hisses into life.

'Nae tea,' slurs Robert.

'I'll take one, hen,' says Bobby, always thirsty, even this far gone.

Now there's no bottle there's no point. The French feels a lifetime ago. The living room is very small and very brown. Francis will be in his rococo nest at the Café Royal, a brute on one side and a princess on the other, his gilded gutter. Lucian will be painting his blond until dawn. Where is Johnny?

Thérèse pops out of the kitchen with a mug of tea for Bobby, repeating the lie all women know, 'It's no trouble.'

'Bed it is then,' says Cronin, twirling Thérèse as if they're at a Viennese ball. He hopes to leave some cheer in the room for their guests. 'See you in the morning,' he says, not wanting to draw attention to sleeping arrangements they all know very well. Outside, the rain tips into a storm, lashing the windows.

'Aye,' says Bobby. 'Thank yous for hospitality.'

He nudges Robert. 'Aye, thanks. You soon find out who your real friends are.'

They start at about two.

Cronin's eyes pop open – he's feels around by the side of the bed for the poker then remembers the Roberts in the living room.

'You don't love me,' Bobby wails. 'You never loved me, not like I loved you.'

Nothing from Robert, not that Cronin can hear.

Bobby, louder: 'You should have gone away wi yer ladyfriend, yer rich lady, and she could put up wi all yer shite!'

A body thumps the adjoining wall.

Cronin sits up. Thérèse snuffles.

'Yer a wash-oot!' shouts Bobby, determined to get a rise. 'A dud! And you've dragged me down—'

'—Ya wee cunt!'

And they're off!

'Fuck you, Bobby MacBryde!'

'How you gonnae dae that eh? You cannae even get it up!'

As one of their two plywood dining chairs hits the wall, Cronin runs through, belting his dressing gown. The living room is blitzed, blankets and pillows everywhere and the couch stripped. The standard lamp is missing its shade. Both men are completely starkers.

Before Cronin can comment, Bobby streaks past, screaming blue murder, followed by Robert stabbing the air with their big kitchen knife. They fly through the front door and out into the storm. Cronin catches up with them in the front garden, his Woolworths slippers instantly sodden. The scene is lit by lightning. The white of their skin glows blue in the electric night. Bobby screams around the rose bush, first one way, then the other. No rose has ever seen the like. Robert slashes at the air.

'Stop!' Cronin shouts, darting as close as he dares with the knife still flashing. 'Just stop! The pair of you!'

He shouts but they're deaf to the world and maybe always have been. A light comes on upstairs and their landlady twitches her nets, rubs her eyes, can't believe what she's seeing. Robert closes on Bobby, both men screaming and swearing and skidding on the soaking grass.

Cronin has got to do something.

Round and round they go, arses flapping, arms flailing as they slip and slide. Cronin pities their wrecked bodies. He kicks off a slipper and, hopping, skelps the first one to come past. Robert falls to the ground clutching his head and Bobby is instantly by his side.

'Ma lover!' Bobby cries, checking Robert's head, hoping for more lightning so he can see. 'You hit ma lover!'

Cronin can't believe it. Still on one foot, he retrieves his sodden slipper and their one good knife and hops back to the flat – the upstairs light is still on, but his landlady is gone, probably slumped on the floor, a feathery hand fluttering over her heart. But she has the phone – the police will be on their way. Thérèse appears, bundled in his dressing gown.

'They're—' she closes her eyes.

'I know,' says Cronin.

Together, they watch as Bobby helps Robert up, showering his head with healing kisses and they stagger back as one.

'Ma heid,' slurs Robert. The electric light in the hallway makes their nakedness blinding. They make a show of covering up, cupping their crotches, but it's too little too late. Not that any of it's little.

Cronin and Thérèse don't know where to look, so stand aside, letting them back into the ruined living room. They retreat to bed to wait for the knock – in her head, Thérèse walks the neighbouring streets searching for 'to let' signs. Soon enough, the knock. Cronin belts his dressing gown and goes to the door doing his best impression of sleepy respectable citizen.

'Morning,' says a constable, pointedly, rain coursing off his shoulders.

'Morning,' croaks Cronin, moderating his already clubbable Irish accent to the appropriate frequency for the law.

The constable steps into the hall. 'We've had reports of a disturbance,' he says, looking over Cronin's shoulder to the front door of their flat. 'Two men fighting out front.'

'Yes, officer,' says Cronin, not bothering to deny what their landlady has doubtless described in Sunday paper detail.

'The witness reports seeing a knife?'

Cronin nods.

'And they were . . .' the policeman glances down at his notebook to spare them eye contact. 'Naked?'

'Yes, well,' says Cronin. 'I've got two old friends staying and they're a bit down on their luck and had a wee bit too much to drink and—'

Thérèse opens the flat door and smiles into the hall.

'Everything alright, miss?'

Thérèse smiles. 'A lot of fuss really, silly boys, you know. Horseplay.'

The constable makes a note. 'Mind if I take a look?'

He walks straight in to their living room.

Miraculously, the room is restored. It is even neater than when they'd left it for Soho. The lamp stands sober in the window, its shade replaced. The pictures are straight. Robert, seemingly fully dressed, is sitting up in the armchair, a gaudy crocheted blanket over his knees, thin hair plastered to his head. Bobby, also no longer naked, lies demurely on the couch. 'Ocht we're awfy sorry, officer,' he says, stretching his vowels from Ayrshire to Aberdeen.

The constable turns to Cronin, snapping an elastic band around his notebook. 'You never said they were Scotch.'

Cronin shrugs.

'Consider this as a warning,' says the constable, heading for the door.

'Oh, we will, officer,' says Bobby, sweetly. 'It wilnae happen again. Promise.'

5 May 1956

Dear Johnny,

I can't believe it about Peter, I'm sure you don't either. The headlines are horrible: Margarine Millionaire! He had so much to live for – I don't mean the money, but that helped. He truly lived for art and artists and I know he ranked you higher than you do yourself, which isn't hard. I'll never forget when I met him in Edinburgh: oysters and champagne and him loving our pictures. I don't know where we would be without him. I don't see how a person can drown in a bath, I really don't. Does anybody believe that? The papers are having a field day – we see the headlines but can't afford the rags and it's probably just as well. I would not write to you if things were not so hard. Robert has not the energy to lift a pen, never mind a brush, so it's me here, again. I don't know if you've got my other letters. He is not well, Johnny – I think that year in the army is finally catching up with him. There's not a pick on him, not that there ever was. We can't get to see a doctor what with having to stay here and there, you really do learn who your friends are. I'm not well myself but that's never stopped me, you know me. I wish we were all still at 77 – I am sorry if I was not as kind to you as I maybe should have been. They were good years. Bombs aside. If you can see your way to sending some funds we would both be very grateful. Robert doesn't know I'm asking. There is talk of a Retrospective for Robert at the Redfern, which has only made him worse because he says that means they think he's over. You should see the stuff he's doing now, he did this riderless horse on the back of a betting slip and I swear if he was anybody else it would be in the Tate. We will pay you back, I promise. You can send it c/o the Old Red Lion in Islington – they are kindly holding our post. I have drawn the landlord's daughter and the picture hangs over the till. We will get back on our feet, I know. If I have ever hurt you, forgive me and believe I was never conscious of hurting. I wish you could love someone else like you say you loved Robert. Never let the bastards grind you down, Johnny!

Your old pal, Bobby

20 December 1956

To Whom It May Concern:
The Artists' Benevolent Fund.

I am writing on behalf of myself and my painting partner Robert Colquhoun in the hopes of a grant. You may be familiar with our work. We graduated top of our class from the Glasgow School of Art in 1938, winning the first ever Joint Travelling Scholarship to Europe, which was cut short by the war. Mr Colquhoun served and was discharged so his talent might be saved for the nation. I was unable to serve due to ill health, which troubles me still. We have been featured in *Horizon*, *Vogue* and the *Picture Post*, among many other publications. No less an authority than John Tonge hailed us as 'Young artists of great promise'. Our work has been shown in Lefevre, the Tate and the Metropolitan Gallery of Modern Art in New York City. Like many painters, we find things hard, as for some time picture buying has been in a slump. We have not 'played the game' but stay true to our aesthetic, which is what we were taught the real artist does. We feel sure you will agree. We have no family money and no savings to fall back on, having always ploughed our takings back into our work and supported younger artists like John Minton. I would not write if I did not have to. I hope you can help us both.

Yours, Robert MacBryde GSA

8 February 1957

Dear Frances and Caroline,

We hope this letter finds you both well. Robert sends his best wishes. I am, as ever, his secretary. We were sad to read about Vanessa Bell – we know how dear she was to both of you and how deeply intertwined your lives were. She is with Virginia now. Duncan must be heartbroken. We know well the loss of beloveds. We still cannot believe it about our dear Johnny Minton, gone last month. He was only the same age as Dylan. It's cruel. But not as cruel as the world that drove him to it. There was not a bad bone in Johnny Minton's body. He especially adored Robert, who is heartbroken and cannot lift a brush. That's Johnny and Adler away. Remember Adler died when we were living under your generous auspices in Lewes? He was another great admirer of your work. We have been thinking, it's years now since our productive and eventful time with you – the ballet was a hit because of the work we did during our stay with you. We are still so grateful. We have an opening in our schedule and wondered about returning – we think often of the view from up on Mount Caburn. In addition to making new work for your press we could undertake some teaching and maybe even private tuition in the town? What do you think?

All thanks and very best wishes, Robert MacBryde

PS We don't suppose you found a bowl of old buttons at Westgate after we left?

14 June 1957

Dearest Elizabeth,

I'm not sure my letters have been getting to you or maybe you think I'm exaggerating. I promise you I'm not. Please believe me when I say we are sorry about Tilty. Let us make it up to you. We are both trying to get teaching jobs and when we do we will pay you back. That old glass was horrible anyway and if it was so valuable the landlord should never have left it lying about in a house with four children! I hope you are still writing – you were always better than Barker, but don't tell him I said that. No, tell him. And you always were a better friend than me. Forgive me? Please?

Your Bobby

PS You can write back to me c/o Dicky and Dennis in Wivenhoe. They have been kind enough to take us in from time to time. It's not that far from Tilty – we could come and see you and the children? They must be so big now! Christopher will be taller than Robert. I wonder if they remember all our games?

18 September 1958

Dear Mr Fleming,

I still can never bring myself to write 'Ian' – once a teacher, always a teacher! Thank you for letting us know regarding the job situation. It seems that everybody is an artist now and I despair when I see the rubbish coming from America! Pop what? It is not true that we have become 'unreliable' – I would like to know who told you that but I understand you don't want to say. If half the stories about us were true we'd be in the jail! Robert sends you his best regards – he is hopeful of a retrospective and him barely forty! Your invitation will be in the post. If the department does have a grant scheme for graduates, please let us know, as it would bridge the gap between commissions.

    Always your student, MacBryde

Suffolk, 22 September 1959

A perfect streak of white starts between the shire horse's ears. It runs down past his blinkers and on to his warm wet muzzle. Bobby thinks back to the Clydesdale that ploughed up the Botanics. Have the flowers grown back? The bit between his teeth seems unnecessary – this animal is the very definition of gentle. He doesn't seem to mind the young man from the BBC fussing around with a camera.

'That it?' the farmer asks, his ancient Suffolk accent making four words out of two as he dons his cap, not waiting for an answer. Robert doubts he usually wears his Sunday best for midweek errands. The two-wheel cart is pathetically empty: three blank canvases are propped theatrically to one side along with a battered cardboard suitcase. No books. Bobby still carries the satchel his mother made. This is all they have to move to their latest place, even cheaper than the last.

'Aye,' says Bobby. 'I mean, yes that's it, Mr Russell.'

'Ken,' he laughs, hoisting a camera onto his shoulder. 'Please just call me Ken. And be yourself.' He can't believe his luck – his first proper film for the BBC! All about this pair whose work dazzled him years before running into them in Soho and being, he admits, horribly charmed. They are dressed almost identically in navy jumpers Bobby has knitted.

The farmer, nimbler than his years suggest, hops onto the cart axle then shins along before sliding onto the horse in a somehow masculine side-saddle. Robert climbs into the cart first, his back complaining. He crawls forward shouting, 'don't film this', then finds a space up front, perilously close to the horse's arse. He extends a hand and Bobby hauls himself up, his ancient canvas bag over his shoulder, as it always has been. He feels the quart of Bell's in his bag, the comforting weight of whisky.

The farmer clicks his teeth and the horse sets off. Ken films them going just a few yards then shouts, 'Stop!' so he can run ahead over a little hill to catch them coming the other way. The hill is jaggy with September stubble, the harvest already in.

'The magic of television,' he laughs as he passes the farmer. He's heard other directors say this — directors, he's a director now! — and hopes it will work for him. The farmer's face gives nothing away. The horse waits patiently.

'A pound a week,' says Bobby to Robert. 'Sell one big picture and we're set for the year.'

Robert looks to Bobby who is taking a deep draw on their last cigarette and glimpses again the boy he'd run away from that first day at the art school. Is he still running? Bobby passes him the cigarette. This village will be close enough to London for them to sell their paintings but cheap enough for them to do nothing else but paint.

'And go!' Ken shouts. Off they roll again, the brass badges on the horse's leathers tinkling in time with its steps. The sound reminds Bobby of a soldier's belt buckle — he shifts the canvas bag over his crotch.

Ken dashes ahead again as the horse nods on down the still outrageously green Suffolk lane; at points it feels like they're in a verdant cave. They pass a church the Normans missed.

'Dear Olde Englande,' says Bobby. Even after all these years down south, the gentle inhabitedness of the landscape never fails to surprise. That church has always been here. This horse has always known these paths. The farmer's great-great-grandfather would recognise this view as will his great-great-grandson. It is comforting. It is cloying. Robert and Bobby will always be strangers here. *Never forget where you come fae.*

The sure motion of the horse lulls them and Robert feels his eyes close as the September sun warms his bones; he can feel his bones these days. Why can it not always be like this? The two of them at peace together under the sun. Why do they have to paint pictures for people who will never see what they see, who only want a clever little thing for their dining room in town? Why do they have to make art that makes money? Why do they have to take their wares to London and hoor about like Soho tarts? Why were they not born with enough to do what they want, like Johnny, like the fucking Bloomsberries, like so many people they never hear from now? Why won't the world just leave the two of them alone?

Robert's eyes flutter as the horse halts.

'Here,' says the farmer.

Ancient House lives up to its name. It's striped like a bumblebee with wattle and daub and the glass in its many tiny windows is thicker at the bottom of each pane than at the top – time is liquid after all. Bobby remembers London was full of such amber windows before the war – he glimpsed them just before they disappeared for ever: the new glass is relentlessly clear.

Bobby looks up at their new front door and is surprised to see a letter box. The house is sandwiched between two identically olde abodes and mirrored by a row across the road. There are no faces at any of the windows. Maybe a plague has carried them all away. Or fairies. More likely, these are now the weekend homes of stockbrokers and this is a Wednesday. There are no streetlights, not even any cobbles. No pub. It's not even a hamlet.

Robert sits up. 'Hold it,' says Ken, appearing again, his face camera obscured. He has fused with it, a marriage of man and machine, an image Robert knows Francis could make a hundred guineas from.

'Can you get down slowly for me?' Ken asks.

Bobby resists a joke, doesn't want to set Robert off before today's fresh start. He climbs down then puts up his hands to take whatever Robert hands him. The larger canvases, then the smaller canvas. Bobby leans them by the front door while Robert passes their case over, then a carrier bag of bits. Bobby glimpses the album of *Donald of the Burthens*. The ballet dances through Bobby's head: their megalithic blues and greys, their Caledonia in Covent Garden, the first bagpipes in the Royal Opera House! Bobby lays the bag by the door – it's years since they had a record player. This house has no electricity anyway. It takes less than two sad minutes to empty the cart. Robert wipes his brow as he climbs off. Ken slips the farmer a coin – this setup was his idea. He'd bought the canvases too. The horse plods off again and Bobby imagines it going on all the way to Ayrshire where rich black fields wait to be ploughed.

The front door is unlocked – there's nothing to steal and nobody to steal it. Ancient House is the same inside as out. There are two floors and two rooms on each. The beams might come from a ship, the walls are a ripple of horsehair plaster scorched by centuries of candlelight. Even Bobby has to duck through the doors. A tin bath hangs by the back door, which leads to an overgrown garden where the toilet must be.

'A studio each!' says Bobby walking ahead, his boots announcing his arrival to any resident spirits. His voice fills the empty rooms. There is not a stick of furniture, not a rug. It echoes like their attic. Robert remembers the rug Bobby made with scraps from the Barras, all the hours lying on it, dreaming up their future. Here they are.

'Have you any cigarettes?' Bobby asks. 'For props?' Ken hands over a pack and they split it between them, then head upstairs.

'It's romantic,' says Bobby, at the top of the stairs.

'Shhh,' says Robert, mindful of microphones.

Ken suddenly feels like he's intruding. He knows not to ask who will sleep where. It's not as if he can use this moment – the BBC would never show such a thing, two men making a home together. But they will show two Bohemian artists struggling in picturesque poverty.

'We need to catch the light,' Ken shouts up the stairs.

'We know all about that,' Bobby sing-songs down, amping up his accent. After all, their film is to be called *Scottish Painters*.

Robert is already setting up in the top back room, which leaves the front for Bobby. It's not like there'll be any road noise. They unpack completely in less than half an hour.

'Ready?' Ken shouts up, his eye on the light now peeking over the warm red slates sleeping on the roof opposite.

'Ready,' Bobby shouts down.

'I'll do Mr MacBryde first, if that's alright,' Ken says, coiling the microphone cable around his arm as he enters what is already Bobby's studio. He is halted by the picture on the easel. It is, as expected, a still life. But the pear seems angry, its core roiling in its flesh and next to it an apple thrums with cosmic potential. Bobby holds one half of a tired-looking melon. He is fixated, barely turns to Ken.

'Why do you always return to still life?' Ken asks, microphone held out.

Because Robert does people and I do things and that's the way it's always been and I couldn't change it now even if I wanted to because that's how love works, you share the world between you and if your world is not to end then things must stay where they are.

Instead, Bobby says what he thinks Ken wants to hear, in the accent he knows he wants to hear it in. Robert listens across the corridor and tries not to laugh. This whole thing was Bobby's idea – *It will get us noticed again! Beam us right into the rooms where our pictures should be! Think of Francis's face!* He will play along. Besides, the young man from the BBC is suitably deferential and they've already had several Soho nights out of him.

Bobby continues, 'I do not know why, for instance, I cut a cantaloupe in half or a lemon or an apple etcetera.' He puts down the melon. 'But I suppose cutting it reveals a sort of pattern inside that I can cope with.' He takes a pencil and draws an outsize lemon on a sheet of *The Listener*, the headline reads *Problems Before General De Gaulle*. 'Perhaps I use cantaloupes and lemons because I especially like yellow. Not every yellow but the yellow of citric fruit – not that the cantaloupe is – but particularly in lemons, that kind of lemon yellow screams.'

Bobby rolls the RRRRR in screams for so long that Robert nearly laughs out loud.

The tape rolls on and so does Bobby, 'It's a scrrreaming kind of yellow. It's like the inside of the fruit, perhaps. And that's why I like that particular kind of yellow. I don't have a special arrangement of anything on a table that I am making a copy of. I simply use things almost where they are in the room, so I seem to work more from still life than anything else.'

At this point in the film, Ken thinks, he will show close-ups of MacBryde's finest works – zoom inside the fruits, often outlined sharply in black, even the tiniest seeds. Dazzle the viewer with ripeness and crispness of outline and the world of colour beyond the black and white of their television screen.

'But you do paint figures?' Ken asks, almost apologetically.

'Yes, I do.'

'But even then the figures you do paint move towards the oval patterns of your still lifes?'

Now Ken will show MacBryde's lesser-known work – strange figures with black pits for eyes, like the masks in Greek tragedy, arms raised in outrage or pleading.

'I would like, of course, to try other things. For instance, the other morning, sitting in the garden, suddenly I think, for the first time, I noticed a trellis of roses.'

He trills the *trrrellis* and Robert hoots then coughs.

'Noises off,' Ken calls over his shoulder.

Bobby blushes and hopes it won't show in black and white.

'Can we get that again?' Ken asks.

'Yes, *we* can,' says Bobby, pointedly.

'I noticed a trellis of roses and the fact that they'd been pruned … the ends and I suddenly saw a way of using them. And again, it's a problem, you see. When you think of the word rose, my goodness, it has such an effect on you: *a rose is a rose*. But as I say, there would also have to be a sort of contemporary way. I'd have to approach the painting of the rose like I do the still life otherwise one becomes sort of untrue to oneself. But that, immediately creates a problem, which of course is for me to solve – now.'

As he talks, Bobby realises that garden is no more, those roses are gone. But he's getting into the swing of talking like people expect artists to. He might actually be about to paint something. He feels that delicious old impatience build.

'Great,' says Ken, clicking STOP. 'That's perfect.'

'Already?'

Ken notes the light moving across the room. 'I think the ordinary viewer will be fascinated to learn about your process.'

'Mr Colquhoun,' Bobby calls, knowing it will give Robert a kick. 'Your turn.' He recalls all the times he sent a man to his lover and vice versa and blushes again in black and white.

Ken pauses. He needs something else. 'Mr Colquhoun?'

'Aye?' Robert calls from downstairs.

'Do you think I could get you bringing up Mr MacBryde a cup of something?'

Bobby laughs. 'First time for everything!'

'We've not got anything,' shouts Robert from what passes for a kitchen.

'I've a flask in my bag,' says Ken. 'You can use that.'

'Is it coffee?' Bobby asks, suddenly thirsty.

'On my way up!' shouts Robert, holding the banister and proceeding carefully with the brimming cup, wondering if it ever had a saucer.

Ken steps across the corridor, uncoiling his cables and hits RECORD. Robert hands Bobby the cup and Bobby looks at it like it's a miracle wrought from thin air. Robert nods as if he made it himself then goes across to his studio to pose in front of his easel, already covered with a large sketch he's just unrolled, the ends still curling. He wipes his brow with the back of his hand and stares at this puzzle of his own devising.

'Mr Colquhoun, your first skill was as a draughtsman, do you think this is what informs your interest in form, in always painting people?'

Ken has seen countless Colquhoun figures, often in pairs, many weirdly sexless, most frozen in a state of almost biblical suffering, their eyes even deeper and darker than those in the MacBrydes. He will dare the viewer to look into them.

'Most of my earlier paintings, let's say *Hebridean Woman*, peasants doing something or other,' says Robert, a cigarette waggling on his bottom lip.

Peasants? Bobby thinks. He means my lot.

Robert pushes on, occasionally darting forward to make a mark with the end of his brush handle, which he's rubbed in charcoal dust. The ghost of a horse emerges.

'I think I was quite conscious of the fact that they were nostalgic and came out of rather romantic memories of the place I came from.' The place I came from as you imagine it, Robert thinks. There were no peasants in Kilmarnock, not the shawled, stooped crones he bewitched London with. He realises he's been painting Bobby's memory of the Hunger Marchers filing through Maybole. Does it matter?

Robert stands back. He speaks, Ken notices, like he's being made to read an essay aloud at the front of class.

'Most painters seem to have a stock in trade – a group of objects or figures painted in a particular way, which they use over and over again, hoping, I suppose, that each painting will be better than the last, that they will be an improvement. They put their faith in this way of doing it, since they must.' He paints a white zig-zag down a dress, one hand trying to stop the other shaking. 'I have used figures for a long time. These figures are usually female figures. Maybe not very prepossessing. They have funny hats and wear peculiar dresses. I don't think that they would ever approximate to the Venus de Milo, but in that I think lies their interest. But all of them are always an exercise in the use of paint and shapes. This I think is because I am interested in the human figure, almost as a thing in itself – it has a value, which is always changing and ending; you can ring the changes on it for ever.'

Robert is haunted by figures. Boys pouring out of Kilmarnock High as the last bell rings, their legs all going like one rippling millipede. His mother and father sitting on their couch, space opening and closing between them. Bobby and him together in a thousand different ways. Sun through a glass of chianti in Rome, both their hands around it. His own hands raw from scrubbing latrines in the barracks, his back broken by sandbags. Men steaming in the Turkish baths, men kneeling in the park, men moaning in the black-out. Filling bloody buckets with Francis when their ambulance got to where they could do no good. Figures are a value always changing. Robert scratches his sides and counts his ribs.

Ken will be spoiled for choice making Colquhoun's montage. He will include his one official war commission – *Weaving Army Cloth* shows two women sitting at a loom, almost trapped by the machinery. Then definitely a print of *Boy with Birdcage*. The star will be *Figures in a Farmyard*, a farmer and his daughter standing by a gurning pig, its face a miniature *Guernica*.

Robert takes his cigarette from his mouth with his left hand and leans against the easel. 'Bobby?' he calls.

Bobby appears as if he's always been there.

'Aye?' he walks over, already appraising.

'This is not for the camera,' Robert says.

'I won't use it but it's easier if I don't have to turn everything off and on again,' says Ken.

Robert nods.

Ken keeps rolling.

Robert winks at Bobby and goes on. 'No artist ever wants any interference with his work while he's working but very often a painter can work for a long time on a canvas and convince himself that everything is going very well, but at the back of his mind he knows there is something wrong, something which is usually fundamental, now because of some blind spot he can't see this.'

Bobby points to the top-left corner of the picture, barely touched as far as Ken can see. Robert nods and draws deep on his cigarette. Bobby says: 'I think this thing perhaps of someone who is knowing your painting coming into the room, seeing that you're almost sort of blundering about and you're half looking for assistance as it were and sometimes they're able to tell you – it's like restoring your sight, things fall into place again. And you're able to continue the painting.'

Bobby picks up Robert's brush and makes a seemingly tiny adjustment. Robert nods then turns to Bobby and puts his arm around him. Ken coughs lightly and steps forward, pressing STOP on the tape which clunks noisily.

'So, when will Hollywood come calling?' Bobby feels able to laugh now. He knows people don't want artists to laugh. Art is supposed to be painful, like the prices paid for it.

'Any day,' says Ken, suddenly worrying his tapes will be blank. It occurs to him that the Roberts don't have electricity, never mind a television. 'Do you mind if I get a few more shots of this place? It's perfect.'

'Aye it is,' says Robert, glancing at Bobby.

Ken leaves them together, trailing his cable down the narrow stairs. Inwardly he narrates the end of his film: *They will go on working here until they find a studio going for even less than a pound, and then they will be on the move once more, taking with them the essentials of their own world.*

He glances back up at them, glimpses one step towards the other as the door swings shut.

THE END

Epilogue

47 Museum Street, London

Just before dawn, 20 September 1962

Bobby's not touched a drop, except for a wee nightcap with Muriel. There's a bottle of Bell's under the sink in the kitchenette. It will have to wait.

There's hardly time for the paint to dry and it's got to be right. They need this. It's Robert's big comeback tomorrow – well, today – in the gallery downstairs. Bobby's got half of Soho coming.

Robert is so focused he barely notices Bobby come back in. Bobby steps into the kitchenette and hums to himself as he rinses Robert's brushes in a jar of turps in the cracked sink beneath the high sash window: 'Three Lovely Lasses from Banyon.' They've got brushes again, a sink, a studio, albeit tiny. He looks down on to Museum Street where the last of the night people and the first of the morning people do their best to avoid each other in the rain – heads down, not noticing galaxies bursting on the oily pavement. The rain turns to sleet. It will be a cold winter.

Folk see that little, Bobby thinks, and only what they want to. Maybe him and Robert have seen too much. There are some things he would like to unsee, maybe undo. But not as much as some might think. This show is another chance. Once it's up, the critics will be raving again and the buyers buying and this time they'll not give it all away.

The brushes are stubborn. *Young artists of great promise. Much influenced by each other.* Bobby has had to beg, borrow and steal these brushes for Robert Colquhoun: top of their year, the man once described as 'Scotland's finest artist', the man he knows many say would have been better off without him, the man who is — even now, in this poky wee cupboard — advancing towards greatness.

To assuage their backers, this will be a solo show. But Bobby knows he's in every one of Robert's pictures and Robert knows it too and that is all that matters. *One organism.* Bobby plunges the brushes back in the jar and watches the turps bloom with the reds Robert can't leave alone right now. A MacBryde show will surely follow. He swirls the brushes, careful not to stub them. Bobby still has things he wants to say but he's done with painting things: that coffee pot, lemons, cucumbers; the critics had loved his fruits, seen so much in them. Bobby was always thinking of Robert, is always seeing Robert. So, Robert is what he will paint next.

A match strikes in the studio. Robert will be taking his first gasp on a Mayfair and standing back. He always hates what he's just finished and it's no good telling him otherwise. Bobby long ago learned to join in, to pile on until Robert is forced to defend his choices and only then can he see any good.

'Here,' Bobby shouts, as he flicks the bristles. 'I've done a Pollock in the sink.'

The joke isn't the best but merits at least a dry sigh. 'Robert, a wee sink Pollock, worth a thousand easy, come and see?'

Silence.

Then a short sharp gasp, like a swimmer coming up from deep cold water.

Still holding the brushes, Bobby runs into the studio.

Paint glistens red-wet on the paper at the easel in the middle of the room and, clutching both sides, his knuckles the white of butchered meat, is—

'Robert!'

Bobby half-catches him as he crumples, sliding him to the floor, cradling his head in his lap.

'Help!' Bobby shouts, putting his hands over Robert's ears. 'Help us!'

Robert looks puzzled. A brush still in his left hand, a cigarette burning in his right. He tries to move his lips, the lips Bobby has drawn and kissed and cursed.

'Shhh,' says Bobby. 'Don't. Help!'

Robert's eyes stare at a single point above them. His lips twitch. Bobby leans down.

'Rabbits, Bobby. Rabbits.'

The brush slips from Robert's hand and rolls along the floor trailing red. Bobby takes his cigarette but can't bear to put it out. He holds it to the paper Robert was working on then pulls it away. A figure is emerging from the paint – the top half is, unmistakably, a skeleton: mad jigging bones, the *Danse Macabre*. Did Robert know he was coming? Did he invite him in?

As Bobby lets Robert slide onto the floor he realises how light he is – *I could carry him*, he thinks. Bobby passes a hand over his eyes, closing them gently, like people do in films. Then he lies down beside Robert, reaches back and takes his arm and drapes it over himself and holds on. The pair of them lie there together, curled like commas. And somewhere up above them the high-blue wind blows.

Afterword

The Two Roberts is a novel but Robert MacBryde and Robert Colquhoun were very real people and very real talents, even if they're not as celebrated now as they deserve to be. They were both born in Ayrshire and did indeed meet at Glasgow School of Art in their first term in 1933. I like to think they met on their first day. They dazzled Glasgow and went on to thrill London and charm the art world. They did, as the *Picture Post* said, 'Live, Travel, Work and Exhibit Together'. They knew everybody and everybody knew them: Johnny Minton, Francis Bacon and Dear Elizabeth. They were the original 'Golden Boys of Bond Street'. They were in *Vogue*. They were stars. They could be terrors. They were, sometimes, their own worst enemies.

Robert died on the eve of his comeback show in 1962. He was only 47. His death made romantic headlines: 'ARTIST DIES AT EASEL!' His body was taken back to Kilmarnock and to this day his grave is unmarked because his family could not afford a headstone. Afterwards, Bobby was taken in by Dear Elizabeth, who eventually forgave him the drama of Tilty Mill – they really were nannies to her children. He was given sunny holidays by Bacon. But nothing and nobody could save Bobby and he never really painted again. He moved to Dublin and was dancing a jig outside a pub when he was hit by a car and killed – the driver was never found. Bobby was 53. His body was taken back to Maybole (briefly lost in transit – very Bobby – another story). His grave is also unmarked. I wish they were buried together.

Officially, Bobby and Robert had to hide who they were or face prison, where many of their friends and acquaintances went. They burned letters and drawings to protect themselves from blackmail – as Morris warned, never write anything down (Morris is my invention). So many stories lost or half-whispered. I have listened as closely as I can – pressed the nautilus to my ear. When asked if he knew his star students were lovers, Ian Fleming is supposed to have said *they were definitely not homosexual in Scotland*. The 'just roommates' narrative persists to this day, erasing so many loves.

Bobby and Robert have been buried in footnotes when, for a brief, glorious time, they were the story. This novel is my way of writing them back to where they belong. They thrived in the temporarily classless art world of the war but lacked the inherited wealth and acumen their contemporaries took for granted. They did not, or could not, play the game. Because their lives ended tragically, I was reluctant to write their story – to add to the gay body count. But I realised the real tragedy would be not bringing them and their work back to life.

This is a novel filled with biographical and historical facts but it is not bound by them any more than Bobby and Robert were – I've tried not to let the truth get in the way of a good story.

So, here, finally, is the ending I wish they'd had.

'Ladies and gentlemen—' The curator tinks his champagne glass and that very particular art hush descends on the packed gallery. 'Thank you.'

'As many of you know, this show has been years in the making and is, I believe, many years overdue.' A murmur of agreement ripples around the room where collectors in stealth-wealth cashmere rub shoulders with the bright young queers who daily call for their downfall in carefully crafted Instagram posts.

The curator reads from his cards, hands trembling. 'This show should have happened sooner – but for reasons we *all* know, it is only happening here and now in 2013. The artists we honour tonight blazed a trail through a world that was on fire – they remained stubbornly Scottish, they made no attempt to hide their working-class identity, they were as out as it was possible to be in a world where their very existence was illegal. They inspired Bacon and Freud, made paintings collected by MOMA and every serious gallery since, long ago leaving behind the lazy monikers of McPicasso and MacBraque. This show is, incredibly, the first major retrospective of their work and—'

Here he looks up from his cards.

'It is my very great honour to welcome here tonight, to our little gallery, the Two Roberts!'

The room gasps and turns as one as the doors open. Bagpipes skirl from hidden speakers. There beams Bobby. Enthroned in front of him, in the wheelchair he's used since 1962, is Robert. Bobby leans down and whispers in Robert's ear and we don't need to know what he says, only that he says it and that Bobby's hand is there when Robert reaches back and that he takes it and holds it and never lets him go.

Acknowledgements

I fell in love with both Roberts during lockdown. It started with a tweet – remember those? – from the Dick Institute in Kilmarnock. It was an image of a still-life by Bobby – one of his bowls of fruit. I was dazzled. Who did this? Who was this other wildly talented Robert? And what did they have to do with each other? That was that. So, thank you to the Dick Institute for that tweet and for ongoing support.

It's the job of a novelist to know what we don't know, to find gaps between facts to make our story. To challenge the facts. That means asking lots of questions of lots of people who know a lot more than me. So, thank you to:

Patrick Elliott, Chief Curator of Modern and Contemporary Art at the National Galleries of Scotland. Patrick brilliantly curated the now iconic 2014 show (which I wish I'd seen), shared his meticulous research and opened many doors.

Simon Martin, Director of Pallant House Gallery in Chichester, for putting the Roberts on walls where they deserve to be and contextualising them in twentieth-century British art, a field Simon is a world expert in.

Jan Patience, one of the UK's best art journalists. Jan has very generously shared her own passion for these Ayrshire icons and connected me to many helpful folk.

Kirstie Meehan and the staff at the Scottish National Gallery of Modern Art for access to their archives.

Michelle Kaye and staff at the Glasgow School of Art Archives who let me loose in the Roberts' Glasgow and European journals (and let me read between the lines).

Alice Strang at Lyon & Turnbull auctioneers for her endless enthusiasm and knowledge, for generous introductions and for letting me handle that double-sided painting by Robert.

Leonie Bell and Chris Carse Wilson at the V&A in Dundee for showing me very rare examples of designs for *Donald of the Burthens*.

I am especially grateful to all the staff and volunteers at Charleston, especially Nathaniel Hepburn, Emily Hill and Shannon Smith. A conversation with Nathaniel sparked the idea for a long-overdue exhibition. 'Artists, Lovers, Outlaws' will open at Charleston in Lewes in October 2025 and we hope to tour it. I'm so thankful to Emily and Shannon for answering all my questions about how to actually curate and for understanding the importance of queer, working-class voices on and off the walls.

One person championed the Roberts and their work when just about everyone else had abandoned them. He was instrumental in saving their reputations and much of their work. This book would have been impossible without the knowledge, generosity and joy of the indefatigable Davy Brown. A much-loved and much-collected artist in his own right, Davy is inspired by Colquhoun especially – they grew up in the same place and even went to the same school (years apart). Davy was a driving force behind the 2014 show and knows everything there is to know about their world and work. He is beyond generous and also a very good cook – as I discovered when he and his wife Jill very generously had me to stay. Davy is writing his own book, about Colquhoun's monotypes, and it will doubtless shed new light. He is a gentleman and a scholar. I'm grateful to Shaun at the Book Shop in Wigtown for introducing us.

My agent, and friend, Clare Conville is the reigning queen of Bohemia. I'm grateful to her for always believing in me and the Roberts and for championing us, and to Lizzie Milne and the team at C&W and Curtis Brown too. Ellah Wakatama edited the book you're holding. At every draft she has seen what I've been trying to do (even when I couldn't) and given me space to ask questions I didn't even know I needed to. I'm so grateful for her insight, passion and care. Thank you to all at Canongate for making this book what it is – Anna Frame, Caitriona Horne, Brodie Mckenzie, Leila Cruickshank, Stephen Parker, Francis Bickmore and, of course, Jamie Byng. Your independence is a very special thing. Madeleine Collinge makes copyediting an art and I'm so very lucky to have had her generous attentions here.

First readers get to see all your efforts, however embarrassing. So, thank you dear David Nicholls for seeing that this is, first and last, a love story and for giving me such honest and useful notes. Robert makes a cameo in Maggie O'Farrell's wonderful novel *The Hand That First Held Mine*. I'm grateful to her for a conversation at just the right moment.

Home is at the heart of this novel – having space to safely be yourself, to be in love, to have a life. And, crucially, to make art. The following places and people have given me space, time and support to write. So, thank you to:

The Society of Authors and the Authors' Foundation for an SoA Authors' Foundation grant.

The National Centre for Writing in Norwich for a week of writing without interruption – Chris Gribble, former Chief Executive, made that possible. And to Sarah Perry for faith in doubt.

Gladstone's Library, for always being a world away from the world.

Gala Wright for a magical island.

Suzanne Williams for putting me up in Glasgow and letting me discover the city anew.

Alasdair Morton for being a true supporter of artists and writers and for being such a good friend.

And, also in Edinburgh, my dear friend Chris Creggan, whose readerly insight and writing I value.

Cate and Nash at Much Ado Books in Alfriston for letting

me back into their village and feeding me and believing in me and just being the most interested and interesting people – they make so many books possible. I owe them so much.

In March 2024 I was Writer-in-Residence at the idyllic West Dean College near Chichester. Thank you to Mark Radcliffe for inviting me and to Sarah Hughes for giving me access to studios there. I found this residency through the brilliant newsletter run by Sian Meades-Williams and suggest you subscribe. Travel to and from West Dean was made possible by a small grant from the Drusilla Harvey Access Fund via the Society of Authors.

Thank you to the novelist Cressida Connolly, whose father Cyril ran *Horizon*, which changed everything for the two Roberts. Her pungent recollections chimed true. A conversation with one of George Barker's now very grown-up children solved a small but relentless mystery, so thank you to them for casting their mind back. Thank you to Polly and David for engineering these chance chats.

I am humbled by the generosity and kindness of Lorna Gibson, niece of Robert Colquhoun, who shared precious family memories of her beloved uncle.

If you want to find out more about the world of *The Two Roberts*, I strongly recommend the following:

Do not miss *The Visitors' Book*, by Jon Lys Turner. It's his compelling biography of his great friends, the artists Richard Chopping and Denis Wirth-Miller. Dickie and Denis were another famous couple moving in the same circles. When Denis was jailed in 1944 for 'gross indecency', Bobby and Robert refused to abandon them. Lots of gay men snipped sex-souvenir buttons from soldiers and constables but few filled a bowl as big as the one belonging to Dickie and Denis. I'm grateful to Turner for his honest and heartfelt book and for letting me put my hand in that bowl. I give Dickie and Denis only the briefest mention in my novel because they are so fascinating and their lifelong relationship so very rich that they merit a whole book on their own. This is a really rich and powerful read.

I am indebted to Roger Bristow for his masterly biography *The Last Bohemians*. He conducted many interviews with figures I have conjured as characters to piece together the Roberts' childhoods, student years, rise and fall. He takes them and their work seriously while also acknowledging their sexuality and humanity. His labour of love directed me to many letters and resources I found inspiring. I have included only a couple of lines from actual letters. Bristow writes in his introduction that 'Memory is a far from perfect source' – his focus is that of a highly accomplished art historian charting careers and movements; mine is that of a novelist and I take liberties Bristow could not.

Peter Parker has completed a work of scholarship that will last the ages in his majestic two-volume series *Some Men in London*. Through contemporary articles, diary entries, government reports, novels and other records, he paints a new picture of life for gay men in London before, during and after the war and all the way up to decriminalisation (in England) in 1967. We meet famous names, like Dirk Bogarde and Kenneth Wiliams, but also everyday men joyfully pursuing their own lives in the face of great prejudice. Parker's research is meticulous and brings them all equally to life. I was delighted to see the two Roberts included along with John Minton, Keith Vaughan and co. One of the stories Parker unearthed is about a man called Andrew Morrison who ended his own life after being arrested in a public toilet. I couldn't stop thinking about Mr Morrison and all the men like him – lives destroyed, stories untold. As a novelist I felt I could do something about this, however small. So, it is Mr Morrison that Bobby witnesses and thinks about thereafter.

Words of Polari glitter throughout my novel. Thank you to my old friend Professor Paul Baker for sorting my Judy from my Lily – do not miss *Fabulosa!*, his totally authoritative and highly entertaining history of Polari, our elusive but enduring queer language.

I would not be able to do what I do without the love and support of my logical family. So, thank you, always, to Professor

Simon Lock, Jawan, Ann S., Brian H., Tinie, Dear David and August, Bakul, Daisy H.B., Mark Vessey, Jeff in SF, Patrick Strudwick, my beloved Yorkshire family and to Alexandra Heminsley, Dee Humphreys and Liney. This book is dedicated to Mike, as am I. My Scottish family are always in my heart. My wee Mum taught me how to read – I fell in love with stories sitting at her feet. She started this book with me but never got to the end. She is in every word I write.

•

The author and publisher gratefully acknowledge permissions granted to reproduce the copyright material in this book.

Epigraph: 'Kiss me . . .' by Edwin Morgan, commissioned by the Scottish Poetry Library for its Valentine's Day text poem project, 2004, reproduced with permission from the Scottish Poetry Library, Carcanet Press and The Edwin Morgan Trust.

Pages 190–192: John Tonge, 'Scottish Paintings', *Horizon*, Volume V, Number 29, May 1942.

Page 214: 'Seven Artists Tell Why They Paint', *Picture Post*, 12 March 1949.

Page 219: *Kilmarnock Standard*, July 1943.

Page 224: *West London Observer*, 12 February 1954.

Page 281: Robert MacBryde, letter to John Minton, 5 May 1956. Uses a line in a letter from Robert MacBryde to John Minton, quoted in Roger Bristow, *The Last Bohemians: The Two Roberts – Colquhoun and MacBryde*, Samson and Co., 2010.